LUCK

ALSO BY NATALIE KELLER REINERT

LUCK

A Novel

The Eventing Series
BOOK FOUR

NATALIE KELLER REINERT

FLATIRON
BOOKS
NEW YORK

LUCK. Copyright © 2018, 2025 by Natalie Keller Reinert. All rights reserved. Printed in the United States of America. For information, address Flatiron Books, 120 Broadway, New York, NY 10271.

www.flatironbooks.com

Designed by Gabriel Guma

Library of Congress Cataloging-in-Publication Data

Names: Reinert, Natalie Keller, author.
Title: Luck : a novel / Natalie Keller Reinert.
Description: First Flatiron Books edition. I New York : Flatiron Books, 2025. I
   Series: The eventing series ; book 4
Identifiers: LCCN 2024047058 I ISBN 9781250387776 (trade paperback) I
   ISBN 9781250387783 (ebook)
Subjects: LCGFT: Romance fiction. I Sports fiction. I Novels.
Classification: LCC PS3618.E564548 L83 2025 I DDC 813/.6—dc23/
   eng/20241004
LC record available at https://lccn.loc.gov/2024047058

Our books may be purchased in bulk for promotional, educational, or business use. Please contact your local bookseller or the Macmillan Corporate and Premium Sales Department at 1-800-221-7945, extension 5442, or by email at MacmillanSpecialMarkets@macmillan.com.

Originally self-published in 2018 by Natalie Keller Reinert

First Flatiron Books Edition: 2025

10 9 8 7 6 5 4 3 2 1

LUCK

1

I WAS DREAMING about dinosaurs. Prehistoric monsters roaring through the night, their heavy tread shaking the ground as we ran through the jungle, cold wet palm fronds slapping us in the face, trying to escape. I stirred and kicked at the sheet wrapped around my ankles, struggling to free myself. The guttering orange of an ancient streetlight flickered across the horse trailer's sleeping loft, an oblong spotlight in the dark.

Why on earth had I been dreaming about dinosaurs? Mentally, I flipped back through the shows we'd watched on Pete's iPad lately, looking for clues.

The dinosaur roared again, just a couple dozen feet away.

I sat up like a shot and promptly hit my head on the aluminum roof. I sank back into the thin pillow, rubbing at my forehead. Beside me, Pete rolled over and pulled his own pillow over his head, apparently still asleep. I wondered what the roaring sounded like in his dreams. Maybe his subconscious brain was more practical than mine, just like his annoyingly sensible waking mind.

Roar!

This time the racket was followed by a thudding on the cold ground outside.

Now *that* was a sound I recognized. I sighed and threw off the covers, goose bumps rushing to my arms as the cold February air swept over my bare skin. I grabbed the flannel shirt I'd discarded along the side of the bed and tugged it on, wondering what time it was.

ROAR!

"Stop it," I whispered, more to myself than to anyone. "Stop it, stop it, stop it."

The thin carpet was cold beneath my feet, and I had to scrabble around for the pajama bottoms and socks I'd abandoned down here when I climbed into bed—I glanced at my phone, 2:35 A.M.— four hours ago.

There's no way to quietly wrestle oneself into flannel pajamas in the claustrophobic living quarters of a horse trailer, and by the time I'd struggled into the Wellington boots waiting by the door, Pete was blinking at me. Of course, the sound of a racecourse just outside was pretty helpful in waking him up, too. The horses' hooves were thudding up and down along the fence line outside, and the wobbly clay soil was transmitting every vibration directly to our feet and ears.

"I'm sure I've got this," I called back to him as I opened the door. Marcus twined his sinuous beagle body between my legs and hopped down the two metal steps to the stubby wet grass that served as our doormat, lawn, and front porch—as if he'd planned the whole thing so he could get in some extra sniffing time.

February in North Florida is fog season, and there wasn't much light outside the dim circle cast by the flickering old streetlight, mounted on the lone electric pole on the property. The two trailers parked beneath it glowed a gentle orange, their silver aluminum skin beaded with water as the fog skimmed their rooflines and trailed ghostly fingers down their sides. The brown winter grass absorbed any ambient light, so that when I turned my back on the trailer door and faced the pasture a couple dozen feet away, all I saw were the faint silhouettes of the fence posts, and the stark white electric tape of Regina's pen.

Luckily, I didn't need light to know Pete's mare had broken out and was leaning over the pasture fence, starting trouble with the boys. Her nighttime wanderings, looking for love, were becoming a semi-regular occurrence. With the approach of breeding season boiling in her veins, she'd gone slightly insane, apparently channeling all of her frustration about being out of work into a deep desire for Dynamo, my previously mild-mannered chestnut gelding. Flattered, of course, by this massively talented and usually standoffish mare's attentions, Dynamo's ego was through the ceiling.

Her flirtation went a little something like this: wait for a fault to knock out the juice to her pen, shove through the inch-wide tapes when they were no longer electrified, saunter over to the pasture where the boys lived, lean over fence, nicker to Dynamo, squeal and kick at Dynamo, repeat. Mayfair, the young mare who was turned out with the boys, grazed as far away as she could without sacrificing the safety of the herd. She thought they were all idiots, and I had to agree with her.

Naturally, *all* the boys went crazy for Regina's antics, prompting Dynamo to turn into a jealous rage-stallion. That's where all the galloping up and down the fence came in, and the enraged roaring. That's where nightmares about running away from dinosaurs entered the subconscious of a perfectly sane horse trainer.

There they went again: the ground rumbled beneath my feet as four or five fairly fit event horses went tearing up the fence line, only to wheel at the corner and come thundering back for more flirting.

I didn't bother telling any of them Regina was only behaving like this because she was on layup from a serious injury. If she had been in work all winter, every ounce of her almost boundless energy would be consumed with tackling both arena work and cross-country courses with absolutely astonishing prowess. She wouldn't give boys the time of day. This was one tough mare, with the endless grinding work ethic of a champion. Horses like her didn't handle bedrest very well.

My eyes were used to picking out dark horses in a darker night, and I could see their shenanigans as I got closer. Regina nibbled at Dynamo's neck and he leaned over to return the favor; she squealed and stomped, Dynamo jumped back, nearly colliding with Jim Dear, who was gaping like a nerdy sidekick who didn't understand how the hero got all the girls. Jim tumbled away from Dynamo's hindquarters and stumbled against Barsuk, Pete's dapple-gray gelding, who pinned his ears and lifted a hind leg in warning. Jim wisely took off galloping, and Barsuk took off after him. Mayfair watched them for a moment and then followed, as if going for a pointless gallop was better than being third wheel to Regina and Dynamo's doomed love affair.

I sighed in exasperation, my breath leaving a white trail in the frosty night air. It was all fun and games until someone got kicked in the knee.

"Can we not?" I asked the herd of insanity.

Regina, remnants of her fence tape dragging around her heels, fastened me with a doleful look as I approached. She could have run away from me, but what she wanted was Dynamo, and he wasn't leaving her side. They were glued to the fence that separated them. *So* romantic. I rolled my eyes.

She didn't protest when I snatched her halter by the cheekpiece and gave her a hard look. Any other horse would've run off along the fence line, shouting for the herd to follow, but Regina played her own game. She was too dignified to protest. The herd of fog-addled idiots reappeared briefly, gathered up Dynamo, and then took off running again. They disappeared behind the slight rise in the pasture, and their hoofbeats slowly faded into the night. I hated it when they went down to the far end. It was a very large field with lots of trees at the end, the kind of field where horses could hide from your sight for hours, making you worry if you were a nervous kind of horse owner, or simply, like me, one who had experienced more than her share of bad horse luck.

Regina tugged at my hand and neighed, disappointed that her lover had left her. I glared at her. "Was this necessary tonight, of all nights? It's foggy. It's cold. I just want to be warm in my bed."

Regina rolled her left eye at me, the sclera tinted orange by the streetlight. *Why would I care?*

As I gave Regina's halter an impatient little yank, getting a sharp head toss in response, the night suddenly turned a luminous blue. I looked up and saw the clouds pulling away from the moon, a fat wedge with a grinning face. I didn't appreciate being laughed at, but I sure did like the extra light. "Thanks," I said, and gave the moon a little wave.

"You're welcome."

I turned around quickly, because while it wouldn't have surprised me if the moon started speaking to me, the voice was at ground level. Pete went sloping by in a pair of jeans and a sweatshirt, the wet grass slapping at his boots, a spool of electric tape and the fence-tester poking out of his back pocket. He looked half-asleep still. I started to tell him to leave it alone, that we'd just put her in the half-finished stall we'd been slowly building in between riding and jobs, but I let the words die in my throat. Pete liked to have things done, and every minute things weren't in order around here pained him. He'd see fixing the electric fence as the least he could do tonight.

I dragged the stubborn Regina over to the pasture gate where a tangle of lead ropes and halters were hung over a massive fence post, waiting to be made useful, and extracted a faded cotton rope from the pile. I snapped it onto her halter and let her drop her head to browse through the brown winter grass while I knelt and pulled at the tape dragging around her forelegs. She'd gotten the nylon webbing wedged under her therapeutic shoe again, the one that was helping hold her cracked hoof together while new wall grew in, agonizingly slowly. In the fall she'd caught her leg in a wire fence and damaged the coronary band, among other things. The farrier thought that with six months of new growth the coronary band might heal and the hoof would resume growing naturally. Or perhaps grow in with a slight wavy, wobbly pattern in the hoof.

Or, at worst, the crack would never mend itself and she'd be forever reliant on therapeutic shoes, no more than a dicey broodmare prospect. For a horse who had been so close to her first Advanced level three-day event, the uncertain prognosis was hard to live with, but it was better than no hope at all.

Apparently her second chance at life hadn't taught her to stop pawing at fences.

I tugged and seesawed at the tape stuck between the shoe and hoof until it popped free, frayed and tearing. Regina grazed on, ignoring me. At this point in Regina's life I could have completely reset all four shoes without her looking up from her grass. Her hoof had been prodded and poked so constantly for the past few months, she'd given up caring what we did with any of them.

"I'd give anything for you to just stay in that damn paddock, Regina," I told her. "You're making this way harder than it needs to be."

"That's her motivation," Pete said from somewhere down the fence line. Sound carried on these cold, foggy nights. "She's the easiest horse in the world . . . when she gets her own way."

"Such a mare." I started to sit down in the grass, then remembered it was drenched with chilly dew. I sighed and straightened up again. "How bad is the fence?"

"Just one panel is down," he called. "But then I have to figure out why the electric turned off again. So I won't be back in bed for a little while. Go without me."

He knew I wouldn't go to bed without him, but it was nice of him to offer. He always did. Yes, this was happening with enough regularity that I could say "always." It was high time we finished that stall so we could stick her inside at night, I decided. Tomorrow. If there was time. I ran through the day's calendar in my mind. There wasn't.

"Come on, miss." I tugged at Regina's lead rope until she reluctantly lifted her head, and we walked down the pasture fence toward her pen.

Regina's paddock was located about a hundred feet away from our little homestead of horse trailers. The "farm" we were renting was essentially a huge rectangular pasture with a strip of open grass running along the western short side. There was enough room on the strip of grass for our trailers and trucks, and the half-hearted shed we were hoping to turn into a one-sided shed row. Regina had a rectangular pen built of electric tape and metal stakes, connected to a solar-powered electric fence charger some former tenant had left. There wasn't any sign of electric fence anywhere else on the property, so we didn't know what they'd used it for. Maybe they'd had a great idea and not enough cash to see it through.

I could certainly identify with that.

Regina dipped her head again to graze as I stopped at the hot box. It was mounted to the fence on a rickety platform of rotting plywood, and the dimly glowing orange light indicated it was on and charging. It was ticking rhythmically, like a click bug that never stopped, day or night.

Well, the fence was definitely on, so something was killing the charge somewhere along the fence. Time for a recon. I started to pick up the slack in Regina's lead when the night suddenly went pitch black around me. Pete cursed with the eloquence of a man who just wants his bed. I looked up at the swath of cloud that had just enveloped the moon.

"For heaven's sake," I said. "Isn't that just typical."

I listened to Regina's teeth pulling at the deep dry grass and the occasional thud of her hoof as she took another step forward, her entire being immersed in the constant struggle to find more, better green stuff to devour. Horses were so powerful, so majestic, so emblematic of everything strong and enduring, and yet they were really just interested in eating grass. There was something very comforting about that at three o'clock in the morning. All our hard work and ambition was just feeding our silly human egos, while our horses nosed around looking for sweet clover.

A whip-poor-will rustled, probably shaken from sleep by our noise, and began to sing in the pine woods at the end of the fence: *whip-poor-will,* with a little chuckle at the end of each note, as if he thought Will's predicament was the funniest thing he'd heard all night. I looked up at the sky again; the moon was still buried in cloud. I couldn't even see if it was going to clear up again shortly or if this was some mass of northern cloud soaring in to overtake us for the next day or two. That happened in the winter sometimes, making everything gray and depressing, making me long for the unbearable heat and humidity of summer, because at least we'd have some damn light. I was a true Floridian. I'd lived here all my life, and I was addicted to glaring white tropical sunlight, long hot days, and the growling of distant thunder.

I tucked my straw-colored hair into a ponytail, bound it up with a rubber band that had been wrapped around a bundle of track bandages from the feed store, and leaned against the fence post where the fence charger was propped.

Less than a second passed before I jumped away, grabbing my arm. "Ouch! Damn!"

Regina looked up at me, her ears pricked, her jaw arrested mid-chew. I could see the whites of her eyes piercing through the darkness, considering taking off.

"What happened?" Pete called. He had his phone out, propped against a fence post, and was using the flashlight app to help him finish stretching the electric tape back into place.

I looked at the fence post, barely visible in the darkness. "I think I found where the fence is losing its charge."

The moon suddenly broke free, and the pasture lit up again in a silvery glow. On the rise in the distance, I saw the herd grazing peacefully, their fight over Regina forgotten. Regina saw them too. She whinnied shrilly, clearly missing the fun and games. Someone looked up, ears pricked.

"Shush!" I reprimanded her, then turned back to Pete. "Can a wooden post be electrified?"

Pete came over and studied the post. Unlike the others, which had more in common with walking sticks than telephone poles, this one was massive and fat, like a chunk of tree trunk had been dislodged from the neighboring forest and deposited here to cement the entire rickety fence.

Or it had been left here when someone lopped off the other trees to create this pasture.

He leaned in close and I thought for a moment he was going to touch his ear to the post, but then he straightened up again and fixed the post with a cocked eyebrow. "It's ticking."

"What?"

"The fence post is ticking in time with the hot box, you can hear it when you put your ear up to it. The box isn't grounded properly, and there's a current in the fence post."

"But it's wood." I didn't know a lot about electricity, but I knew wood wasn't supposed to electrocute a person.

"The wet is what's doing it, I think. Because we got that rain earlier. Is that the first time it's rained since we moved here?"

I considered the past couple of weeks. We'd been at this pasture in a forgotten section of North Florida for three weeks, since the beginning of February, so we were in the doldrums of the dry season. Yesterday afternoon a cold front had gone howling through, with an icy, piercing wind and a quick burst of rain that had everyone running for cover.

Pete and I had sheltered in the horse trailer, a damp Marcus panting by our sides, and looked helplessly back at the little shed row of stalls we were in the middle of constructing. Eventually everyone would have a stall. But for now, the pasture horses had a run-in shed and Regina had an oak tree. These were the closest things our previously coddled horses had to a barn. Luckily, they all seemed able to tough it out.

"That was the first rain," I confirmed. "So the post is hot when wet?"

"Basically. But that's not why Regina's fence isn't charging. It's just a kind of funny thing."

Regina stopped chewing for a moment, and we all contemplated the mystery of the un-hot hot wire together. Sometimes you realized just how loud a horse's chewing could be. She paused, and the whip-poor-will paused, and in the sudden silence left behind, I heard another ticking sound coming from behind me, and lower down. *"Grass,"* I realized aloud, turning and pointing.

Pete bent down and looked around the post, then eased himself through the fence boards and looked on the other side. "Ah," he said eventually. He reached up and switched off the fence charger. The rhythmic ticking stopped and the night seemed to exhale slowly, as if the repetitive noise had been driving it crazy for the past few weeks. I wondered if you could go insane from living next to a pasture hot box. I wondered if I even needed another reason. "You're right. Loose piece of wire and long wet grass."

I listened to him uprooting the grass. The pastures grew tough prairie grass up here in the pine wood clearings; it grew in thick clumps and when it was very long the edges seemed to grow serrated. It could draw blood if you weren't careful when you pulled at it. In my head I called it wiregrass, which was a term that popped up a lot in novels about Old Florida's cowboy days. Whether it was actually wiregrass or not, the horses loved it and grew fat on it. I hated it because the clumps made our attempts at field dressage training even tougher.

Regina went back to pulling at the shorter blades on this side of the fence, snorting loudly through her nose as she went.

"That'll do it," Pete said eventually. "Don't touch the post." He reached around and switched on the box, and it resumed its proud ticking with the air of a soldier returning to his post. He slipped back through the fence and pulled out the tester to check Regina's pen. "That's better," he called. "Let's put her back in."

I tugged Regina's lead rope and she followed me sullenly.

Pete clipped the tapes together again behind me, while she watched with an expression so clearly annoyed you could see it with only the moonlight.

"That's one pissed-off mare," I observed.

"I'm going to have to hire a cowboy to put her back into work."

"A bull rider."

I admired Pete's guts at even saying anything about riding Regina aloud, especially on a night when she'd already been loose and could have seriously injured herself (again). The eventing gods didn't usually like bold moves like that. They preferred to keep us guessing and vulnerable at all times. "Let's go back to bed," I said finally, pulling at his arm. "You're cold."

"It's chilly," he admitted. "You cold?"

I plucked at my plaid sleeves. "L.L. Bean, man. This is what they sleep in up in the Maine woods."

"I heard your mom say that, but I didn't know you'd take it to heart." Pete took my hand and started across the grass to the trailer. The thick blades rustled around our Wellington boots.

"I wish she'd bought you a pair." Christmas Day, nearly two months ago now, had meant a rare meeting between myself, my parents, and Pete, who was practically an orphan, since his parents lived overseas. I wanted him to feel like my parents were his parents, and I wanted them to treat him like a son. He was still having a hard time with the loss of his grandmother, who had basically raised him, and I thought he could use a little family love and support. But they hadn't really gotten the memo and had treated him with the sort of distant suspicion I guess most parents would treat a boyfriend they'd never met before. They bought me the flannel pj's, in deference to my upcoming winter living in a horse trailer, and bought Pete a travel mug from Starbucks, which he used every day without fail, as if to prove to me he was really very happy with the outcome of family Christmas with Jules.

And for all I knew, he was. Pete was never easy for me to read at the best of times, and he'd gotten even quieter and moodier since we'd left Briar Hill Farm. So I let well enough alone. I wasn't the sort of person to badger someone to share their feelings. Usually, I didn't even care how someone besides myself was feeling. Pete just happened to be an exception.

Still, I really did wish he had a pair of these magic pajamas. The temperature had to be down in the forties and I wasn't even that cold.

The trailer steps creaked as we climbed in, and Marcus pushed his way in front, hopping onto the little couch next to the door. He thumped his tail against the worn blue fabric, happy we were all home from our wee-hour adventures together. I leaned down and pulled at his long, silky beagle ears; even in the darkness I knew just where he was. When you reside in a horse trailer, you very quickly learn every inch of your surroundings, and just how far your hand has to reach to touch a panting dog in the darkness.

Marcus gave my hand an appreciative lick, then he sighed heavily and dropped his head, apparently slipping instantly back into deep sleep. I pictured him, curled up like a ball in the thick flannel blanket (another present from my parents—at least they considered Marcus a son), as I climbed up the short ladder to the bed over the gooseneck of the trailer. I missed having Marcus in bed, but there wasn't room for him even if he could figure out a way to get up there.

Marcus, having taken over the small couch and finding the extra stretching room delightful, did not seem to mind the separation as much as I did.

Pete snuggled up against me as soon as my head hit the pillow. "You're warm. Give me some of that."

"This is why we need a dog up here," I said. "What about a Jack Russell? We can get one of those tiny ones."

Pete laughed at me, then fell asleep almost instantly, while I lay awake, gazing into the dark and listening to the whip-poor-wills calling out in the pine forest. It was magically quiet here in High Springs, even quieter than Ocala. At Briar Hill, we'd heard the distant hum of the interstate on wet nights like this. Now whole hours could go by and I'd hear nothing besides the fence charger, and even that drifted away if the wind was from the north or west. Sometimes the silence was like a roaring in my ears. The little night birds chuckling and whistling out in the woods were a welcome break.

Some nights I used this quiet time for planning out conditioning calendars and show schedules; some nights I just spent it worrying. Lately, I'd been trying something else.

"I'm lucky," I whispered, turning away from Pete so my words fell into my pillow. They were only for me. "I have Pete, and Marcus, and a warm place to sleep. I have Mickey, and Dynamo, and Jim Dear, and enough money to keep them fed. I have a sponsor. I have Pete. I have Marcus. I have Mickey."

I thought about Mickey for a while, then. So talented, so gorgeous, so going places—and with me on his back. No matter what else happened, as long as I had a horse like Mickey, with easygoing owners like Mickey's, I was lucky, all right.

I rolled over again and looked at Pete, sleeping in that shaft of orange light glowing through our little window. He didn't think we were lucky; he wouldn't agree with my assessment of my blessings. Nights like this were a reminder to him that we didn't have what we needed. We didn't have enough fencing, we didn't have enough stalls, we didn't have enough of anything a pair of upper-level event riders needed to be successful.

And I knew he was right.

I was content, though. Against all odds, I was happy with our unconventional lot.

I'd gotten here expecting to hate it. How do you leave one of the best equestrian centers in Ocala for a ten-acre field with no conveniences in the middle of nowhere? What I hadn't expected was the feeling of peace that had washed over me almost immediately. That very first night, after dealing with all the predictable difficulties of moving six horses and setting up camp, I'd sat on the trailer steps and looked up at the stars.

There were so many here. If there were plenty of stars in Ocala, there was plenty of light, too, city sprawl replacing pastures with increasing speed. Someday the "horse capital of the world" would be nothing but subdivisions named for famous racehorses and the great farms their lawns replaced, and that someday wasn't far away. I loved Ocala, but anyone could see that it was being paved over.

Up here among the pine plantations of northern Alachua County, the sky was awash in stars so bright, I could see by starlight on clear, moonless nights.

I remembered that first night here, trying to make sense of what had happened. I'd been worn out with pretend optimism. All I had wanted was to move and put Briar Hill behind us, but once we'd actually done it, I wanted the feeling of being at home even more. And I couldn't imagine feeling at home in this weird frontier of lonesome pine trees. Then I'd looked out and seen that magical starlight, that soft, luminous glow that seemed to flow from all around, casting no shadows.

I'd left the trailer, stepping onto the strip of grass where we would make our home for as long as this exile from horse country lasted. Maybe others would follow us from the expensive fields of Marion County, and we'd just stay. Maybe this would be the new horse capital, and we'd long for the silence we'd once had, and move out even farther. At this point, I didn't know what I wanted anymore. To be still, maybe. To stop feeling like I was on the run. Two farms gone in two years; too many.

I opened the gate soundlessly and slipped into the pasture, walking out into the darkness that wasn't.

Their teeth tore at the thick grass, which hadn't been grazed or mown in months. Their tails were still. There was no pond nearby, and no standing water, and so there were no mosquitoes.

I walked among the horses as they slowly moved, step by step, toward the middle of the field. We were about halfway when the starlight seemed to thicken and whiten. I stopped, though the horses didn't, and I stared, though the horses didn't lift their heads.

Among their warm, hungry bodies, I watched the first silvery wraiths of a fog rise up from the ground, gathering up the starlight.

My breath caught in my lungs and refused to come out again. The grasping, drifting fog was spreading like a greedy ghost across the lower end of the field, and it was both the most beautiful and the most frightening thing I'd ever seen. I turned to Dynamo and wrapped my fingers into his mane. He paused in his grazing to regard me, head cocked, ears pricked. "I'm getting on," I told him.

I imagined him shrugging. *Whatever.*

Mounting from the ground wasn't my strongest suit, but I managed to heave myself over his back after a few practice hops. Once I was up there, Dynamo decided I was worth paying attention to and obeyed the combined pressure of my seat, leg, and hands to turn back toward the barn. There was no light except the small shining rectangles of the trailer windows. All around them the formless glow lit the field with a blue so faint it was nearly imperceptible. I didn't turn around to see the luminous fog; I kept my eyes on the shadows where Pete and Marcus were waiting for me.

And as I slipped off Dynamo, rewarding him with a stroke on the neck for allowing me to interrupt his grazing, I realized the other horses had come along too. We were all together in the starlight. They crowded around me, certain I'd brought handouts, and as I fended off eager lips and nibbling teeth, I thought: *This is happiness.*

There was no one here but the horses. And except for Mickey, they were our horses. There were no owners with differing opinions on training and show schedules, no one breathing down our necks to go farther, faster. There was no one but us.

Now, as I had that first night, I lay awake, in a horse trailer parked next to a big pasture, without a barn, without an arena, without anything that we should have to run a successful eventing business. And I felt free.

I wasn't sure I'd ever felt free before.

I looked at Pete again, still sleeping in his patch of orange light, and felt the earth spinning away with us lodged safely in our trailer atop it. We were better off here, even though we were making do with less than we'd ever had before—I *knew* we were. I wished he knew it, too.

2

PHILOSOPHY AT THREE in the morning is one thing; waking up to start morning chores a few hours later is quite another. I would have given anything to have back my neat center-aisle barn, my horses nodding at me over their stall grills, my tidy feed room with the morning feed buckets lined up in rows. Life without a barn was chaos, especially at feeding time. Had I really thought this would somehow be better? Feeding six horses loose on ten acres was just the kind of adventure I didn't need in my life.

"Can you get them in the catch pens okay? I'll set up feed if you're good."

I gave Pete the thumbs-up. It was too early for words.

The catch pens were little stalls we'd built along the fence in front of the trailers. Maybe "stalls" was a strong word. They were small holding pens with just enough room for a horse to walk in and eat his grain without another horse leaning over and taking it. Breeding farms used them for pastured horses. They were the convenient way to catch broodmares or yearlings and feed them without everyone sharing a bucket, and to keep horses handy while waiting for the vet. I'd seen them around Ocala, but I'd never used them before. At riding and training barns, we typically just brought horses inside when we needed them.

Neither Pete nor I had ever kept horses on pasture board, and our ignorance had showed quickly. At first we'd had this naive hope we could feed everyone in the pasture if we just spread their feed buckets far enough apart. This hope lasted about forty-five seconds, when Mickey discovered Jim Dear had some grain that was probably way more interesting than his and went plowing after it with his ears pinned, chasing poor old Jim off his bucket.

Jim, who had briefly roughed it before I'd gotten him, sulked for barely a minute before he went trotting up to Mickey's abandoned bucket, but at this point Dynamo was feeling opportunistic and had already gone to investigate Mickey's bucket, during which time Barsuk was eyeball-deep in Dynamo's bucket . . . it was a mess. Feeding time dissolved into dominoes.

The good thing was they'd only had about a half scoop of feed in each bucket, in the interest of experimentation, so no one ate someone else's expensive vitamins, or had too much if they gorged on more than their share.

After this, Pete decided we should build catch pens. We'd just spent a couple thousand dollars on the first month's rent and security deposit, so there was no extra cash to buy fence supplies, but the property had an old rubbish heap behind the run-in shed. We found some flimsy round fence posts, the kind cattlemen used for barbed wire, piled up and slowly rotting under a brown blanket of dead kudzu vines. We dragged those out, with a lot of screeching on my part when the inevitable giant brown wood spiders came scrambling into the light, and hauled them over to the fence near the pasture gate. We had been at the new farm all of three hours, and we were starting to build things.

I picked at a splinter in my thumb while Pete surveyed the pile of posts. A few were rotted nearly through in the middle, but a dozen or so were fairly intact. Enough, if we stood them out twelve feet from the pasture fence, to set up the skeleton of six catch pens.

Pete rubbed at his scruffy beard, which had popped up while we'd been busy with moving horses and our life. It was a reddish brown, darker than his burnished copper hair. "We need some boards," he announced eventually, as if this was a great revelation.

I had to make allowances for Pete sometimes. He was a horseman of the landed gentry variety. He was not exactly handy with a hammer, or quick with the engineering plans. But he figured it all out eventually. Sometimes it just took a little longer than I would have hoped.

"We don't have any boards," I informed him. "We do have another spool of electric tape." It was left over from building Regina's pen.

"Can we use that to build catch pens?" He looked doubtful.

"If they're big enough, maybe." I'd never seen anyone build stalls out of electric tape, but Regina was living in a pen built of electric tape and it was keeping her in . . . *So far,* I reminded myself. Of course, at this point, we'd only been here since noon and it was now about half past three. Still, we just needed these things to work for twenty minutes at night and twenty minutes in the morning, and only until we got the stalls built. "Maybe we don't even have to hook them up to the hot wire. Probably just the visual of the fence will be enough to keep them inside," I added hopefully.

Record scratch, narrator voiceover: *"The visual would not be enough."*

Now, three weeks later, we were older and wiser and knew the true limits of nonelectrified electric tape.

For an actual visual a horse would respect, we'd gone back to good old wood. Just one board, nailed to the top of each fence post, plus a rubber stall chain to keep horses in their catch pens until we were good and ready to let them out.

This lesson had cost us one spool of electric tape, making a serious dent in our precious inventory of DIY horse stabling supplies. Every time Regina tore some fabric in her nocturnal escapes, we lost a little more. Now I cast a desperate glance back over at the framework of the shed-row-to-be. It was like a skeleton of wobbly lumber. Somehow it felt hard to imagine we'd turn that into a workable barn.

Back to reality. The geldings were being idiots, as usual. Barsuk and Jim Dear were sparring over the same catch pen. Mickey was watching with pricked ears, evidently ready to join the fray. Dynamo was still standing at the other end of the fence, staring at Regina. Mayfair was already in the catch pen she liked, waiting for her feed with ears pricked and one hind leg cocked. No one messed with Mayfair, but she liked to hold her leg in firing position anyway, as a reminder.

"Knock it off!" I shouted, and everyone turned and stared at me with wide eyes.

I slipped through the fence and clapped my hands at Barsuk, startling him out of the catch pen he'd tried to claim from the cowering Jim Dear, then snapped up the stall chain before Jim could follow him back into the pasture.

"Why do you always want to go with him?" I asked Jim. "He only wants to kill you."

I patted his haunches before I moved on to push Barsuk into the next catch pen. I felt sorry for my plain bay gelding. Jim Dear was the farm punching bag. Once I actually watched a squirrel chase him from the shade of an oak tree. He was the nicest, sweetest gelding you could ever hope for, and he'd jump the moon if you just gave him the right stride for it, but he was essentially gentle

Ferdinand the Bull deposited into a bull ring, and every other horse was a matador out for his blood.

Barsuk, disgruntled, pinned his ears at me and shook his head as if he was ready to charge and run me down. I scooped up a handful of sand from the trampled-up ground and hurled it at his chest. "Don't even *think* about it." I tried to roar, but my voice was still hoarse with sleep. Wasn't that crazy? The rest of my nerves were tingling, ready to go into battle with these mad horses, and my voice was still trying to wake up. "I'll make you sorry you were foaled!"

The dapple-gray gelding turned tail and trotted into the catch pen next to Jim Dear, ducking his head into the empty bucket and rattling it violently to let me know there was nothing in it and he was outraged.

"I know it's not full yet, you idiot," I told him. "When have I ever dumped feed before I locked you lunatics in your stalls?"

Barsuk flattened his ears, arched his neck, gripped the green bucket between his long teeth, and gave it a fierce yank. The bucket's snap popped off the screw eye and went sailing through the air, never to be seen again. Barsuk held the bucket for a moment, considering his next move, and then with one fluid swing of his neck, threw the bucket into the air. I watched it sail up, over the fence, and whack poor Jim Dear on the neck. Jim had a fit and nearly ran right through the stall chain, his eyes huge.

"I got a real problem with you," I told Barsuk. "You're a talented horse, but you shouldn't be living with other horses. You're a sociopath."

He shook his head at me, a little habit of his I hadn't noticed before we moved out here.

In my mind, I had a phase two for our little farm: building two fences right through the pasture, making three big paddocks.

There'd be one for Barsuk, one for Mayfair and Regina once she was off layup, and one for the other boys, who weren't so violent with Barsuk's bad influence out of the way. Of course, they'd need sturdy wooden coops built between them, for all the fun little cross-country jumps I wanted to build out there.

My Farm 2.0 was a *secret* dream, though, because Pete didn't have a phase two in mind. He insisted we were here temporarily, before we landed our next big break, and there was no reason to start developing infrastructure. This was the term he used whenever I brought it up. "This isn't a place where we should spend time developing infrastructure," he'd say, like he was Henry Flagler choosing where to build his next railroad.

So I didn't mention phase two more than a few times before I let it go. But if I didn't say anything out loud, you better believe I was dreaming it. In my imagination, I had us build this little scrap of pasture into a full mini equestrian center, complete with a single-wide trailer (from the used-trailer lot, to save money) to take the place of living in the horse trailer, within the next six months.

All I needed was to pick up maybe one nice horse and sell him for a tidy profit.

"Hop on in here, Mickey," I told my gray horse, and he shook his head at me, his little white forelock wagging, before he entered the catch pen. "Did you learn that from watching Barsuk? Because he's a bad influence on you. Try to learn from Dynamo, instead."

Flipping a project horse from green-broke to ammie-ready in six months didn't seem to be a stretch. I'd turned out amateur-owner horses like a machine back before I moved to Briar Hill. Then, my ambition to only train upper-level horses had gotten in the way. And look at me now: just three horses to my name.

"Four would be fine," I said to myself, pushing a compliant Dynamo into his catch pen and snapping up the chain. "Plenty of time to spend on you guys, and a project horse to bring in some cash."

"Everyone in?"

I looked over my shoulder. We'd parked our two horse trailers back to back to create a little settlement. Pete's trailer had nicer living quarters than mine, so we set up household in there. My trailer was the combination feed and tack room. Pete leaned out of the back of it, one arm full of buckets.

"All in," I confirmed.

Pete jumped down. The horses saw the food coming and roared their approval.

There was an important lesson here: horses really don't care where they live, as long as there is food.

With everyone munching, I settled down on the lip of the open trailer doorway to watch them. Their contentment spilled over and softened my worries. They were happy, so I was happy. Sometimes, being an equestrian was as simple as that.

Marcus came flowing into my lap, wagging his whippy tail. "You were licking up whatever Pete spilled, I guess?" I asked him. "Think you're a horse?"

Marcus closed his soulful brown eyes, appreciating the rubdown I was giving his ears. He didn't think he was a *horse*. He thought he was a *person,* which was probably my fault.

There was a wan suggestion of sunrise over the tall pines at the far end of the pasture, a dirty pink beginning to soften the gray clouds. Pete stood watching it, empty buckets in both hands, as if he was waiting for a sign.

He spent a lot of time like that these days. It worried me. Some girls wanted a soulful man. I found the idea problematic. We didn't have time to sit and be soulful. We had work to do.

And you couldn't dwell on disaster too long in the horse

business. There were simply too many disasters and not enough time. Unfortunately, that was exactly what Pete seemed to be doing. So things weren't exactly going as planned. I mean, obviously they weren't—a few weeks ago we'd kept our horses on one of the best eventing farms in Florida, and now we were renting a ten-acre pasture with a very basic, possibly illegal RV hookup about a fifteen-minute hack from shared arenas at High Springs Equestrian Center, a very grand name for a very basic boarding stable.

Of course I missed Briar Hill, but I didn't miss it the way Pete did. I missed it the way a person misses a castle from a dream; it was a good dream, the kind you try to cling to as wakefulness comes to rouse you back to reality, and I'd be happy to dream it again, but this was real life. A pasture, a leaning skeleton of a shed row, the living quarters of a horse trailer—and Pete, and the horses, and Marcus. If that was all I had right now, that was fine.

Pete wasn't taking it quite so well.

Briar Hill had been *his* farm, and we'd spent a fortune trying to keep it from going to that Old South college Pete's grandmother had willed it to.

We knew she would have changed her mind and left it to Pete if she'd had half a chance; Pete was doing exactly what she'd demanded of him, that he find a way to make it to Advanced level and onto the international stage. The problem, of course, was that she didn't expect to die. That's the problem for most people, I imagine.

So Briar Hill would be going to people who couldn't possibly use it. They'd eventually sell it, probably in pieces, a little farm here, a little farm there, and there was really nothing we could do about it. The best thing to do was put it out of our minds. No more Briar Hill Farm.

Of course, the farm that sucked us dry was now, ironically, paying our bills.

There was just enough money coming from the renters living in our old house and using Pete's old barn to keep us going. For a little while longer, Briar Hill was keeping our horses in hay and grain, and us in soup and crackers.

I was ready for the cycle to be over, though, even if it meant the rent money dried up. Losing a farm was starting to feel like a broken record for me, and I was tired of that skipping song, playing over and over: you need owners to pay your bills, you need to win to keep your owners happy, you need to hurry hurry hurry and get that horse going, oh and by the way, here's a storm to blow away your house, here's a hurricane to flatten your farm, here's a lost legacy to ruin your chances.

I had already learned the lesson Pete was trying to ignore now: nothing lasts, and everything hurts . . . for a little while, anyway. I was hoping he'd come out of this haze with the same vagabondish tendencies I had acquired—the feeling of being a transient, light on responsibilities outside of our own horses.

I *liked* things the way they were right now.

The horses finished their grain and started on the alfalfa we'd thrown under their buckets, hoping the hay would catch spilled pellets so they didn't dig them out of the sand.

The sun slowly lifted above the pine trees, its light muted by the thick cirrus bank stretching across the sky. Today would be a northern day, cloudy and cool. A sensible woman would spend it in bed, under the covers. I was not sensible.

Marcus yawned, his tongue curling to touch his black nose, and stood up, shaking his floppy ears. He fastened his brown eyes on me and made the most beseeching look a beagle can make, which is almost deadly. *Time for breakfast, lady.*

"I agree. Pete, honey?" I called. "Let's have some coffee, okay? I'm making it."

It was usually Pete's job to make coffee in the morning. We'd picked his horse trailer for our home because the living quarters were almost luxurious, but the electric outlet in the kitchen made me nervous. Unfortunately, it was becoming quite clear that if I wanted coffee today, I was going to be responsible for it. Pete was leaning on the fence, gazing into the distance, evidently not in any hurry for caffeine.

I sighed, and hopped down from the trailer. "Come on, Marcus." Marcus followed, grunting a little as he hit the ground— Marcus, like the horses, was not following the strict austerity diet we humans were on, and he was a roly-poly. I opened the screen door of the living quarters and my boots clanked on the metal steps. Marcus sat down in the grass and eyeballed me, as if he would prefer his breakfast served alfresco this morning.

"You're the smartest one here," I told him.

Two short steps and I was across the trailer's living area and standing at the kitchen counter, where a little sink, a half-sized fridge, and a tiny microwave were wedged into place like puzzle pieces. To the fridge's right was the wall where the gooseneck began, and our bed rested atop it, at chin height. To the kitchen's left, there was a little bathroom with an adorable shower like something you'd build for elves, crouching behind an accordion door. Against the wall next to the door was a dark blue loveseat. That was all.

These few square feet were where we lived now.

The tack room at Briar Hill had been larger and more comfortable, I reflected, but it also had its share of electrical problems. The time the air conditioner almost caused a barn fire while we were peacefully sleeping right next to it, for example. "I just hate electricity," I said out loud. "Couldn't we learn to power our lives with something that can't kill us?"

"Everything can kill us," Pete said with impressive gravity from just outside the trailer. "Just some ways are more interesting than others."

"Horses, for example," I suggested.

"Of course. Are you really going to make the coffee?"

"I said I was going to, didn't I?"

"You say a lot of things. You said you were going to drive down to the phone company's offices and burn them to the ground if they didn't figure out our data plan by last Thursday, but I drove by yesterday and the damn place is still standing."

"Give me time. Here it is Tuesday and they still haven't fixed anything. I'm sick of driving to the truck stop to use Wi-Fi every time I want to check my emails." I took a deep breath and plugged in the coffeemaker, shoving the plug home with a grunt.

There was a *pop!* and an acrid smell, but no obvious sparks, and the coffeemaker's little power light turned on, a satisfying amber that meant soon we would have caffeine flowing through our veins and all would be well with the world.

Except for the obvious fire hazard in the room.

"Pete, you have got to have this thing fixed."

There was silence.

I turned around and saw he'd wandered away from the open door, staring up at the leaden sky again as if it held the answers to whatever questions he kept asking himself.

Well, I sure didn't have them. Maybe the sky would start talking and do us all a favor.

I busied myself pulling out our travel mugs and the slim jug of milk from the fridge, while the coffeemaker hummed and rattled to itself. We'd have some coffee, we'd do some chores, we'd ride, we'd go to the local farms where we made a few bucks teaching and training. Just another day in this mad, mad life of ours.

"Are you going to work on the barn today?"

We were a couple gulps of coffee into our mugs and Pete's shoulders appeared to have sagged a few inches away from his ears, meaning he was loosening up enough to perform polite conversation. I leaned my plastic patio chair back so my head rested on the cool aluminum skin of the trailer behind me. Pete was leaning forward, his forearms resting on his thighs, his coffee mug clenched in both hands. He looked over at me and considered the question for a moment. "I think I can get another stall walled off today," he said. "If Penny Lane doesn't want me to ride too many."

I bit back my initial thought, which was that those rich fancy-pants owners over at Penny Lane had better put him on a set schedule with regular horses to ride if they didn't want him to go to a competitor who would, with Pete's help, start kicking their asses at the HITS winter show circuit every weekend. This was not a helpful thing to say. I knew this for a fact, because I said it yesterday, and Pete did not say anything in response. He didn't say anything for a good two hours, just went and hammered at the stalls until he'd bloodied his thumb and given me a headache.

He didn't necessarily enjoy his job, giving weekly tune-ups to ring-sour jumpers at Penny Lane Equestrian Center, but their facility was nice and nearby, and, most importantly, the manager let us use their Grand Prix arena for jumping schools once a week. Between that and the little hunter course at High Springs Equestrian Center, just a hack away, we were able to keep our horses from forgetting how to jump a course between events.

"Well, that's great. We can give that stall to Mayfair when Regina's not in it," I offered instead, trying to turn the construction project Pete was woefully unprepared to complete into a positive. Really, getting a new stall *was* a positive . . . if you didn't count the money that wouldn't be going into Pete's pocket from riding a few troublesome warmbloods, and the possibility of a serious medical bill should he fall off the roof. "She could use some stall time away from the boys. Rein in that attitude of hers a little bit."

"Oh, she's just feeding off Regina." Pete shrugged. "Hormones in the air. Regina wants a man and Mayfair doesn't disagree. But I think we should give the stall to Dynamo. He'll need his own stall once he starts galloping again and needs his legs done up afterward. Mayfair's not working hard enough to worry about that right now."

"Good point." I gave in because Dynamo was the most important horse on the farm right now. Pete was right that Dynamo needed a stall for icing and poulticing after conditioning gallops, but so was I—Mayfair really did need to be pulled in from the herd and reminded she was not in charge of the farm. She'd been a model citizen since the day Pete brought her home, but the sudden change in status from lesser filly to boss mare had found its way into the riding ring, and I didn't think for a moment it was all hormones. She just really loved being in charge, and she was testing the limits of that power. She had a surprisingly powerful buck, as we'd recently learned. These were facts you didn't necessarily want to know about your horse.

Still, it was a reminder that we really couldn't reintroduce serious endurance work, the tough stuff that called for icing or poultice afterward, if the horses didn't have their own stalls. They'd tear down the catch pens if they were left in for too long, and needed room to walk and lie down. It was another reason we had to hustle on the barn.

At least Mayfair and Jim Dear were just going Novice and Training level. With Dynamo about to step up to Advanced, and Mickey and Barsuk schooling Prelim, their legs needed all the pampering they could get.

In the catch pens about twenty feet away, the horses had finished their breakfast alfalfa and were glaring at us, waiting to be let out into the field. It was only a matter of time before they started dismantling the entire structure.

Infrastructure, I thought suddenly, and suppressed a giggle.

"You want to ride right now?"

"Might as well," Pete said, shrugging. "Get it out of the way."

I watched him push out of the chair and shuffle toward the trailer's tack room without enthusiasm. Something essential was missing; not all of Pete had come with us to High Springs. I sighed. Why was I the only hopeful one?

I'd known he wasn't impressed when we'd come to see the property. I'd taken his hand and asked why we shouldn't give it a try. Maybe we weren't big-farm people. Maybe we were horsemen who just needed a handful of horses and low overhead. Maybe we'd succeed this way when the traditional route had failed us.

Some of the words had even come from Grace, the trainer I'd spent last summer working for down in Orlando. She'd told me my strength was in my ability to get close to a horse. She'd been the one to put this idea in my head in the first place, the idea of having just a handful of horses, horses I worked with closely every day, becoming a true partner to each one.

A month after talking Pete into this patch of grass and sagging fence, I still thought we'd made the right decision. We'd succeed with this place, once we overcame the first obvious hurdles: the lack of a barn, the lack of jumps. We could build those things. We could buy an old mobile home, with a little savings.

My infrastructure plans could work out.

I was willing to wait and prove to Pete I was right. That our future was right here, on this big rectangular pasture, if we could just hold ourselves together long enough to build it.

3

THE MORNING SUN was gleaming through the tops of the pine trees by the time we were cantering around the pasture, and the silver fog was slowly receding back into the trees at the far end of the field with its dry summertime pond. The grass grew in thin clumps down there, and the exposed clay was cracked, with a peeling skin of green moss in places. Birds fluttered up as we thundered along the fence line, riding side by side like a pair of knights errant.

Or a cowboy and his sidekick. Only, who was who? Something told me we'd both applied for the same job.

We'd dragged some old pieces of wooden lattice I'd found in the woods into the field and propped it up on some convenient tree stumps, and now I let Pete pull ahead and canter Dynamo over the makeshift jump before I guided Mickey onto the same path. A far cry from our massive cross-country course back at Briar Hill, but I'd made a couple of these little fences and scattered them around the far end of the field, and they made a fun diversion from slogging up the long trail to the arenas at High Springs Equestrian Center, where we did most of our training now. Pete tolerated them because they weren't permanent and didn't fall under his forbidden category of infrastructure. They were literally just trash in the pasture we could jump the horses over.

I had fun plans for actual cross-country fences, though— maybe when the pond filled in, we could throw a couple poles in front of it, and have a water splash. It would be good for the younger horses, anyway.

I circled Mickey and hopped him over the lattice again, and after the jump he dug his head down against the bit, eager to push on and gallop for bigger fences. The web reins, stiff with old sweat, dug into my fingers and rubbed old calluses.

"We don't have anything else right now," I told him. "Sorry, buddy."

Pete had pulled up Dynamo and was surveying the motley collection of brush and old building equipment. "I think we can make some gymnastics out of some of these, and turn those old poles into a skinny V," he said thoughtfully. "It's great galloping over some basic jumps, but we really need to work on precision if we're going to be ready to get back in the game. A month off can be a long time when we're talking about these technical courses we're going to see."

I'd much rather just gallop at high speed over brush fences, but I knew he was right. We'd taken enough time off from serious jumping work. Everyone would need a refresher before Mill Pond. When we'd first inked it into our calendars, the early-March event had seemed perfect, the culmination of four straight months of increasingly tough competition on the Florida winter circuit. We hadn't expected taking a surprise month off while we threw all our energy into getting moved, getting settled, and getting new jobs to pay the hay man.

Now there were points to chase if we were going to level up horses and get to the fall championships, and we were facing the end of the Florida season in just two more months. We had a lot of catching up to do in March and April, or we'd have to travel north to get the finishes we needed, and there was no money in the budget for long-haul trips with the horse trailers.

"We can work on some jumps this afternoon," I offered. "I don't have to head over to teach until after four. We have time to work on the stall and put together some jumps."

"Well, I have to work after all," Pete said glumly. "Denise texted to tell me there were four to ride before their owners start showing up after five. I'll be there at least until six. And we need to get the rest of the stalls done before anything else."

Then why did you say anything at all? I wondered, but I didn't say it out loud. "That's fine, then. I'll work on the barn this afternoon. I can swing a hammer."

"Don't try to get that metal sheeting up there by yourself again," he warned.

"I wouldn't even consider it." The struts were in place for the entire shed row to get a roof, but the sheet metal came in big heavy rectangles that caught the wind and threatened to cut off heads and arms (ask me how I found out). We needed an extra person, preferably one who had actual experience attaching sheet metal to wooden struts. "I can nail up some of the boards between stalls, though."

"That's fine." Pete nodded as if he was a foreman and I was one of his workers, and I pressed down another snotty response. *Be nice, Jules. Pete's got a lot on his mind.*

So do I!

Just be nice and don't worry about it, okay?

"Fine," I said aloud.

Pete glanced back at me as he started to walk Dynamo back toward the top of the pasture. "What's that?"

"Oh, nothing."

I gave Mickey a pat, noticed he was barely warm, and sighed. Sure, the morning was cool, but we just didn't have enough equipment to challenge these horses at all, let alone get them fit enough for a horse trials. Or accept in any client horses. I knew that was bothering Pete, too. He was supposed to be on the look-out for a good horse, an upper-level prospect, and the question of where we'd keep this horse was definitely a bridge we couldn't cross yet.

Rockwell had introduced Rick Delannoy to us back at Glen Hill Three-Day Event while we were still admiring our ribbons, and Delannoy had insulted me, plain and simple, by having eyes only for Pete. That sandals-and-socks-wearing snowbird wanted a top event horse and he wanted a big-time rider for him, but he didn't have the dough to chase after someone with more mileage than raw talent, so Carl Rockwell handed him to us . . . well, to Pete. He'd looked right through me.

Delannoy had been itching to go horse shopping right away, but Pete kept pushing it off. I knew he was trying to avoid letting Rick find out about our barn, or lack thereof. Part of Pete's reputa-tion had simply come from Briar Hill Farm, one of the best eventing properties in Florida. By keeping the farm name on our equipment, including the *Briar Hill Eventing* decal Alex had put on our trucks, the word on our recent self-eviction was only out to the most con-nected members of eventing society.

Pete was sure that once Delannoy and Rockwell actually con-nected our new mailing address with the reality of our rather sparse base camp, his star would begin to fade. I didn't think the entire eventing community was that shallow, but I knew Rockwell was, and there was no reason to think his buddies would be any different. So I cropped all evidence of our reduced facilities from any pictures I uploaded to social media. For all anyone knew, we had decamped to High Springs for our health, not because we were too broke to afford a proper training facility.

The upshot of all this deception by omission was that Pete had been unwilling to play the Delannoy card. He'd told Delannoy he would call him when he knew he'd found the right horse, not before, and we'd just assumed that would be no time soon.

But when he found the horse . . . we'd have to have somewhere pretty to put him. And somewhere we could get him fit for a busy competitive season, just like the rest of our horses.

"Pete? Should we trailer down to Alex's place to do a gallop?"

"All the way to Ocala?"

"Mickey needs to get back into fitness work. There's not enough room here."

"I suppose," Pete said, "but won't Alex want a lesson, too? That makes it a whole day away."

"Well, yeah," I admitted. "She's been bugging me." Alex had been keeping her off-track Thoroughbred, Tiger, with us before we'd left Briar Hill. She'd been disappointed to take him back to the training barn of her Thoroughbred farm, but there was no way she could drive an hour and change to High Springs every day to ride. It was one of the nagging problems I couldn't quite brush away; we were just so far away from our community.

Pete opened the gate, a hand on Dynamo's chest to keep the horse from shoving past him before there was enough space to safely pass through.

"It's safer to gallop them on the groomed track than on our pasture," I reminded him.

He nodded, looking back over the pasture as if he was looking for the smoothest route through its clumps of wiregrass and half-hidden burrows where gopher tortoises tunneled. "I can see doing it this week, but we need to find a local place."

"Maybe there's a state park with riding trails around here," I said. I pulled out my phone to check while it was still top of my mind, and it almost immediately started buzzing in my hand.

I was so startled I nearly dropped the damn thing, but I caught it just before it rolled beneath Mickey and presumably was trampled under his hooves. The screen told me it was Eileen, Mickey's half owner. That was weird. It was only nine o'clock in the morning, very early for her to be calling. "Hello?" I said cautiously into the speaker. Mickey flipped his ear back with interest.

"Jules?"

Who else would it be? "Yeah, hi, Eileen, what's up? It's funny you called, I'm literally on Mickey right now—"

"Listen, Jules, I don't have a lot of time to talk. Things aren't good. I'm really sorry to call you like this, but things just aren't good."

My hand started trembling on the phone and I slid it under the harness of my helmet to keep it from slipping out of my grip. *I'm lucky,* I reminded myself. *I'm so lucky to have Mickey, lucky lucky lucky—*

"I'm selling," Eileen gasped, sounding as if someone had punched her in the stomach. "I have to sell."

"Sell?"

"Mickey."

"Eileen, what happened?" *This isn't happening.*

"What always happens? I don't have the money." She sniffed, then seemed to pull herself together. Her next words were much stronger. "I can keep my young horses if I sell my horses in training. That means Mickey."

"You love Mickey," I said wildly, nearly shouting. "You're crazy about him!"

Mickey flicked back his ears, possibly because I said his name, or more likely because his rider was clearly going insane while still on his back.

"I love my babies too," she insisted. "And they're here with me. Mickey is in Florida. He'll never be mine again. And he's talented. I don't want to squander that."

"We can work something out," I babbled. "Let's talk this through."

"I can't, Jules. I'm sorry."

"Is Carrie buying you out?" Eileen was only the half owner, after all. The other owner was an established member of the eventing community, with half a dozen top horses in her name. "Carrie can buy Mickey's other half, problem solved."

Eileen sniffled. "I'm really sorry. But Carrie isn't going to buy him. Carrie wants out, too. She asked me to buy his other half and that's when all of this got really clear to me."

It was a shot in the gut. Everything stopped around me; the world went silent. Only Mickey went on, walking steadily, his mane rough under my right hand, holding the reins connected to his living mouth. Only Mickey was real.

"Why would Carrie want out?" I croaked, finally finding my voice, or something like my voice.

"She has too many horses," Eileen said grimly. "She's looking to pare back. Jules, I'm so sorry."

"Don't apologize," I said, not because I didn't blame her, not because I didn't want her to feel bad, but because I wanted to get down to business. "Have you talked to anyone yet? Any buyers?" It had to be another owner who would want me to ride Mickey. It couldn't be another rider. Or someone else's owner.

"No . . . but Carrie might have. I told her last night."

And Carrie knew everyone. And everyone knew Carrie. It would probably be all over the blogs by afternoon feeding that Carrie Donnelly, top owner, was looking to sell her interest in Danger Mouse, that up-and-coming gray gelding she'd unaccountably given to Jules Thornton to train. People would be calling her. Owners, trainers, riders. Mickey wasn't just a big horse for me. Mickey was a big horse, period.

That's why I'd been so damn lucky, up until about five minutes ago.

4

"DOWNWARD TRANSITION TO trot in the corner, half halt, half halt, half—good! Check your diagonal, that's right, now bring him down *aaand* halt."

The teenager I'd been shouting at ran her hand down her bay gelding's neck the way I'd shown her, a soft slide rather than a big clapping pat on the neck—a moderate motion that wouldn't dislodge her seat from its balanced position in the saddle. Her mouse-colored ponytail swung beneath her green schooling helmet and across her expensive (Rockwell Brothers) technical-fabric polo shirt, also green, above black breeches and black field boots. Jordan's mother liked her turned out well, and matchy-matchy, at all times. Jordan didn't care; she just wanted to ride, hopefully event, if her mother would let her. Mrs. Reynolds was on the fence about eventing versus hunters. Mostly her debate was about body count, like it was for a lot of moms, but so far local eventing had been having a happily safe season.

"He felt super nice and easy in those transitions," Jordan panted, because she knew I liked feedback. The truth was, I wasn't a great riding instructor and had always hated the gig, but I was finding that if I got the students talking about what they were feeling or not feeling from their horses, the lessons kind of built themselves.

Today, still in a haze from Eileen's morning call, I was together enough to notice Jordan's riding faults. Being judgmental was kind of my thing. Why hadn't I realized that was the basis of riding instruction? Maybe I'd been running from my true calling all these years.

"He *did* look nice. But what happened to changing diagonals by rising two beats? Didn't you feel him bobble when you sat two beats instead? I thought we had that down."

"I forgot." Jordan sighed. "I always forget something." Her face was already red from the chilly breeze, or she would have blushed with embarrassment. I'd only been teaching Jordan for three weeks, but I'd already learned she was a nervous wreck when criticized.

"That's okay, Jordan. If you don't forget something, I will."

She relaxed a little and her horse ducked his head toward his hooves, pulling the reins through her hands. She yelped and dove to recover them. I watched the horse stagger into an unbalanced walk. So much for keeping them together in a neat package for more than two minutes.

"Let him stretch out on a loose rein and then we'll do some fences," I called, and sat down on the mounting block in the middle of the covered arena. I dug out my phone and checked for messages from Pete.

He'd had to go ride at Penny Lane right before noon, so he'd only managed to nail up a few boards on Mayfair's stall before he had to pull on his white Penny Lane polo shirt and head over to ride four horses who were back for a hot minute from the Ocala showgrounds to get their heads screwed on straight again. The horses went through the same pattern every couple of weeks: they lived in their stalls at the showgrounds, cantering in classes half the day and standing by the in-gate the other half, won a few ribbons, went a little bananas from the stress, and had to come home for some turnout and a come-to-Jesus meeting.

Pete was the priest in these proceedings. Once he'd exorcised the horse show demons and baptized every good little citizen, they went back on the trailer and returned to the horse show hamster wheel. He didn't love the job, but it paid him decent money and gave him the potential to meet new clients and network with hunter/jumper types, which was something he was more interested in than I was.

Sometimes they had nice horses who wanted to be event horses instead, and I knew he was on the lookout. The potential owner he'd picked up back at our last event was in the market for the right prospect, and Pete was anxious to find him a horse with mileage, even show-jumping mileage, so he could move it up the levels quickly.

Pete's forays into the hunter/jumper world sometimes backfired because he a) was completely gorgeous in a pair of Tailored Sportsmans and b) really worked that glittering smile of his when he was "networking," and so things with his most recent sales partner, Amanda, had ended rather awkwardly. I didn't miss Amanda the Hunter Princess one bit on a personal level, but I did miss her potential to make Pete lots of money by selling some of his show-ring prospects to her clients. And I felt bad about the way the whole thing had gone down, with her so obviously in love with him, and me . . . well, in the way. She thought she deserved Pete more and since she was gorgeous and well-dressed and even reasonably nice, for a hunter princess anyway, I could kind of see her point.

But while I might regard getting dressed up as wearing clean jeans and slicking back my hair with leave-in conditioner, I wasn't a total ogre. I had good cheekbones, possibly because I didn't have enough to eat on a regular basis. I had a fantastic tan and my hair was an interesting mix of dark brown and white-blond thanks to the bleaching Florida sun. I had really amazing biceps from galloping racehorses for a few months in the fall. So I wasn't the stuff of fashion show runways, but I was just fine. And temperament-wise, I was improving a lot. I hadn't verbally abused anyone in months, and the blogs had been quiet about me for some time now. Last summer's online drama, when I'd been the subject of entire posts calling out my antisocial behavior, might as well be a million years ago.

Still, even with Amanda finally out of the picture, I wasn't thrilled to see Pete back in hunterland. I was always afraid he'd stay there, or at least ride more jumper classes. The prize money was good, the horses sold for more, the clients tended to throw more cash into training and lessons. If Pete had developed champagne taste working with Amanda, he might not like the cheap beer that was all our eventing lifestyle could afford.

Plus, it meant he was gone a lot, at a point when we needed to really invest time into putting our farm together. I hadn't even had time to tell him about Eileen's call—I'd been waiting for a quiet moment when he wasn't stressing about a hundred other things, and that moment just hadn't come.

So he left, and with four hours between me and my evening riding lessons at High Springs, I figured I had two options: I could panic over the potential of losing Mickey, or I could work on the barn. The idea of panicking over Mickey without a side of alcohol was not particularly alluring, and as it was too early to drink, I took up hammer duty for a few hours. I managed to get up boards between most of the stalls that had uprights. Maybe they didn't have proper walls yet, or a roof, but if we needed to contain horses in something more substantial than our wobbly catch pens, we had something.

At three it was time for me to make more coffee, wincing at the machine's inevitable electric pop, before heading over to High Springs Equestrian Center to teach.

Our rented pasture belonged to the owner, and it was a fairly quick ride through a belt of pine woods and up a slope between paddocks to reach the barn and arenas. At first, the deal had just been to rent the pasture and use the arenas during the day, when things were quiet around the barn. But Rosie, the lapsed Brit who owned the place, had quickly sussed out the state of our bank account and lured me into teaching some of her more advanced students. I'd agreed to a trial run, explaining that I was no riding instructor, but things had lasted three weeks and I was still showing up for lessons four afternoons a week. At this point, I supposed, the job had moved from trial to steady.

I'd spent years avoiding teaching, but wasn't it really just putting off the inevitable? The surest way for a trainer to make a living, or at least afford a little bit of protein, was to teach riding lessons. And really, I was finding, it wasn't the worst thing in the world after all.

The kids who rode at High Springs Equestrian Center didn't seem particularly overprivileged, and I'd never seen any of them bully a working student or try to hand off a hot horse to a groom. Instead, they all dug into their work with the same grinding determination I'd had to show at their age, working their asses off just to pay for the sheer privilege of being at a barn and near horses. Even if they had parents with checkbooks to pay their bills, they still groomed their own horses and were nice to the help. It was like another planet for me.

I was starting to think maybe I should have gotten out more, maybe tried riding at more than two barns in my life. Between Osprey Ridge, the high-end barn near Tampa where I'd grown up as a working student, and Seabreeze, the posh boarding stable in Orlando where I'd spent last summer as a working student, I'd apparently only seen the extreme end of the boarding/lesson category.

Jordan was a good example of the kind of student I spent a few afternoons a week yelling at: skinny and frizzy-haired when she took off her helmet (rarely), about fourteen years old by the calendar and about forty-five by attitude, certain she could do way more with her horse than her horse thought he could do with her, and showing hunters because all her friends were doing it and she'd been told eventing was "scary" and "only for insane people" and "would probably kill her."

All potentially true, of course, but there was no reason I couldn't try to win over a few kids to my team. She had been secretly longing to event, she had confessed to me on the first day, but her private dream didn't owe itself to her being a poor kid surrounded by hunter princesses, as I had been. She just thought it looked amazing, and her friends didn't tease her for thinking she could abandon the hunter ring for the cross-country course. They didn't seem to tease each other about anything.

There was only one student lurking around the tack room who reminded me of being back at Osprey Ridge, where I'd spent my lonely teenage years mucking stalls and riding auction rejects while the entire cast of *Gossip Girl* rode in vicious circles around me, and she was my next lesson. The thought of dealing with Lindsay's mocking smirk and downturned eyes made me dig my fingernails into my palms even while Jordan was still doing delightful Jordan things, like throwing herself onto her horse's neck in some sort of arabesque swan maneuver that she adorably believed to be a crest release. I could only assume she'd gotten it off the cover of a catalog.

Probably *Rockwell Brothers Saddlery*. They should have put *me* on the cover. I'd have shown them a textbook release.

"Let's take Sammy over the outside line," I called to Jordan, pointing out a basic five-stride line along the long side of the arena. "Keep gentle contact, now, don't throw your reins away over the fence."

Jordan cast me a terrified look. "Won't I tug on his mouth?"

"Not if you put your hands in the right place. It's only two-six, Jordan. He could step over it from a walk, so don't overthink this."

Jordan flushed a deeper red. Overthinking was kind of her thing.

When we were done with the lesson (both of them survived gentle contact over the fence) Jordan rubbed Sammy's saddle mark as hard as she could with a rubber curry comb, panting with the effort, while I talked about sitting in the middle of one's horse, and establishing a straight line from shoulder to heel, and creating a firm anchor with one's leg in case of uneven terrain or a stumble at landing. I actually liked this part, taking on my favorite role as Professor Thornton, Expert Equestrienne.

"You can't let your lower leg swing around while you're jumping," I warned her. "It's got to stay right at his girth. Dig your heel down for stability."

"Melanie's trainer ties her stirrup to her girth at shows," Jordan admitted, but at least she sounded doubtful of this strategy. "She uses fishing line so it won't show."

"Melanie's trainer is going to Hell," I informed her solemnly, and Jordan's intent face cracked into a smile. I'd noticed the younger teens really loved this, when I said ridiculous things with a straight face. I chalked it up to being spoken to like they were adults. Who among us hadn't loved that when we were teenagers? Being treated like an adult at a young age was probably one of the top reasons girls stuck with horses even when the going got tough. It's not easy to get respect when you're a girl, not at any age and definitely not as a teen. Horses don't care what your gender is, though. What a nice change from human society!

Now I fixed Jordan with a stern glare. "You really want to fake it? For a fifty-cent ribbon, you want to fake it? What happens when your horse stumbles at a canter and that fishing line snaps—where's your leg going?"

"Back," Jordan admitted. "Up." She gave up on the curry comb and went for a towel. Sammy rested a hind leg comfortably, happy with the attention. His blocky warmblood head was hanging from the crossties, the halter cheekpieces pulled out at angles from his face. He closed his eyes. *Goodnight, world.*

"And where is the rest of you going?"

"Over his head."

"That's right!" I leaned against the wall and took a gulp of Diet Coke. "So it's all worth it."

"Is it, though?" A new voice, monotone and bored, cut into my happy teaching moment. "I mean, prove this is all worth it. You can't do it."

"For God's sake, Lindsay." I closed my eyes, tilting my head against the wall. I felt my ponytail push apart and reached back to free it from the rubber band. My hair slid along my shoulders, nearly to my elbows—too long, but haircuts cost money and took time, neither of which were in my possession. "This is not about the meaning of life. It's about riding horses."

"Why?" Lindsay led her horse up the aisle slowly, his hooves sliding along the concrete because he wasn't picking up his feet properly. It was such an annoying sound. Much like Lindsay's voice. "Tell me why we're doing this."

I shrugged. "I don't know, Lindsay. I don't know why *you're* doing it, anyway."

Every week it was the same old story with this girl. Lindsay hated horses, as far as I could tell. She'd been a tough junior for a long time, and then the torch just burned out. Now she was sixteen, and wanted nothing more to do with horses. Her mom wasn't having it, though. She'd already spent a small fortune on Lindsay's riding, and apparently was the only non-equestrian mother I'd ever met who would be furious if her daughter didn't spend more time riding than studying. She'd moved Lindsay's classy bay Hanoverian, William, to High Springs when it became apparent there was no point in spending a fortune every month on the A-circuit barn where they'd been since Lindsay was in pigtails and garters, but otherwise, she insisted on the same regular riding routine Lindsay had been grinding out since she was six: daily riding and at least one lesson a week.

One hour a week with Lindsay was about all I could handle, so I told her mom it was plenty.

Lindsay stopped William in front of me and waited. She pushed a loose lock of green hair behind one ear. The rest of her thin mane, as far as I could tell from beneath her helmet, was still bleached blond; just the one leprechaun streak this week, then. It was always a new color with Lindsay: new hair, new nails, new drawings scrawled on her hands with markers. I liked the fantasy colors; it made a nice contrast with her black clothes. Black boots, black breeches, black riding shirt from Rockwell that perfectly matched one I had in my drawer back at the horse trailer.

"Your hair looks good," I said, pushing off from the wall. "Maybe we can get you a green-piped saddle pad for your next show."

"I'm not going to a show."

"That was a joke. No one should see your hair in the show ring."

Jordan waved at me frantically. "Is Sammy's coat good enough?"

I looked over the dark chestnut gelding, pretending to appraise him like a bloodstock agent at a Thoroughbred sale. Sammy was sixteen and looked older, a lifetime of cantering hunter courses nearly every day of the week catching up with him, and his coat was edging toward old-man woolly, too. He needed clipped. Sammy looked like what he was: a rather tired, bedraggled horse with a little too much hair for Florida life. "He looks great," I told Jordan. "Nicely done."

Lindsay looked at me as we walked out to the covered arena. She was my height, which made it hard to remember she was still a teenager and I couldn't completely act with her the way I might have with Lacey or Becky, my old working students who had been in their early twenties. "Sammy looked like crap," she said accusingly. "You lied to her."

I sighed. "Sammy looks as good as he's gonna look this afternoon. He worked hard, he needs a clip job, and all he wants is to roll in some sand and eat some hay. What would you make her do?"

"Give him a bath."

"He'll never dry before it gets colder this evening. He has too much hair."

Lindsay glanced back at William, as if assuring herself that her warmblood was still young and beautiful, and didn't say anything else.

My phone buzzed in my pocket. I pulled it out and was surprised by the name on the screen: *Grace.* "Go ahead and warm up," I told Lindsay. "I have to take this."

"Hey, what's going on?" I said as Lindsay stalked away, William walking cheerfully by her side. He clearly didn't know he wasn't the center of her life anymore. "I haven't heard from you in forever."

"You either," Grace said tartly, in that way she had that never let me forget she was several decades my senior. "It's a two-way street."

"I don't have a lot of time for correspondence."

"Like I do?"

I sighed. "I think we're getting off on the wrong foot. Which is weird, because *you* called *me,* and you clearly want something."

Grace laughed rustily. "You're such a pill, Jules Thornton. Why did I think I should keep in touch with you?"

"Because I'm the best working student you've ever had?"

"I wouldn't be so sure. Most of my working students don't screw around with my good horses and nearly get them hurt at shows. Or threaten my junior riders. Or—"

"That's fine, that's fine," I said hastily, looking around the yard to make sure no one was around to overhear any incriminating words spilling from the phone's speaker. "But now I'm worried. If I was so bad, you must really be scraping the bottom of the barrel looking for help."

"It's more like I'm checking in, just in case I do need help. It's easier to ask for help down the line if you say hello once in a while. Anyway, I was *paid* to take you on, don't forget."

I chuckled. Grace had been on my mental list of people to call about Mickey. Her advice was more timely than she knew . . . or did she? I wondered, with a sudden shiver of horror, if the gossip mill already knew Carrie, Eileen, and I were about to part ways. I sat down on a bench next to the covered arena and watched Lindsay walk William around the ring. "Okay, consider yourself checked in."

"Is that all? Tell me about yourself. You ditched Ocala for the wild north. How is that working?"

"Well, I'm teaching lessons in the afternoons at a mid-level hunter/jumper barn. I've got my horses in a rented pasture and I'm living in a horse trailer with Pete and Marcus, both of whom seem to require more space than me. But it's working." I paused, considered my words. "Or, I thought it was. Pete might not agree."

Grace laughed again, but this time it was a sympathetic laugh. A *this is what happens when we try to have nice things* laugh. "And so Briar Hill's gone?"

"As good as gone. We decided it was better if we got out before we were kicked out. Just trying to maintain a little dignity and keep the blogs out of our business. They still are, obviously, but not in the same way as if we'd been evicted. We're brave, instead of bankrupt."

"I would do the same thing."

Something in Grace's voice just then made me sit up straight. Something heavy, and resigned. "Grace? Is that what this is about?"

Silence.

I pushed up from the bench so quickly I startled William, who was just a few feet away. He spooked to one side before catching himself, looking thoroughly embarrassed. Lindsay scowled at me as she gathered up her reins and poked her feet back into her stirrups. I ignored her attitude. She ought to have been sitting firm enough that a little spook didn't dislodge her. Let it be part of the riding lesson.

I swallowed and tried to focus on the call. "Grace. Is it the farm?"

Grace's property, Seabreeze Equestrian Center, was a living dinosaur, the last farm left in a former agricultural community that had been swallowed up by the vacation machine that was Orlando, Florida. I'd spent last summer there, working for Grace in a coerced attempt to boost both my dressage and my people skills (the attempt worked, by the way). It was a condition of my sponsorship with Rockwell Brothers, and I took out my anger and humiliation at being forced into it on Grace, but she'd made me a better rider despite myself.

The problem with Seabreeze, and the reason she'd taken me into her program at all, was that it had become valuable as anything but a riding stable.

The property all around was being plowed up and bulldozed to build vacation homes and hotels, but Grace was determined no one would develop Seabreeze. It had been her grandfather's farm. If it was a relic of another time, so be it—there was plenty of room for nostalgia in tourism and parenting, the two major economies sweeping around her in glittering resorts and subdivisions. She'd worked hard to build up a tourist and after-school business at the same time.

Keeping horses relevant in our urbanizing world was the most noble job I could think of, and Grace had been successful at it.

So far.

But Grace was also one of the most practical people I'd ever met, myself included. She'd get out when it was time, sentimentality be damned.

"I may have to sell," she said finally, her voice tight. I wondered if it was the first time she'd admitted it out loud. Saying terrible things aloud was so final.

What if I said right now, *I'm losing Mickey,* what would that feel like? What if I said, *I don't know how to talk to Pete anymore,* would the air feel more breathable once the words were made real?

I wasn't that brave.

"Shit, Grace," I said instead. "I'm so sorry."

"Thanks. I am, too."

We were both quiet for a moment. In the arena, Lindsay nudged William into a trot. The big Hanoverian cheerfully agreed that trotting was a great idea. His gait was a pretty daisy-cutter, but he pushed out his nose ahead of him like a donkey following a carrot. It was the same with all the horses at this hunter barn.

Didn't these kids feel like they were riding a bouncy two-by-four? Maybe if Lindsay learned a little dressage and put him together so he was a comfortable ride, she wouldn't be so over the sport.

Hmm, I thought. That wasn't actually the worst idea.

"Well, Jules, I was going to see if you wanted to work out some stall rental at Briar Hill. But that's fine, I guess. Do me a favor and just keep an ear to the ground. I might be in the market for something, about twenty stalls, nothing too crazy. I'll have to downsize. Not that many boarders will be able to come with me if I go too far north of the city."

For a moment I considered how much her land must be worth, so close to the theme parks. "You could probably buy Briar Hill if you can wait for it to go on the market," I said lightly, but my heart was squeezing tightly in my chest.

Imagine if Grace bought Briar Hill! Maybe we could move back, at least to the guesthouse . . .

"I'm not going to make *that* much." Grace chuckled. "I have to live on whatever I make, too. I'm looking at my retirement fund here. Briar Hill's off Millionaire's Row, isn't it?"

"Yeah," I admitted.

"Not happening."

I nodded, then remembered she couldn't see me and cleared my throat. The guttering little dream I'd harbored of taking Pete home finally flickered out. *Not important,* I told myself. We were making a new life, a different kind of life, and it was going to be better. No point in getting nostalgic for Briar Hill now. "So what price range are you thinking?"

"God, I don't know." Grace sighed. "I hadn't wanted to really work that out, it will make it so real, you know?"

"I know."

"Anyway, it can't cost a king's ransom. But twenty stalls. Paddocks. Arena. An apartment. Close enough to town that I'm not taking a cooler to the grocery store to get my ice cream home in."

"What kind?"

"Cookies and cream, unless there's triple chocolate."

"So a Publix."

"Of course, a Publix. I'm a Floridian just like you!"

I considered her requirements. "Well, it's a tall order."

"I have to at least try. I'd like to have some students and boarders still, and they'll need amenities. Some of my adults will still ride with me on the weekend even if it's a drive. I've got a few who are definitely ready to move with me as soon as I say the word."

"You sound really serious for someone just testing the waters," I pointed out. "This doesn't sound like something you're just kind of, I don't know, trying to keep your options open on."

"That's all it is right now," Grace said. "But things can change real quick."

"You're telling me."

"Well, it sounds like you landed on your feet all right. You're teaching, you've got your horses."

"Close." I paused. All of a sudden I knew I had to tell someone, and Grace was probably the right person . . . better even than Pete. Definitely better than Pete, I amended. He was so distant, I wasn't sure he'd notice it was bad news. "I got a call I didn't like this morning. About Mickey. Losing him, I mean."

"Lose—you mean they're taking you off him?"

"They're selling. Both owners want out."

Grace was quiet for a moment. I watched William trot down the long side of the arena with his clueless nose leading the way. "Any idea what they want for him?" she asked.

"No clue. But he won't be cheap." I wondered if Grace might consider buying him for me, then I shoved the idea aside. If she came into enough money to buy a horse like Mickey, it would be because the farm she loved was on its way to becoming a resort with a name like Tuscan Grande Lakeside Villas, and I wasn't going to wish that on her.

"I'm sorry," Grace was saying. "That's hard."

I swallowed, trying to push away the sudden lump in my throat. It *was* hard. It was too damn hard. Lindsay was circling William around me, but instead of the bay warmblood, I was seeing my gray Thoroughbred, with his big goofy face and his silly short forelock and his black-tipped ears, and I thought my heart was going to break.

Then I got hold of myself. "Well, I only just found out this morning," I said stoutly, pushing past the telltale croak in my throat. "There's still plenty to talk about. Maybe we can reach some kind of deal."

"Of course," Grace said, but she didn't sound like she meant it. Grace wasn't one to sugarcoat things. If you've been in the horse business long enough, you give up on that. The only sugar around a barn is what the old-timers bring to hand to their grandkid's lesson horse. "Keep me posted."

"Same to you."

Phone back in my pocket, I lifted my eyes from William to his rider. Lindsay was watching me intently, and I wondered how much she'd heard.

5

"ARE YOU READY for me yet?" Lindsay asked, her tone as acidic as her chemical-spill hair. "I've been riding for at least ten minutes now."

"More like five," I snapped. "And it's time you learned to have your horse warmed up *before* the lesson, not after. Your mom isn't paying me to tell you how to walk and trot on a loose rein before you start working."

"I'm not sure what she's paying for," Lindsay drawled. "Since I ride hunter and jumper classes, and you're an event trainer. But I don't actually give a shit if she wastes her money. That's her call, not mine."

I squeezed down all the rage in my swirling brain. *You cannot yell at teenagers, you cannot yell at teenagers.* If I'd learned anything at Seabreeze, it was that entitled kids with an internet connection were dangerous. Their parents could be pretty scary, too. Picking a fight with Lindsay would end badly.

Plus, I reminded myself, teaching riding was a job, just like grooming at Seabreeze had been a job, and in order to keep a job, you had to avoid felony assault, getting killed by an insane horse, and insulting clients. There were a few other rules on the books, but those were the most important, in my experience.

Still, being on one's best behavior didn't mean you couldn't have a little fun on the job. And what was the best way to have fun as a riding instructor? Besides committing to No-Stirrups November, of course?

Introducing a little light dressage to the curriculum! It's so unexpected, you see. That's where the real comedy lies. And even more than just amusing myself by making Lindsay have to work for something in the saddle, I might actually make a difference in her life.

Here's where I was going with this. Maybe, if her horse was more pleasant to ride, if she forged a deeper connection with him in the saddle, she'd remember what she used to love about it. Drilling eq patterns and circling around hunter courses couldn't do anything for rider burnout. It was the empty boredom of riding the same patterns, day in and day out, that had gotten her to this point in the first place. But that astonishing first moment when a horse moved onto the bit and lifted his spine up to meet a rider's back—*that* had the potential to change everything for Lindsay.

I considered my options for a moment. I didn't have to commit to anything real here. Lindsay was perfectly willing to let me coast through our weekly hour together. I could shout "More leg!" and set up fences for her while my brain was off working on my actual problems. I didn't have to do anything serious like get invested in her riding.

But I didn't want to think about big problems like Mickey right now. Or Pete. I just wanted something to distract me.

Tag, Lindsay. You're it.

I took a breath. "Lindsay, listen to me for a second."

Lindsay glared at me, then realized she was showing too much emotion and rearranged her face into its usual bored blankness. She looked like a mannequin in a goth shop, but beneath all those black clothes and empty features, her elegant seat was anything but plastic and rigid. Lindsay knew how to sit a horse and look pretty. I wondered what else she knew, or if it was all a pose.

She pulled up William. "Well? What do you want?" She narrowed her eyes at me, but at least the blank stare was gone. I had her attention.

Now I just had to figure out what to do with it.

"Well," I said slowly, as if the idea had just occurred to me, "let's see if we can bring William's nose in a little and ask him to carry his weight better. Right now he's moving flat and on his forehand. It would be more efficient and comfortable for him," I went on, guessing she loved the horse enough to be swayed by an argument for his well-being, "if he moved off his hind end, instead."

Lindsay glanced at me, guarded interest in her expression. "Okay. How?"

Did kids these days even read riding manuals under the covers after bedtime?

"Half halts," I replied. "You're going to close your fingers and sit down as if you're going to whoa, wait for his balance to shift back, then push him forward instead."

"That's *dressage*." She spit out the word like I was suggesting she commit a ritual murder. Although with her current goth look, maybe ritual murder was more Lindsay's style than dressage. Well, I didn't have any enemies close by, and dressage queens wore black coats, anyway. We would stick to the original plan. She'd probably love a top hat, the little show-off.

"What does it matter what name you call it?" I asked in what I hoped was a reasonable tone, rather than the mocking one my vocal cords were more prone to. "He'll move better, he'll feel better, and it's something new for you to do. You know how to trot and canter in circles, Lindsay. You can jump a course. This is a waste of your time and you know it. Hell, it's waste of William's time."

"And of your time?"

I wasn't going to say it, but if we came right down to it . . . I swallowed the cheeky response and went with a more practical approach. "Nothing's a waste of my time if I'm getting paid. And your mom is writing me a check either way. I could ignore you or I could work with you, same difference. Why not try it?"

"*Fine.*" Lindsay ground the word out through clenched teeth. I refrained from suggesting she loosen her jaw in order to loosen up the rest of her body. I would save that little tidbit for when she was less likely to bite my head off.

On my command, Lindsay closed her fingers and sat deep, or as deep as she could with her shortish stirrups. William nearly sat down in his hurry to halt, but then she opened her fingers and pressed her legs to his sides, and he darted forward, more strung out than ever, and rather wide-eyed over the whole affair.

Lindsay stuck out her lower lip. "Well, that didn't work."

Something told me she hadn't been challenged in a long, long time.

"Not quite," I replied gently. "That was a little too much of . . . well, of everything. Let me show you. If you want," I added, putting the ball in her court.

Lindsay halted William with hands and seat, and he seemed relieved to be allowed to stop for real this time. "This, you know how to do, right, buddy?" she said to him. I smothered a smile. Yeah, she loved her horse, even if she hated everything else in the world right now. I'd let that be my motivation. Because I definitely knew where she was coming from.

I felt a little strange taking her hands and manipulating her fingers, then placing my hand on her back, showing her exactly what I wanted her to do with hand and seat as she half halted. I couldn't remember ever going this far before with the few students I'd had. Alex needed me as an extra pair of eyes; she was more than capable of training her off-track Thoroughbred herself, even if she didn't realize it. My two working students had ridden horses who had basic dressage down, so I'd gotten away with shouting the instructions and getting halfway decent results from the horses before their riders had really figured out what was going on.

"And what about my seat?" Lindsay asked. "Am I sitting correctly?"

It was the first time in our month together Lindsay had asked me a question about her riding. I didn't let my face betray my excitement, just put my hands on her hips and shifted them. A few moments later, when she trotted back out to the rail, I could see her biting her lip as she tried to replicate the subtle shift in her pelvis without my guidance.

Learning new tricks kept Lindsay occupied right up until the end of our hour.

When she finally dismounted, the sun was sinking behind the tall pines that separated my pasture from the equestrian center, and a frosty briskness was settling over the arena. I slid on my riding jacket as she led William to the crossties and started untacking. The hunter-green technical fabric was stretchy and form-fitting. Between this jacket, the slim long-sleeved polo shirt, and the hip-hugging breeches, I was basically wearing a dark green catsuit.

"That's a nice jacket," Lindsay said, surprising me. "I mean, I guess you get nice clothes for free, right? Since you're Rockwell's ambassador?"

"Sometimes," I admitted. "For the first six months they sent me almost nothing to wear, just loads of horse stuff, but I got a couple packages for me over the past month. I guess it was to pay me back for doing well at the three-day event. Otherwise I'd be wearing cheap fleece pullovers from Old Navy all winter."

Lindsay grinned knowingly. "You're not exactly making a ton of money at this, are you?"

"Most people don't." I sat down on a tack trunk next to the crossties. Now that lessons were done, my mind was heavy and sluggish with worry over Mickey. "Most do better than me, though."

"Mind if I ask why?"

"Partially because I never did much teaching. Partially because at my age most people think I should still be working for some big-name trainer, maybe even as a working student. But I won't do that again."

Lindsay slipped the saddle from William's back. "Why not?" she asked, looking at me with curiosity as she placed it on a metal stand, tossing the dirty saddle pad on top. "Wouldn't you be better off riding at some big fancy barn with a big-name trainer? I mean, you're renting the back pasture and living in your horse trailer, right? That sounds a little nuts."

"It's a lot nuts. But I like it."

She scoffed. "There's no way you like it."

"I do." I thought about our little patch of hillbilly heaven, just me and Pete and the horses, Marcus, and Barn Kitty, who was rapidly returning to her feral roots, slinking along under the horse trailer and stalking lizards in the woods. No one to impress, no one to avoid, no one but each other. But that was a dream version of our reality, I reminded myself. Pete wasn't happy, so my vision of it was skewed. "I like being away from all the owners and barn politics, anyway," I said. "I'm not really, what do you call it, a team player."

Lindsay grinned at me and it was a real grin this time, not ironic. "Me neither, girl."

I'd never heard her speak to me in a voice full of genuine warmth, and I was surprised enough to sit quietly for a moment, skipping over the dressage lecture I'd planned to deliver. I watched her curry-comb the sweat spot out of William's back. A voice in my head said I should get going, it was time to head back and feed; but I was comfortable on the tack trunk, and enjoying the way William was leaning into Lindsay's hard work, his upper lip stretching out in that funny way horses had of showing you when you'd found their itchy spot.

"Are you losing one of your horses?"

I looked from William, who was straightening up and licking his lips, slowly returning to the world after Lindsay stopped rubbing his back, to her thin, elfin face with its wisps of green hair tucked behind her ears. Her carefully blank face gave away nothing. "Yes," I said. "I have a really good youngster and he's going be sold."

"Because of you?"

"No, because the owners need out."

"What are you going to do?"

"Do? I'm going to wait and see what happens, I guess. Call the other owner I haven't talked to yet, and ask her not to sell, maybe, but that seems a little desperate." Could you be too desperate to keep a horse you loved? I didn't know. "I honestly don't have a plan. I just found out this morning. How do you even know? You overheard my call?"

"The phone call. Rumors."

I sighed. "Naturally."

"There's always rumors about you. If you had a Google Alert set up for your name, it would never stop hitting your inbox."

"That's why I don't."

She grinned. "That's fair. You have any cookies?"

I dug in my jacket pocket and came up with a Rockwell Brothers Artisan Apple Yummy Wafer. "Here you go."

"Thanks." She handed the cookie to William, watched him crunch it with obvious delight. I watched the wheels turning in her head, and wondered what she was up to. "Why don't you start a syndicate and buy him for yourself?"

"Well, a syndicate needs lots of people with money, and I don't know anybody with any money, so . . ."

"Jules," Lindsay laughed, "you're a brand ambassador for the biggest saddlery company in the US. You have thousands of followers on Facebook and Instagram. You know as many people as you *want* to know."

This was true. I'd never thought of it quite like that. "Are you telling me to just ask people I don't know for money?"

Lindsay nodded. "That's exactly what I'm telling you. People do shit like that all the time. One time I gave a guy five bucks to buy a cockatoo."

"Did you know him?"

"No. He just really wanted a cockatoo so he made a crowd-funding page and I thought, 'Sure, bud. Go make your dreams come true.'"

She unhooked William's crossties and walked him down the aisle to his stall. I didn't bother scolding her for not using a lead rope. She was too old to drill on Pony Club technique. I knew, because I'd been her age just a few years ago, and I'd already learned that saving time felt better than saving traditions. William wasn't going anywhere but right alongside Lindsay, because he didn't want to be anywhere else.

I wondered if she realized what a special thing that was, to have a horse who clearly adored you in the passive, ear-flopping way a hound dog adored you. I wondered if she even knew he felt that way about her. Maybe Lindsay didn't know that much about anything, and she just gave the impression of being world-weary and all-knowing because that's what a sixteen-year-old with an all-black wardrobe and a rainbow collection of hair dye bottles under her bathroom sink was trying to do, all the time.

Let that be the truth, I thought. *Because I don't want her to be right about a syndicate.* I trained my eyes on my boots and told myself the truth, while I knew what it was, before I was too scared to think of it again.

Truth: I wanted to buy Mickey for myself.

Truth: having other people in the mix would ruin everything.

Truth: Mickey was my horse.

Truth: no, he wasn't.

Truth: but I wanted him to be.

I had a ten-year plan for Mickey, one that involved growing experienced and wise with him, traveling around the world with him, eventing on the world's stage.

I wanted Mickey to be like Dynamo, a beautiful eventing machine I'd created myself. I wanted Mickey to be like William, a loyal friend who walked by my side without a lead rope. I wanted Mickey like a high school girl who wanted her crush, all to herself forever and ever—forgetting college was coming, change was coming, life was coming to wreck all her plans.

I'd always known I was way too attached to Mickey, but I hadn't realized until a few moments ago, when Lindsay spoke so matter-of-factly about selling pieces of him to dozens of people, that I loved him the way a girl loves her heart horse. The way I loved Dynamo.

"Never fall in love with someone else's horse."

There was no one around. I was just telling myself, far too late.

6

I STOPPED BY Penny Lane to watch Pete riding before I drove home. The winter sun was long gone, and I was in no hurry to get home to deal with the horses alone. Besides, sometimes it was therapeutic to just lean on a fence, hook one heel over the bottom board, and watch somebody talented ride nice horses. It could take your mind off things. Call it "Operation: Pretend Nothing Bad Is Happening."

Standing between High Springs Equestrian Center and Penny Lane was a large income gap and five miles of county highway. Tonight the lanes stood wide and empty beneath a half-moon, its lazy face expressionless as it drifted through the clear, dark sky. This was timber country, not horse country, and thousands of acres of ramrod-straight pine trees lined up in tidy rows, playing tricks on my eyes if I turned my head to try and focus on them. Every now and then I drove past a little clearing, home to a rusting trailer with a pit bull sleeping on the sagging porch, lit in a pool of orange spilling from a streetlight overhead, his domain a weedy yard decorated with bits of farm machinery and dented cars. We were back in old North Florida now, all the money and cultivation of Ocala's glitzy farms far behind.

Except for Penny Lane.

From the two-lane highway, Penny Lane seemed to leap at you out of nowhere; just pine trees for miles and then, suddenly, a broad expanse of green rolling pasture with picturesque black-board fences, a Kentucky-style barn with a central rotunda and cupola, and a massive covered arena and outdoor jumping arena side by side. The farm looked wildly out of place here, as if a piece of Ocala or Wellington had shaken loose from its moorings and settled down without regard for its surroundings. The way subdivisions always seemed to do when they replaced farms, come to think of it.

Tonight, Penny Lane glowed gently in the moonlight, the empty pastures glistening with evening dew. I parked my truck in the gravel lot in front of the barn and carefully walked around the side of the barn to avoid being asked any questions. Technically I didn't have any place here; being the girlfriend of a glorified exercise rider wasn't a good excuse to wander around a farm with a collection of million-dollar warmbloods and a tack room holding the French cowhide equivalent of a small island nation's GDP. The barn aisle's fluorescent lights formed square patches on the grass outside each stall window, but that was nothing compared to the light pouring from the covered arena, where Pete was cantering down the long side, lit up like a football star.

I loved watching Pete work with these horses. They were big, powerful, over-the-top show jumpers, but they were shown by relatively unskilled amateurs. So to keep them jumping and in the ribbons, they were over-bitted and over-ridden, their high spirits strangled by gags and martingales and figure-eight nosebands. Some of them barely lasted a week at the showgrounds before they had to be hauled back, wide-eyed and sweating, to the farm for a few days without the loudspeaker in their ears and a ribbon-hungry rider hauling on their faces.

It was Pete's job to bring these jumpers back from the brink of nervous breakdowns. He had a simple trick to figure out every horse's individual quirks—he treated each horse the same for the first ride, just to see how they'd react. One by one, he slipped the same simple bridle over their heads, took them out to the arena and told them they could open their mouths, duck their heads, stretch their necks, look around . . . do everything except bolt, rear, and buck. And the horses didn't know what hit them. Or rather, what *didn't* hit them.

Of course, there was no telling what they'd do with such basic tack if one of their amateur riders tried to take them around a course at a big A-circuit show. Probably nothing good. Pete held these horses together with an electric seat and sticky legs and sympathetic hands. The idea of his extra schooling with less equipment wasn't to shame anyone who didn't spend all day, every day in the saddle building those physical tools, it was to fix all the day-in, day-out desensitization that has to happen when you're using heavy equipment on tender nerves.

Pete was cantering a big powerful gray who reminded me of Grace's stallion, Ivor. Same high head carriage, same huge movement at the trot and canter. This horse had longer legs, though, and a slimmer neck. More Thoroughbred in him than Ivor, I supposed. More *very tall* Thoroughbred, I amended on a second glance; Pete's heels didn't even reach the bottom of the horse's barrel. He must be nearly eighteen hands. A giant. His legs were elegant but solid, and an Irish term rang in my head, absorbed and forgotten from childhood reading: *nine inches of bone.* His cannon bones weren't quite that big around, but I could suddenly see the significance of the words.

As I crossed my arms on the fence and leaned against the top rail, Pete pushed the gray up to a high crossrail. The severe angle of the poles made for a deceptively large effort. Pete loved these fences for encouraging careful jumping, but this gray beast didn't seem to need the extra lesson. He bounded over the X like a kangaroo, then put his head down and bucked, horseshoes glinting under the lights, white tail flicking in the air. Pete, legs forward, body in the middle of his horse, didn't miss a beat. He just gave the horse leg, pushing his nose up, and circled him around to jump again.

After four beautiful bascules, the horse hadn't stopped bucking after the fence and didn't look as if he was stopping anytime soon. Pete sighed audibly and brought him down to a walk. They turned in my direction and I saw Pete's expression. He was grinning.

"What do you think?" he called.

The horse approached with a high head and flared nostrils, as if he wasn't sure just what was lurking in the shadows. "I think that's some fancy bronco you got there."

Pete let the reins swing loose, daring the horse to spook. "He's some jumper, I think you meant."

"If you mean he can jump equally well with his front end and his hind end . . . What's his deal?" I didn't like bucking. It was not my thing.

Pete shrugged and the horse snorted, comfortable I was a human now that he'd heard my voice. "Dunno. He just likes bucking after fences. Nothing malicious in it." He didn't sound concerned. I felt like I would be more bothered over this sort of behavior, but Pete and I had always wanted slightly different things from our horses. Still, I suspected his owner wasn't going to be thrilled when the horse returned to the showgrounds with his bucking habit intact.

"He doesn't look mad about anything," I said doubtfully, letting my eyes run over his easy, fluid motion. "Doesn't look sore."

"Nope, doesn't even pin his ears." Pete regarded the horse's twitching ears for a moment, as if they held the answer. In fact, they could. Catching a horse pinning his ears back when asked for a certain movement could indicate discomfort that might just be a lack of fitness, or betray something more serious hiding beneath the surface. The gray horse's ears weren't doing anything of interest right now, just swiveling to catch our voices. "Just one of those things, I guess. If anything, I'd say he's just bored and looking for more excitement."

Pete reined back in front of me and the horse stretched his neck out to say hello, depositing a dollop of white foam from his mouth onto my arm. I smacked it off with my hand and gave him a poke in the nose as payback. "He likes this bit, anyway," I observed, swiping my arm along my shirt front to remove the layer of goo left behind. "Is the bucking a problem for his owner?"

"She cried and got off at the last show. So yes."

"She cried?"

"And dismounted. In the arena. The clock was running. The trainer had to make her apologize to the judge. Apparently it was a whole big deal."

"No shit."

"I'm about to suggest she sell him."

"How old is she?" I couldn't imagine anyone out of jodhpurs and garter straps doing anything so outrageous in a show ring. In fact, when I'd been in jodhpurs and garter straps, I'd have been lucky if a buck after a fence was all I got. The ponies and horses I'd been riding were more likely to run straight through the arena fence and all the way back to the barn if I gave them so much as a moment to think about it.

"Sixteen." Pete grinned at my shocked face. "I know, right? Old enough to be able to handle something like that."

"I have a sixteen-year-old over at High Springs who'd laugh

her ass off if her horse started bucking. She'd probably encourage him to do it in every class just to be different."

"The problem one you hate teaching?"

"Yes, actually." Although after tonight, I wasn't sure I hated teaching Lindsay anymore. There was something there.

"Well, I don't think this kid is on her level at all. It sounds like she'd be better off trail-riding an old broke Quarter Horse than trying to ride this beast in junior jumper classes. They tell me he doesn't focus until he's really galloping, but then he has crazy talent and jumps like the fences are on fire, only he always bucks. So he cleans up *if* anyone can stick with him long enough to get to the jump-off. And that doesn't happen with his current owner." He tousled the horse's white mane with affection.

I noticed the slight emphasis on the word "current." I studied Pete's face as he ran his fingers through the horse's mane. The look in his eyes was unmistakable: hungry and excited. The expression of someone who has just found the horse they've been looking for. "But you could do it," I suggested, just to see where he was steering the conversation.

"Well, obviously. You saw him just now. Those bucks are small potatoes compared to his talent."

"You want him."

He flicked his gaze back at me and quirked an eyebrow in apparent amusement. "Me? Why would I want a jumper?"

I wasn't fooled. I knew Pete's face better than my own.

"Don't lie to me. You want this horse. You think he can event. You think he's a warmblood who bucks because he wants to get out and gallop, and that's like the magic combination right now." I folded my arms across my chest and gave Pete a knowing look. "How much do you think they'd want for him?"

"He's not for sale yet." Pete looked down again, ran his gloved hand along the horse's hot neck. He nudged him into a walk. "And he's not a warmblood, he's an Irish Sport Horse."

I knew it! *There's your nine inches of bone, Jules.* Still, Pete needed to be talked down before things got too serious. "That's literally the definition of a warmblood: draft and Thoroughbred. Do you need to go back to Pony Club?"

"You know what I mean. And that's the definition of an event horse, too."

I studied the horse again. He didn't look as huge now that he wasn't cantering with that proud head carriage, but he was still awfully tall. I supposed Irish Sport Horses were usually taller than Thoroughbreds, although you didn't see them much anymore. They'd been the kings of eventing for a long time, as the cross of Thorough-bred and Irish Draught was a classic formula for brains, athleticism, and body. They were a famously sound breed, besides, which you couldn't necessarily say for Thoroughbreds, as much as I loved them.

"What is he, seventeen-two?"

"At least."

"Too big."

Pete scowled at me. "Maybe for you, shortie."

"I'm nearly as tall as you!"

"Well, you don't want him and I do. So let me cool him out in peace and I'll be home to help you feed in about half an hour."

"Fine, fine. You're right, I don't want him. I have a gray prob-lem child of my own. This one is all yours." As I said it, I remem-bered my gray problem child was really in trouble this time. The shock of the memory was like a gut punch. I gripped the fence to keep myself from staggering. Pete didn't know, and this wasn't where he was going to find out: at work, on a horse that made him happy. Except . . . this wasn't his horse, or even a sales horse. This was a kid's horse.

"Pete?"

"Yeah?" Pete's voice was absent. He was playing with the gray horse's mane again, absorbed with the salt-and-pepper hairs.

"If the kid wants to keep him, you'll help her figure him out, won't you?"

"What?"

I frowned. I didn't like the idea of Pete convincing a teenager, a child really, that she should sell her horse. It was wrong to put ideas like that in a kid's head unless they were coming from a disinterested party, and Pete was definitely not suffering from a lack of interest. There was something about the entire situation that made me feel . . . hurt. I couldn't explain it. "Just respect that it's her horse, and don't try to manipulate her."

"Sure, Jules," he said, not even looking at me.

That bastard! If we weren't at his fancy job, I'd tell him what a jerk he was being. Instead, I glared at him. I had such a good glare, honed over many years, perfect for shutting people up. But Pete was used to my glares. He turned the horse back from the rail, throwing me a sideways grin to let me know what he thought of it. I should have expected that. Laughing at my constant outrage was probably the cornerstone of our relationship. I got mad, and he thought it was funny, and I had no choice but to let him laugh or break up with him.

So I gave up on the glare and unclenched my jaw as I watched the two of them walk away, both looking like the masters of their domains. Pete sat easily in the saddle, while the horse beneath him strode out and stretched his neck as if he'd never been happier. If he'd been a monster down in Ocala just a few days ago, he was a carefree trail horse right now, all his worries swept away after some time spent with a rider who didn't panic at his little habit of bucking when he was happy.

"That's a good horse for Pete," I muttered to myself. "The mystery problem horses always melt like butter when he's in the saddle." I had to admit, Pete looked relaxed and stress-free for the first time in months. He didn't even look relaxed when he *slept* anymore. That horse might just be magical, and I didn't blame him for wanting to bring him home.

Just one little problem—even if Pete did get the owner to sell. "We don't need another white horse to keep clean, Pete!" I called after them, and he waved his whip at me without turning around, acknowledging my complaint but not in any hurry to do anything about it.

7

AT HOME, WITH the darkness stretching long fingers from the towering pine trees into the bluish glow of the moonlit grass, the horses were watching for me from the corner of the pasture closest to the road. In her nearby pen, Regina stood with her ears pricked, looking like the queen she was. A queen who would behead me if I didn't feed her immediately. As I came a little closer, I could see her impatience mirrored on the other horses' faces. It was nearly seven o'clock, which was midnight in horse hours, and everyone was outraged.

Well, everyone except Marcus, who was absolutely thrilled to see me. "This is why we have dogs," I told him, as he propped his pudgy forelegs against my knees, panting with joy. "Horses don't really care about us. Oh, Marcus! I love you, little flea-face."

I wanted nothing more than to throw myself down on the sofa and relax—wasn't that what normal people got to do after a long day of work? But I wasn't normal, and neither was my life, and my day's work was not yet done. The door wasn't even closed behind me, and I was climbing back down the stairs. Well, at least feeding dinner wasn't the hardest thing a person had to do in a day. And it was especially gratifying when the horses' expressions changed from grave disapproval to slavering delight.

I let Marcus out ahead of me, and he waggled blissfully through the cold, damp grass while I went to my trailer/feed room and started hauling around feed buckets in the moonlight. I could have waited for Pete to help feed, but every minute that passed gave me more attitude to deal with from the spoiled crew in the pasture. In the interest of keeping everyone (and every fence) intact, division of labor was not always feasible.

Mickey was first up. "Pete's in love, and we're going to end up with another white horse," I informed Mickey, spilling grain into his bucket and snapping it into place. He ignored my news and dug into the grain almost before I could secure the bucket; the wooden fence boards, pliable with age and many rainy seasons, sagged dangerously beneath his assault. "Please don't kill the fence, Mickey. It's just food."

There was no time for idle conversation, even if he'd been listening. Down the line, the other horses roared their hunger. One by one I gave them their buckets and watched them grind into their dinner with the special kind of viciousness that herbivores reserved for hard vitamin pellets sweetened with molasses. Over in her pen, which had no sturdy fence posts to clip a bucket to, Regina turned her feed pan over and lipped her grain from the scanty grass.

"It would be nice if you avoided sand colic," I told her sardonically. "Unless you'd love a colic surgery as soon as you've recovered from nearly cutting your leg off." I turned away from the sight of her long, shapely nose digging through the dirt for each delectable pellet. I'd rather worry about the financial implications of keeping three white horses clean for events than the tens of thousands of dollars needed for colic surgery. I was pretty sure the insurance agency would just write Regina off as totaled if we tried to get them to cover another major medical procedure. I'd never had a horse need colic surgery, thank goodness, but Grace had told me a few horror stories.

Marcus came up and lipped at my hand for salt and sweet from the electrolytes and supplements we sprinkled on the feed. "We'll need a new groom to keep all of them clean," I told him. I'd noticed lately that it was easier to change the conversation in my brain by saying things out loud. If that meant I talked to myself more often, so be it.

"We might need one anyway. Who will be competing by this fall? Barsuk, Dynamo, Mayfair, Regina, Jim, this new horse, Mickey . . ."

Unless Mickey's gone.

"Don't even go there," I told myself. "New topic of conversation." I pushed the thought away, to the same place where I kept all my unpaid bills, and the nagging worry that Jim Dear wasn't insured yet, and my increasing suspicion that I didn't fully understand calcium-to-phosphorus ratios in hay. This wasn't the time to think about Mickey, or any of these things. I wasn't sure when it would be.

"Is everyone happy now?" I threw out to the crowd, and though they didn't answer as such, I got the feeling life was good for the herd. Everyone was eating, no one was sniping at one another, and I'd tossed out a flake of alfalfa for each horse to eat after they'd cleaned up their grain. I could sneak inside and fix dinner for myself, and Marcus, and Pete, and come back out in an hour to let everyone back into the pasture. *The perfect mom,* I thought. *Doing it all while Dad's still at work.*

I glanced at my phone: seven thirty. Pete was due back by now, but they'd probably found something else for him to do, another horse who needed his attention before the weekend. He was frequently kept late at Penny Lane—the riding instructors and barn owner seemed to have no concept of time management, or that employees might have their own horses and their own responsibilities. He'd show up late, exhausted and starving. "I should make dinner," I announced, trying to get myself going, but I wasn't in a hurry to retreat to the claustrophobic trailer yet.

Instead, I gifted myself a few minutes of peace to lean on the shaky fence, wobbling as the horses dug at their buckets, and take a good look at everyone. Well, I meant to look at everyone.

I mainly looked at Mickey.

From a distance, he was a shining white charger. The pale gray Thoroughbred glowed in the moonlight, the grass and sand stains left from rolling in the field bleached from his coat by the forgiving North Florida night. It refined the lines of his muscles into smooth arcs and swanlike arabesques, and darkened the peppery strokes of his mane and tail to mysterious shadows. He was a creature of light and dark. He turned my heart over, that big bright horse. He made me think I could die of love.

At least, I thought somewhat more rationally, I felt like I could stare at him all night. And maybe it wasn't the worst idea. Because once he was on the market, he was as good as gone. *I should watch him,* I thought, *I should watch him every waking moment until I've lost him.*

"Settle down, Jules," I said, and he looked up at me, ears pricked as if surprised I was still hanging around, before he went back to his dinner.

Be yourself, I thought. *Be selfish, practical, bitterly determined Jules.* Who never fell in love with anything or anyone, except for Marcus, because a dog's love was sacred and forever and he would never fall out of love with me and leave me, and because a dog was mine the way a horse, the potential victim of bankruptcies and failures and fallings-out, could never be. An owner would never show up with a trailer to steal my beagle away because I wasn't a good enough dog-parent, or sell him off to pay my debts.

I ripped my gaze from Mickey and let it drift over the other horses. They were dark shadows next to his unicorn shimmer. Even Barsuk, with his charcoal dapples, faded into the night. They seemed like unknown entities. But that was crazy because they were my horses, and Pete's, and we'd been together for years. We were a team. It was just the stress of the day (of the week, of the month, of the year) that made the herd feel like a crowd of strangers.

"I love all of you equally," I said out loud, as if to make it come true, and I expected at least as much a response as Mickey had given me—a questioning glance, *Yeah yeah, Mom, we get it,* but now no one so much as slanted an ear in my direction. They ate the food I'd given them, which they considered a right granted by the universe, and ignored me. I considered myself chastened for all that misplaced emotion I'd lavished on Mickey, a horse who was utterly content with his grain and had no idea the upheaval he was causing in the lives of the women connected to him. Horses went on. When we humans were busy struggling to accept the daily burdens of life, horses ate their food and went on.

That was good advice, I thought. Because I was pretty hungry, now that I thought about it.

So I left my little herd to their grain and returned to the horse trailer. Marcus followed, wagging his tail and sniffing at the cabinet where his food was kept. I opened up a tin and plopped the contents into his bowl, then busied myself flicking on the stove burner and getting water to a boil. That ramen-and-champagne life, I thought. Thinking about finding someone to buy us fifty-thousand-dollar horses, while we heat up fifty-cent bags of soup for supper.

Pete clomped up the steps as I was dumping the noodles into the pot, bringing with him a gust of chilly air that raised goose bumps on my bare arms. Another cold February night was settling in. How many months until summer? One or two, and then we would be dying of heat. I didn't have much room to complain about the cold nights that came and went so quickly, but I did anyway.

"Ah, the wife has made dinner," Pete joked, popping off his boots at the door. They immediately toppled over and seemed to take up half the floor. "I am a lucky man."

I gave him a dutiful housewife-kiss on the cheek and handed him a beer. "You most certainly are," I reminded him. "A very lucky man."

He snorted, but he accepted the beer and returned the kiss, so I let it go and returned to my chef duties. The trailer was quiet, just the sound of horses pushing through their alfalfa flakes out front and the electric hookup humming on the other side of the trailer, a disconcerting sound I was not convinced was entirely benign.

"I'm calling Delannoy tomorrow," Pete said. "Tell him I think we should seriously consider this horse."

"I knew it. You're like a little girl when a new pony comes to the barn. But he belongs to a kid."

"So we'll convince her to sell him to us. What's wrong with that? He's no good for her, but he's a good horse. He's a great horse." His voice sharpened. "I think he's my next big horse, which God knows I need in case Regina doesn't come back."

"I just don't think you should go after some teenager's horse because you fell in love on your first ride," I said defensively. "That's not fair to her and it's not a sound business decision, buying a horse because you have a big crush on it."

"Excuse me? This is not a crush. This is me riding a talented horse and spotting his potential. Oh, and you're definitely not afraid to fall in love with horses. I've seen you around Mickey and Dynamo."

"Well, Dynamo doesn't count. I bought him myself. I own him free and clear."

"That's only one of them," Pete said pointedly. "What about Mickey?"

"What *about* him?"

I poured noodles into a pair of chipped white bowls that had lived in the trailer's cabinets for years, knocking into each other every time the wheels hit a bump. They were scarred by life on the road, as I imagined we would be someday. Or, maybe, as we were already. "Eat your slop, I made it with love." I thunked the bowl in front of him.

Pete regarded the soup with actual affection. "Thank you, I'm starving."

"It contains zero nutritional value."

"Salt is a food group," he informed me. "Sit down and eat with me."

I did, but only because there was literally nowhere else to sit besides the lawn chair outside, and the wind was too nippy. I sat stiffly beside him on the hard little sofa, and looked at the bowl on the tray in front of me. I didn't want it anymore.

"I'm sorry about what I said about Mickey," Pete said, noticing I wasn't eating. "I know you guys have a special relationship. I shouldn't make fun of you for it."

I could tell him right now, and it would all be out in the open. I picked up my spoon, poked it into the noodles, and watched the steam unfurl into the cool air.

At my feet, Marcus panted, his eyes pinned on me, ever hopeful I'd just hand him the bowl and call it a night. Maybe if I'd been a different kind of person, one more prone to allowing my emotions a say in . . . in *anything,* really, I'd have just handed it off and climbed into bed.

But I wasn't. I'd worked all day and I had to eat. I didn't have to feel things. There was no requirement for that. "Seriously, Pete, I have to bring this up. This is a real problem to consider. Can you not get like a bay or a chestnut or something instead of this gray? I am so over gray horses. I had that gray stallion at Seabreeze. I have Mickey. Barsuk is getting lighter by the day. We can't afford that much purple shampoo, man. Not to mention the amount of time it's going to take to prep for shows if we're running some kind of unicorn cavalry at every event. We'll need a working student specifically for bathing duty."

Pete laughed. "Don't worry about the expense. Delannoy will buy the purple shampoo. Or we'll put it on the monthly order from Rockwell."

"Rockwell might not keep us on after this spring," I said, trying to keep my tone light. "We've been difficult little influencers for him, refusing to have any good luck with the basics, like keeping a farm for our horses or an actual roof over our heads. I'm not sure trailer-chic is in his summer fashion line."

Before I could stop him, Pete pulled me up against his side, wrapping his arm around my shoulders. He gave me a solid squeeze, and I recognized with surprise that he was actually in a good mood. Pete hadn't cracked a real, genuine smile in weeks, aside from those fleeting moments when a horse he was riding had a breakthrough, but now he was grinning like a benefactor had promised him the moon and he was about to take delivery. "Don't worry about any of that," he told me. "I'll get Delannoy to buy this horse. Then I'll take Dynamo to an Advanced event this spring, come in in the top ten, make Rockwell happy. And then I'll give Dynamo back to you and I'll get this horse rolling next. He's already an experienced jumper, a little schooling in cross-country and some dressage and he'll be at Prelim in no time. Show him off, get some more youngsters in training, save some money . . . *boom.* This time next year we'll have a barn, we'll both have upper-level horses, we'll get a working student . . . and she can scrub the gray horses all day long."

Well, when he put it that way, having a few owners back on the tab sounded awfully good. Without thinking about the implications, I asked, "Pete, do you think Delannoy might buy me a horse?"

I felt his shoulders tense and bit the inside of my cheek, frustrated with myself. I couldn't turn Pete's new owner into a repeat of the Rockwell deal. Even if that had been none of my doing, and Pete had played hardball to get me included in the sponsorship completely on his own, I didn't need him thinking I was going to try and piggyback on every break he got.

"Chill out," I said, nudging him, hoping to turn it into a joke. "I was just kidding."

"I know that," Pete said, but his tone said otherwise.

"I don't even like Delannoy," I went on. "He treated me like a housewife tagging along on your big day. Does he even know women are allowed to ride astride these days?"

"He was rude, I admit." Pete dug his spoon into his bowl. "Maybe when we've been working together for a while, and he gets to know the business, he'll see what you can do and decide to invest more . . ."

"I wouldn't take his money on a silver platter," I declared, even though of course I would. The very statement was ridiculous.

"I like what you're trying to do," Pete said. "Just a couple of horses, one really strong owner partnership, investing all of your time into getting it perfect with them . . . I just don't know if it's for me. But it's perfect for you and I'm sure it's going to be a huge success."

"Me, a success?" I laughed. "I used to think so."

"You and Mickey are going places," Pete said. "Be serious."

"Mickey's going up for sale," I said, and Pete dropped his spoon.

He craned his neck to look at me and I got a good look at his face. The expression: horror. The shock: complete and utter. His face turned white, and freckles usually hidden by his deep tan suddenly stood out like an invading army across his nose and cheeks.

It was slightly gratifying to know he was just as gobsmacked by the news as I had been. At least that meant I hadn't been wrong. At least that meant I hadn't missed the signs, or been doing something wrong all this time. I was in the clear.

Slightly gratifying, but completely alarming, because it also meant things were every bit as bad as I had thought.

I saw his lips try to form words, and then just give up, his cheeks collapsing. I could tell he'd been going to say *It's okay*. And he'd been struck with the conviction that it wasn't, and that maybe lying was worse.

Of course it wasn't okay.

This was a disaster of the first order. What had I been thinking, working through my whole day as if nothing was wrong? I pressed my lips together to stop my chin from wobbling as the realization swept over me. I'd been such a fool today. My life, my *career* was collapsing around me, and I'd nailed boards up in the barn and taught riding lessons as if nothing was wrong!

I should have been in panic mode; I should have been getting into my battle station, prepping my plan of action. Instead, an entire day had passed and I was no closer to owning Mickey, and he was a day closer to leaving my life forever. I felt an uncharacteristic urge to have a panic attack, an actual hyperventilating, pulse-racing, nerves-twitching event.

Deep breaths, Jules. You've handled worse. Your barn blew away with you still inside it, remember?

Deep breaths were hard to come by; my throat was closing up and my lungs were collapsing. But that wasn't me. That wasn't Jules. I didn't have panic attacks, I *gave* people panic attacks. Maybe that wasn't something to be proud of, but it was true I'd caused a few of those one-rail-remaining, Jesus-take-the-wheel moments in my competitors' lives. And I'd taken home the blue rosette and the check, besides. I didn't have nerves, and I knew how to keep my heart in check. I didn't have anything that could get in my way. Sometimes I just had to remind myself of how tough I was.

Pete was softening me up, I thought with grim amusement.

But I would be resolute, face my disaster head-on, attack it, destroy it. The Jules way.

Or, I would in a minute or two. When I had everything under control.

I sat quietly and concentrated on getting my breath back while Pete said things, his mouth moving slowly, his eyes blinking rapidly. I couldn't hear him, but that was fine. I had to think. *Think, think, think!*

I frowned down at my soup. The noodles curled over and over one another, helplessly entwined. You had to really break the package up with your hands before you opened it, or you had a mess on your hands, long noodles slipping from your spoon, splashing back into the salty broth, splashing your little table that had to double as your work desk because you lived in a horse trailer, you lived in a horse trailer, *you lived in a horse trailer* . . .

8

"I DON'T WANT a syndicate," I announced a few minutes later, my head between my knees, my forehead pressing into the drop-down table. "But I am going to buy him. I don't have any idea how, but I have to do it."

Pete's hand was on my back, his head tilted over me. He was close enough for a kiss, but he wasn't looking for anything but reassurance I wasn't cracking up completely. There was plenty of good reason to believe I was. A swooning spell and a nosedive into my soup bowl was not exactly typical behavior for me.

I didn't think I'd actually fainted, but the rushing in my ears and the dizzy spell that came with it had been close enough to startle us both. Now Pete closed his fingers, rubbing my back through my shirt in the same reassuring pattern he would use on a foolish horse. *Because that's what we know,* I thought, my brain moving at a slow, observant pace; my thoughts crawling along and taking a good look around now that my heart rate had quieted. We had retreated from the world to recover, to live alone with our horses, the only thing we truly understood, but the world had followed us, so now we had to deal with it.

What was the right way to counter the assault of an entire world we didn't want any part of? Was there a deeper wood we could settle in, and if I took Mickey there, could we hide from his owners forever?

"Everyone syndicates," Pete was saying. "It's totally common. We can do it. The only crazy thing is that we haven't done it yet."

I didn't want to do it. A syndicate—multiple owners, each with their own piece of my horse. Each wanting their payout in the currency of bragging rights, photo ops, visits with friends to show off their investment, saying "This is my horse, Mickey," while I stood by, holding the lead rope and relegated to groom in their eyes. I had an awful vision in my head of Mickey, standing at attention, tacked and braided and gleaming, waiting for the awards presentation at a big event. He was surrounded by a crowd of owners, all jostling for his reins, all pushing to hand him a carrot. I wanted to get to him, to tell him what a good job he'd done, to fix his rosette to his bridle, but there were girls and women snatching it from my hand, plaiting it into his mane, tugging at his reins to lead him off to a big parade I wasn't invited to, because he wasn't my horse.

He was theirs.

"We'll have to talk with a lawyer, get a business filed, and we'll really have to keep careful records for taxes, but other than that, it shouldn't change anything," Pete went on.

Pete was so calm and confident! But it wasn't his horse.

Mickey wasn't my horse either, I reminded myself.

Wasn't there another way? I tried to think. I could beg Pete's new owner for the investment. *You love Pete, love me too!* I could go to Rockwell, hat in hand, and promise to do better if he'd just buy Mickey for me. Wouldn't he agree since I was already part of the company, even though he'd never wanted me for his brand?

No, that wasn't the answer. It couldn't be the answer. For one thing, I couldn't embarrass myself like that. I'd already debased myself enough for Rockwell. I'd already spent last summer in Orlando, tacking up horses for rich suburbanites when I should have been on my own farm. Sure, I'd gained a great friend in Grace and I'd admittedly improved my dressage considerably, but I'd also lost what little business I'd had. I'd ended up here, in a horse trailer, chasing the noble but possibly deluded goal of trying to build a three-horse eventing business. Rockwell's influence in my life was definitely a mixed bag.

So then, what? Suppose I panicked, refused to try and build a syndicate on the principle that it would be terrible, and I did absolutely nothing?

Then Mickey would be gone. He would leave quietly on a trailer (bless that horse, he loaded well), and he'd go to someone else's barn, and I'd have to endure seeing him only at events, only at a distance, only with someone else on his back.

Unbearable.

Wouldn't it be better to keep him close and keep my legs wrapped around him, even if a horde of owners did lay claim to him on paper? Even if they did lead him away and spoil my victories? At least I'd get to bring him home at the end of every weekend. At least he'd always be with me. He was the horse I couldn't lose, he was the best hope I had of a partner who would go all the way with me, just as thrilled by big jumps and long gallops as I was.

I'd do anything to keep that horse.

But there was one more thing. And it was Lindsay's idea. Of course Lindsay had been right. *Why don't you let the internet buy you your horse?* She'd chipped in five bucks to help a guy buy a cockatoo. I was guessing he didn't owe her a five-dollar share in his bird.

I'd been a teenager like her not very long ago, with a clear-eyed knowledge of the ruthless steps a girl had to take if she was going to keep her head above water. I'd gotten to this point in my career, such as it was, by making big moves and not looking back. I'd keep climbing the same way.

Lindsay must have thought I was an idiot to not start a campaign immediately. She was right. I should have done that the second I hung up with Eileen. *Donate to the Save Mickey Fund!*

I should have told Eileen not to worry, I'd find the money. Why had I wasted so much time? Maybe I was too tired to think clearly. The time for that sort of indulgence was over. There were no more excuses.

"I'm crowdfunding this one."

Pete looked at me, startled out of his monologue on syndication. "What?"

"I have fans, right?"

"You certainly have an interesting position as a celebrity."

"I'm using it. I'm going to get the money to buy Mickey. Websites, Facebook, Instagram, everything. I'm going to make a sob story and people are going to give me money to buy Mickey, and in return they can join . . . I don't know, a fan club or something, Friends of Danger Mouse. And they'll get to do the things syndicate owners would do, but they won't own him. I won't give them a piece of him. And they won't have to deal with payments or anything in the future, so there's that. It's a onetime buy-in. But they get to be members forever."

Pete raised one eyebrow, considering. I waited.

"Good," he said eventually.

"You think?" I'd been talking out of thin air, actually.

"For one thing, I'm not sure anyone else has done this. So it will get press. And the wider an audience it reaches, the more likely people are to join in. Maybe you could even get it beyond eventing. Get it on *Good Morning America* or something."

I considered the possibility of doing a livestream via my iPhone to *Good Morning America,* live from the pasture, Mickey at my side. I didn't think our signal was good enough.

"Well, this is what we're doing."

"Good," Pete said again. "I think it's great."

I smiled suddenly, blinking down at my toes inside their argyle socks. Pete was on board. I lifted my head, possibly too quickly, judging by the little wobble of dizziness that came over me, then gave him an impulsive kiss. I grabbed my spoon and slurped up a salty spoonful of ramen. "So it's settled," I said around noodles.

"It's settled." Pete's spoon clattered against his bowl, and then we were eating as if nothing had happened, Marcus keeping watch from his position against the refrigerator door in case we dropped a noodle. I pulled my tablet out from the little book rack next to the couch and propped it up in front of us, and pulled up a show I'd downloaded the last time I was in town and had some Wi-Fi, and for a little while, we just accepted that things were weird, and up in the air, and we were going to handle them . . . later.

9

IF I WAS excited about my crowdfunding campaign to buy Mickey, I was still annoyed at Pete's decision to try and buy the horse at Penny Lane. First thing the next morning, Pete called Rick Delannoy and suggested they go look at a horse together.

A horse, Pete said casually, not specifying just how much he wanted the gray jumper. Just "a nice horse I've run across," he said. "A ton of potential, in the wrong discipline right now, dying to be let loose to run."

He sat outside in the early golden sunlight, trying to eke a little warmth from its rays before they disappeared altogether. The sky was busy prepping something special for the afternoon, with a west wind roaring in the pine trees and white clouds scudding anxiously under a high pale sky. A huge gray-white blanket of cloud, high and flat, was pulling itself over top of us as if we were being tucked in for the night. I didn't have to check my weather app to know there was a storm on its way, which would probably arrive just in time to spoil the afternoon for riding. So I was a little bit annoyed that Pete was on the phone when we should have been tacking up.

I showed my irritation in a perfectly healthy and not at all passive-aggressive way, by clomping up the little fold-down metal steps into the trailer living quarters, slamming the door behind me, then storming out again as if I'd forgotten something vital in the feed trailer.

All Pete did was take his conversation from the canvas folding chair just outside the trailer door and move it down to the skeleton of the barn, where he leaned up against a spindly strut and continued his wheeling and dealing with Delannoy. It became very clear we weren't going to start grooming and riding as soon as the horses finished their hay. So I flipped up everyone's stall guards so they could go out and browse in the pasture, then grabbed a manure fork, dropped it into the big orange wheelbarrow, and trundled over to Regina's pen to do a little cleanup. The liver chestnut mare glanced at me without actually lifting her head from her hay, her eye landing on me without any real interest.

Since she was still on layup, she only got timothy and alfalfa hay, not straight alfalfa, and it took her the better part of a morning to find every tiny green leaf of alfalfa and nibble it up before she grudgingly worked her way through the timothy. This required great concentration and I was not permitted to distract her.

Picking out a stall or a pen or a pasture is the best therapy in the world—it doesn't matter how big the space is, cleaning up manure is when equestrians do their best thinking. If everyone had access to a horse and could spend half an hour a day cleaning up after it, the world would be a more thoughtful and coherent place. Also, there would be fewer flies.

I cautiously pushed Regina's hindquarters over to reach the piles she was blocking. The mare flicked her tail and stomped one hind leg viciously, letting me know she'd kill me if she wasn't so busy with her hay, but she shoved over nonetheless so I let the bad manners go. So Regina wanted to kill me. So there was going to be another rich guy throwing money at Pete while apparently never realizing I was alive. So the preferences of the man with the money would be put ahead of mine. So what. Big deal.

I just had to remind myself periodically, every five minutes if necessary, that I had Mickey, and I had to put all my energy into keeping Mickey. There wasn't going to be room for adolescent jealousy in the next few weeks. Even though it was one of the emotions I was best at expressing.

I glanced over Regina's back and out to the pasture, where the boys (and Mayfair) were grazing in a tightly bunched pack. White and steel-gray, red chestnut and bay, they were all lovely, but I knew Mickey was the loveliest of all. He'd grown in the nearly two years I'd had him, and was almost seventeen hands tall—a little big for me, really, and taller than the other Thoroughbreds in the field. He was elegant, perfectly shaped, and, if you asked the rest of the eventing community, way too good for me.

I smiled to myself. Even if the partnership was falling apart, the fact it had happened at all was something. I'd scored a Donnelly horse, and Donnelly horses were the gold standard in eventing. So I hadn't moved the dial with Delannoy—so what?

He'd never been interested in backing a lady rider. There were always going to be chauvinists like him in the horse business. I had nothing to be jealous of, and everything to be proud of.

Plus, if Delannoy bought Pete a horse who could go upper level this year, there'd be no question of his keeping the ride on Dynamo . . . the ride I'd given him to keep our sponsor happy after Regina had gotten hurt. I'd have my big horse back.

"Prelim this spring," I muttered. "Intermediate next winter . . . and I'm getting Dynamo back, so I'll go from no upper-level horses to two, that's not bad . . ."

Regina snorted into her hay.

"You'll come too," I told her. "You'll get better. Then Pete will have you, and Barsuk, and get whatever he ends up getting this guy to buy for him going at least Prelim, so next winter we'll all be so busy we won't be able to see straight, and it'll be great." It was exactly what Pete had said to me.

Regina just shook a fly from her ear and went on digging through the timothy. She was nobody's fool. If she was going to make a comeback from her injury, she probably already knew. The rest of us would just have to wait and see.

Pete finally came over as I was easing the wheelbarrow out of her pen. I looked up as he crossed the brown winter grass, phone in hand, face unreadable.

"Well, what did he say?"

"He's coming up this weekend."

"Well, that's great news." I waited, but there was no celebration in Pete's expression. If anything, he looked a little annoyed. "Isn't it?"

"He has three other horses he wants to look at."

"That . . . that *he* picked out?"

Pete nodded slowly.

"Oh boy."

"Yeah."

"So he's going to be one of those."

"An owner with zero knowledge of horses and an overriding urge to be part of every decision?"

"Uh-huh."

I started pushing the wheelbarrow toward the manure pile along the far tree line. "I'm sorry," I said. I glanced back, and Pete just shook his head ruefully.

Well, that was the way this game was played. When you needed an expensive horse, you needed a benevolent rich person or a collection of highly passionate fans. Both were liable to want to have a say in where their money was going every month. I didn't know how I'd managed to get such quiet, hands-off owners in Carrie and Eileen. I'd just gotten really lucky, I guess.

Well, that was over now, wasn't it?

Suddenly, I didn't want to be here anymore. Not around Pete. I put the wheelbarrow away, went inside, and pulled on riding clothes.

"Where are you going?" Pete asked as I stalked past him. "Those are your fancy off-the-farm boots."

I glanced down at my shining dress boots, which I usually only wore to events. "I'm taking Mickey up to High Springs for a jumping school," I said.

"Am I invited?"

"I think I could use a little time alone, to think."

Pete slanted an eyebrow at me. "Okay," he said.

I found the jumping arena empty, as I'd hoped, and hopped off Mickey's back to start dragging jumps around. I needed a challenge. I needed something *hard,* that was going to take my mind off Pete and Rick and Eileen and everyone else running roughshod over my life.

I pulled three jump standards into a narrow formation and was eyeing the result when Mickey tugged back on the reins I'd looped over my shoulder. I turned to see what had his attention and found Lindsay walking up to join us, wearing paddock boots and bright purple riding tights. Of course, when I went off alone to clear my head, Lindsay would show up. I put my hands on my hips, waiting for her inevitable snide remark.

She tilted her head at my handiwork. "You're going to jump a triangle?"

"A skinny corner," I said. "These are pretty common on cross-country and you have to be precise or you'll get a runout, or your horse's shoulder or hip might hit the flag and knock it down. That gets you penalties."

"Where's the flag?" Lindsay asked.

I tapped the standard next to me. "This would be the flag, on a course."

Lindsay nodded. I thought she looked guardedly impressed. "Maybe I could help you set fences while you jump," she said.

"That would be great."

"It looks like you'll knock down the poles a lot," she added. "This'll save you getting up and down constantly."

I rolled my eyes as she grinned. "Thanks."

Lindsay popped two poles into place, forming a triangular jump that was only a few inches wide on the left, but three feet wide on the right. With only a few feet between the jump standards on either side, Mickey would have to be dead straight to the fence or one of my fancy off-the-farm boots was going to get a big scuff on the way over.

I sent Lindsay off to set a few more jumps to a similar height and cantered Mickey around the arena as she finished, making sure he got a good look at the corner jump. They were common on upper-level cross-country courses, sometimes in pairs that were slightly off-set, to make them that much tougher to get through. A horse that felt he couldn't jump it perfectly was apt to run out, racking up refusal points that were impossible to recover from in the final score. Or, in a misfire slightly less costly but still enough to kill a good finish, take out the flag mid-jump.

After hopping a few straightforward fences, I cantered Mickey up to the corner. He blew hard on the way in, and backed off about a stride out, before ballooning over the jump. I laughed as we soared over it, in no danger of hitting the standards—they were well below my heels. He landed hard, snorting, and tossed his head as we cantered away.

"Wow!" Lindsay called. "That horse can *jump*!"

I grinned, patting Mickey's neck, and sent him around the ring again. Once more he huffed hard at the jump, but this time, he went over it without losing momentum. The third time, he twisted a little, and his hip brushed the single standard. The feel of hitting the fence annoyed him, and he bucked after landing, reminding me of Pete's dream horse.

"That was still good," Lindsay said appreciatively. "Maybe lose the bucking."

"Good idea," I said, pulling Mickey up. I gave him a long rub on the neck as he ducked his head, snorting. "I'll try it without the rodeo next time."

When we were finished, Lindsay walked over to the arena gate and opened it for us without my having to ask. She stood with her hand on the gate as Mickey walked through, eyes on the horse. "That was pretty cool," she said, and I thought I heard a note of envy in her voice.

"Would you like to try a jump like that in your next lesson? We could make it a little wider to start, but I'm sure William would be fine with it."

"Not much point," she said, lapsing back into grumpy teen mode. "No jumps like that at the horse shows."

"But if you were to try eventing . . ." I let my voice trail off, hoping I sounded tantalizing. Mickey turned in a circle and shoved his muzzle, sloppy with foam, against Lindsay's chest.

"My mom will never let me, remember?"

"Maybe we can work something out," I said.

Lindsay looked back at the corner jump, and I could see the longing in her expression. The girl was dying for a challenge. And I wanted to be the one who gave it to her. Maybe I couldn't stop Pete from making a bad decision, but I could stop Lindsay from giving up on horses.

10

DRY WEATHER TOOK over again, the short days passing by sunny and warm, giving way to long, brisk nights. We had one of those weeks where every day seemed exactly the same as the last: chores, riding, chores, bedtime. Only lessons with the kids up at the equestrian center, and Pete's frequent trips to Penny Lane, helped me keep track of the dates on the calendar.

On what I was pretty sure was a Thursday, although I wouldn't like to bet on it, Pete had a rare day off from Penny Lane and suggested we ride Mickey and Dynamo together up at the equestrian center. We'd both been so preoccupied with our own problems, the invitation felt like a date. I tacked up happily, and joined him on the trail, for once not even feeling the slightest pang at seeing him on Dynamo.

Mickey stretched his neck out and stealthily reached for a few trailside leaves as we strolled along the wooded path to the arenas. Beside us, Pete sat Dynamo with his usual easy elegance, his slim, muscular legs hanging just a little too long for my chestnut Thoroughbred's shortish, stocky build. Pete needed tall, elegant Thoroughbreds, like Regina, I reflected, letting my eyes linger on the curve of his calf beneath his black leather half chaps. He really shouldn't be on anything under sixteen-two.

"What are you thinking about?" he asked, grinning. "I see you eyeing my chaps. You planning on stealing them? Because I put my initials on the inside. With a Sharpie. That's permanent, I'll have you know."

I flushed and turned my attention back to the trail ahead. We were nearly through the little wood between our pasture and the equestrian center's neat paddocks, and we always had to be careful about the other horses causing a fuss when they saw us come riding up the path between their turnouts. Still, I didn't need to maintain eye contact in order to continue a good snark session. "I have my own chaps, thanks, and they're brown, to match my boots. I'd look pretty ridiculous with black chaps over brown boots. It's called style, Pete. Learn about it."

"You could start a new trend," Pete suggested, unperturbed. "Put them on your Instagram and the Little Juleses can all copy you."

The Little Juleses was his nickname for the sudden flood of tween and teen adoration my Instagram feed had started attracting. The mean comments were still coming in strong, but a serious fan base was starting to build. I attributed my newfound popularity to two things: Mickey's strong resemblance to a unicorn, and the blush-inducing piece that *The Chronicle of the Horse* ran in their online edition, all about my selflessness in lending Pete the horse I'd had since I was a teenager, rescuing my boyfriend in his hour of need. There were a lot of girls out there who thought they were going to meet a handsome bronze-headed eventing gent with a very slight English accent, and I was now their inspiration and idol. If Jules could do it, anyone could.

I wondered if grouchy Lindsay would respect me more, or less, if she knew about my loyal army of Instagram followers. Less, I suspected. Lindsay didn't strike me as a person who would follow the crowd. If everyone else was peering suspiciously at a cliff, she'd jump off it just to be different.

"They might, but I don't want to mislead my Little Juleses." I sighed. "My mom told me brown never mixes with black, and it's one of the only fashion things I've ever remembered. Maybe because it was so applicable to tack. Imagine if you rode with a brown bridle and a black saddle. Good Lord almighty."

"That's what I'm talking about, Jules. Make it happen," Pete urged. "Take advantage of this newfound power and use it for evil. I know it will make you happy."

"Never," I vowed. "I will only use my power for good, and to make sure everyone has matching tack, and also to try and get rid of bling browbands forever, because I hate them."

"Gold clincher or get the fuck out," Pete agreed solemnly. "Just like my grandfather always said."

"You see? It's time-honored."

"If you get rid of bling browbands, you could probably bring back long format."

I considered the possibilities. "You're not wrong. Are there no limits to my power? I mean, I really am like the Jesus of eventing right now."

Pete cracked up so completely he nearly fell right off Dynamo. I couldn't help but burst into laughter myself, and Mickey took advantage of my inattention to rip an entire branch off a tree and try to chew it up, despite the flash noseband keeping his mouth strapped closed. So we were occupied in our own separate endeavors—me trying to fish the tree branch out of Mickey's mouth before it became inextricably tangled up in his bridle, Pete trying to regain his composure—when the High Springs horses noticed strangers in their midst and came galloping like wild Mustangs to the corners of their paddocks, whinnying anxious *who-goes-there*s at the top of their lungs.

I was on the ground before I knew what happened, the air huffing out of my lungs in one painful rush. There was a flash of red and brown and white over my head and then the sound of thrumming hooves. I laid very still for a moment, thinking about how much my back hurt and how very hard the ground was in the dry season, and then I cautiously sat up and looked around.

Next to me, Pete was doing the same.

Ahead of us, galloping up the hill toward the arenas and barn, while the horses in the paddocks raced in circles, went Mickey and Dynamo, neck and neck like they were running their own private match race.

"Shit," I muttered, or I would have muttered if I had enough air in my body to form sounds.

Pete stumbled to his feet, brushing sand off his breeches. "What are you . . . waiting for . . . get up," he gasped, still trying to get his lungs back to full capacity.

"No rush," I panted. "They're already . . . halfway . . . to the barn. Relax."

Pete subsided, then doubled over and put his hands on his knees to steady himself. "Christ. That hurt."

I peeled myself up. He was right about that. After a month without much rain, the ground was as hard as pavement. I limped over to Pete and put a hand on his shoulder. "You okay, babe?"

"Nothing's broke, anyway."

Up at the cluster of arenas and barn, I could see people running outside, reaching for the cantering horses. Mickey was the first to allow himself to be captured, then Dynamo. I saw them disappear into the barn. "They're safe. Let's take a slow walk up there and shake it off."

Pete reached out and took my hand. "You just wanted a romantic walk through the forest."

"Romance isn't dead, Pete, not while I'm around."

"So what do you want to talk about?" he asked, squeezing my hand. "Romantic things? Farrier appointments and whatnot?"

I rolled my eyes at him and unclipped my hard hat with my free hand, swinging it from my head and slipping my wrist through the harness. I carried it like a fashionable purse; hell, it cost as much as a designer handbag. Thank goodness I hadn't had to pay for it. The quiet stretched out between us. There were a million things we could discuss and none of them were anything I wanted to think about. "I hear silence is nice," I suggested.

Pete shrugged and held a finger to his lips, eyes twinkling.

"Thanks," I whispered.

"Shhh," he hushed.

Thanks, I mouthed, and winked.

"Your horses are down here," a voice called as we walked into the barn, still hand in hand, still quiet, although every now and then Pete turned and waggled his eyebrows at me, and I giggled. Rosie stuck her head out of the tack room halfway down the aisle. She was round-faced, with short-cropped brown hair and an unending wardrobe of sweatpants and black hoodies, covered with hay and shavings and cat hair. "In the crossties."

"Sorry about that, Rosie," I said.

"No one to bother but me," she said with a shrug. The big center-aisle stable was empty of boarders or students. Weekday mornings were the sole property of barn managers, trainers, and grooms. "Set your horses free on a Saturday and we might have a bit of commotion."

She emerged from the tack room with a saddle on her hip and waited for us to limp down the aisle. Both of us were favoring one side; me the right and Pete the left. "Well, you're a lopsided crew today."

"We'll get it straightened out once we're riding," Pete said with a grimace. "We need a little more rain to soften that ground."

"You're getting soft yourselves, from always riding in arenas." Rosie chuckled. "When I was a kid we rode in the fields. If your pony got you off and ran away, you had to walk home. You learned not to fall off. I'm pretty surprised a pair of your experience can still get tossed that easily."

"We weren't paying attention," I said. I didn't mention how rarely we rode in arenas anymore. She owned the pasture where we did our riding. She knew.

Rosie nodded. "Just like your student," she said cryptically. "You leave and they lose all their sense." She started across the wide aisle toward a stall where a spotted horse waited for her, his head over the stall guard and his ears pricked, the picture of a Very Good Boy.

"Oh no," I said, catching her hint. "Did someone fall off after I left last night?"

"Jordan did," Rosie said nonchalantly, slipping the saddle onto a small dowel of wood clipped to the stall front. She picked up a grooming tote and ducked into the spotted horse's stall while he rumbled a friendly greeting to her.

"Jordan? But she was done for the night! She was out grazing Sammy when I left."

"Lindsay convinced her they should prance around bareback,

and then she trotted her horse away. Sammy spun around to go with him and Jordan slipped right off his side."

Ugh, Lindsay! She did it on purpose, I *knew* it. That girl needed an attitude adjustment. "Was she okay?"

"Fine, fine, but I told her she'd better learn to stay on without a saddle as well as with one. You'll have to change up your lesson plan, Miss Riding Instructor. *I'd* put her on the end of a lunge line and take away her stirrups. But I'm not her trainer anymore." Rosie bustled about, currying her horse's coat, as if she was bored with the entire affair. She was very good at dosing out occasional instructions without acting as if she really cared one way or another, which happened to be perfect for me.

I clenched my fists at my sides as I marched on down the aisle, thinking furiously of poor Jordan and how embarrassed she must have been. Like a lot of the younger girls here, she idolized Lindsay, if only because the teenager had a driver's license and a pretty serious show record. Lindsay never did a thing worth their attention, though. She just pulled mean tricks like this.

"That girl's a problem," I muttered. "Even if she was an excellent jump-setter the other night." Sweetening me up with her sighs about wanting to event. Probably she'd made it all up.

Belatedly, I reminded myself the idea to crowdfund Mickey's purchase price had been Lindsay's. But since I had no idea how I was going to pull it off, I didn't feel like I had to give her much credit.

I caught up with Pete, who had taken off Dynamo's polo wraps and was running an assessing hand over his legs. "All good," he said, straightening up with effort. He put a hand on his back and groaned. "Why did I stand up? Now I have to kneel down again to rewrap him. I'm too old for this."

"Makes me wish we just used gallop boots. Did you hear what happened to Jordan?"

"Which one is she?"

"The sweet one with the older horse."

"Let me guess, the nasty teenager caused it?"

"Of course." I dropped to my knees next to Mickey and started unwinding his polos. "She's so awful! She hates everyone, thinks she's better than everyone . . . What?"

Pete was gazing down at me with his trademark quizzical expression, one eyebrow tilted in amusement. "Oh, nothing. Just wondering, who were you more like when you were a teenager? Jordan . . . or Lindsay?"

I stuck out my chin at him. "Neither," I informed him. "Because I was always working and no one talked to the help."

"Okay. Which one would you have been if you could have been on equal footing with the other riders?" Pete's gaze was steady.

"I hate you."

"I know," he said cheerfully, and went back to wrapping Dynamo's legs. "You two would have been a formidable team, is all I'm saying."

I watched him for a while. Watching people wrap legs always put me into a zen-like state.

"There's just one problem with hating Lindsay," I said eventually.

Pete had moved on to Dynamo's hind legs. He was tying the horse's red-gold tail in a knot to get it out of the way. "Only one?"

"How many problems do I need?"

"Oh, one's fine. Let me guess . . . is it that her mom pays you?"

"That and . . . I might need her help," I said slowly, testing out the words.

"For what? Do you want to hire her as a weekend groom? I'm not sure we have the money."

"No. It's about the crowdfunding thing, to buy Mickey. It was *her* idea. And I think she would know how to do it. Me, I don't know where to begin. I have all these followers because Rockwell says I have to and people are nosy and want to know what I'm up to, but come on. I'm really no better online than I am in person. I don't know how to talk to people. I wouldn't know how to convince them to give me money, not like that, not when most of them probably are looking for the money to buy a horse *they* love."

"But, not everyone's in your boat," Pete observed. "Is that what you think? You only attract the penniless enthusiasts?"

"If they're a fan of mine, they're probably broke," I said with a shrug. "Rags to riches is all I've got and . . . well, they don't know it's already back to rags over here."

"It won't be rags forever," Pete said.

"We hope."

Pete slowly straightened. He placed a hand on the slope of Dynamo's shoulder and thoughtfully rubbed his fingernails into the horse's coat. Dynamo leaned into the rub, his ears at half-mast, eyes rolling back in his head. "So you're going to ask a teenager to run a social media campaign in order to raise, what, fifty or sixty thousand dollars? Think that's what they want for him?"

"I'm guessing that much." So far nothing had come up about Mickey's sale—not even a call from Carrie, which I found disappointing. But he was bringing home ribbons and almost ready to go Prelim, he was young, he was sound, he had the potential to go Advanced . . . sixty thousand wouldn't be a stretch. It might be a bargain. I hadn't had a horse on the market at this level before, and I didn't pay a lot of attention to their prices, who was selling who, and for what. "Who better to run a social media campaign than a bored teenager?"

Pete laughed. "You have a good point."

"Now I just have to get her to do it. And not kill her along the way."

That might not be so easy, now that I thought about it. Pete was right—we were really alike. Which meant we were pretty hard to get along with.

"Let's ride," Pete suggested. "The answer will probably come to you while you're in the saddle. And if not, we'll ask Rosie if you can muck any of her stalls for free."

We wove our horses in and out of one another's path in the farm's outdoor arena, their hooves barely raising dust from the watered surface. Late morning was the best time of day to ride here, after Rosie had set out the sprinklers to get ready for a busy day of training and lessons. By seven o'clock tonight, when the last of the boarders were getting ready to ride, the orange footing would be rock hard, with a fine layer of dust lifting up to coat everything, horses and boots and faces alike. Unless, of course, those gathering clouds in the northwest made good on their promise of flooding rains before then.

Mickey moved through a many-looped serpentine with grace, his neck arched and his mouth soft on the bit. With little time to ride while we were trying to settle in at the new property, I'd concentrated our abbreviated training time on dressage: plenty of suppling exercises and lateral work to keep him stretchy and strong despite a lack of jumping and galloping work. The extra schooling showed in every step now. His nostrils fluttered gently under his flash noseband with every breath, and each time we changed direction, he mouthed the bit and dropped a big gob of foam onto his chest and knees. He felt spectacular, a floating horse rising up to meet me.

Pete passed us in the center of the arena, Dynamo dancing his own light-footed trot as the pair flashed by. My bright red chestnut was stockier and harder to put together than Mickey, but Pete had his measure and knew how to balance Dynamo so that all his pieces moved with the same grace as a more naturally elegant horse like Mickey. I turned Mickey to the left at the rail so I could look across the arena and watch Dynamo a little more. In the corner, Pete shifted slightly and Dynamo hopped into a collected canter without changing pace. The muscles in his crest bulged beneath the ripple of his mane. "Beautiful," I whispered, and Mickey cocked one jealous ear to listen.

I stayed on the rail as they cantered down the arena toward us, keeping to the inside as the fastest-moving horse in an arena should, and then in my own corner I asked Mickey to canter. He sprang into his wonderful rocking-horse gait, and I kept my eye on Dynamo in the other corner, finessing Mickey's speed until we were traveling exactly opposite of the other horse and rider.

Pete saw what I was plotting and with a few pointed nods we managed to put on an impromptu pas de deux, passing each other in the center of the arena as we changed directions, changing leads at the same time. I was concentrating so hard on matching Mickey's strides to Dynamo's, all the way across the wide arena, I could hear nothing but the thudding of hooves. The rest of the world, the whinnies from the paddocks and the cars on the highway and the tinny country music escaping from the barn aisle, receded and disappeared. It was just the four of us, a perfect quartet.

When we finally decided to come down to a trot, and then a halt, we did so with style, lining up our horses nose-to-nose in the center of the ring. I dropped one hand to my thigh and nodded a salute to Pete. He did the same to me. Then we dropped our horses' reins and they shoved their noses together, saying hello as if they'd never met.

I laughed breathlessly. "Pete, that was the most amazing thing we've ever done."

He looked dazed as well. "I know," he said wonderingly. "I've never ridden with someone like that before." A smile crept across his face. "Who knew you could ride without being competitive?"

I shook my head at him. "Never tell on me."

A gust of wind lifted Mickey's salt-and-pepper mane over his sweaty neck, reminding us the riding window was short today. "We better go back," I said.

Pete picked up his reins and brought Dynamo alongside Mickey. His boots pushed against mine as he leaned over to kiss me. "Thank you for being the perfect dance partner," he said gently, and as my pulse began to race, I thought I wouldn't complain one bit if it rained all afternoon, and kept us inside.

11

THERE WAS AN email from Grace that afternoon, reminding me of everything she'd said on our phone call a few days ago: the sort of farm she was looking for, the insistence she wasn't ready to jump ship yet, the slightly suspect excuse that she just wanted to be ready. I scrolled through the message slowly while Pete changed into a clean pair of breeches and a fresh polo shirt before he went over to Penny Lane.

I couldn't quite believe Grace was really thinking of leaving Seabreeze so soon. It was barely six months since I'd left her barn, and although she'd mentioned the possibility of moving up to Ocala, there'd been no indication she was in a hurry to go. Now her words seemed to have the same bitter urgency my thoughts had in the weeks just before Pete admitted he was ready to leave Briar Hill. Even before I'd gone public with my decision to let Briar Hill go, I'd already given up. I felt like Grace was doing the same thing.

"Grace might leave Orlando," I told Pete.

He was pouring cold coffee from the carafe into his travel mug. "And go where?"

"Here," I said. Then I remembered our status as exiles. We

weren't "here" anymore, we were an hour north. "Ocala," I amended. "She's looking for a farm. Not too big, she says, about twenty stalls."

"Well, good luck to her."

His voice was dismissive, as if he had too many problems of his own to worry about someone else's. Well, he really didn't know Grace, except as a person who had been only marginally more insane than me last summer. He didn't know that in the end, I felt like we'd kind of hit it off.

Or that she'd suggested we work together in the future.

I waited until the sound of his truck had faded down the road before I sent Grace a reply.

If you still want to go in on something together when you get up here, I'm listening, I typed. *I'm in the middle of nowhere in High Springs. I'll make this work, so this isn't me asking for help, but I'm just saying . . . I'm open to a partnership.*

Then I clicked Send before I really knew if it was a good idea or not. I closed my eyes and tipped my head back against the wall. Why did I want so many things at once? I wanted us to make it on our own, and at the same time, I wanted a big farm again. I wanted to spend time getting close to my horses, really figuring out what made each of them tick, and at the same time, I knew I would jump at the chance to work with a dozen more. I felt like I was standing at the crossroads of a cluster of barricaded roads, waiting for the gates to lift and not sure which one I really wanted to take.

My phone pinged while I was still just sitting on the couch, staring at nothing, imagining all my potential next moves. I picked it up and saw a text from Alex.

Hey are you busy tomorrow afternoon? I can't make our lesson Friday because we have a horse in at Tampa.

I thumbed over to my calendar and squinted at Thursday's

entries. Just one late lesson to teach, at five. *I can do 3 but have to be at other barn by 4:45 to teach.*

I'll bring him and be there at 2:30. Thanks!!!

No problem. Bring coffee.

Duh!

Well, at least there was a little Starbucks in my future. I checked the weather forecast; tomorrow would be pretty cold, the afternoon just barely reaching the mid-forties. She'd be bringing hot coffee instead of iced for once, and hopefully her full attention, because Tiger was going to be a maniac with that cold wind blowing up his tail. I once knew an amateur rider who was very accomplished in the show ring, but skipped most winter shows because she had a hard and fast rule: never ride a Florida horse when the temperature dips below sixty degrees. It was a pretty smart rule to live by, considering the way most Floridian horses reacted to the slightest taste of cool air.

The wind was roaring in the pine trees outside, sounding like ocean waves pounding on a shore, and I knew the bad weather wasn't far away now. I had two lessons to teach, one at three and one at four; by the time I got back, it would probably be raining and turning colder with every hour. I went to the trailer door and leaned on the frame, looking at the horses grazing happily in the pasture, their tails to the wind. This was when I had to make one of those annoying decisions about who came in and who stayed out in the weather. There were just a couple of basic stalls with enough boards tacked up to keep a horse inside—and not entirely out of the rain, unfortunately, as the roof wasn't finished.

After a moment's thought, I knew the chosen few would have to be Regina, Mickey, and Dynamo. I felt bad for Mayfair, whom I considered briefly before giving Dynamo her spot. She was a lightly built Thoroughbred, so slight and slim it seemed as if the wet would affect her more. Possibly not true, but either way, she was the one who needed a stall next. Barsuk and Jim Dear would put up with the weather no matter how bad it got, although Jim was a little spooky in high winds and would probably gallop around like an idiot when the storm front finally broke over the property. I would love to keep him inside, so I could be assured he wouldn't do something truly stupid like run through a fence. But I just didn't have the stalls.

This puzzle alone would be a good reason to abandon whatever this experiment in bare-bones horsemanship was, and go into business with Grace. This business just required money, and a lot of it. That was the hard truth.

Maybe eventing on a shoestring *used* to be a thing, but it wasn't a reality for us, not in the twenty-first century. Not with anxious owners to please and expensive horses who needed coddling. I might have gotten Dynamo out of an auction pen two feet deep in mud and muck, but he wasn't a youngster anymore and he couldn't be expected to get soaked in a cold rainstorm and stay healthy, let alone stay in top form. Mickey might have lived in Eileen's backyard when he was coming off the racetrack two years ago, but he was a valuable and promising athlete now with too much potential for me to risk his catching a respiratory infection on a cold, stormy night. The same could be said of all the horses.

"Real life or metaphor?" I muttered to myself, chuckling grimly. Low white clouds raced beneath a higher shield of steely gray. "Go easy on us," I suggested to the sky. But I knew all too well I had no sway with the weather gods.

I threw hay into the pasture and into the three makeshift stalls, then brought in Regina, Mickey, and Dynamo. Horses prepped as they could be for the impending weather, I shut Marcus in the trailer with a new bone, put out a fresh can of food for Barn Kitty, wherever she was wandering, and got into the truck to drive the long way around to the equestrian center, hoping for the best.

The cold front didn't arrive until I was midway through my last lesson. It had been a quiet hour with an unassuming teenager named Lizzie who did what she was told, stayed out of her horse's way, and managed to make riding look boring. She would probably go through her entire life accomplishing nothing of note in the show ring, but she'd never upset a horse, never yank on a tender mouth, and never spoil a promising youngster. There was an awful lot to say for that.

As she wrapped up a slow, unremarkable canter around the arena, the drama arrived with a gust of cold wind. Behind her horse's silhouette, the northwest sky was an angry sea of dark clouds blotting out the sunset, and the wind rushing through the oak trees was shockingly cold. Lizzie's horse, an unflappable bay Quarter Horse gelding, actually lifted his head and managed to look astonished as a plastic bag went sailing through the covered arena and hooked itself on a rafter, rattling with every gust of wind. Lizzie promptly hopped off and ran up her stirrups with a businesslike manner.

"But we can keep going for another fifteen minutes!" I protested, pointing at the dusty clock hanging over the barn door. "Don't you want to hop over a course?"

"I think we're done for the day," Lizzie said with the firmness of a high school guidance counselor. "Thanks for a great lesson, Jules." She clucked to her horse and the two of them went back to the barn, leaving me standing in the center of the arena.

The riding instructor life was certainly not what I'd expected. I'd had no idea how different every student was going to be. If I'd realized there was this much variety to a day, maybe I wouldn't have been so adamantly against teaching for such a long time.

On the quick ride home, a few raindrops hit the windshield, their patter surprisingly loud, but when I hopped out of the truck, the weather was still merely threatening to unleash the apocalypse, not actively doing so. Lightning flashed through the clouds with that peculiar brilliance reserved for fully matured thunderstorms, showing me the outside horses were all in their catch pens, heads lowered to their feed buckets. To my left, Pete's truck was running, the headlights aimed at the barn. Pete waved, hammer in hand, from within the stalls, then went back to hammering.

Hammering? I hurried across the crackling grass, rubbing Marcus's soft head as he jumped up on my legs to say a rapturous hello.

The row of stalls was rapidly transforming from three to six—Pete had somehow wrestled down another half dozen panels of corrugated roofing onto the supports he'd already put in place earlier in the week. Now he was finishing up a quick skeleton job below: a board down the middle to create two stalls, a board across the fronts, another at the end for a back wall. He grinned at me as the last nail went into place. "A roof for their heads."

The sky growled and the ground seemed to quiver in response. "This is incredible," I shouted. "How did you get those panels down in all this wind?"

"I got some help," Pete admitted. "I grabbed the maintenance guy at Penny Lane and promised him fifty bucks if he'd help me finish the roof before it rained. He left about half an hour ago."

"Jeez, that was fast. I've only been gone about two hours."

"Matt's really experienced. I think he built his house."

"Guess that's pretty typical for up here."

We looked at the skeleton of stalls in silence. It was basically a pen with a roof on it. The first three stalls had half walls in the front, and rear walls about six feet high, with a gap between the roof and the wall for air flow. The new ones had only a few boards to keep horses contained. They would be soaked if the rain was blown sideways by wind, which was exactly what was about to happen. Still, it was better than nothing. And Pete looked really proud of himself.

"Let's get them inside, then," I said. "Any chance of nails on the ground?"

"Nope. Matt went over the place with a magnet before he left."

"Perfect."

We brought the horses, spooking and snorting, over to their new stalls, the stall guards from their catch pens slung over our shoulders. Pete hadn't had time to drill holes for the screw eyes, so we tied them up with baling twine and a stern admonition for each horse to not break out and cause trouble in the night.

We did the same with water buckets, minus the lecture, then everyone got a nice pile of hay in the front of their stalls, as far away from the open back of the barn and the impending wall of water as possible. With the help of headlights, lightning flashes, and muscle memory, we got everyone secured in the barn despite the inky darkness of the early night.

"We should get the power company to install a second street-light over here," I said, as we'd both said about two dozen times since we'd moved here and parked our trailers under the only light source for a half mile in any direction.

"Good idea," Pete replied, as we'd both replied each time. It seemed like in daylight, we never remembered the things we needed so desperately at night.

The trailer rattled with the force of the storm when it finally hit, making me wonder if we should've concentrated on building ourselves a room to live in before the horses, but the wind and light-ning were short-lived and then it was just a soaking rain, cold and hard. Just thinking of the horses out in such awful weather made me thankful Pete had managed to get them all under a roof tonight.

"I'm really amazed you got so much done in such a short amount of time," I told him over a bowl of blue-box mac and cheese, a warm and comforting supper with the temperature dropping outside. "I was just thinking today that we might want to go into business with Grace when she moves up. I sent her an email to feel her out. And then you manage to get the barn up! I was wrong. We're doing fine. You did an amazing job tonight. That's how I know we're going to be okay."

"Well, like I said, I had help," Pete said. His voice was cool. "What's that about Grace?"

"I told you she's thinking of moving up to Ocala, so I said hey, maybe we should go into business together, tell me what you'd think that would look like . . . Anyway, it took a month to get up the first three stalls and now we have three more in a couple of hours? That's amazing. You're a workhorse, Pete."

"The supports were already in place," Pete said defensively. "There was a lot of setup to be done, all we had to do was get the roofing nailed down."

"I'm just saying, it took so much less time than the other stalls, you did such a big job so fast."

"Are you saying the rest of the barn took too long to get built, Jules?"

I froze, hand hovering midway between my bowl and my mouth. Pete looked slightly wild. *That's it,* I thought. *The pressure's too much for him. The kettle is whistling and no one's turning down the heat.* I spoke carefully, slowly, as if to a yearling on the edge of a tantrum. "That's not what I was saying at all, Pete, I just meant—"

"God, I can't do anything fast enough to please you," he

snapped. "You're always full of plans. You want catch pens. You want stalls. You want separate paddocks. You want jumps. You think I'm just going to build you an equestrian center, Jules? That's insanity. What, you think I owe you after losing Briar Hill? And if you don't get it fast enough, you're going to pick up and move back to Grace's barn? Why can't you just wait it out, Jules, and let us get our lives back in order in some kind of natural timeframe? What is the goddamn rush?"

I stared at his angry face, his cheeks reddening, his eyes wide. The first emotion that came flooding over me wasn't reciprocal rage, although maybe it would have been once. Instead, I just felt confused. Where had this come from? I would never understand men, I thought. Or maybe it was just other people in general. Either way, I didn't want a fight. But my feelings were hurt, and I wanted him to know it.

"Pete," I said finally, my voice thin, "how could you say that?" I couldn't think of anything else to say. I genuinely wanted to know the answer.

"But that's it, Jules," Pete replied icily. "I'm right. Why don't you just say it? You think I better get on the ball and give you the farm you deserve, since I lost the last one."

I put down my fork. Clearly, dinner wasn't happening now. Not even comfort food was going to solve this crisis. I fixed Pete with what I hoped was a warm, loving, understanding expression that in no way reflected the disappointment I felt on the inside.

"Pete, don't be an idiot," I said.

Oops. So much for warm, loving, and understanding. Although I'd kind of said it with all those things in mind. Anyway, I had to carry on. Pete was looking like he might leap out of the trailer and drive off down the road at any moment. I took a breath and tried again.

"Sorry. Just listen to me for a moment. First off, I don't think having plans to improve the property is some sort of unreasonable series of demands, it's just planning, and I've been working just as hard as you. Second, how could you think this has anything to do with Briar Hill? You didn't lose it, Pete. It was *taken* from us. And third, for God's sake, of course anything we do with Grace we do together." Although I couldn't quite recall the wording of my email. Had I made that clear? Well, it was just a tentative first step, after all. Nothing had been offered, nothing had been set in stone, and she had to know I came as a package deal. "I would never go anywhere without you."

It was a big statement, but he didn't receive my assurances with the same spirit of generosity. Instead, Pete continued to glower at me, and I suddenly wished for a full-size table between us, a full-size room around us, enough space to hold all this emotion and upset. We had a full-size life but not nearly enough room to contain it.

He spat out his next words. "All I hear from you is *I want, I want, I want.*"

I leaned back a little despite myself; his anger was that alarming. "Well, what's wrong with wanting things?" I protested. "It's not like I told you to go and do them. Did I say, 'Pete, I demand you build me a barn'? When did I say that?"

"Maybe not like that, but you obviously want a barn. And if you want a barn, who is going to build it? Are *you* going to build it, Jules? You use the back of a dandy brush to knock loose boards into place."

"There's nothing wrong with that. Maybe I can't build a barn. You think I would have just said, 'Well, I can't build it all by myself, so guess I'll never get a barn'? No, I would have taught more lessons and saved up and paid somebody to do it." I sat back and leaned my head against the flimsy wallboard. It was cold; outside the rain was pelting against the aluminum, and no amount of cheap cardboard between us and the elements could keep out the creeping chill of a Floridian winter rain. I was exasperated. "I would have made the money and outsourced the job, like a normal person! When did you stop being normal? What is happening right now? What are you even arguing with me about? We *needed* a barn, that's not exactly an empty wish!"

Pete got up and very deliberately put his bowl on the floor. Marcus sprang into action; this was the moment he'd been waiting for. I watched the beagle dip his long nose into the bowl and devour the rest of the mac and cheese I'd made for Pete while he'd been showering.

I hadn't had time for a shower yet, but Pete could shower and eat the food I made for him and still find time to start an argument. *Seems fair,* I thought. *Seems legit.*

Marcus's ears dipped into the cheese and came out tinged with orange.

"Storm out," I told Pete. "Make a big scene."

Pete looked ready to take my advice, but then he looked around the little trailer as if he was just realizing there was nowhere for him to go. Cold rain outside and my cold face inside, waiting for him to apologize or make things worse.

It was his call, I figured.

He sat back down.

I waited.

"I'm sorry," he said.

"Thank you."

"I'm very tired."

"I'm sure."

Silence ticked between us for a few minutes. I took a bite of dinner, then another, my eyes on Pete's bowed head. Part of me wanted to take mercy on him, to say I understood what he was going through.

The other part of me knew he couldn't be allowed to get away with this. I was tired, too. I didn't act out because of it. I'd conquered that part of my personality; now it was his turn.

"I just feel like your dreams are too big for me right now," Pete said suddenly, his eyes flicking up to meet mine.

The words hit me with an intensity nothing else he'd thrown at me had been able to match. I dropped my fork. It bounced onto the floor and Marcus pounced on it gleefully. "I don't know what you mean," I said faintly.

"I mean all of your big, ambitious Jules-plans. I love them, I do. I love that you're always on to the next thing, the next *five* things; nothing slows you down. But right now I just feel like I need to move slowly and wait to see what happens next."

I felt dizzy. I caught my forehead in my palm before I tilted forward. So this was vertigo, I thought detachedly. Some people live like this all the time. I wasn't sure I was strong enough to handle more than a few seconds of it. One of my saving graces in life was that I was always in control of my body, even when my life was spinning out of control.

But Pete really needed to pick a speed. Either he was taking on the world at full gallop, or he was backing off hard, waiting for the jumps to come to him.

"Jules? Are you okay?"

The worry in his voice was real, and suddenly that was too much for me.

How could he say he didn't want to be part of my plans, and

then act concerned about my well-being? Didn't he know life was all or nothing? *Either care or don't, Pete,* I thought. *I don't want half-and-half.*

"I'm fine," I muttered, and just like that, I really was. The dizziness subsided; I picked up my head and faced him again. I was Jules, and I was tougher than him, tougher than life, tougher than fate.

I took in Pete as if I'd never seen him before. His blue eyes, his tan cheeks, his slanting eyebrows, his dark fox hair, his pointed chin. I loved him, even when I hated him. He was part of my *life;* he was part of my five-year plan, my ten-year plan, my life plan. I hadn't asked for him, heaven knew, but now I couldn't write him out of my story without doing some serious damage to the page. I'd have to tear it all up and start over again and God, I was so tired. "Pete, listen to me."

He leaned forward, and that slightly subservient gesture gave me courage. I plunged ahead without any doubts about what I would say next.

"I'm sorry you don't like this farm. I'm sorry you don't think I have us on the right path. But I'm going to keep making plans for both of us, because right now, I'm in charge. If you don't feel like you can make these decisions, that's okay. I don't expect you to do anything more than what you just said: figure out how to make Delannoy happy, get a horse out of him, and get Dynamo conditioned for Advanced. That's it. Everything else, leave to me. Until you're ready to jump back in, I'll handle things for both of us. Got it?"

Pete was still for a moment, staring at me. Then he nodded slowly. I let go of a breath I hadn't known I was holding.

"You're going to be fine," I told him confidently. "Just leave everything to me."

12

"JUST LIKE THAT? You just told him you were in charge from here on out?"

"Just like that."

Alex tugged up on Tiger's girth. "That's fantastic. Holy shit. If I ever did that with Alexander, you can bet the world would be coming to an end."

I slipped Jim Dear's bridle over his ears. We were going to ride over to the equestrian center to use their arena for Alex's lesson. Ordinarily a trainer wouldn't be allowed to bring an outside student over, but I'd wheedled the favor out of Rosie in exchange for an extra tune-up ride on one of her lesson horses each week. I didn't have that many to ride right now anyway, so I could use the extra saddle time for basic fitness. "You know Pete. He's nothing like Alexander. He puts on a good front but deep down he's not the most confident guy."

Alex looked at me over the stall's half wall. "I don't think that's necessarily true."

"About Alexander? You'd know better than me."

"About Pete. I think you've got him wrong, there, Jules."

"Oh, do you?"

"This is the guy that drove through the eye of a hurricane to rescue you and your student, right?"

"Yes," I admitted. "What about it?" But I knew where she was going with this.

"And crawled under your house to dig out your dog, also during this same hurricane."

"Uh-huh."

"I don't think he's got a confidence problem."

I didn't have a response to that. I finished buckling up Jim's bridle in silence.

"I'm sorry," Alex said eventually. "I didn't mean—"

"No, it's fine," I said shortly. "I just . . . I'm a little bummed out. If it's not confidence, what's his problem? Do I know this guy at all?"

Alex laughed. "Jules, he just lost his farm. Oh, and his grandmother? Who practically raised him and he made it his life goal to make her proud? That's a lot to take. The difference between the two of you is that *you* move right on to the next thing. You lose ground and see it as an opportunity. He loses and he's got to take some time to mourn. He's not ready to make his next big move. He moved to High Springs to hide out, not to plot his stunning return to the spotlight. Not everyone's as ice-cold as you, you know," Alex added, "and I don't mean that as an insult at all. Just a fact."

I led Jim out of the stall, stretched his legs and checked his girth, and mounted up. Alex did the same with Tiger, with her trademark addition of a little shimmy to avoid his habitual attempt to bite her as she was halfway into the saddle. We all learn to accommodate our horse's habits.

"How would you be feeling right now if it was you and Alexander starting all over again?" I asked as we started off for the path through the pines.

"Like giving up horses forever," Alex said seriously. "I'd be on a plane for the Bahamas and I'd sit on a beach and think of all the wonderful things I could be doing besides ever getting back into horses. And Alexander would do exactly the same."

"But you wouldn't be serious."

"I'd be dead serious. For about three months. Then we'd probably figure out a way to get started again. But it wouldn't be instantaneous. We wouldn't handle it like you." Alex smiled at me.

Alex hadn't been riding Tiger regularly since we'd left Briar Hill, and we could both see the difference immediately. He'd been going in a nice Novice dressage frame before, and jumping a course without getting too silly, but now he was running through her hands and rushing fences. I dismounted and handed her Jim's reins so that I could quickly pull some jumps together, building a gymnastic with a couple of trot poles, a bounce, and a one-stride to a small vertical. Alex sighed at the return to basics, but she dutifully walked Jim alongside Tiger until the jumps were built, and then gathered up her reins to trot Tiger over the little series of fences.

What happened next was pretty special.

Tiger tugged at her hands and burst into a canter about five strides before the jumps, then realized there were trot poles before them. He tried his best to canter through them, stumbled when he stepped on one, then slid through the gymnastic with the aplomb of a two-year-old who hadn't yet learned where all his legs were, pulling down every rail. Alex cursed. I laughed and set the fences again, Jim dutifully following me like a school horse who knew the lesson routine by heart.

"He won't do that again!" I shouted as she trotted around the arena a second time. "He's going to go through this time quiet as a sheep."

And I was right: Tiger was a smart horse, and he didn't need to be told twice that he'd screwed up. He put his head down to scope out the trot poles, picked up his legs smartly to avoid stepping on them, and then jumped slowly and carefully through the gymnastic, cantering out with his neck arched and his ears flicked back to Alex, listening for her praise.

"What a good boy!" she told him obligingly. "What a smart boy!"

"You see?" I said to Jim, who was watching with interest. "Everyone learns from a little stumble or three."

After they jumped successfully through the gymnastic a few times, I decided to be generous and let them go out to the hunter ring to try some lines. "See if you can get him to trot in and canter out of the outside line there," I told her. "It's an easy five strides. If he pulls you, bring him down to a halt and then make him pop the fence, even if you're really close to it."

"Got it," Alex said, straightening her helmet, and off they trotted.

I leaned back on the picnic table by the arena while Jim pulled on the reins until I let him crop the short grass within reach.

Happy with the new arena and the cool breeze nipping at his tail, a gift of last night's cold front, Tiger decided to tug on Alex again, and she dutifully sat down and brought him to a halt just a couple of strides before the first fence. I was enjoying the startled expression on Tiger's face—he really hadn't seen that coming—when I heard footsteps approaching. I turned, surprised; it was too early for any of the boarders to be here on a weekday.

But here was Lindsay, her dark fringe of bangs swaying beneath a frayed Ariat baseball cap, a shocking pink braid draped over her shoulder like a bough of cherry blossoms against her usual black clothes. Her tight riding shirt had a plunging neckline studded with tiny buttons, the top few left open to show off a hot-pink sports bra. She looked like a burlesque girl dressed up as an equestrian. It was an especially daring outfit considering the chill in the air; the day had scarcely managed to warm past fifty. In Florida-degrees, that's just above freezing.

"That's a new color for you," I observed, although it probably wasn't good practice to point out my students' lingerie. "You lightening up?"

Lindsay twisted her mouth in a possible smile. She nodded at the arena and I turned back just in time to see Tiger deer-jump the second fence in the line, popping up from a near standstill. Alex clung to his neck as he landed heavily, then got herself together and kicked him back to a trot to try it again. "Whose deer is that?"

"That's not a deer, that's a Tiger," I said, grinning to myself.

"What?"

"His name's Tiger. That's my friend Alex. She rode with me at my old place. They've had a few weeks off. Hence the deer-jump."

Lindsay settled onto the picnic table next to me. I resisted the urge to ask her what she wanted. Maybe she just felt friendly. Maybe she was plotting my demise. Either was equally possible, but she'd definitely never tell me to my face. "Does she event too?"

"She trains racehorses, but she'd like to event."

Lindsay swiveled to face me. Suddenly her blank expression was animated. "She's in racehorses?"

"All in," I confirmed. "Major horses. Cotswold Farm, down in Ocala."

"Wait." Lindsay looked at Alex, trotting her horse up to the piddly little two-foot fence like a short-stirrup rider, and then back at me. "That woman trains Personal Best. That's Alex Whitehall."

"Yup. I had no idea you liked racing."

"I like anything that isn't *this*." She gestured at the plain brown hunter course. "And Personal Best is kind of a big deal. I can't believe you know Alex Whitehall!"

Interesting, I thought. All of a sudden, I had something Lindsay wanted. I decided to use my power for good. In an evil kind of way. Casually, I said, "Maybe I'll introduce you."

"Maybe?" Lindsay sounded hurt.

"Well, you tend to be nasty to people." I kept my tone nonchalant. "I heard what you did to Jordan. Not sure I want you representing my students to Alex."

Lindsay watched Alex longingly. Eventually, she said, "I've known Jordan a really long time. That's just how we are with each other."

"Does Jordan think that, too? And everyone else in the barn?" Lindsay chewed at her lip.

"What if she'd gotten hurt? You should have been more careful," I said, losing patience.

"*Fine,*" Lindsay muttered. "I'm sorry I got Jordan dumped off her horse. But in my defense, I didn't know she'd fall off."

"Always assume the worst, with horses," I said. "Just call that a life lesson."

By the end of the hour, Tiger was jumping the line courteously and Lindsay had recovered her steady cool. I brought her over to the gate as Alex was riding Tiger out, his nostrils flaring.

"Hey Alex, this is Lindsay," I said. "One of my other students."

Alex grinned and leaned down, holding out a gloved hand. "What's up? I'm Alex."

Lindsay took her hand uncertainly. Teenagers were cute when they were introduced to adult conventions, pretending they knew all about it and then immediately flubbing minor courtesies. "Jules told me you have racehorses," Lindsay said, her voice nervous.

"That's right, this is one of my ex-racehorses." Alex steadied Tiger as he crab-stepped, throwing his head up. Lindsay didn't back away. Her eyes followed the dark bay hungrily.

"From the Florida Thoroughbred Makeover."

I looked at Lindsay sharply. How much did she know about Alex?

Alex was grinning, delighted her favorite had been recognized by a fan.

"That's right! You know about Tiger? That's so cool! Well, he and I have had a lot of uneven training, so Jules has been helping us get our shit together. Oops—can I say shit in front of teenagers, Jules? I don't know the rules."

"She knows worse things than you do," I assured her. "Teenage life is very dark now."

"Oh, there's no way it's as bad as adulthood. I thought so too when I was a teenager, but now I'm a racetracker and the world is filled with unimaginable darkness." Alex laughed. "Sorry, Lindsay. Anyway, do you have a horse? What do you do?"

Lindsay looked at the ground. *She's embarrassed,* I thought incredulously. *Lindsay the Teenage Nightmare is embarrassed. The marvels of hero worship never cease.*

"I just horse show," Lindsay muttered. "Not so much anymore. I have a Hanoverian named William I used to do children's jumpers with."

"Well, that's cool. What's wrong with that?"

"Nothing, I just . . ." Lindsay looked up, her dark blue eyes full of hope. I was seeing so many new sides to Lindsay today, I felt dizzy. "I want to gallop at the track. I want to get into racing."

"Holy shit," I said. "You never told me that."

She glared at me, an expression I was much more used to. "You never told me you knew anyone in racing."

"How old are you?" Alex cut in. She started to walk Tiger in a slow circle around us, and he dug down at his bit and swished his tail, expressing his irritation at the delay in action. I itched to get on him and take him around the course six or seven more times, until he got over his attitude. But Alex never seemed to notice his shenanigans. Years of riding young racehorses had given her an enviable seat that sat tight no matter where the horse beneath her swayed and bounced. For Alex, the only things strictly off-limits were bolting and bucking.

"I'm still sixteen," Lindsay admitted begrudgingly. "But I can ride—"

"Of course you can. I just can't help you until you're eighteen. Insurance, you know? But in two years . . ."

"A year and a half," Lindsay offered.

"In a year and a half, we can talk about getting you onto the training track. And then . . . who knows?" Alex smiled brightly. "I know exactly how you feel. I wanted to ride racehorses, too. I just had to wait it out. And now look at me. Back in the schooling ring, but for fun this time."

Lindsay looked half hopeful, half chagrined, as if this was both the best and worst news she'd ever gotten. I knew how long the gap was between sixteen and eighteen, between the false freedom of a driver's license and the soaring independence of escaping to start the life of your dreams. I realized the three of us had a lot in common. But it was likely that at the root of every equestrian's ambition there was a restless spirit longing to escape the fate of that tedious, everyday life society had promised them. Of course we had that in common.

"In the meantime," I said, "if you want to learn to gallop horses and keep a seat through everything a rotten youngster can throw at you, let me introduce you to a little sport called eventing."

Lindsay looked at the ground. "I know. I asked my mom. It didn't go well . . . Let's just say my mom will never let me. She wants me to ride more but she doesn't want me going cross-country. Not with William. She said he's worth too much. And I won't let her sell him, either, to get a new horse. So I'm stuck." The emotion in her voice was real, a complete departure from her practiced monotone.

I looked at Alex and she stared back at me, eyebrows raised. Had we just discovered a lukewarm corner of Lindsay's frozen little heart?

An inkling of an idea formed in the back of my head and pushed its way forward. "Lindsay, if I convince your mother that eventing is the best possible thing to do with William, will you help me with that crowdfunding thing we were talking about?"

Alex blinked at me, and I realized I hadn't told her about Mickey. But before I could explain, Lindsay was looking up, eyes wide. "Are you serious? You want my help with it?"

Okay, all this emotion was unsettling. "Are you interested? Because I don't know the first thing about any of this. I post things online because Rockwell told me to, not because I have some burning desire to share my entire life with strangers."

"First of all, sharing your life with strangers is way more interesting than sharing it with people you actually know, who are usually just the boring locals that school and family have thrown you in with," Lindsay declared, suddenly very much in control of her emotions again. She looked older when she was feeling authoritative, even with the pink braid looping over her shoulder. "Second, I would love to do this. I'm a social media genius. You're so lucky you know me. I probably would have done it without you even offering to talk to my mom, but now that you've offered, I'm holding you to it."

I shook my head. Impossible. That was all, she was impossible. But she wanted to help, and I needed all the help I could get. "Deal," I said, and we shook hands. "I'll fix things with your mom, and we'll get started on this social media thing as soon as possible. What's your schedule look like for the rest of the week?"

Lindsay grimaced at me. "Dude, I'm in high school. What do you think it looks like? I'm available after three thirty every day. Except for today, because sometimes I need a mental health day."

Alex laughed, clapping her hands together like a little girl presented with a puppet show. "I have no idea what's going on," she chortled, "but I have to tell you, I really love the two of you together. You're going to be the most bad-tempered power couple ever."

So what's the deal with my new fan club member back there?" Alex was rubbing the sweat marks out of Tiger's dark bay coat; the day was too chilly to give him a shower. I had given Jim a quick once-over with a towel and turned him out; I had to rush back over to the equestrian center to teach in about five minutes. "And then tell me why you're buying Mickey."

"Lindsay's a funny story," I said. "Mostly in that she's awful. But apparently she loves you and her horse and no one else. And she won't admit it about the horse."

"Awful how?"

"Just the usual teenager-awful I guess. Pete says she's just like me."

"Oh, that's bad all right. And he's totally right, by the way. She's basically a teenage version of you. I bet you were just like her in high school! Oh my gosh! Teenage Jules! What a nightmare. I bet you wore all black, too."

"So anyway," I went on, pointedly ignoring her while she laughed at me, "she only rides because her mother won't let her quit, burned out from too much A-circuit stuff, blah blah blah. It's funny because my instinct is to really dislike her, but if she wants to event, maybe we'll start getting along okay. And, of course, we're going to be working together on this project."

"Which is?"

I took a deep breath. "Mickey's going up for sale and we're going to try and crowdfund enough money to buy him," I said in one big rush.

Alex nodded, calmly accepting the news of Mickey's owners dropping me with the aplomb of a horsewoman who has been there a hundred times herself. "And social media is going to save you?"

"Lindsay says that you can get total strangers to buy you stuff if you ask them nicely."

"Big, if true," Alex said, sounding a little skeptical. "Social media can also be a total shitshow."

"I know. I've had plenty of run-ins with blogs and mean girls online," I said.

"But did you get hounded out of your horse racing career and forced to make a public show out of retraining your recently retired racehorse at a Thoroughbred Makeover event in order to clear your name after being falsely accused of horse abuse by keyboard warriors on social media?"

I looked at Alex. That was a mouthful. "Um, no?"

Alex laughed. "Sorry, that was just me showing off that I've been more bullied than you."

"Yikes, sorry, that must have sucked," I said lamely. I thought I'd had a rough time online, but it sounded like Alex's thing was much, much worse. Trying to avoid awkward silence, I plowed on. "So, you get it, though. Social media's not my fave, but if there's money up for grabs, I can't really turn it down."

"Well, even my thing worked out, because look at Tiger and how great he is now. And even Lindsay knows who I am because of that Thoroughbred Makeover competition we did! So, I can see this working. I really can. How many followers do you think you have?"

"Like, four thousand on Instagram and half that many on Facebook, I think. Those are the only things I post to."

"Good numbers." Alex tossed the brush back into her grooming tote and gathered up Tiger's lead rope, ready to load him up and head back to Ocala. "And Lindsay's going to show you how to wring ten or twenty bucks out of each of them?"

"Something like that. I guess we'll have to talk about it." I grinned. "Looks like I'll be seeing a lot more of Lindsay than I ever planned. Especially if she wants to event, too."

"You know, Jules, riding instructors make a really big difference in their students' lives. And this is even bigger than just teaching. You might be getting more involved with her than you realize. That's a big responsibility."

I busied myself picking up Alex's tote and stowing it inside the trailer's tack room, inwardly fussing over the gravity of her words. She was right, of course.

When I'd been a teenager, my trainer Laurie had practically taken over as my mother. I'd spent all my time at the barn, following her around, trying to please her, and ultimately turning into someone with a lot of her attributes. She'd taken me on as her responsibility without hesitation, though at the time, I'd just thought she kept me around to do chores and make her life easier. Maybe I hadn't given her enough credit for everything she'd taught me.

Shaping a teenager's future was *not* a responsibility I wanted. Wasn't I already responsible for fixing my future, and Pete's? Wasn't that enough trouble for anyone?

"She's just helping me with this one thing," I said, trying to dismiss the idea. "It's not a big deal."

"Jules Thornton, youth counselor," Alex persisted, chuckling.

"It suits you. Sometimes the most troubled youth become the most inspiring adults."

"Shut it, you."

"In all seriousness." Alex led Tiger up the ramp into the trailer, and after she had closed the door on his hindquarters, she turned back to me. "I know you don't like teaching, and you're only teaching *me* to be nice, and you're only teaching Lindsay to make money. But this is real. This is your chance to help this girl follow her dreams."

"Her dreams of . . . what?"

Alex smirked. "Imagine! No one else was ever going to do it for her. She'd already given up. And then she met you. And through you, she met me. And we're both going to enable her to do more with horses than she'd wanted to do in a long, long time. To think, she could've just gone to college and probably law school judging by her excessive and alarming confidence, and then continued into a successful career, possibly becoming a state attorney or a high-powered corporate lawyer. But you're saving her from all that."

"You're so bad at sarcasm," I said. "You're not even being funny."

Alex latched up the back doors of the trailer. "Maybe, but if she really gets into eventing, or comes to gallop for me in two years . . . well, how does it feel to mold the next generation?"

I thought about it. "This is definitely too much responsibility for me."

"Nothing is too much for you," Alex said cheerfully, looking over the trailer hitch one more time. She ran her fingers over the connections with the special obsessive quality reserved for horse people who have been reared on a thousand horror stories told 'round the feed store counter. "You're a rare breed of crazy. And that's why your fellow crazies love you."

And with that final summation, she hopped into her truck, shut her door, and started back to Ocala.

I hastily called Marcus back into the trailer, settled his frowning hound face with a new rawhide chew, and jumped in my truck to get back to work. Alex's words stayed with me as I drove over to the equestrian center, as I met my evening student in the barn, and as she led her horse out to the arena. I looked at the horse and rider combination without pleasure.

Kelly was in her mid-fifties, had just taken up riding again after a thirty-year gap, and recently purchased a flashy pinto half-warmblood with auto lead changes and a bland, bored expression in his eyes. She was like one of Grace's adult students, I thought, coming back to childhood dreams she'd forgotten. The opposite of everything I'd ever wanted from my own life. Was this Lindsay, thirty years from now, leaving work early every Thursday to fit in a riding lesson? Alex told me I had the power to stop it from happening to my students. I could give Lindsay a riding life even though she believed it held no more joy or surprises.

Or maybe Lindsay would just quit, and be done with horses forever, because some busybody riding instructor kept pushing her in a direction that made her miserable. She might not like eventing. William might not like it. She could get hurt. William could get hurt. And in the middle of it all, we'd have this thing with Mickey, whatever it was we were doing.

"I don't need this responsibility," I muttered.

"What?" Kelly asked, alarmed, as she trotted by on the wrong diagonal.

"Check your diagonal," I said automatically.

13

I WAS FEEDING in the dark again, and this time it was bitingly cold. But at least the horses had stalls now.

I threw grain into everyone's buckets and they dug in with gusto; the chilly wind that had been whipping through the pines and down the pasture's empty slope all day was really good for building up appetites. Igor, the robot voice who spoke from my weather radio, promised tonight would be a cold night, with a frost by morning, and I had to get everyone rugged up in warm blankets. Their clipped show coats were looking a little ragged as spring neared, but they still weren't woolly enough to cope with a freezing night. Regina hadn't been clipped at all, but she really hadn't bothered to grow a winter coat—none of them would have. They'd all spent too much time indoors, and too much time in Florida.

By moonlight, I hauled blankets out of my trailer tack room and threw one over the front rail of each stall, where they swayed atop the stall guards in cheerful plaid patterns. Mickey nosed his blanket thoughtfully, still chewing his supper, grains of sweet feed tumbling from his lips and sticking to the fabric.

"Don't do that," I told him, "or you'll end up with ants in your pants after you lie down tonight." He dribbled oats on my arm and then went back to his bucket for another monster bite.

Everyone was a bit muddy after a few good rolls in the damp pasture, the thick North Florida clay clinging to their withers and hip bones like old glue, so I had to knock the dirt off each horse with a stiff brush before I could throw a blanket over their backs. By the time I was done, I was sweating through my hay-covered fleece and my hair felt like it was standing on end, crackling with static electricity. I was pressing my cold hands against the wooden plank between two stalls, hoping with unscientific optimism that it might soak up a little loose static, when I heard a thoughtful *woof* from Marcus, and I looked over the backs of the horses to see Pete driving up the lane, headlights bouncing through the makeshift barn.

"I'm almost done," I called as he climbed out of the truck. "How was Penny Lane?"

He strolled over, one careless hand rubbing at Marcus's ears as the disloyal pup stood on hind legs to welcome him home. In the moonlight, his tan face looked almost white; his eyes were dark shadows, unreadable even from a few feet away. "I think I have the owners ready to sell," he said in a low voice, as if it was a secret. "Things are looking good."

I handed him a lead rope and pointed at Dynamo, who stood with his head over his stall guard watching us, ready to be turned out.

Pete took the rope without looking and kept his gaze fixed on me. A grin creased across his stubbled cheeks. "Congratulate me," he murmured. "I'm going to get a new horse."

I regarded him for a moment. We hadn't really spoken since last night's fight and my firm assurance that I was in charge of our future for the time being.

Apparently whatever had gone down with the horse's owners at Penny Lane had turned his mood right around. I wished it was for any other reason. "Pete, can I ask you a serious question?"

His mouth twisted as he realized I wasn't going to shower him with affection and congratulations. He took the lead rope from me and marched over to Dynamo's stall, abandoning his foolish hope I would be jubilant over whatever game he was playing. "Fire away," he said without bothering to turn back around. He snapped the lead to Dynamo's halter; Dynamo shoved his head at him, ready to get back outside. Pete pushed him back gently and I had a moment's guilt at what I was about to accuse him of. Pete was a good person, a good *horseman*. He wouldn't screw anybody to get ahead.

Which was precisely why he would never get ahead.

And he knew it.

"Be honest with me. Did they want to sell that horse a week ago?"

Pete dropped Dynamo's stall guard against the ground. The hose had leaked when I'd filled buckets earlier, and the snap fell with a wet thud into the mud by the door. I hated it when stall guard snaps were allowed to touch the ground. He knew I hated it. He shrugged. "They do now."

"*Did* they?" I persisted.

"They hadn't said so out loud." He led my horse past me, hooves sucking at the mud. The grass was already gone from in front of the row of stalls, and last night's rain was giving me a preview of what the wet season would look like here if we didn't put down some rubber mats or something, fast. "But I don't talk to them much. I talk to their trainer."

"And now they've said so?"

"The girl doesn't want to ride him anymore. She told me yesterday. And she went home and told her parents last night. She wants a hunter. Something dead quiet, with auto changes. Her exact words. I'm not robbing her, Jules. I'm helping her."

I watched them, Pete and my big red horse, moving through the moonlight.

Beneath the dark sky, all the color was drained from the world. The two of them were shadows of their real selves, hooves and boots whispering softly through the dew-damp grass. Thank goodness they made a noise when they touched the ground, I thought. On these lonesome nights, we were all ghosts out here.

Sometimes I thought we needed the reminder that we were made of flesh and blood, or we'd just float away, forgotten in the middle of the pines.

Behind me, Mickey neighed and shoved his chest against his stall guard, very much flesh and blood, very much alive. The wood groaned in response, cheap nails squeaking in their burrows.

"Knock it off," I snapped automatically, but my heart wasn't in it, and Mickey just pushed again, until finally the screw eye popped loose and the stall guard fell to the ground. He bolted forward but I was standing nearly in front of him, and it was a simple thing to reach up, snatch his halter, and spin him around, bringing him to a screeching halt so that he was facing me with wide eyes and flared nostrils—or at least it was a simple thing for me. After all these years of dealing with rude horses, I could nab a bolting horse with little more than muscle memory.

"You're a punk," I told him, and gave the halter's noseband a yank to let him know he was in trouble. Mickey jerked his head up in response and then he pivoted around me anxiously, frustrated his buddy was already in the pasture and he was still stuck over here with mean old Mom.

"First, you behave like a gentleman." I snapped on the lead rope I'd had slung over my shoulder and led him back into the stall, where we turned a slow circle before we headed back out. By the time I got to the gate, Pete had already gone back for another horse. He didn't look at me as he passed me, and I couldn't make out his expression. But I figured he could only be thinking two things— either he was ashamed of whatever it was he was doing with that gray horse and that teenage owner, or he wasn't bothered at all, and he was angry at me for trying to make him feel he should be.

Why was I so hell-bent on poisoning this deal for him? Something about it made my gut twist, that was all I knew, and I wasn't willing to dig into my memories to look for the answer. Some things were better left buried. We were the only ghosts we needed.

When everyone was out and Regina was snug in her pen, picking through her T&A for the bits of alfalfa, I called Marcus and opened the trailer door. Light flooded out; there was warmth and comfort inside. Pete followed me in, Marcus at his heels.

"Sit down," he said. "You did all the feeding. I'll heat us up something."

I settled down on the couch and peeled off my socks, and tugged up the tight ankles of my breeches to give my sore legs a rest. Marcus clambered up next to me and put his head in my lap. I pulled at his ears and waited.

Pete was quiet, pulling a couple of little frozen pizzas out and heating up the toaster oven. They would take ages in there, I thought, but let it go. He'd sit down and have a beer with me, and explain what he was doing with this horse.

This horse, I thought. I didn't even know its name.

"What's the horse's name, Pete?" I asked.

I watched his shoulders stiffen and knew the reason. He didn't even want to talk about it. God, what was going on? Was this horse worth so much plotting and subterfuge?

"It's Rogue," he said finally. "Gallant Rogue."

I had to grin. No wonder he'd been keeping it quiet. "That's a romance novel name."

"I know, it's awful."

"That's his registered name? It's not, like, Z Diamond ESOL?"

"He's Irish, remember, not a Hanoverian or something. Although they do have a bunch of Diamonds in that breed. And Clovers."

"Diamond Rogue would be even better," I mused. "How much does it cost to change? With a horse named like that, you could be the next Fabio. Now that's gotta be a lucrative gig—paintings of you on Diamond Rogue, shirt pulled open, kilt pulled up, in the romance section of every airport bookstore. Tack shop sponsorships are so passé. Models are where it's at. And I'd be the envy of the industry."

"And that's all you ever wanted." Pete pulled two beers out of the fridge and settled down next to me. Marcus, annoyed, wiggled halfway onto my lap to make room. I bent over him and kissed his domed head. "So listen, about the kid . . ."

"The horse's owner?"

"Yeah, that one." Pete hesitated. "I wouldn't be pushing her to sell if I thought she wanted the horse at all."

"How can you be sure of that, Pete? She must love her horse. Maybe she's just mad at him right now and you're giving her an easy excuse to keep feeling that way."

"Maybe I am. What's wrong with that? She's mad at him, he's not a good horse for her, she gets a new horse, she's happy. We're all happy."

"It feels icky," I insisted.

"I'm so glad you're the ethics panel now," Pete said crisply. "You and your reputation for a heart of gold."

"Hey! I've never done anything unethical. I'm just . . . very publicly grouchy."

"I know, I know." Pete took a long swig of his beer.

"Pete, just promise me you won't push her to do something she'll regret. I know about teenage girls and their horses, okay? We get emotional and make the wrong choices sometimes."

He leaned over and pressed a kiss to my hair. "I promise," he vowed. "If only because you just admitted you might have been wrong once."

14

I COULDN'T SAY why it bothered me so much. I just couldn't believe a girl could go from wanting to get her horse back to the show ring one week to wanting to sell him the next. Granted, I didn't know anything about this girl. She might have been ready to give up riding, like Lindsay. But I did know that even if Lindsay got her much-talked-about wish and wasn't forced to ride anymore, she'd put up a fierce fight before she let anyone else near William.

There was something in the way she handled him, something in the way she spoke to him, that said she loved him beyond any value he might have as a show horse. The way horse girls do.

Then again, William had never done anything to scare Lindsay. Fear was a powerful motivator, especially when you were in the saddle and being judged. It could motivate you to try harder and be a better rider, or it could motivate you to hop right off that horse you thought you'd love forever, hand over his reins to the first person available, and run away. Giving up on a horse wasn't always a mistake, but when it was, it was usually impossible to recover from. Horses rarely return once they're gone.

I had a feed store run the next morning, which pushed riding off to midday.

This was another big change from keeping horses in Ocala, where everything could be delivered and you didn't have to take hours out of your day to drive to the feed store, load up the truck, schlep back home, drag the fifty-pound bags out of the back of the truck and stack it all up again. By the time I got back, Pete had finished riding his horses and was nailing up some plywood to create half walls around the unfinished stalls.

"I stopped at Publix for subs," I announced, presenting a plastic bag bulging with foot-longs.

Pete dropped the hammer. "You are a queen among men," he told me, and I accepted his tribute.

That afternoon, once we had recovered from an overabundance of meats, cheeses, and sweet teas, I rode Jim Dear over to the equestrian center alone. Pete had gone over to Penny Lane to talk to Rogue's owner and her parents. He was going to tell them he was prepared to make a serious offer based on what he felt the horse was worth—enough to buy the girl a new, more suitable horse. That way, he'd explained to me through a mouthful of Pub sub, it would be out in the open and he'd know if they were going to ask a ridiculous price for the horse or stay in line with what he thought he could get Delannoy to pay.

It was all more subterfuge than I felt like I could deal with. Another reason, I thought, to stay well clear of all those sponsorships and syndicate games. If only I wasn't getting dragged into it with Mickey's situation. Grace had told me to keep my stable small, to take extraordinary care of the horses I had and not worry about acquiring more.

That's going to be your edge, she'd explained, *to be deeply in*

*tune with your horses, not someone who got on ten horses a day
and handed them back to a groom, ride after ride.* But that wasn't
reality. Grace's idea was a kind of equestrian utopia, and it took a
lot of money to fund a utopia. I felt the ground sloping back toward
the old model: a big barn, lots of horses, owners and sponsors. Pete
wouldn't mind that at all, but I had hoped we could hold out for
something better.

Jim nodded his head as we walked briskly up the slope toward
the arenas. It was almost three o'clock, which meant a steady
trickle of boarders would start to arrive, starting with the high
school kids and ending three hours later with the last of the adults.
I sometimes taught a Friday-night group lesson as a stand-in for
Rosie when she took a horse to the mini prix down in Ocala, but
she was around this weekend thanks to a badly timed hoof abscess,
so I had the night off.

Once I finished with Jim Dear, I was going to feed early, grab
my computer, and drive into town for some Wi-Fi and supper. I
was hoping Pete finished up with his stuff by then, but if he didn't, I
was going alone. I had entries to finish and no internet at the farm.
Closing dates were getting dangerously near and we had horses in
dire need of competition.

I turned Jim into the covered arena and nudged him into a
working trot. A quick warm-up, a little lateral work, some transitions, and we'd call it a day. Jim was developing into a steady, ser-
viceable horse in the dressage arena. He wouldn't light up a Grand
Prix competition, but he got the job done with pricked ears and a
spring in his step. Good enough for the lower levels, and we'd see
once we got to Prelim whether he tuned up into something bigger
and better, or if I would sell him as an amateur adult horse. Sometimes average horses surprised you when they hit the upper levels

and reached a new level of fitness. The confidence turned them into new versions of themselves.

Some of them even grew downright dangerous for anyone but an experienced professional; others just got full of themselves and needed careful handling.

I hoped Jim managed to surprise me without getting crazy. He was a nice horse and I'd had him sitting around doing very little for a long time, waiting for the stars to align so I could get him into steady work and showing.

This past year, despite the move and the break in training, had been a nice slow uptick in work for him. By fall, I'd know if I was keeping him for myself or selling him on. Well, if nothing else happened to slow down our training schedule. Of course, there was no guarantee with horses; they kind of loved creating unplanned time off for themselves. But after last year, didn't we deserve a run of good luck?

"What a year," I muttered, watching his ears flick back to catch my words. "What a crazy, hellish year it's been. And every damn time I think things are settling down . . ."

"Talking to yourself. You know what they say . . ." I turned my head; Lindsay was standing at the in-gate with William's reins in her hands. She grinned at me. "Hi. Want a riding buddy?"

I focused my attention back on Jim, who had bobbled a little, losing his self-carriage, the moment I looked away from the path in front of us. "Come on in," I called, as if I had a choice in the matter. It was the boarders' arena, after all. I was basically a poor relation.

Lindsay mounted up and took William for a couple slow loops around the arena, then pushed him into a trot and caught up with us. She rode alongside Jim, letting William match his strides with that long, flat hunter's trot I found hopelessly irritating. How could people ride that way? Why didn't she pick up her reins and put him together in a frame? How could she stand riding a horse with his nose poking out in front of him like a donkey chasing a carrot? No wonder she'd tried to stop riding, if this was the best version of her horse she'd been taught to expect.

"You left school early?"

"Cut my last class. It's PE. Like, is that a joke?" She flexed her arm and an obedient bicep arched under her stretchy black riding top. "I'm not chasing after a ball like some kind of animal. We evolved beyond that."

"Why would you cut class and come riding, the thing you constantly tell me you don't want to do?"

"Where else would I go?"

This was a stumper, I had to admit.

"Anyway," Lindsay said, "I don't hate riding. I was just bored."

"Fair," I said.

We rode in silence for a few minutes. William leaned over to lip at Jim's bridle, and Jim nipped back. They squabbled like a pair of old hens while we watched them, not bothered enough to stop the silliness.

"So what do you want?" I asked finally. "You didn't come out here to sic your scary gelding on my little Jimmy."

"Okay, so about eventing, like we were talking about yesterday," Lindsay said quickly, as if she'd been waiting impatiently for me to make the first move. "I can help you with the whole crowdfunding thing, but be serious with me for a minute. Can William even do it? I mean, eventing is hard, right? He's a teenager and I wouldn't want to push him. He *can't* get hurt."

The passion had returned, lighting up her usually guarded face. I closed my fingers on the reins and Jim flung up his head, tossing white foam from his mouth. A glob landed on my cheek and I swiped it away. "That seemed over the top," I informed him. "Could we react with a more appropriate level of disapproval next time, please?"

"Okay, so is that dressage? You just speak to your horse like you're in *Downton Abbey* and he arches his neck?"

"And we dress like Masterpiece Theater at horse shows," I replied, shrugging. "Lindsay, you're fine. *Of course* William can event. Any horse can event. You just have to get him fit and ready first. You avoid ninety-nine percent of accidents with fitness and good training. The other one percent can't be avoided. They're just bad luck." I pushed aside the nervous voice that had popped into my head yesterday, warning me that if anything happened to Lindsay and William on the cross-country course, it would be my fault.

"But could he do it, like, well? Like, win. Because while I don't really care about ribbons, my mom does. And actually I do care. A lot."

"Eventing's not about winning. It's about finishing," I announced. Sure, this was an old proverb that grew less and less true every year, because the sport grew more expensive and the prize money and sponsors grew more necessary, but I would stick with it until the bitter end. Until someday, maybe, it became the truth again.

"Well, let's start there, then," Lindsay was saying. "Can we finish an event? I know he needs to be really fit. What else do we need? We can jump, obviously."

"*You* need to be fit, too. You're up there galloping and balancing him for a lot longer than just a two-minute jumper course. It requires a ton of fitness for a rider to get their horse through cross-country."

"Are you trying to tell me no? Is this because I cut PE?"

"Of course not. If you want to event, let's do it. But we have to start with dressage. And in the meantime, you'll have to work out, too. You don't do barn chores, so it will have to be a gym or something." I waited for her to change her mind.

"We have a workout room at home," she said instead.

I nodded. One test passed. "And what about dressage lessons? You have to finish on your dressage score. There's no point in hoping everyone else will screw up the cross-country or jumping phases."

"Well, can I get William to move like your horse does?" Lindsay nodded at Jim Dear, who was back on the bit and chugging along like a dressage steam train at a very pronounced medium walk.

I smiled. "I've been wanting to fix William since the first day I saw you ride him. His upside-down neck muscles haunt my nightmares."

"Well, I'm here to make your dreams come true," Lindsay drawled. "Let's start tomorrow, okay? I'll put my name down on your lesson book for two o'clock. I do the dressage, you talk to my mom about the cross-country, and we get you the money to buy your horse. Everyone wins, except me, because somehow I do twice the work here."

"What if I'm busy? I have to look."

"You don't have anywhere to be at two o'clock on a Saturday. The only place you'd be would be one of your events, and you would have talked my ear off about that already."

"I wouldn't tell you if you asked me," I retorted, sticking out my tongue. "And we have to start on . . . whatever it is we're going to do about Mickey. Because his owner is not going to wait around for me to make an offer. I'm surprised she hasn't sold him already."

Lindsay laughed. "Two o'clock tomorrow. And then we'll talk

about Mickey." Then she pulled up William, as if this conversation had been the only reason she tacked up, and leisurely rode him out of the arena and down the barn lane.

Jim watched William go with pricked ears, evidently wishing he could go on a hack too, and I gently pushed him into a serpentine, partially to get his attention back, partially because I just loved how bendy he was, flowing around curves like a snake. So now I had an extra lesson tomorrow. And it was going to be starting a hunter/jumper rider in dressage! I decided I'd better drive over, and bring my dressage saddle along. Nothing was more frustrating than trying to develop a long dressage leg with a flat jumping saddle.

Eileen called again while I was riding Jim Dear back to the barn. The early-evening air was crisp and the sun was at a steep, chilly angle, golden light slanting through the pine trees. I was shivering a little, wishing for a sweater, when my phone buzzed in the slim pocket of my riding breeches. I slipped it under the harness of my hard hat so that I could talk while my hands stayed securely on the reins, my stomach queasy with dread. Besides getting a promise of help from Lindsay, I hadn't done a thing toward figuring out how I'd acquire Mickey from Eileen and Carrie. I hadn't had the time.

Or maybe I had, but I just didn't know where to start on my own.

Eileen's voice was brisk, as if she'd talked to Carrie since our last conversation, and gotten a pep talk on how to divest herself of previously loved horses in a businesslike manner. "I'm sorry, but we have to move this along as quickly as possible. Carrie's helping out with logistics. We're going to send out a photographer and she'll want to do a little video as well, but of course chances are he'll sell just based on his record and Carrie's name."

"People are going to wonder why Carrie is selling him, though,"

I pointed out, though I knew I was grasping at straws. "Don't you think it looks bad, when she's selling a horse who supposedly had so much potential?"

Eileen brushed away my admittedly feeble attempt to sway her. "Every owner has horses of different levels and they make decisions about which ones to keep and which ones are no longer the best investment for them. Carrie never went around telling people Mickey was the next big thing. Honestly, Carrie never said anything at all about him. She was really just helping me out, because she knows how I feel about him. When I got him off the racetrack, I didn't know what my next step would be, so I asked her advice and . . . here we are."

I bit my lip and looked down at Jim's swaying mane in front of me. Way to steal my thunder, I thought. Way to tell me my position as their horse's rider/trainer had never mattered at all, that all the points I'd *thought* I'd scored by getting the ride on a Donnelly horse were imaginary. What if everyone knew it? What if the entire eventing world knew I was just riding an average, everyday off-track Thoroughbred and Carrie Donnelly had put me on him because she was doing a friend a favor?

But that couldn't be true. I *knew* how good Mickey was. Pete knew. Grace knew. Even Carl Rockwell knew. Eileen was the one who had no idea what she really had when he was sitting in her backyard, waiting for his real life to begin. She'd just thought he was pretty.

"Eileen," I said slowly. "Can you give me a little time?"

"Time for what, Jules?"

"To get the money together and make you an offer."

Eileen was quiet for a moment. When she spoke again, her voice was sympathetic. "Jules, from what I understand, you're not in a position to buy him."

I bristled immediately, and since Eileen was on the verge of becoming an ex-owner, I didn't see any reason to hide my temper. "Excuse me, but what exactly do you know about my position? I happen to have just downsized in order to concentrate on a select few horses and we've cut down costs considerably—"

"Is that your press release?" Eileen asked bitingly. "Because I like it. I do. But I know exactly where you've got that horse—*my* horse, I remind you—and it's not the kind of place a trainer with enough resources to run a stable would choose. Unless she absolutely had to because she couldn't afford a proper barn."

I bit my lip and didn't say anything.

Eileen sighed and swallowed audibly. When she spoke again, her tone was calmer, her words paced more slowly. The way a woman would speak when she wanted to comfort a pitiable fool. "Jules, I'll be honest with you. I need Mickey sold this spring. I didn't make that up. But I *want* Mickey sold as quickly as possible, because neither Carrie nor I believe you are financially stable enough to be trusted with him for very much longer. We talked and decided we're not going to embarrass you by taking him away and sticking him in another barn to sell. As a *favor*, Jules. So do us a favor in return and have him ready for the photographer next week, okay? And pretty soon we can put this all behind us. I really do wish you the best, but this partnership is over."

As she finished, her voice hardened again. This steely Eileen was a new development, and before I could get my head around it, she was gone. I pulled the phone from my helmet harness and looked at it. Call Ended.

"Fucking hell," I said out loud, and Jim Dear's ears flicked back to me. "Son, I have to fix this right now or I'm completely out of luck." My voice cracked on the last word. *Luck*. What a silly god to have chosen to worship.

15

I CALLED LINDSAY as soon as I had Jim Dear groomed and turned back out.

It was technically suppertime, the sun sinking behind the pines, and the whole herd was a little astonished, Jim included, when I shut the pasture gate on his hindquarters and retreated back to the trailer. I knew there'd be nonsense, but I left them to their tomfoolery.

Jim was kicking out his heels and showing off to Mayfair, who eyed him with distaste, as I dug out Lindsay's number from my lesson planner and dialed.

I hoped it wasn't too weird, me calling a teenager to ask for help. Or for any reason at all.

"Yeah?" she answered on the first ring. I figured her phone had been in her hand already, thumb scrolling through some endless feed of jokes I would never understand.

"Lindsay, it's Jules."

"Oh. Hey. Are you canceling on me already?"

"Canceling? No. I'm ready to get started."

"With what?"

"With your help?"

"My help?" I heard a spark of interest in her monotone voice and I thought: *This is what she's been waiting for, someone who actually needs her for something.* "What could I do for you?" Lindsay went on, a note of wonder in her tone. "Wait—I can't get weed for you. Who told you that?"

"This is not about weed, Lindsay. *Jesus.* It's about the whole social media thing. Getting the money together to buy that horse."

"Oh! Shit. I forgot. Uh . . . yes. Now is not a good time."

I narrowed my eyes, as if focusing my gaze on the pasture beyond would help me zero in on why Lindsay sounded so vacant and confused. "Lindsay, are you . . . are you high?" I winced as soon as I said it. What a grandmotherly thing to say. *Are you smoking the grass?* I should have said, just to make a full job of it.

"Oh my God, Jules, are you for real? No, I was just asleep and you woke me up. And I kind of forgot I had put dinner in the oven and . . . yeah. I, uh . . ." There was some rattling from her end, a fumbling with the phone that translated through the ether as thumps and rustles. "I . . . uh . . . have to call you back later."

"Lindsay? Is your house on fire?" I asked, but she ended the call without answering.

Well. I sat back on the trailer step and watched the horses watch me. They were lined up along the fence, heads over the top rail, ears pricked in my direction. When I made eye contact with Dynamo, he nickered encouragingly.

Feeding's easy, anyone can do it!

"Fine," I said. "It's better than feeding you monsters in the dark."

As soon as I stood up to get started, my phone chimed. I looked at the text from Lindsay:

House didn't burn down

Thanks for asking

You go first with my mom, then we get your horse

"Thanks a lot," I told the phone. "Why do I feel like I'm being blackmailed by this kid?"

Mickey whinnied and everyone else joined in, a chorus of *We're so hungry, Mom, feed us* trembling on the cool winter air.

"Fine," I announced. "Fine!"

Pete came home in the twilight and helped me put blankets on everyone. The stars were twinkling furiously in the dark sky, promising another bitterly cold night. Was this the coldest March ever? We should be done with this nonsense by now. This was *Florida*. I glared at Mickey as he waited, ears pricked, for me to get his rug on. There were always more chores. All I wanted from life was to hustle into the trailer and get into my flannel pajamas. The minute I had Mickey's last buckle fastened and deposited him back in the pasture, I ran inside, Marcus panting hot on my heels.

Pete came in a few minutes later. I was already buttoned into my super-strength jammies. He took one look and laughed at me.

"Like you're not cold," I retorted.

"It's maybe forty-five degrees."

"I don't want to talk about it."

He shook his head, still laughing. "Get under the covers and I'll make you some supper."

I cuddled up under a fleece blanket and watched him throw together a salad while water boiled for a box of pasta. The tiny counter was just big enough for a small plate to chop veggies on, and he had to balance the bowls on the one burner of the stove that wasn't occupied by the little saucepan. Our salads would be warm, I thought. Who knew cold salads were a luxury?

"Delannoy comes tomorrow," he said eventually. "I'll be out all day with him."

"I have lessons," I said. "And I'm talking to Lindsay's mom about her moving into eventing."

"Think she'll go for it?"

"Didn't you talk Rogue's owners into selling their horse? I can talk Lindsay's mom into letting her daughter try a new discipline. The horse is already an experienced jumper. She could probably go out and win at Prelim if she could just get through the dressage. I'll play down the cross-country and just focus on improving Lindsay's equitation. And getting her excited about riding again. That's all her mom really wants, anyway."

Pete turned around and frowned at me, looking vaguely threatening with a knife in one hand. It was as if he'd only heard my first sentence, the one about *him*. "I didn't talk them into selling their horse. I helped them decide Rogue wasn't the right horse for their daughter. Which happens to be true. I didn't make that up. You saw the way he bucks."

I shrugged.

"She's never going to be good enough to ride that horse safely," Pete said, reading my thoughts, and turned back to his chopping. "Anyway, after we're done, let's talk about the eventing calendar and make sure we're all set for the next few horse trials. I don't want to get caught by surprise after all these weeks off."

I picked up my lesson book and flipped through it. "You mean like the one in two weeks?"

He sighed. "Exactly like that. I thought we were still farther out."

I ran my finger under my own scribbled handwriting. "Mill Pond. Georgia border. In two weeks. Taking everyone. Except Regina, of course. We can get them all into your trailer, but we'll have to take out the hay and everything else stored in there."

"We can use one of the stalls in the barn. It will be empty. Except for Regina, of course."

Problem number two. Pete sighed as I said, "But we can't leave Regina alone all weekend. What were we thinking?"

"Maybe we can take her up to Rosie's barn?"

"She'll pace all night. That won't be good for her leg."

"It should be fine by now," he insisted. "It's healed up."

That was mostly true. The deep wound through her fetlock had healed; now we were just trying, with firm bandaging and a commitment to keeping her as still as possible, to fully heal the section of coronary band sliced through by the fence wire back at Briar Hill. If the coronary band didn't close up properly, she could end up with a permanent crack in her hoof wall, which would be the end of her career.

Pete said, "In two more weeks we're really at the end of the bandage stage. That's when we're going. By then, we'll know. She's either better or she isn't."

I pushed that ultimatum aside and thought of the next one. "Well then, if we're all going eventing in two weeks, time to cross-country school."

"We absolutely have to school this coming week. Maybe twice."

I smiled at the thought. It had been way too long since we'd tackled a cross-country course.

"I'm going to ask Haley Marsh to school us over the Intermediate course at her place."

My smile faded. "*School* us? I don't want a lesson. And when did you talk to Haley Marsh?"

"I ran into her tonight at Penny Lane. Have you ever met her?"

I shook my head. Haley Marsh was a member of the Canadian Equestrian Team. She wintered in Ocala, but we'd never been introduced. Her big four-star horse, I remembered, had belonged to

Carrie Donnelly before Haley's clients bought him. She'd know Carrie.

She'd be very interested if she found out another good horse from Carrie's barn had hit the market.

She might already know, from Carrie herself.

I felt sick suddenly, the idea of Carrie emailing and texting her buddies in the five-star community, asking who might want a nice gray horse who was stuck with an amateur in over her head.

Pete poured the pasta into the boiling water. Drops of water splashed and hissed as they hit the gas flame and turned to steam. He pulled his hands away quickly. "You're going to love her. Really nice, super rider obviously, and she's got a gorgeous course at her place. She asked if we had a place to school and when I said no, she offered a free coaching session. She said it was the least she could do for two eventers who'd had such a rough winter so far."

All that was the least she could do, to scope out a nice upper-level prospect being sold from under its current rider. I didn't want to take Mickey anywhere near her. "I don't know, Pete, seems a bit odd that she'd offer that for free."

Pete turned around and quirked his eyebrow at me. "What are you saying, she's trying to sabotage us? Think she's going to give us some sort of monumentally bad advice and we'll just blindly follow it? Come on, Jules. She just wants to help. She's ridden at the Olympics. Two World Equestrian Games. She's finished Badminton four times. She's better and more experienced than both of us by every marker. This is a really generous offer and it's going to help us out tremendously at Mill Pond, along with everywhere else we ride this spring."

I pulled at Marcus's ears as he snored gently, head on my lap. How could I explain to Pete that I didn't trust Haley Marsh, or anyone who might be in the market for a potential upper-level horse? Because wasn't that everyone we knew?

Jesus, I thought, *even Delannoy might be interested if he found out Mickey was for sale.*

A nightmare scenario that had never occurred to me suddenly presented itself, took off its hat and gloves, and settled down, not in any hurry to leave.

I could get over a lot, I thought. But I would not be able to get over Pete getting the ride on Mickey.

He wouldn't take it . . . would he?

Of course not.

I looked at Pete, eyes full of suspicion, as if the contract had already been signed. Pete glanced back at me and raised his eyebrows. "What?"

"Pete, if Delannoy wanted to buy . . . nothing. Never mind."

"What, seriously?"

"Mickey," I muttered.

"What?"

"*Mickey!*" I shouted. "What if he wants to buy *Mickey?*"

"Oh." Pete considered this. "That won't happen," he decided.

"Why not? He's perfect for Delannoy. He's ready to move up, he's coming off a successful winter season, he's perfectly sound and moves beautifully . . . the minute he hears Mickey is for sale he's going to be sniffing around."

"No, he's not," Pete said. "Because he doesn't know any of those things. He only knows what he's told. And I'll tell him . . . I'll tell him Mickey's a piece of crap."

I slapped Pete with a sofa cushion. "You can't tell people that!"

Pete looked at me with consternation. "Then I have to be honest, Jules, I don't know what you want me to say."

"There's no right answer," I admitted. "To anything."

"Call that girl and get her busy on that social media thing," Pete suggested.

"She said I should talk to her mom first—"

"Who's the adult, Jules? Make her start now."

Grumbling to myself, I texted Lindsay. *We need to move on this social media thing.*

To my surprise, she texted back a series of images almost immediately. I flicked through them. She'd gone through my posted pictures, pulled all the best shots of Mickey, and edited them with text. In a few short lines, she spelled out the problem—Mickey's for sale!—and the solution: We can save this partnership!

"Whoa," I said, showing my phone to Pete. "This is really . . . good?"

"Really good," he agreed. "Has she posted any yet?"

"No, we haven't started yet."

"What are you waiting for?"

16

THERE WERE PROBABLY a million reasons not to give Lindsay access to all of my social media accounts, but none of them would help me keep Mickey, so when she said she needed the passwords and full access, I handed them over. The graphics she'd created were gorgeous, and when she added a few videos to our text exchange, I was hooked. This girl had done her homework. I gave her access and before the night was out, I'd started receiving emails assuring me I was signed up for new things, including a crowdfunding page and an entirely new email address, just for the Danger Mouse Project.

Do I need to do anything? I texted after the last update came in.

Not a thing, came the reply.

"She's on it," I told Pete, and he gave me a thumbs-up.

On Saturday afternoon, while Pete was out horse hunting with Delannoy, I met with Lindsay's mother and gave her a quick lecture on the benefits of eventing for bored show jumpers and, even more so, bored teens. The thrills of cross-country were offset by the discipline of dressage, I explained—it was like hiding veggies under melted cheese so your kid would eat them.

"And there's a fitness component," I added. "Since Lindsay is only riding one horse per day, she'll have to work out to make sure she's physically capable of getting through all three phases and having the strength to hold herself up and help her horse out. There's no leaning on the neck when you're tired. You're out galloping for ten or fifteen minutes, jumping twenty-some fences over up-and-down terrain, and you're both getting tired. So that eats up some free time after school, when she'll be running or swimming or lifting weights." I knew that moms hated teenagers having any free time. It had never come up in my family, because obviously I'd spent every waking moment (and some sleeping ones) at the barn, but I'd seen enough of overscheduled kids and satisfied moms to know.

Lindsay's mom, who was a terrifyingly thin woman in heels, navy slacks, and matching blazer despite it being a Saturday, nodded her head. "She's not interested in anything else at school, so it's riding or nothing. But obviously making her ride William an hour a day isn't cutting it. She's up half the night doing who knows what on her phone. I'd much rather she comes home late, eats dinner, and passes out from exhaustion. Is that wrong of me?" She tittered, red-lacquered fingertips pressed to her mouth.

I hid my broken nails behind my back and smiled politely. "I think that's what most moms want. I can't get her on a fitness program, but I can convince her she needs to figure one out."

"Lindsay's father keeps a beautiful little home gym," she assured me. "Weights and everything. Looks like it's time it got some use."

I didn't know if forcing Lindsay into a weight-lifting regimen was really part of the deal we'd made, but I reminded myself of what Pete said: *Be the grown-up.* I was the one who got to make the rules in this relationship. "So it's agreed? We'll evaluate Lindsay and William over the next couple weeks and then find a Starter level event to point them at. Maybe in the fall."

"In the summer," her mother corrected.

"There aren't many events in the summer," I hedged. I really had no idea how much time it would take to get a good dressage test out of the pair, and I wasn't about to take a student with plenty of show mileage to an event without at least a shot at a blue ribbon. I had a reputation to uphold. Sort of.

"That should make it easier to narrow the right one down," she said, lifting one plucked eyebrow at me.

"Late summer," I said. "If they're ready to win."

"I'm sure they will be." She smiled. "You're working with a pair of champions. I expect them to continue to excel, or else we'll find someone else."

I managed to keep my jaw from dropping, but barely. Lindsay was not joking about her mother being a hard-ass. Still I'd handled worse than her. "Enjoy the rest of your weekend," I said politely. "I have lessons to get to."

Lindsay poked her head from around the corner of the barn, where she'd been eavesdropping. "What the hell, Jules?" she whispered. "That didn't sound like what we talked about!"

"You wanted to event, you're going to event."

"I wanted to have some fun. Now Mommy Dearest is going to be breathing down my neck about getting bulked up and being ready to win at my first competition. Just what I needed—a repeat of the A-circuit!"

"It's not going to be like that," I said soothingly. "Everything's going to be totally different now."

"How can you say that? How can you know?"

"Because you're going to love this so much, it won't feel like work. I promise you."

Lindsay glared at me another second, then she pushed her length of bright pink hair behind her ears. They were almost pointed, giving her an elfin look that made me start a little. Her face softened. "No one ever said something like that to me and meant it," she said. "But you really do."

"Eventing is like a drug, Lindsay. Once you get a taste, you're not going back to being sober."

Her face broke into a satisfied smile. "Don't ever say that to my mom. The woman already thinks I'm high half the time."

"Are you?"

"Not even close. More like a sixteenth of the time."

"Well, it's about to be none of the time. Because you aren't going to have any extra time to kill." I grinned. *Look at me, the grown-up.* "I meant what I said about the workouts. You have to get fit to ride with me."

"I hate you and I regret offering to help you," Lindsay informed me.

"I wish I could care." I sighed. "But your mother is giving me money to make you miserable, and you know I'm all about them dollar bills."

Her slim eyebrows came together, and I knew someday she'd be just as terrifying as her mother. It was my job to make sure some of that ice-cold conniving was tempered with warmth and empathy. "Go tack up your horse and let's get on with things," I told her. "I want to go out for dinner with my boyfriend tonight."

Lindsay stalked off, muttering something about how crazy it was that anyone would ever go out with me, a sentiment I happened to agree with. With her mother gone and Lindsay's angry face out of mine, I breathed a private sigh of relief and slouched against the barn wall. A horse lipped at my ponytail through his stall bars, huffing warm breath on my neck. I reached up to tickle the whiskers on his nose.

"Horses are so complicated," I whispered. "You seem so simple, and then it's nothing but emotional warfare from the first ride on out. Parents, coaches, sponsors, owners . . . Why do you make everything so awful?"

The horse wiggled his lips against my fingers and then very delicately pressed his teeth against my palm, giving me a good pinch. I yanked my hand away and turned around to face him. He jumped back in alarm, eyeballs rolling, evidently certain he was toast for trying to bite me.

But I didn't care enough to get on his case. I didn't even know him. He was just some horse standing in a stall at a boarding barn, chewing on whatever handy person came his way. "Dummy," I told him, and left it at that.

Luckily, teaching Lindsay was not as tiresome as talking to her. She was a naturally talented horsewoman. Not every rider is, and I'm sure there are good riders out there who made it up the levels through sheer force of will, but Lindsay was one of those lucky girls (like me, if it's not bragging to say so) who picked up new riding skills easily because her body was naturally attuned to her horse.

By the end of our hour, she was figuring out half halts and beginning to understand why William's flat head and neck carriage made me so crazy.

William, to his credit, even tried to mouth the bit for her as they trotted in an endless twenty-meter circle around me, working as a team to find a little flexibility in his spine and her elbows. She sat down to ask for a halt and he shuffled down to a walk and then a square halt that took an agonizing number of shuffling half steps to achieve, and then arched his neck grandly and chewed at the bit like a Grand Prix horse slurping on his curb and bridoon.

"That was good," I lied. "Look how nicely he's carrying himself."

Lindsay leaned forward and patted her horse's neck, sweat beading her forehead and her normally white cheeks flushed pink. When she should have sat upright again she stayed slouched, leaning gently over William's withers like a messenger who had galloped all night with a declaration of war in her saddlebag. I'd never seen her this worn out after one of our riding lessons. Her mother was going to be thrilled.

"Let him walk a few times around the arena and then you can take him in."

She nodded and gave William a little nudge with both heels. He picked up his feet and strolled away, stretching his neck out and looking pleased with himself.

"You tired?" I called.

"I'm dead," she said. "This is my ghost talking."

"Well, that's exciting. Are you still mad at me from beyond the grave?"

"I don't know. This was confusing and I have to think about it."

"Fair enough."

I went into the barn to wait for them and found Rosie sitting outside the tack room in a lawn chair, drinking a Diet Coke. She saw me eyeballing it and gestured to the open door behind her. "In the fridge. Help yourself."

"Thanks." I pulled out a can and popped it open. "I think four o'clock is the sleepiest time of day. I always need a little caffeine about now or I feel like I'll fall right off my horse. Wish I felt that tired when I went to bed."

"Guilty conscience keeping you up?"

I looked at Rosie's broad face in surprise, but she was grinning at me. "All those murders." I took a long swig of soda. When I came back to earth, she was still grinning at me. "What? Did I miss something?"

"You hear what your boyfriend's up to today?"

"He's horse shopping . . . why?"

"I got a call a little while ago from an old friend. She says this guy Pete is trying to buy her daughter's horse. I thought it might be our Pete so I ask, is he an eventer? And she says yes, he's been schooling the horse before her daughter takes him back down to Ocala, and damn if he didn't talk to her and convince her to sell the horse. And she loves this horse. Pictures of him all over the house. So now she can't figure out what he said to make this kid change her mind. And he's coming over to see the horse with his checkbook ready, and she doesn't know what to do."

My mouth went dry. I was staring at Rosie, but I couldn't think what to say.

It occurred to me I must look like an idiot. A guilty idiot. *All those murders*, I thought again.

"What did you tell her?" I finally managed.

"I told her that didn't sound like Pete, but I've only known him a couple weeks, and anyway, there's no telling what someone ambitious like that might do. If he decided he had to have the horse . . . what's to stop him from talking some little girl out of keeping him?"

"She's sixteen," I said defensively, though I hardly knew why. "She's not a little girl. She can make up her own mind."

"Can Lindsay? Lindsay says she doesn't want to ride anymore, but is that true?"

With perfect timing, William's hooves rang out on the paved aisle behind me. I turned to see Lindsay walking alongside him, the reins gathered in her left hand.

She was looking at him the way little girls look at their horses.

Rosie chuckled behind me. "Sixteen is still a piece of clay, if you know how to mold it. You're showing Lindsay how to ride William in a new way. I just think it's . . . *funny* . . . Pete didn't try that with this other kid." The deliberate pause before and after "funny" told me Rosie knew exactly what Pete was up to.

"He's not her riding instructor," I said slowly. "He was hired to school her horse, nothing more."

"He could give her some pointers. He could offer. But he didn't. Why not?"

"I don't know what he does over there, okay?" I spun back around on Rosie and her eyebrows went up in surprise. "I don't know what his relationship is with the kid, or the family, or anything. For all I know, he didn't even know them before this past week. Because she can't ride him, did you know that? He bucks after every fence and she can't ride it. She's scared of him. How is that Pete's fault?"

"You're very defensive," Rosie observed.

"I don't like to hear gossip about my boyfriend," I retorted. Which was the truth, because even if I didn't agree with Pete's decision to go after Rogue, he was still my partner, and I'd defend him against all comers. He'd do the same for me. "This is a perfectly aboveboard situation and you're turning it into drama. I thought we were friends, Rosie."

Rosie's eyebrows came together and I had a sudden, horrible feeling we weren't friends at all. We were friendly, a different thing altogether, and now maybe we weren't even that anymore, which was going to make daily life very awkward. Seeing as how she was my landlady and employer.

"What are you guys talking about?" Lindsay had come out of

nowhere. I spun around and she was standing there in the aisle, her right hand tangled in William's mane, a gesture of love and possessiveness I'd never seen her show with her horse before. But Lindsay's previous lack of public affection didn't mean her love for William hadn't been there all along. She was young and inexperienced, and she'd mistaken boredom for a change of heart. Maybe Lindsay's mother was the only one who had known her daughter was still in love with her horse. Maybe she wasn't such a villain for forcing Lindsay into the saddle every day, after all.

I wondered what this other girl's mother had said when her daughter told her Pete wanted to buy her horse, and she wanted to sell him. I wondered if she had some special insight into her daughter's heart, and had known it was a mistake.

It seemed likely, since she was calling Rosie for advice.

Rosie answered when it was apparent I wouldn't. "Lindsay, if William was behaving so badly you couldn't ride him, would you sell him, or try to learn how to ride him differently and see if that fixed the problem?"

"Of course I'd learn to ride him differently," said the girl who hadn't wanted to ride him at all a few days ago.

"That's a setup," I argued. "No one's going to answer a hypothetical question with the easy way out. You have to really be in the position to know what you'd do."

Rosie shrugged. "Well, I'm just telling you what I've heard. I won't be the only one in town wondering about this. Word gets around fast."

I followed Lindsay down to the crossties and watched her untack William.

He was sweating despite the coolness of the afternoon, which meant he'd been trying really hard to figure out how to please Lindsay with these strange new commands she'd been giving him.

Horses try so hard, I thought suddenly, and does anyone even know why they do it? Everything we trained them to do, they'd willingly done for the past two millennia, without ever stopping to wonder if there was a good reason for any of it.

It really was a reminder to not just do right by horses, but to give them everything you ever could. Because we could never repay the debt we owed to our horses.

Lindsay unwrapped a butterscotch candy and William pricked his ears, reaching out with his upper lip to snatch at the treat. "You wait," she scolded lovingly, and then handed it to him. "Silly boy." She glanced up at me as William crunched the candy between his teeth. "Was everything okay down there? Did I say the wrong thing?"

"No, yeah, it's fine. Rosie has a story backwards, is all."

"Okay. Hey, listen—is it okay if I use *all* the pictures on your Insta? Not just the ones of you and Mickey?"

"For what?"

"Internet Things," Lindsay said in a solemn tone.

"Sure," I said, shrugging. "Have at it."

17

"SAW YOUR NEW website this morning."

"Saw what now?" I pulled up Mickey alongside Tiger and gave Alex a confused look. What was she talking about? Ahead of us, sunlight shimmered on the training track of Cotswold Farm, but galloping could wait. If I had a new website, I needed to know details.

Alex grinned as Tiger tried to bolt, reining him back. The horse threw up his handsome head, showering us all with white foam from his (soft and proper) mouth. "You have a new website! Guess who showed it to me?"

"I have to guess Lindsay but I don't understand why. She's texting you now?"

"We're besties."

I felt oddly jealous.

"You jealous?"

"No," I lied. "But I'm annoyed." That part was true.

"The micromanager has lost control of her media!"

I shook my head. Mickey pulled at the reins, trying to run his nose along Tiger's neck. Both horses were hyped up, excited to head out to the track for the first time in months.

Pete was somewhere behind us on Dynamo, having gone back for his phone, left in the truck. In no rush while we waited for Pete to catch up, we were dawdling along the horse path under the oak trees, enjoying the shade from the midday sun. Today had dawned hot and dry, as if the previous week's blustery cold had never happened, and the horses were sweating a little under their ragged old body clips.

Tiger jumped sideways, snorting at a squirrel who ran across our path, and I had to laugh. "He's just looking for trouble, isn't he?"

"Just because the track is up ahead. He knows exactly where we're going, the brat." Alex gave him a boot in the side to straighten him out and Tiger brought his dancing hooves back to the path. "So anyway, she sent me the link this morning, which is how I learned that Jules Thornton of Briar Hill Farm has launched her new website and is excited to announce she is seeking participants for a crowdfunding campaign to purchase her horse Danger Mouse, who is being sold out from under her."

The words, said out loud, were terrifyingly real. We were really doing this. I was really doing this. "Did she actually use the words 'sold out from under her'?"

"Yup," Alex said. "Shots fired."

"Shit."

I'd set Lindsay loose on the world to convince people to buy Mickey for me, but I was not prepared for the actual reality of it. What would people say? If this failed, what would it do to my career? Carrie Donnelly would never work with me again, that was for sure. What other owners would look at that damning phrase and think I was an unprofessional firebrand?

Then again, didn't most of them think that about me anyway?

"Do you think anyone else saw it, or maybe it's still a secret?" I asked hopefully. Maybe there was still time to take it down.

I'd figure something else out.

Anything.

"Nope, I've already seen it on *Eventing Chicks* and *Red Flag on Right*," Alex announced cheerfully, citing two of the most popular eventing blogs in the country. "I clicked around and it's everywhere. The internet loves it, by the way. People are always excited when someone pushes back against the status quo. Even *Eventing Chicks* thought it was great, and they're not your best friends."

"Shit." So much for hiding my head in the sand.

"So this isn't what you wanted?" Alex turned around in the saddle. "Oh, Pete's coming. Are we keeping this quiet?"

"No, it's fine. He's going to find out anyway, if it's all over the internet now." I steadied Mickey with one hand on the reins and pulled out my phone with the other, using my thumb to click open Instagram. "Oh . . . shit again." I couldn't think of anything else to say.

"What is it?" Pete had arrived. "Bad news?"

"Five hundred and thirty-two notifications on our Facebook page," I said, holding the phone out so the Briar Hill Farm page was showing.

Alex burst out laughing. I glared at her.

"What?" she asked innocently. "This is good news. What if it's five hundred and thirty-two people who want to give you a hundred bucks each? You'd have, what, fifty grand? How much do you need?"

"I don't know because I haven't asked yet, genius! Oh my gosh. You know Carrie and Eileen have seen this by now." I started thumbing through the comments while Mickey danced underneath me.

They weren't all, or even mostly, offers of money . . . but some of them *were*.

Some of them were even worded with punctuation and everything, as if an adult had typed them. "'My trainer and I would be interested in getting involved,'" I read aloud. "'Please email us.' And an email address . . . at Apex Eventing." My eyes went to Pete's, which had widened gratifyingly. "Apex Eventing!"

"Who are they?" Alex asked.

"Really wealthy West Coast barn," I explained, passing the phone to Pete so he could see for himself. "They don't come east very often, but when they do, they come to win. Lolly Bowers is an amazing trainer."

"Maybe she could give you lessons, too," Alex teased.

"Rude."

Pete handed my phone back over. "Well, the good news is, I think you can buy Mickey," he said.

"It sounds great, except I still don't know how to put all these pieces together. Lindsay's asking for donations on a whole separate website." I didn't know how many people would go from commenting on a Facebook post to actually clicking to a new site and pulling out their credit card.

"I know who we can ask," Pete said. "She just did a big syndication."

"But I don't want to do a syndication," I reminded him. "I want to buy him."

"Don't rule it out—Apex would be quite a coup, if they wanted to buy into him," Pete insisted. "You should call them."

"You should look at all your options," Alex suggested. "Wait and see what the public demand is, and then you can decide if you can really get enough money donated to just buy him outright. If not, you can always put together a syndicate."

"And I know who we can ask," Pete said again.

"Don't say it," I warned him.

"Amanda."

I groaned. "Are you crazy? We can't ask Amanda."

Pete shrugged. "She said to ask anytime we need anything."

"Yeah, well I'm sure that was before the little incident at Glen Hill when she had her heart broken. By you and me."

Alex was discreetly quiet, nudging Tiger up the track so Pete and I could ride together, facing each other down. Maybe she knew what would come next. She had more relationship experience than I did.

"It was after," Pete admitted. "It was last week."

I reined back, the webbing pulling through my gloved fingers as Mickey tugged back at me, mouth gaping around the bit. "You're talking to Amanda?"

"She was at Penny Lane . . ."

"What?"

"To see a horse for sale. A horse I'd been riding. I showed him to her."

I was speechless. I looked away from Pete, concentrating on the neatly furrowed track ahead of us. We were nearly to the gap, and Mickey danced sideways in an excited jig, placing me eye-to-eye with Pete again. He looked ready to start talking. *"Later,"* I growled, and loosened my reins, letting Mickey plunge ahead to jog alongside Tiger.

My anger seemed to set off sparks in the air, and the horses felt the electricity and fed off it, bursting with excitement. Next to us, Tiger's neck was bent and his chin was nearly touching his chest, completely on the muscle, his entire being straining toward getting his hooves onto that groomed surface. Alex chuckled and shook her head as she pressed her fists into his withers, muttering something about using her exercise saddle next time.

I let Mickey jog up to the gap in the fence, pulling him up just before we entered so as not to perform the cardinal sin of going through a gateway at a pace faster than a walk. Trot into an arena, you'll soon gallop out again, Laurie used to warn me. Mickey pulled at the bit and jigged sideways, nearly as excited as Tiger.

"Whoa, whoa, whoa," Alex commanded in a deep voice. Okay, no one was quite as excited as Tiger. The bay gelding was digging against the bit, shoving his head down toward the ground in an effort to throw Alex off-balance so he could push off into the gallop he was craving. I watched for a moment as they went bouncing past us, frankly impressed with how conniving the old campaigner was. He knew exactly how to manipulate his body to throw even an expert like Alex into momentary turmoil.

But Alex wasn't an old hand at riding young racehorses for nothing. No sooner had he tried to rip the reins from her hands than she was standing in her stirrups, bent at the waist over his curving neck, with the reins bridged in her hands and wedged against his withers. Now when he pulled, he was yanking against himself. Tiger tested her grip once or twice, then snorted and floated away from us in a smooth trot, settling into a familiar groove along the outside rail.

Pete watched with admiration. "Bridge your reins like that in the gallop lanes on cross-country," he said, switching on teacher mode. "Let your horse balance himself and save your energy for the fences."

"I *know*," I hissed, even though if I was being perfectly honest with myself, I'd never taken a grip quite like the hold Alex had on the reins right now, not even when I'd been riding young racehorses myself last fall. She looked like a jockey, while I was sure I'd never looked like anything other than an event rider in the wrong saddle. I hated being honest with myself, though. And I certainly wasn't going to admit anything to Pete right now, Mr. Let's-Hang-Out-With-Amanda-the-Hunter-Princess-and-Not-Tell-Jules. "Let's go, then."

I let Mickey spring after Tiger, trying to catch him with a long ground-eating stride that *almost* made up for my not letting him canter yet. Dressage extensions for the win.

We warmed up with one long trot all the way around the track, and I immediately wished we'd started at first light like racehorse people did. The footing seemed to reflect the baking heat of the midday sun up at us. It was hard to believe I'd worn a hoodie yesterday. Florida's spring weather was a roller coaster, hurtling between frostbite and heatstroke every few days.

Sweat rolled into my eyes and I tugged up my shirt collar to swipe it away.

Mickey felt my hand leave the reins and tried to bounce into a canter, straining to pass Tiger, but I dropped the stretchy fabric and took another steady hold, squeezing the reins until he relented and arched his neck against the bit, trotting like a Standardbred who just discovered dressage. Behind us, I heard Dynamo's breath fluttering through his nostrils. I was glad Pete was still riding him through the spring, because it made this off-site conditioning possible. If I had to do the gallops on both horses, we'd be here for hours, and neither of us could be away from our side jobs for so long every week.

Through the spring . . . my mind floated away to consider calendars and closing dates as Mickey's even gait bounced against the cushion of the training track. We had two more months of spring eventing before the temperatures shot up to red-alert levels and the competition ran north. Barns would be selling horses who had done well on the winter circuit, lightening the load before they pulled up stakes and went home for the summer. The market was about to flood with horses who had cross-country mileage.

I could remind Pete that with the spring sales rush coming up, he would be better off waiting to buy a new horse. If his new investor had enough money to buy a successful show jumper, wouldn't he have enough to buy a successful eventer? Putting that money into a young up-and-coming horse with plenty of experience at Prelim would make a lot more sense than buying a horse like Rogue . . . or like Mickey, for that matter.

In the backstretch we rode along the skeletal hedge separating the neighboring property from Cotswold Farm, and I shook my head at the scruffy makeshift training oval tracing a faint path through the overgrown pasture. It hadn't been that long ago I'd been riding a wild-eyed filly around that oval, chasing a man who had the nerve to tell me my galloping scared the boss. Didn't matter, apparently, that they'd given me shoddy equipment and stirrup irons with no pads or latex to give grip to my boots. I thought my stirrup-free gallop had been pretty impressive, actually.

"Looks like Mary Archer cleared out!" I shouted to Alex.

"Yeah, she just kind of disappeared a couple weeks ago," Alex called, glancing back at me over her shoulder. "I think she went to South Florida."

She was welcome to it, I thought. South Florida was too paved for me, and too hot, even for a Floridian like myself. I'd stick to Ocala, thanks very much. If I was going to live with horses, I was going to live in horse country . . . or as close to horse country as I could afford.

At the first turn we pulled up and turned our horses to face the rail, racing style. We probably shouldn't have; Tiger was having a conniption at the thought of real exercise-style work, and Mickey and Dynamo didn't seem to have too much trouble recalling their racehorse days, either.

"You guys are being ridiculous," Pete announced as Dynamo threw his head up and down, threatening to rear. "You know you're here to do a couple of gallop sets, not breeze before the Breeders' Cup."

"Yeah, but Tiger doesn't know that." I nodded at the dark bay, who was literally trembling with excitement, standing still as a stone otherwise, in that weird statue pose Thoroughbreds sometimes assumed right before they went completely ballistic. "We better get going before he blows his top completely."

"He doesn't know if he should go up or down or backward or forward."

Alex snorted. "Let's get moving." And she dropped her hands, freeing her grip on Tiger's mouth so that he burst from his frozen pose with all the energy of a massive coiled spring.

They were past us before Mickey and Dynamo knew what happened, and then our two were tugging at the bridles and taking off after them, their hooves thudding on the track with the satisfying rumble only a perfectly primed galloping surface could provide.

There was probably a time when I forgot all my troubles while I was galloping, but those days had slipped away, relics of a more carefree time. Had I ever been carefree? It was hard to imagine. Maybe I'd just been better at clearing my head. Now I bent over Mickey's neck, the way Pete had taught me even though I'd fought him at the time, and looked between his two pricked ears at the groomed track ahead of us, and I thought about problems.

Amanda was a problem I'd thought I was done with. She had made her pass at Pete, it hadn't worked, and she'd been embarrassed.

I thought it was over. The fact that Pete had not mentioned she was back in our lives already did not make me happy.

I dropped my hand a little as we came into the first turn, gave Mickey a discreet nudge with one leg, and he swapped to the left lead with a seamless skip in stride. To my right, Pete did the same with Dynamo, and to his right, Alex did the same with Tiger. Our horses ran in tandem, forelocks flung back in a breeze of their own making, utterly content with life. And I wished I could feel the same.

We came into the backstretch and the horses changed leads again, Mickey doing it without being asked, a good little racehorse. "Good boy," I said out loud, and saw Pete turn his head, flash a smile at me, as if I'd meant him.

He *was* good, I thought resignedly. He was kind of out of his head right now, but hell, I'd been out of my head last year and he'd stuck with me. I was going to have to support him through this whole thing with Rogue. We did have to talk about Amanda, as much as the thought made me squirm. *But for right now,* I told myself, *can't you just be happy? Can't you just gallop your horse?* I looked through Mickey's ears, and I felt his hooves roll beneath me, and for a minute or two more, I let myself be content.

18

THE FIVE HUNDRED and thirty-two notifications had blossomed to a full thousand by the time we had cooled out the horses. We were standing around in the grass in front of the training barn, letting them dry from their baths in the ferocious tropical sunlight. Pete was the first to suggest I be brave, take out my phone, and see what was new in the world of Jules fandom. Since I considered him to be on thin ice after his Amanda announcement, I decided against taking his advice.

"Don't want to," I said mulishly.

"Could be the Little Juleses are pooling their allowances to get you the money. Or maybe you happen to have a rich fan who will want to buy him for you," he mused, flicking an unseasonal horse-fly away from Dynamo's back with the loose end of the lead rope. Dynamo flicked his ear back at him reproachfully. "I didn't mean to hit you," he assured the horse, who snorted and went on with his grazing. "What's better, a syndicate or a single owner? Isn't it better to have one person? I mean, so much easier."

"I don't think so," Alex said thoughtfully. She was leaning against the rail that ran around the outside of the shed row, while

Tiger dug at a patch of thick grass that grew lushly where the grooms habitually dumped water buckets. "One owner has full veto power. That's basically where Jules is at right now, with two owners who both want out. A big group of owners just needs a majority vote. That could come in handy if you want to do something they might not like."

"Like what?" Pete challenged, curious.

"Like choose between Kentucky Three-Day Event and Badminton," I suggested cheerfully, thinking as big as I possibly could. I rubbed at Mickey's neck as he pulled fiercely at the short grass near the driveway. "Some might not want to go to the UK, some might think it's way better than Kentucky."

"Whose team would you be on?" Pete teased.

I shrugged. "I'm just happy to be included."

"Well, then you lobby them to get your way," Alex said. "That's probably the best-case scenario. An owner could just decide which event they want you to go to."

"Sounds tiring," Pete said dubiously. "Having to work for a vote every time you make a decision?"

"What isn't tiring about the horse business?"

"Good point."

"Maybe it doesn't have to be that complicated," I suggested. "Maybe the contract can state I have full control of training decisions."

Pete looked skeptical. "Who would sign that?"

"A bunch of amateurs," Alex said. "Amateurs who love Jules and want to help her succeed. That's the goal, right?"

I ran a hand along Mickey's neck, feeling the heat pulsing beneath his salt-and-pepper mane. "That's the dream," I agreed. "A syndicate of fans who want me to succeed, not a pair of owners who want their horse to look good no matter what. But you're all ignoring the fact that I don't want an owner at all. I just want to buy him for myself. That's the number-one goal, even if it sounds crazy . . . no owners. No more of their bullshit."

"They were good owners," Pete said. "Be fair."

"Sure, until they weren't anymore." I slipped my phone from my pocket and looked at it warily. There were many, many red circles on my icons. All the social media apps, plus the email box, plus something from Starbucks. I clicked that first—hey, double gold stars through next week!

"Good news?"

My caffeine addiction was affecting my work. "Haven't looked yet."

"Start with Instagram," Alex urged me. "That's where most of your followers are, right?"

"Yeah, but I think they're all kids," I said. I clicked on the camera icon anyway. There were 627 new notifications. Lindsay had just posted a new photo to the account. It was a good one: I was jumping Mickey over a Novice level fence at Sunshine State, a fence he knew so well from schooling sessions and events it was practically cheating to include it. He'd charged the palisade wall, a fence that could still be pretty scary for a horse at that level, and jumped over it like a hedge in a steeplechase, with his back in a full bascule and every inch of him striving to honor that arch. Even his upper lip was stretched out, reaching toward his straining knees. I was sitting chilly in his center, my hands just a smidge past his withers with my fingers soft, a textbook automatic release I wasn't always capable of performing. But when I did, that move was a knockout.

I thumbed down to the caption first. I hadn't even wanted to look at what Lindsay had posted. *This unicorn isn't going anywhere if we have anything to say about it. Help Jules Thornton keep Danger Mouse! Comment here if you want to contribute to his purchase and be part of #TeamBriarHill.* There were a lot more hashtags after that. I scrolled down.

A lot of the comments were hearts, or sad-face emojis, or some variation on "noooooo not fair!" There were still a few "Jules Thornton doesn't deserve this horse" posts, and I knew there always would be. Those that couldn't, criticized. I was past caring about them.

But a surprising number of comments went a little deeper.

I'd be interested in getting involved. PM me.

This is a team I can get behind. Here's my email.

No one is taking our unicorn. We're in!!!

"How many are actually talking money?" Alex asked.

"Not a lot," I admitted, scrolling down. As my eyes scanned the screen, new red hearts and comment bubbles appeared in a continuous stream. Was this what it looked like to go viral? "But there are definitely some people interested. Some email addresses and requests for messages." I bit my lip and looked at Pete. "How am I going to get in touch with all these people?"

Pete smiled at me. "Make a spreadsheet? You know how to use a computer, right?"

I glared at him, suddenly annoyed. He had a wealthy owner who was giving him hell, so he didn't have to figure out how to balance all of these interested buyers and turn them into a united coalition, complete with checks written "pay to the order of Juliet Thornton." Did he know how good he had it right now?

Alex spoke up. "Won't Lindsay handle them?"

I didn't know. I hadn't thought about it. I hadn't expected this kind of response. And this was just Instagram . . . what was happening on Facebook? What was in my inbox? There were seventy-seven unread emails, and that wasn't just because I usually didn't bother checking my email. Most of those were dated today, so they couldn't all be sales messages from SmartPak. "I gotta text her," I mumbled, my mouth too dry to say much more.

Lindsay, please tell me you have a plan for the hundreds of people who are responding to this.

About ten seconds went by, then her response: *duh.*

"What did she say?" Alex asked.

"She said, 'duh.'"

Pete laughed. "That's just perfect."

I tried to swallow my panic. My heart was thudding in my chest. "I really hope 'duh' is teenager code for 'of course I have a plan, and I will execute it flawlessly.'"

"How did you get that so spot-on?" Alex laughed. "Urban Dictionary?"

I gave her a blank stare.

"Jeez," Alex said. "You really do spend all your time in the barn."

Pete offered to pack up the trailer while I caught up with Alex for a few moments, perhaps recognizing that even I still needed girl talk once in a while. Alex and I retired to the training barn office, where she retrieved Diet Cokes from an old green fridge in the corner. I settled into the leather desk chair where I'd seen Alexander sit in the morning, back when I'd ridden horses here, and swirled it from side to side with the tip of my toe. Like a little kid, because every now and then I felt tempted to just be a kid again. Being an adult was exhausting.

Alex slipped into the tattered office chair on the other side of the desk and slid the soda can across the laminated wood to me. "So," she began, popping open her can. "Are you okay with everything?"

"You mean with Mickey?"

"Yeah."

"Or do you mean with the farm?"

"Uh . . ."

"Or do you mean with Pete trying to convince a new owner to buy some kid's horse?" Alex looked around to make sure Pete wasn't about to stroll into the office. "Yeah, why don't you tell me everything," she said. "But maybe hustle on the Pete story, before he gets back in here."

"I just don't love the way he's behaving about this horse. He's riding it because the kid can't, but the kid wasn't ready to sell him . . . so now Pete's convincing her family it's the right thing to do. Because he wants him."

"Oh." Alex frowned. "But if she can't handle the horse . . ."

"Maybe she could, with the right training."

"Maybe it's not the right horse for her, Jules. Maybe Pete's helping this girl and her family make the right decision."

I popped open my Diet Coke and took a long drink, letting the bubbles clear my head. Okay, Alex was on Pete's side. Fine. We would move right along. "Next," I choked, trying to speak before the hot fizz in my throat had subsided. "The farm situation seems to be under control. The college is taking over Briar Hill as soon as the tenants leave in May, last I heard. I don't know what they're planning on doing with it, but it's out of our hands. We'll stop getting rent checks, that's about the only thing that will change."

"What about where you go next?"

"I don't want to go anywhere next."

Alex shook her head. "Jules, come on. I know you're taking a break from the politics and everything, but you gotta get back out there. You two need a real barn. And you need to get back to Ocala. You're spending your whole day trailering down here to use the track, and you have to spend a whole other day trailering to a cross-country school. Even if you don't have your own track or course for a while, you should be within hacking distance of one."

I sighed. "You don't understand."

"What's not to understand? It's fun playing hooky for a while, but that's not how business works. What about Grace? You said she was thinking of selling. Why don't you go into business with her?"

"We've talked about it," I admitted.

"And?"

"And nothing. I left the ball in her court. She hasn't responded. Maybe she isn't ready yet, I don't know."

"You have to make the moves here. Find a property and convince her to buy it and bring you guys onboard."

I shook my head; I wasn't going to do this right now. I couldn't talk about the uncertainty of my future with a person who was secure on her own property, and had never had to face the kind of constant paranoia that came with relying on other people to pay all of your bills. I knew what I wanted was impossible, but I wasn't ready to give up my little dream yet. "What's next on the agenda, Mickey?"

"Yes," Alex said. "Syndicating Mickey. If you can't get the money to buy him. And let's be real, a lot of people want you to buy him, but they're also going to a website filled with appeals to save starving horses—hell, starving people—and it's going to feel weird to them to donate to you after seeing those campaigns on the way in. I think buying him is a long shot and you should have a really good plan B."

I looked at the ceiling. It was a standard white popcorn ceiling with a fan and a globe light, nothing interesting, but I kept my eyes on it for a while. Without looking back at Alex I said, "I'm fine with syndication."

She huffed impatiently. "No you're not. But it's better than losing him."

"Exactly," I said. "But you have to understand, I'm not giving up on the idea that I can get the money to buy him."

"I just think that's really optimistic."

"Call me an optimist."

"Weirdly, that doesn't suit you."

There was a moment of silence. Outside the office, the world went on with its day. I heard horses pacing in their stalls, rustling the straw; I heard a mockingbird calling out with the songs of six other species of bird; I heard Pete slamming the door of the tack compartment, finished with packing up our things and on his way back to the office any minute.

"Alex, can I ask you a question?"

I heard her shift in the chair, the creak of old springs. "What's up?"

"Could you . . . can you . . ." I stopped. I couldn't do it. I wouldn't beg from Alex.

Then Alex's face was in my vision, blocking out the sagging ceiling fan. She leaned in so close I could see her freckles, dark specks on her tanned skin. She pushed her blond hair back behind her ears and gave me a kiss on my forehead.

I was too surprised to move. "I wish I could," she said softly, sadly. "Everything is wrapped up in our own horses right now. Things are tight. My hands are tied."

I blushed, not from the kiss, but from the fact that I'd asked at all. "I shouldn't have said anything."

She leaned back, settled one hip bone onto the desk, and regarded me from above. Her eyes were still sad, as if she'd disappointed herself.

I reached out and took her hand. "I'm okay with it," I said. "Because whatever it takes, I have to keep him."

Alex nodded, her lips squeezed tight together, and I felt hot pricks behind my own eyes, like a warning of emotions I didn't want, and so I took a big gulp of Diet Coke and promptly choked on it, and Alex whacked me on the back, and we both ended up half crying, half laughing, and that's how Pete found us when he came back into the office, ready to load up and head home.

19

MONDAY SHOULD HAVE been our day off, but since we'd used it to gallop, everything was out of whack. Pete went out to work on the barn in the late afternoon, but I couldn't sit still, and I wasn't ready to talk to him about Amanda yet. Instead, I went to Lindsay's house, using the address I'd found on her mother's checks, and surprised her by knocking on the door like some sort of cheerful stalker.

"Can I . . . help you?" she asked doubtfully. She was wearing her usual black, but in the form of ripped leggings instead of breeches. Her bangs sported a new shade of teal today. It was a nice change from the pink.

"I like your hair."

"Are you hitting on me?"

I snorted. "Don't be an idiot. I'm here about this." I held up my phone, which was still receiving new notifications every few minutes. "Why is my phone imitating a Christmas tree?"

Lindsay took the phone from my hand and smiled at the red bubbles dotting the screen. "Oh, I know all about this. Your accounts are on my phone, too, remember?" She held up her phone. "Twinsies!"

"Very charming. And alarming. So what are we going to do about it? Do you have a plan?"

"*You're* the idiot," Lindsay said cheerfully. "Come upstairs and I'll walk you through it."

Lindsay's bedroom was surprisingly tidy, a neat rectangle sporting a desk, two stuffed bookcases, and a bed with a frilly white bedspread I was just dying to tease her over. A palm tree tapped against one of the tall windows. I peered out at the view, overlooking a neighborhood of identical beige houses with identical red-tile roofs. Depressing. I sat down on the girly-girl bed while Lindsay pulled out a Swedish desk chair and popped open her laptop. She pulled up a file: "The Danger Mouse Project: Campaign Plan."

"So, you really do have a plan. Like, literally."

Lindsay scoffed. "You didn't believe me? Christ, Jules, you entrusted me with getting buyers for your horse. You gave me your Facebook password. That's practically your social security number. And you didn't believe me?"

"I didn't think it would be like this," I admitted.

Lindsay pushed her laptop to one side of her desk. Downstairs, the housekeeper was running a vacuum and singing along to a reggaeton radio station, the bass thumping up through the floor. "That beat is driving me a little crazy," she said.

"I can't stand any beat," I said. "I think we're just old people in young bodies."

"That's probably it. Anyway, everyone who sends their email is entered onto this spreadsheet. I click here, this is everyone who sent a Facebook message or whatever. Anything without a real email address. I'm marking them off as I get their emails. Got that?"

I nodded, squinting at the spreadsheet and thinking, *This is what businesspeople do, in their offices all day. They look at spreadsheets*. I didn't have the right kind of brain for this. Or if I did, I'd buried those neurons under tons and tons of horse knowledge years ago. The letters swam together, ignoring the confines of the neat little boxes Lindsay had constructed for them. I pretended I could read it and nodded with great confidence. "Looks good, then what?"

"Everyone goes into this email list on this site." She clicked over to a website tab, where a smiling cartoon monkey greeted me. "And from there, we send them a mass email with our message."

"Which is?"

"Which is whatever you and I are going to write, as soon as Charyl finishes vacuuming and turns off that radio. I need quiet to write properly."

"Okay," I agreed. So this was it. We were going to write the pitch letter, asking everyone for money. Now that the moment was here, I didn't feel ready.

What on earth could I possibly say? What if people really gave me money? Where would the money go? What if there was too much, or not enough? Did it get refunded somehow? I tried to push back a wave of panic. "I wish I had this business plan under control first."

"You need to talk to someone else about that. You know anyone with experience syndicating?"

"Why is everyone using that word all of a sudden? We started this by talking about crowdfunding enough to buy him."

"You need this in your back pocket. It's called being realistic. So do you know someone?"

"I do, but I don't want to talk to her."

Lindsay grinned. "I'll bet you have so many enemies."

"You have no idea."

"Is it that hunter trainer, Amanda?"

I gawked. "How the hell do you know that?"

"I have an internet box just like you." Lindsay pointed at her laptop. "It wasn't hard to do a little research and figure out what you've been up to for the past year. Or your BF."

"He wasn't up to anything."

"And you'd rather he doesn't decide to."

"Oh my God, Lindsay, really—" She was pushing all my buttons. "Can you not?"

To my surprise, her grin faded. "Sorry. Just playing around. I know it sucks to have someone making you feel like that."

"Like what, insecure?"

She nodded. Downstairs, the vacuum, and then the radio, were switched off in quick succession. There was a bang of a closet door, then the front door, and Charyl was gone. "Time to get to work," Lindsay announced. Sharing time was over.

The letter, when we were done with it, seemed to get the idea across simply, in a few basic sentences. Lindsay said that was how people on the internet preferred to read things. Lots of white space, she said, and I nodded like that made sense to me.

Thank you for your interest in joining our new opportunity in eventing ownership. I'm excited to welcome you to the Danger Mouse Project!

Mickey, as we call Danger Mouse, is currently offered for sale by his owner partnership. I'm sure I don't need to tell you how much potential this young event horse has. You've seen the pictures and the videos of his tremendous jump, gorgeous dressage, and wonderful temperament.

And I don't need to tell you how much fun it is to own an event horse! As members of Team Briar Hill and supporters of the Danger Mouse Project, you'll enjoy perks like joining us at events, special meet-and-greet opportunities, and being a proud supporter of one of the hottest young horses on the circuit. This is a team you definitely want to join!

In the next week we will be sharing details of the Danger Mouse Project and how you can take part. In the meantime, please indicate your interest by clicking the investment level below. We'll reach out to all interested parties with our updated ownership information.

Welcome to the team! It's going to be a great ride.

Sincerely,
Jules Thornton

The words bought us time to figure out the technical side and gauge just how interested people were, without using the word "syndication." Plus, it gave us time to determine the finances of a potential syndicate: the level of investment needed to buy-in, the splitting of maintenance costs on Mickey. Vet bills, farrier, feed and hay, event bills, even tack: all of it would need to be split fairly among the investors if it came down to a syndicate. I didn't have the first idea how to do it, but that was where Amanda came in. If I could deal with talking to her about it.

"Well, I think this looks good," Lindsay said, effectively winding up my visit. She stood and I followed suit. "Let me know what Amanda says. If you want, I can come . . ."

"I'm going on a weekday, you'll be in school."

Lindsay sighed and looked away. "Did I tell you I'm using this for a class project?"

I laughed. "No, but I think you probably should have. Shouldn't you have my permission?"

"Are you saying I don't have it?"

"Of course you have it. If we get this horse, you'll get an A for sure."

"Oh, you'll get the horse," Lindsay assured me. "I'm a straight-A student and that's not about to change."

20

I RODE JIM Dear up to the equestrian center to teach on Tuesday afternoon, feeling pretty chipper about my future. The day felt wintry, with a brisk wind that rattled the dry leaves of the live oaks, and as we trotted along the trail, Jim was happy to kick up his heels. We arrived at the farm with a spook and a clatter of hooves that took us right inside the barn aisle. I hopped off once Jim found it within himself to halt, and found a cluster of kids and horses gathered around the crossties in the middle of the barn.

Everyone stared at me.

"Oh," I said. "Hello."

They kept staring. I looked down at myself, hoping I hadn't brought in a giant spider or something. "Is everything okay, guys?"

Jordan's eyes were big. "You rode *into* the barn," she said.

I realized I'd broken one of those sacred barn rules kids are brought up with: never ride inside the barn.

"Whoops, guess I did. No one tell Rosie, okay?"

Rosie waved from the tack room. "Hi, Jules!"

I cracked a grin and eventually the little crowd broke into nervous laughter. Jeez. They could be a buttoned-up bunch. "What are all of you doing in the aisle together?" I asked, loosening Jim's noseband. "I'm supposed to teach Heather and Melanie in privates today, right?"

Lindsay stepped up, looking like the designated speaker. "We thought maybe we could have a group lesson."

It was my turn to stare. "What, with *all* of you?" There were seven kids here. The arena was big enough to hold all of them, but I wasn't sure my brain was capable of keeping track of that many horse-and-rider pairs at once.

Lindsay nodded. "We have some questions."

Jordan sidled up to me and whispered, "And we want to keep this quiet."

They all looked deadly serious.

"Okay," I said. "Sure, I guess."

The kids flew into action, and in a few minutes we were all mounted in the arena. I was happy I'd brought along Jim Dear, because I needed the additional height he gave me to get a good look at everyone. "Why not circle around me, guys?" I suggested, not sure where to get started. My usual lesson planning was to let the kids warm up and see where they were falling short. How could I do that with seven kids?

They rode closer than I expected. Jim snorted, finding himself the vortex in a ring of children and horses.

"Fine," I said. "Will someone tell me what's going on?"

Heads swiveled, everyone looking to Lindsay. She glanced over her shoulder, as if making sure no one from the barn was watching us. "Okay," she said. "First question. Tomeka wants to know if it's true that you jump telephone poles instead of regular jumps in eventing."

Tomeka, who was about twelve years old and always wore a

serious expression when she rode, clucked her tongue in annoyance. "You weren't supposed to say *names*," she told Lindsay.

"Sorry. Just trying to keep track of all the questions."

I let Jim Dear turn in a small circle, riding him alongside Tomeka's horse for a moment. "We don't jump telephone poles," I told her, "although we do jump logs. But you never jump anything you're not ready for. There's no rushing cross-country work. We're very, very safe about it so that everyone has fun and no one gets hurt."

Tomeka nodded solemnly. "That's good to know, thank you."

"Melanie," Lindsay said, "you're up."

Melanie was about Tomeka's age. She squirmed in the saddle. "Okay, um, do you have to have three sets of saddles and tack and stuff for eventing? Because my mom said I can't get another saddle until I grow out of this one."

"Nope," I said. "You can do all three phases in one saddle as long as you and your horse are comfortable in it. Same goes for your bridle and your show clothes."

"That's great," Melanie said. "I'll tell my mom."

"Wait a minute." I held up a hand and the little carousel stopped spinning. "Why am I answering questions about eventing? What is going on here?"

Jordan spoke up. "Lindsay was telling us that she's going to start eventing, and we might want to, too."

"All of you?"

Seven heads in riding helmets nodded.

"And you came out here to ask me about it so . . ."

"So Rosie won't tell our parents," Melanie said.

"My mom is scared of eventing," Heather added.

"Mine too," Jordan said.

"And you talked Lindsay's mom into it," Tomeka said.

I looked around at them, shocked and a little delighted. All these barn rats wanted to get off the horse show circuit and train with *me*? That was pretty flattering.

And scary, sure, but I decided to focus on the flattering part. "So, do you want me to talk to all your parents?" I asked.

Tomeka shook her head. "Not mine, not yet. I'm still not sure I can do it."

"Everyone's kind of nervous," Jordan said. "Me included."

"But we want to *think* about it," Melanie said. "We have more questions."

At that moment the wind, which had been ruffling the horses' manes and sending cold fingers down my back, picked up and gusted through the arena, whistling through the lattices in the jump standards and knocking down a few water bottles left on the railing. Tomeka's horse jumped, and Jim Dear skittered sideways to save himself. I guided Jim away from the other horses so no one got run over by my Thoroughbred's silliness.

"That's some wind!" I called over my shoulder. The kids were gathering their reins and trying not to get caught out in a spook, but everyone probably would have been fine if a branch on a tree alongside the arena hadn't chosen that exact moment to give up on life. It came crashing to the ground with a surprisingly loud thud, tiny twigs and leaves flying through the air around it.

And that was when every horse decided it was the tree or them.

Jim was never a horse to keep his head in an emergency, but this time I really needed him to manage his nerves. As horses began fleeing the scene, kids shrieking and leaning back on the reins, I tightened my own grip on his mouth and kicked him toward the most panicked-looking rider. It was Heather, whose horse was streaking across the arena with his tail flagged. I pointed Jim at the galloping horse and put my legs on. Jim wasn't a cow horse, but he figured out the assignment pretty quick—*Follow that pony!* We were after them and in a few quick strides, we'd caught up with Heather's horse. She was losing her balance, one stirrup gone and her whole being focused on not getting bounced out of the saddle. The horse side-eyed Jim, but let me take the inner cheek strap of his bridle in my hand, and he slowed to a walk willingly as Jim responded to my left hand reining him back.

Heather kicked her left foot back into the stirrup and her hands choked up on the reins again. "Thanks," she gasped.

I had a real urge to answer her in a John Wayne accent but I couldn't think of any lines, and there were a few other horses still bouncing across the arena, so Jim and I set off to slow the next one in line. Tomeka's horse was probably already winded but we made a show of catching him anyway, and Melanie's Arabian pony probably could have galloped all day, but Jim cut the little horse off and we grandly restored the slipped reins to Melanie.

The wind quieted as we got everyone under control, as if it had done its mischief for the day. I expected the rattled riders would dismount and head inside, but they brought their dancing horses back to Jim and I found them circling around me once again. "We're still doing this?" I asked, surprised. "Are you guys sure?"

Melanie held her tugging horse in check as she nodded. "I want to ride like *you*," she said.

"Well, okay." I looked around at them. Everyone gazed back, waiting for instructions. "Let's talk about emergency stops."

I floated home after that lesson, Jim still feeling fresh under the invigorating chill of yet another wintry evening. The kids now knew the emergency, or "Pony Club" stop, everyone loved me, I was going to keep Mickey, despite everything Eileen had threatened, and things were going to be fine. The other problems—Pete's perplexing obsession with another person's horse, his desire to move to a bigger farm, the radio silence from Grace after I'd left that message suggesting we go into business together—we could work out, after the situation with Mickey had been tidied up. Whether I owned him outright or I had to form a syndicate, I'd have my horse, and I'd accept the results.

"Everything is coming up Jules," I sang to Marcus, and he looked up at me from beneath his saggy beagle brows and sighed before he went back to sleep, slowly sinking into a Marcus-shaped dent on his favorite spot on the couch. Pete would be home from Penny Lane soon and he'd be starving. I'd decided to fix dinner before I finished with the horses for the night; we could heat it up afterward and spend less time sitting around starving, getting crankier and crankier. Maybe we'd get along better in the evenings if we weren't eating after eight every night.

The future dinner was sizzling in a pan, a bag of Chinese vegetables and chicken, and I'd put water on the boil for rice. "Pete doesn't know how lucky he is," I told Marcus, and threw him a nub of baby carrot. He stirred just enough to chew it up, leaving orange curls of soggy carrot to fall onto the floor, and went back to sleep.

I was scraping the carrot shavings off the floor when my phone buzzed. It was Lindsay, telling me the initial email had been sent out and she'd follow up with everyone who opened it, but didn't click the investment button, in a few days. "Get your lawyer on it," she said. "Because we're going to have investors in no time at all."

I didn't see any need to let her know I didn't have a lawyer. Not yet. We'd figure my attorney situation out after I talked to Amanda. And yes, I was even resigned to talking with Amanda now. Anything to make this happen. I'd done a little research into how syndication worked, and was pleasantly surprised by how easy it seemed. Obviously I wasn't going to do any of the legal work or accounting—that was way over my head, to say nothing of taking far too much time. But I was already feeling a little less reliant on Amanda's advice.

I tipped a bag of white rice into the boiling water and danced away from its hisses and spatters. While I was turning down the heat, my phone buzzed again.

I eyeballed the name on the screen, and half entertained the idea of letting it go to voicemail. But no, that would only be worse. I'd have to wait for the message, freaking out the whole time, and then I'd just have to call her back. I picked up the phone again and swallowed, steeling myself. *Here is my perky voice,* I thought. *Let's give it a try.* Green button, go. "Oh, hello, Eileen!"

Perfect, Jules. Nicely done. You sound so—

"What's going on down there?" she snapped. "Is this some kind of joke?"

"What?" I blinked into the steam as it lazily whirled into the cool air, slowly pushing a fun-house fog through the trailer's living quarters. I watched it bump into the overhead lamp and twist in protest. "Is what a joke?"

"This email—someone forwarded it to me. You think you can build up a syndicate to buy Mickey? That's not happening, Jules. We've been over this."

Her voice warbled and arced, as if she was being jostled by electric waves, and I realized the connection inside the trailer was threatening to cut us off.

Would that be such a bad thing? Yes—she still owned Mickey, so she still owned me. I turned the stovetop off and went outside, Marcus resignedly hopping down the metal steps at my heels.

"Eileen? I don't think you understand—we've got the money in place. We have buyers lined up. I just need you to wait long enough for us to get the legal stuff worked out."

"I told you not to do this," Eileen said icily. I fell silent, still unsure how to deal with this new, mean version of her. Or had she always been a dangerous opponent just waiting for the moment I crossed her, and distance had kept me from seeing that side of her?

Horsewomen were frequently like that. Anyone in the business longer than six months could tell you—this was a profession propped up on broken promises and partnerships gone bad.

The stranger that was Eileen went on talking. "I told you I was not going to sell you Mickey. I told you that you aren't in any position to keep him, and we aren't comfortable with your situation right now. So you can just drop this little scheme of yours, all of it. I'm sending a van to pick him up tomorrow."

I sat down on the ground, hard. I realized dimly my legs had simply given out. They couldn't hold me anymore. Nothing could hold me up any longer. I was just going to stay down here on the cold March clay, the damp soaking through my breeches, until the end came and my horses were loaded up one by one, and my trailers were stripped of their tack, and I was left here with nothing.

"Have him ready by three," Eileen said. "That should be plenty of time. I'll forward you the email so you'll know the company's name."

She didn't even have a van lined up. It was breeding season and show season and shippers were crisscrossing every lane in Ocala, dragging their valuable loads from barn to barn at all hours of the day, and yet she was so determined to get Mickey out of my clutches, she was going to call every transport service in town until she found someone who would come out here immediately.

I ended the call without a word in reply. She'd been saying something more, but I couldn't understand her. Language had lost meaning. The phone fell at my side and sat silently. She didn't call back. Whatever she'd been saying apparently wasn't that important.

Pete returned home as the sun was setting, orange light glinting off the chrome of the truck's grille. I was still sitting on the ground, my head against the tire of the trailer, Marcus leaning against my side. I didn't turn my head; I didn't want to tell him. I didn't want to talk to anyone at all.

Marcus certainly did; he ran over to Pete with his tail wagging. Such a traitor.

"Jules?" Pete's voice was cautious as he climbed down from the truck. In the pasture, the horses set up a cacophony of whinnying; they'd all given up neighing at me ages ago. Maybe they couldn't even see me anymore. Maybe I'd simply faded into the environment, nothing but a shrub, or a weed, growing up against a horse trailer abandoned in an empty pasture somewhere in North Florida, miles from civilization.

I closed my eyes, just to be extra sure I was invisible.

It didn't work. Pete crouched down next to me, and put a hand on my shoulder. I felt his warmth and realized I was cold. The chill had been seeping into me, creeping through my clothes and skin and bones, and now as the sun was fading, the cool March evening felt positively freezing. I started to shiver, and Pete exclaimed something softly and pulled me up against him, his hands tight around my wrists. I whimpered, a sound I dimly realized I'd never made before, and tried to pull them free.

"Shhh," he whispered. "Let's get you inside."

The horses must be so disappointed, I thought as he closed the trailer door behind us against a symphony of outraged whinnies.

"We can't live like this anymore," he said.

He'd dropped me on the couch, and now he was standing a

few feet away from me, but it was across the room—as far away as he could get in our tiny quarters. I didn't know if the distance was accidental or on purpose, but the couple dozen inches felt like miles. I was wrapped in the duvet from the bed—he'd dragged it down and swaddled me in its folds like an infant—with Marcus half on my lap, half on the sofa. There wasn't any room for Pete to sit, I realized, and though I felt a stab of guilt, I didn't push Marcus down, either.

"I know," I whispered.

"I wish this wasn't what it took for you to understand this farm had to be temporary."

"I just didn't want it to be temporary."

He ran his hands through his hair and sighed. I had an unwelcome flashback of my parents doing much the same, every time I wanted to do something equine that interfered with what they thought a normal child ought to do. I couldn't please anyone, could I? That was why I'd stopped trying to please anyone a long time ago. Anyone but myself. But that kept getting me into messes.

"If I promise Eileen we are going to move . . ."

"But we aren't, are we? Not right now. We don't have anywhere to go. We don't have any prospects. That's been my question all along—how is this better than getting ourselves set up somewhere else? Somewhere permanent?"

Impatience rose in me. "But we can't just make something permanent appear out of thin air! There should be a way to make *this* work. We're doing fine. People need to stop being snobs about fancy barns and photogenic properties."

"So you're saying that the system should change, not you?" He gave me a ghost of a grin. "Let me know how that works out for you."

"If we get out there on course and show everyone we're the same team that crushed it in the fall, they'll see—"

"No," Pete said. "I know you think you know best. Most of the time, you probably do. But I'm telling you, Jules, you're wrong about this one. They're not going to give us any leeway. If we don't find a proper farm and fix our image, we're going to lose everything we gained last year."

He didn't have to elaborate. I could see the future spreading out before us, and it was short and it was bitter. I would lose Mickey, and that was a professional and emotional blow I wouldn't easily recover from. Delannoy would grow impatient with Pete's farm situation, and decide against buying him a horse. Rockwell would be finished with us after our contract was up in May, and our stipend and equipment pipeline would end. We would have a handful of horses, and the pittance we got from teaching and training. And that would be it.

Except we wouldn't sit around and wait for that to happen.

Pete was right this time. We couldn't give up our careers over this.

I'd been holding on to a silly little dream, so foolish it was going to bring us both down, for so long he probably thought I was never going to snap out of it. But he was wrong.

I sat up and pushed down the duvet. *No more panicking*, I told myself. Time to take charge again.

"What do we have to do, right now, to convince someone to take us on as barn managers, or resident trainers?"

Pete shrugged. "Tell everyone we know to tell everyone *they* know that we're looking, for starters."

"Then we'll do that. We'll find a farm that wants us and we'll go."

"This is a pretty sudden change of direction," Pete said. "What happened to keeping things small? Only having a few horses? That big dream you got from Grace?"

Oh, this is about Grace, I thought. He blamed her influence for all of this—her telling me to slow down and focus on my horses instead of expanding my business. Oh, the irony, when I never would have met Grace if not for him. I couldn't help rolling my eyes. "Okay, what the hell else do you want from me, Pete? You didn't want to be here. You told me, over and over again, this was a pit stop while we got situated. Okay then. I *accept* that. We're situated. It's time to move on." I stood up, letting Marcus slide from my lap and back onto the couch. "We have an event in ten days. If we're going to turn things around, there's no better time to draw a line and say this is when we change course."

Pete still looked grumpy. "You sure turned that mood around fast."

"I'm a woman, Pete," I said matter-of-factly. "We don't have time to sit around moaning. We have to get on with it. Now come on, let's go feed the horses. They're probably furious with us for making them wait this long."

The evening so far had felt like a roller coaster, but the repetitive tasks of taking care of horses—feeding, watering, blanketing—settled my nerves. With hungry horses pulling at their lead ropes as we led them into their stalls, the numbed, shocked feeling left my limbs and my usual sense of purpose came back to my brain. I had these horses to take care of. Their lives were in my hands, and I didn't have the luxury of falling apart.

Pete took the flat cart over to the hay trailer to pull down a few bales for the evening, and I busied myself with the muddy garden hose, pulling it down the row of stalls and reaching over the front boards to fill each water bucket. Most of the horses ignored me, too busy with their grain to bother inspecting my work, but Regina took the time to pin her ears and shake her head at me, and Mickey gave me a curious once-over, rubbing his soft lips against my light jacket and leaving behind a trail of sticky oats. I placed my free hand against his forehead, the whorl of white hair between his eyes. His forelock didn't quite reach that point; it was still short, fluffy, and silly-looking after he'd severed it the first night he'd been in my barn. If Eileen had been able to deal with her beloved horse scalping himself in the first few hours he'd spent under my care, why on earth couldn't she handle him living on rough board in a barn that put the "shed" in "shed row"?

"You *can't* leave tomorrow," I told him, and my throat closed up despite my strong-willed intentions. Mickey only snorted, depositing scattered droplets on my jacket front I was better off not contemplating, and went back to his feed bucket, digging his nose so deep into it the snap screeched against the screw eye. "You have to stay with me."

The whining of a wheel that wanted greasing told me Pete was coming back with hay. I pulled myself together and went on to the next stall, kinking the hose so I wouldn't add to the already muddy ground in front of the barn. I didn't need him to see I was still falling apart inside.

21

WHEN YOU HAVE horses, any major life change is nearly impossible to fathom. They always need cared for, day in and day out. If they're in work, let alone entered into competitions, training can't cease.

So it was with good intentions that we said we'd call, text, and email every horseman in town, and it was with stress bowing our shoulders that we neglected this task and went on with our daily lives, the cycle of feeding and mucking and training and teaching and feeding and mucking again. There were gallops to schedule and complete. There were cross-country courses to school. The next event was looming on the calendar. I had horse show nerves for the first time in years. It had been months since we'd competed, and now we had to make up for lost time—all while I knew Mickey was out there, in someone else's barn.

Because Mickey was gone.

He had stepped onto the trailer and they had driven him away.

I was left with my remaining horses and a wall of facts blocking me from going after Mickey, a barrier that seemed insurmountable. The lack of facilities, his owners' refusal to sell to me, specifically because of that lack—what was I supposed to do about it? If they were really determined to ally themselves against me, what was the point of fighting for him?

I knew there would always be more horses.

But I loved Mickey. And no matter how many times I told myself there would always be more horses, that I had very nice horses in my care *right now,* horses who had potential to step up the levels and show everyone what I was made of as a rider, as a trainer, that didn't stop me from mourning my big gray Thoroughbred. I swallowed my tears, a thousand times a day, until my throat was always raw.

And I texted Lindsay, constantly, asking her what we could do. When we could make our next move. *How* we could make a move, when Mickey was for sale to everyone in the world except me.

I'm working on it, she replied, again and again. *Calm yourself and write "thank you" to everyone commenting that they'd love to buy into the Danger Mouse Project. All of them!!!*

At least all those "thank you" comments took up some of the time I'd probably have spent mooning over pictures of Mickey.

And the rest of the time I spent preparing for an event that was supposed to be our triumphant comeback. In the saddle, putting in the hours and miles, schooling our horses through all their rough spots, and polishing their strengths. Jim Dear needed to practice his downward transitions for the dressage, and Barsuk and I needed more time over fences together. I schooled him with Pete up at the equestrian center, trying to find our rhythm over low fences before we were tested over much more challenging questions at the event.

"Once more for me, and then you go over them!" Pete called, and I looked up from whatever it was I'd been contemplating— the white rings on Barsuk's dappled coat, maybe, or the intricate pattern of rubber and nylon knitted into the reins resting on his withers. I hadn't really seen any of it. I blinked to force myself to focus on Pete and Dynamo, cantering in the arena before us. Off to one side, Jordan leaned on the fence, soaking it in and serving as our assistant when poles needed raised or lowered.

Smooth as silk, Dynamo soared around the course we'd set up at the equestrian center. Pete balanced in the center of the saddle, heels down, eyes up, shoulders back, chin out. His equitation would probably be called old-school, but it was the way his grandfather had taught him, military-precise. A straight line from shoulder to hip to heel whether he was cantering between fences or hovering in the air over a leaping Dynamo's balletlike bascule. I remembered how Jordan had described her friend's trainer tying her stirrups to her girth—this was the effect her silly trainer was trying to reproduce, but without actual skill or strength required.

I wasn't quite as strong as Pete in the saddle, which meant Dynamo, a long-bodied, short-coupled horse who needed a lot of leg to keep him balanced and on the bit, looked better with Pete. Perhaps only marginally better, but I found even the slightest edge over my riding annoying, and doubly so since it was Dynamo.

They completed the course and circled at the top of the arena as if they were in the hunter ring, and then Pete walked Dynamo out of the gate, reins loose. The horse stretched out his neck, dropping his nose toward the ground, nostrils puffing. It was a cool day, but he'd been working hard for the past hour.

"Your turn," Pete said with a grin. "How was that?"

"You could have held him together through the in-and-out better."

"Literally always," he replied, shrugging it off. "Those are tough for him."

"Everything else was flawless," I allowed, shaking my head.

"As you will be with Barsuk," Pete said chivalrously. "You ride him better than I do."

"We're *not* doing a permanent swap."

Pete laughed.

Barsuk wasn't jumping at the same level as Dynamo, so I waited while Jordan scurried into the arena and started pulling down jump cups, dropping everything down a few inches to Preliminary height. Pete was taking him Prelim this weekend, as well as taking Dynamo Intermediate and Mayfair Novice. I was taking Jim Dear in Modified, the step-up level before Training. I had planned to take Mickey in this division, too, but now Jim was the only horse I was eventing this weekend.

Eileen had been nice enough to pay me back the nearly two hundred dollars I would forfeit by not showing up with Mickey. Maybe she just knew I had a case against her if I could afford to go to small claims court. But why bother?

Mickey was gone.

A judge couldn't bring him back. A few hundred dollars wasn't going to change the fact that he wasn't in my barn anymore.

Jordan finished and gave me a thumbs-up. I squeezed my calves against Barsuk's slab sides and he stepped forward with his quick, trappy gait. The ex-racehorse was narrow between my legs, his black mane ruffling over his dappled neck. A few jagged cowlicks threw the smooth line of his muscled crest into disarray. He had the kind of mane that always had to be braided, I thought absently, even for schooling shows.

Slight where Mickey was substantial, slim where Dynamo was broad, Barsuk was a different kind of Thoroughbred from the other two in my life. I'd often thought there were three distinct body types in the breed, and my current experience was bearing this out. Dynamo was the big-chested bulldog; Mickey the commendably elegant wolfhound; and Barsuk the swift, racy greyhound. His girth was two sizes shorter than the one I used on Mickey. My hands on the reins, loose enough to have loops in them, felt like they were practically at his ears.

I'd get used to him, though. I was still the ten-horse-a-day trainer, even if I only had two horses . . . and only one to event myself. Hell, maybe I *would* just sweet-talk Pete into letting me event him as long as he was still showing Dynamo. Not a trade, but a temporary catch ride. I'd find my seat on Barsuk and bring home a few ribbons, get a few photos on the blogs riding a different gray horse.

I was that kind of rider, after all, the kind who could mount up on any horse and make him into a competitor. Sure, there wasn't time for deep personal connections with that kind of training schedule. You got on, you got off, you handed the reins to a groom, you got on another one. But what good had all the my-horse-is-my-BFF philosophies done me? I'd invested myself far too deeply into two horses, and I didn't have the ride on either of them right now.

"Barsuk, buddy boy, we are going to form a temporary partnership." His black-tipped ears flipped back to listen to me, then pricked forward again as we neared Dynamo and Pete. I struggled to get my head in the game. This was my career. Riding new horses was what trainers did to stay alive. I took a deep breath and let my weight sink into my heels, pushing everything but my feel of this horse right out of my head. Two strides into the arena, and I'd feel like I'd been riding Barsuk, and only Barsuk, my entire life.

That was the plan, anyway.

As we passed Pete and Dynamo, Pete gave me the wide smile of a man who is happy with his horse. "We're going to turn some heads next weekend," he said. "He's absolutely humming with fitness."

I only had eyes for Dynamo's flared nostrils, the veins standing in high relief along his sweat-darkened neck, the flutter of foam resting in the crevices of his eyelids. "He's really blowing," I observed. "You better keep him walking for a while. And here . . ." I reined back Barsuk, then leaned down and unbuckled Dynamo's flash noseband, letting the leather hang loose around his nose and chin. "Unbuckle your girth a couple holes, too. Give him some room to breathe."

I noted the dark look Pete gave me and filed it away for a future argument. It didn't matter right now. That was my horse he was sitting on, and I didn't want to hear tales of how talented my horse was while he was still hot and blowing. I *knew* how talented he was. I had uncovered that talent myself.

"I know how to cool out a horse, Jules," Pete called after me, but I was already in the arena and moving on with my life.

I flicked Barsuk's sides with my calves. He gave a little jump and he was cantering, his shoulders rising before me and his neck arched with theatrical flair. His body was so narrow I had to drive my lower legs forward, my heels near his sharp elbows, to sit his powerful collected canter without pumping my upper body back and forth. I felt about as graceful as a drunk college girl on a mechanical bull at midnight, but I knew I looked steady and secure in the saddle all the same. *Ten horses a day,* I told myself, *and not a single one canters the same way.*

We circled methodically at the top of the arena like a pair of hunters before an amateur/owner class, missing only a standing martingale and a total lack of impulsion to fully look the part. Outside the ring, Pete stalked back and forth on Dynamo, a red blur at the corner of my vision. *Shut him out,* I thought. Time to focus. Time to stay ahead of all my worries for just a few minutes.

The course we'd laid out wasn't complicated: a vertical set perpendicular to the in-gate, a hard left turn to a five-and-a-half-stride figure-it-out line with a big oxer at the far end, a big looping right-hand curve to a triple combination of the traditional sort—vertical, two strides, vertical, one stride, oxer—and then a cut back through the center of the ring to a skinny lattice, a quick turn left, hoping one wouldn't hit the arena fence on the way, to a high vertical and then a bending line back to a Swedish oxer near the top. Kid's stuff.

It was the kind of course a riding instructor builds when they have low-level riders and not a lot of space, just with the fences hiked up a bit. Prelim wasn't terribly high, but it was enough to make things interesting, considering the limited space in the arena.

I bent Barsuk out of his circle and straightened him out with barely three strides available before the first fence. He tucked up into himself, his nose behind the bit and his legs drumming nearly straight up and down. Bunny-hopping to the first fence, really? I bit my lower lip, sat down, and drove him forward with my legs and pelvis, pushing like a deranged steeplechaser at the last long furlong of a two-mile race. Talk about pumping my upper body.

He took the hint and plunged forward; the last stride before the fence was three times the length of the one before that. His launch was more like a bullfrog hop than a bascule, but I tucked myself low along his withers, clinging for dear life from my thighs to my heels, and managed to avoid getting left behind the motion and looking like a total novice.

After the fence he bolted, his saintly arched neck turned inside-out in pursuit of more giraffe-like heights, and I had to shove my leg in front of his elbows again and thump down like a potato in the saddle, letting him know with grinding seat bones that I was going to make his life very uncomfortable as long as he was hollowed out like a pacer.

He came back to my hand with a suddenness that nearly threw me off-balance, holding the bit so delicately I could have believed it was a sharp-edged curb instead of the gentle snaffle Pete always used. But in the end all that submission was fine, because we had to make some decisions very quickly about the uneven line approaching us with alarming rapidity. I went for a slow and steady six—like every good show jumper would, right?—and Barsuk happily jumped out of my hand on each fence, looping around the bottom of the arena with measured strides and a look of transcendent compliance on his speckled face, turned inward to match the arc of his circle just enough for me to see his dark eye.

I sat down and breathed as we took the long way around the turn, nearly brushing against the fence, so leisurely were we in our bend toward the line up the side of the arena. I figured jumping toward home on a horse this capable of turning himself upside-down had a high potential for disaster, so the slower and calmer the better in the run-up to the first element. Also, I was really enjoying this version of Barsuk, this calm and collected canter with a darling *huff* rushing through his flared nostrils every time his forelegs hit the pockmarked earth.

Such pleasures can't last, and deserve to be savored.

Here it was: a high white fence with two more beyond it, and the invitation of the gate and the barn in sight just beyond. He jumped the standards on the way in, scrabbled midair over the second element, and tried to chip an extra half stride in before the oxer on the way out, as if he'd suddenly lost faith in the redeeming power of the exit route dead ahead. Again, with knee and heel and hand I shoved him up and over the fence, his hind hooves rapping the last pole but not enough to drop it, and I had to concede that even if it was ugly, we were still jumping clear.

Somehow I got him back between my hand and my leg and we jumped the skinny, the bending line, and the final oxer without more drama. I was no catch rider, and learning a horse's jumping style for the first time over a course wasn't my usual strategy, but as I pulled him up and let him stretch his neck to the ground, I thought we hadn't done too badly.

Pete came back into the arena on Dynamo, whose breathing had noticeably calmed in the two minutes I'd been tearing around the arena alternating between continental and American riding styles, and matched our walk.

I glanced over at him. "That was not my prettiest riding."

He threw me a wry smile. "Barsuk's not the easiest to jump. You did fine. You didn't pull anything, and I thought your pace ended up good, even if you took the scenic route in the middle there."

"I liked the way he felt down there. I was trying to keep that mood."

"He has on and off modes. That was his off mode. He switches back on really quick, though. As you found."

"Not a lot of in-between."

"No."

I thought about Dynamo, who had an entire spectrum of movement and mood to choose from. Riding Barsuk had been like driving a manual and skipping a few gears between first and fifth. Dynamo, when warmed up properly and held together with plenty of leg, was like a very smooth automatic.

That's the way it always feels after your first good horse, though. You make a horse and then you have to make another one, to prove you can, but you find it never feels the same way twice.

Bitterly, I realized I'd never have such a pure feeling on a horse again. I kept reaching for it with Mickey, but what I had with Dynamo was a one-time thing, born of years and years of trial and error, getting to know his bones and his muscles so intimately. I had made him in my image, and now he would always be perfect the moment I sat astride him. He would arch into me because that feeling had become so familiar, it was part of who we both were.

A partnership like this could be once in a lifetime.

Or, at least it was when you were a ten-horse-a-day trainer.

"You okay?" Pete asked.

"With what?" Barsuk paused to rub his sweaty face on his foreleg. The sun began to toy with the pine trees at the edge of the farm.

"With everything."

"When you put it that way, no."

"With Barsuk."

I rubbed my hand along his neck, feeling the cooling sweat beneath his rug of black mane. "Yeah, I'm okay with Barsuk. I think you should let me have him for a while. Until you're done with Dynamo."

"Yeah, I figured." Pete sighed the sigh of a boyfriend whose girlfriend has discovered his most comfortable T-shirt. "After next weekend."

"Thanks."

We rode home with our fleece jackets pulled over our thin riding shirts, emblazoned with ROCKWELL BROTHERS SADDLERY on the chest, keeping warm against the spring's evening chill with the gifts we expected to stop coming very soon.

Unless, of course, something miraculous happened.

22

WHEN GRACE CALLED me at last, it was after nearly three weeks of silence on her part. I wasn't expecting her tone to be quite so brusque, although I probably should have. She was blessed with the same social graces I was—that is to say, none at all—and I'd sent her an admittedly cryptic message about losing Mickey and needing a new farm position as soon as possible. Naturally, she was annoyed with me for not being more forthcoming. Grace did not enjoy beating around the bush.

While Grace talked, I left Pete to finish feeding the horses, all of them leaning over their flimsy stall chains with the same bright expression of toddlers anticipating snack time, and retreated to the camp chairs by the trailer door. The nylon seat, shaded all afternoon, was cold through my full-seats. Marcus sidled up for a pat and I dropped my free hand into his fur, thankful for the warmth.

"There was nothing I could say to change her mind," I responded as soon as Grace paused to take a breath. "She thinks I'm irresponsible for coming up here and letting the horses live out for a few weeks. She won't sell him to me, and I've got dozens of people lined up trying to help me buy him who are just hanging on by a thread, getting fed emails every couple of days to say an update on how to invest is coming soon. Meanwhile, Carrie could be quietly passing around a sales video to her favorite riders and getting ready to field offers on him. I'm going to lose my chance!"

"Are you done complaining?" Grace said with a sigh. I imagined her standing in her dusty office, looking down through the window at her little empire below: dozens of horses, dozens of students, grooms rushing around with halters and ponies and hay carts. All of it on the edge of ending, bulldozers waiting to tear it all down the moment she gave the signal. Did Grace have more problems than me, or were we about even? She would probably say more.

"I don't think I was complaining. I was just stating the facts. If my reality sounds like one big complaint, that's just an unfortunate truth."

"How long ago did she take him?"

"Last week."

"And you just sent me this message today. Tuesday. How am I supposed to help you when you don't tell me things?"

"I didn't expect you to do anything about it." Also, time passed without my realizing it. Depression plus unending work had a way of making the calendar meaningless.

"I could have found a way to help you."

"I thought you had your own stuff going on," I said lamely.

"When has that ever stopped you before?"

I was quiet. I didn't want to point out that I almost never asked for help, from anyone, because she had told me before this was a foolish philosophy.

"You should never have given her the horse," Grace declared. "You should've stalled, told the drivers she was trying to claim the horse illegally and you'd have them arrested, something like that.

You have to have something in your contract about thirty days' notice, for God's sake."

I didn't have a reply to her logic. Of course I hadn't had the forethought for anything of the sort. I'd taken Mickey as a gift from the eventing gods, and I didn't look that sort of thing in the mouth. The contract had been my basic training-board contract, taken out of a big paperback book of equestrian legal documents. It had never occurred to me I'd need anything more. I never thought I would ever be in this kind of situation. I didn't think someone would just say, "We're taking back this creature we trusted you with, that you loved like your own child, and there's nothing you can do about it."

Why hadn't I seen this coming? People were cruel.

Grace understood my silence. "Oh, you foolish girl," she said, her voice sympathetic.

"I was just starting out. He was my first big break. I didn't know it could end like this."

"You knew you were dealing with horse people, though, and that nearly always ends in tears and bad feelings. So where will your second big break come from? You shot yourself in the foot with this one, Jules. I'm sorry to say it like that, but it's true."

She was right, of course. I shouldn't be surprised at any of this. I should have *expected* things would end this way. The horse business thrived on deceit, overwrought emotions, and hearts ripped in two.

I chewed the inside of my cheek to keep my jaw from wobbling, willing myself not to shout or cry or throw the phone into the tall grass along the fence, which would definitely propel Marcus into a happy game of find-and-chew. (Marcus did not fetch. Marcus destroyed.) I could not afford another phone.

I pulled myself together again, mainly through the pain of biting down on my own tender mouth. Better get on with things. Better not dwell on mistakes.

Worrying was the kind of fun I could save for the middle of the night, when I woke up and remembered anew that my world was in some kind of slow, painful implosion sequence.

"Grace, we're going to start over," I explained, starting over with our start-over story. What better place? "We're looking for a barn management situation. We'll work out of someone else's barn and pick up the pieces that way. The normal way everyone does it. No more maverick-style Jules-doesn't-need-owners. It didn't work, and there's no use trying to be a trendsetter in a business like this. I'm going to follow the formula, do things by the book."

Grace was quiet for a moment. I imagined her chewing at her lip, trying to regroup the same way I had. When you're passionate about something, but you don't want anyone to know just how much it affects you, you have to reboot or risk sharing your emotions.

I felt a burst of gratitude for just how much I mattered to Grace. I wasn't sure what I'd ever done to deserve it, but it felt good to have someone so thick-skinned and dangerously driven on my team.

"Well, I'll keep my ear to the ground for you," she said eventually, her voice vibrating with repressed emotion. Anger? Sadness? I didn't know. And she wasn't going to tell me.

"Thank you," I replied. I dug my fingers deep into Marcus's wiry ruff of spotted fur. "Thanks so much for being there for me."

Grace chuckled, a rusty sound. "I have to keep my eye on you. You know too much about me."

"Who was that?" Pete asked when I came back over to the shed row. Everyone was eyeball-deep in their buckets, plowing through their feed like they'd been starved for days.

"Grace," I said. "To berate me."

"That's nice. I'm sure you needed that."

"Somehow, I always feel like when she does it . . . maybe I did."

Pete grunted, clearly not convinced. He started gathering up Regina's rug from the makeshift blanket racks we'd strung up, made from narrow PVC pipe and baling twine—the hallmarks, along with duct tape, of every struggling equestrian trying to get through winter with just a little class. "I think heavy blankets tonight. It's supposed to be pretty cold, and this wind isn't helping."

So we were moving on, I thought. Back to the practicalities. No more conversation tonight. Probably for the best, though. Barn chores left plenty of room for introspection, and combing through one's memory for old contacts to call up, begging for a job.

With everyone hayed up, watered up, and rugged up, we clambered back into the trailer to wait out the cold night. Marcus scrambled up the steps ahead of us and claimed the couch before Pete and I could get out of our boots.

"So why did you need it?" Pete asked a few minutes later, as he was stepping out of the shower. Water pooled around his feet and soaked into the stubby whorls of the industrial-gray carpet.

"What?" I was already halfway out of my breeches, ready for my own shower. Water hummed to itself on the stovetop, anticipating the addition of hard coils of rotini.

"Why did you need Grace to berate you?"

"Oh . . . maybe to remind me to do things right for a change, instead of doing whatever I want."

"That doesn't sound like you."

"And here we are, in a horse trailer."

Pete grinned and leaned in for a kiss. His lips were damp from the shower. When I pulled back, he winked. "There's a bed in this horse trailer."

"Nice try." I laughed. "But nothing is standing between me and a shower. My feet are frozen." I pushed past him toward the tiny stall.

"I've got a text here asking me to come ride Rogue tomorrow," Pete said. "He was apparently a bit of a brat at HITS all weekend."

I paused and looked back at him, only halfway into the shower. One foot cold and dry on the couple of squares of linoleum that comprised the bathroom floor, one foot hot and wet in the slippery shower stall. "Have they given you an answer about selling yet?"

"No, not yet. It's time, though. I need to sit that girl down and say, 'This horse isn't right for you, but I'll buy him and give you enough to get a horse who is.' No more dancing around the truth."

I bit my lip and looked away from him. *This horse isn't right for you, but I'll buy him* . . . Something about that sentence clawed at my insides.

I would have loved a ten-minute shower, but two minutes was closer to the reality. There was just enough hot water in the trailer's tiny heater for both of us, if we were quick and efficient about it. I often mourned the lack of shower-thinking time. I'd figured out dozens of training problems while hot water drilled like little hailstones into my skull: horses who wouldn't go on the bit, horses who refused every other fence as a matter of course, horses who crow-hopped and bucked after fences, like Rogue . . .

My eyes opened and met Pete's, sitting on the sofa a few feet away. He had the grace to flush a little. No doubt hoping I'd come out with my feet warm enough for a little play. But my thoughts weren't on fun. "Pete," I began, stepping out of the cooling water and sliding the faucet to the off position. "Why is Rogue so important? You know there are a million horses out there. And you're annoying Delannoy by pushing so hard for this one, when you could be buying any number of horses who are actually for sale, this minute."

His smile faded. "You want to talk about this right now?"

I wound myself into a towel, covering up his scenic view. "I remembered something. And I think it's important to talk about it."

Pete stood up, cinching his fleece robe around him. I thought he was going to cross the few feet between us and hold out his arms to soothe away whatever insecurities I was feeling right now, and I steeled myself against the comfort of his touch. I didn't need comfort until he understood the depth of my disappointment in him. Then he could decide if he wanted to embrace me, or give me a little distance . . . a very little distance, considering our cramped quarters.

But he didn't. Instead, he passed me and reached for the stove, turning down the burner. The water was bubbling and chattering, threatening to toss the corkscrew noodles onto the floor, where Marcus had positioned himself in hopeful anticipation.

"I forgot to tell you, I figured out the line where Rogue stops bucking and starts thinking," Pete said, his back to me. Apparently he wasn't in a hurry to hear what I'd remembered.

"Oh?"

"I took him into the woods next to Penny Lane and jumped some logs and a creek."

"You took Rogue into the woods," I said blankly.

"Yes." Pete popped open a jar of pasta sauce.

"Those horses don't go out of the arena."

"I wanted to know what he'd do." He shrugged. "The horse was amazing. He loved it. He jumped everything I pointed him at. Jules, there's this huge oak tree back there—it would be a terror if it was at Badminton. And he just bounced over it like it was nothing. Roots in the air like claws . . ." He faded off, remembering the monster jump. "And then we went back to the arena and went around a full course without a single buck. Ears pricked the whole time. Down to business. It was like I found his magic button." Pete turned around, his eyes wide and his face full of light. "He's a born event horse, Jules."

I looked away from his happiness, shrugging into my own robe, pulling it tight and slipping my feet into a pair of fleece slippers. It was going to be a very cold night, I reflected, so we'd better fix this before bedtime. This wasn't an evening to forgo a good snuggle, and he was going to be upset with me. "Get me a beer, will you?" I asked, since he was blocking the fridge. "And then I have something to tell you."

"What am I, the butler?" he asked amiably, and pulled out a pair of bottles. "What's going on?"

I accepted the bottle gratefully and pressed myself into the corner of the couch, ceding the other side to Pete. "This happened when I was a kid," I said. "And I just remembered it. You know how when you suddenly remember something and it just shocks you?"

Pete's face was wary.

"It's not that," I said quickly. "There weren't any men around at my barn. Total girls' club."

He exhaled.

"But it's about Laurie. My trainer."

Pete nodded. "She was like a mother to you."

"A cool aunt, let's say," I corrected him. "I've been thinking about this. A cool aunt who worked me to death and never paid me a dime."

"That's the business."

"I know. I'm guilty of it too, and I'm going to do it again and so are you. But I didn't mind hard work. And no one who really wants to be in the business is going to mind it. Because she was building me up into the person I am, and she gave me so many horses to ride, so many late-night lessons, let me keep Dynamo for free . . ." I trailed off, thinking of the lonely evenings riding Dynamo after everyone else had gone home and the barn chores were done. Even Laurie, who never seemed to leave, would often be done and out the gate, her office locked behind her, while I was still trotting in endless serpentines and circles, trying to teach balance to a poorly built Thoroughbred who had been on his way to the killers when I found him.

"He didn't win anything at first, because he was a mess. You know how hard he is to put together. He's not a dressage horse. He's barely a hunter. His natural way of going is flat and falling apart. Laurie told me to get him going low-level and sell him, buy something better. I ignored her. And then he won. And won again. And he started winning all the jumper classes we entered, and most of the events, and Laurie was quiet about it. Didn't tell me to sell him for a while. Then one day she sat me down and . . . this is what I just remembered," I said slowly. "It's one of those things you put out of your head. She said he was never going higher than Training and to sell him. And she'd buy him for a school horse and that way he'd still be around the barn."

Pete's eyelid twitched, just once, and I knew he'd recognized where this story was going.

"She talked to me for half an hour. It was late. My mom was so pissed when I got home past nine, homework still waiting for me, no dinner left. And I couldn't even do my homework because I was so confused about what to do with Dynamo. I trusted Laurie. She was my best friend. She'd taught me everything. But I loved this horse and I could see his potential—I'd thought anyone could see it, I thought it was obvious—and she was telling me he was trash.

That she would do me a favor by making him a school horse, but she wasn't going to pay that much for him. I was just completely lost."

"Well, you didn't sell him," Pete offered, his voice gravelly. "And you stayed with Laurie. So you guys worked it out."

"Yeah, we did. I said I couldn't sell him and she said okay. And if I ever changed my mind, to let her know first. She'd take him. And I moved on and we kept winning, and I put it out of my head. And I forgot all about it. But Pete . . . she manipulated me. Or she tried. A teenager who trusted her. I thought Laurie was my friend, my best friend in the world, and so I shoved that night out of my head. But it happened. She really did that to me. She lied to me to try and get my horse." I put my head down on the table and took a deep breath. There had been far too much emotion today, even for a normal person who was okay with having feelings. I was exhausted.

"I know what you're trying to say," Pete sighed, rubbing my back. "But this is a different situation. This girl isn't my student. I barely know her. There's no trust issue at play here. I'm not betraying her or lying to her about her horse."

"No, but you're not giving her a chance to make things right with her horse, either. You're just telling her the horse is too much for her, which might not be true. And which isn't your job. You could tell her the horse wants to event, and that you finally stopped his bucking, which is what she wanted. You could help her decide if she wants a discipline change in order to keep him."

"Teaching her isn't my job either," Pete said, his voice tensing. "I'm not her trainer. I'm not here to tell her anything about her riding. I was told to get on the horse and get him ready for shows. I've done that. If he starts up again while she's at the show, well, I sent him down there ready for the show. If she can't ride him that's on her trainer, not on me. If she asks my opinion and I say I'm not having a problem, when *she* clearly is, that's on her to either try and do something about her own riding, or sell the horse."

"But she's a *kid,* and you're an adult. And she's a student, and you're a professional," I reminded him softly. "And so when you say something, she believes you. And if you tell her a half-truth, if you leave out the important part, which is maybe she could ride the horse with the right help, and under better circumstances for the horse, then you're lying to someone who trusts you. You're lying to a kid about her horse. Even if it's just a lie by omission—she expects more from you."

Pete sighed.

I lifted my head from where I'd still been resting on the table, my cheek cold on the Formica. "I expected more from you," I whispered.

He pulled back as far as he could in the tight space and regarded me with a lifted eyebrow. I felt like I was on the defense against that arching eyebrow's accusations.

"So this has been your problem from the get-go with Rogue? Your old trainer tried to trick you into selling your horse to her? And you're taking all this out on me?"

It was a painfully bald statement to make about Laurie. She'd given me everything. "I told you I just remembered it. And I wouldn't be here without Laurie," I said carefully. "But what she did was wrong."

"Oh, you'd be here," Pete replied, chuckling ruefully. "Maybe not in this trailer, maybe not in High Springs, maybe not with Dynamo, but you'd still be a professional trainer, Jules. You would have found a way. *No one* gets in your way."

"Laurie got me here," I said firmly. "Even if someone else could have done it, and done it better, she was my trainer. And that's what makes what she did so awful. A kid trusts a trainer. That's why you can't do it to this kid."

Pete started to protest, but I got up and went to the stove, to stir the sauce and drain the pasta. My back to him, it was easier to say, "Pete, it might not be the same to you. But it's the same to me, and I won't tolerate it if you continue to try and trick this kid into selling."

23

CROSS-COUNTRY SCHOOLING WAS just about enough to get me out of my funk. Haley Marsh's glorious spread was dotted with live oaks and offered a schooling opportunity for nearly every type of question we'd be asked at an actual event. There was a water complex with a variety of walls to jump over and banks to jump out of, a hillside dotted with logs and coops offering all sorts of angles and slopes to gallop up and down, and even a clear stream running through a shady forest to pause at, letting the horses splash and drink. We put everyone in my six-horse trailer, having cleared the storage from it early that morning, and stabled Jim Dear, Mayfair, and Regina in Haley's barn while we rode out on Barsuk and Dynamo for the first round. We'd come back for Jim and Mayfair after we'd schooled the first two horses.

Haley rode out with us on a wide bay gelding named Forest. The old horse had been one of her upper-level mounts. Now, at age twenty-one, he had white hairs mixing with the brown on his face, and his lower lip never met his top lip—it just hung down, showing a centimeter of yellow teeth and pink gums. It gave him a permanently relaxed look.

"Oh, he's been on permanent vacation his entire life," Haley said when I commented on his expression, and she leaned forward to give him an affectionate rub between the ears. "I swear, until he's focused on jumping, I do all the thinking for this horse."

"You've had Forest since he was a colt, right?" Pete asked. He found it easy to be casual with her, since he'd met her years ago at Briar Hill Farm, but I was still a little starstruck in her presence. Haley Marsh was one of the good ones, a rider I could honestly say I wanted to be just like when I grew up.

"Yes, I got him as a two-year-old and did all his training," Haley said. "My first big-time horse! You have to make your own, you know. I really believe that. Buying someone else's work won't get you to the top."

Someone should tell that to anyone thinking of buying Mickey, I thought bitterly.

"I hope you're wrong," Pete said, grinning. "Because this horse is all her handiwork." He pointed down, indicating Dynamo.

"I heard about this." Haley glanced at me, and I thought I saw admiration in her gaze. I sat up a little straighter. "Whatever it takes, right?"

I nodded. "That's right."

"Let's go jump some fences," she said, letting Forest walk past us and take the lead. Dynamo and Barsuk fell in behind her, heads bobbing. Back in the barn, Jim Dear whinnied after us, but the others were quiet, happy with their hay even in unfamiliar surroundings.

Out in the spring sun, a gentle breeze playing around us, the world started to make sense again. Hoofbeats, and a flying mane, and the sound of a horse blowing with every stride—this was my element. I listened to Haley's suggestions as I gathered up Barsuk for the fences, jumping two or three at a time before circling back to her side to watch Pete take a turn on Dynamo. The horses were happy to be out in open fields for the first time since we moved to High Springs, and it was easy to let them stretch their legs, to give in when they pulled and asked for more running room. Haley was full of praise for both horses.

"You're on the right track with these two," she said as we walked back toward the barn, three across. Forest had been allowed to jump a few small logs and he swung his head with the same swagger as the other two geldings. Despite arthritis and age, he was still an event horse, too. "I wouldn't take off any more time, though. Keep them going through May."

I nodded. May was when eventing in Florida slowed from a drizzle to a drought. If we kept our heads down and competed every few weeks from now until then, we'd be able to take off June and July without feeling like we were falling behind again. Dynamo would move up to Advanced with Pete, and maybe he'd find another horse by then, too.

Rogue, I supposed, but there was always a chance some other horse would pop up.

Either way, I'd get Dynamo back for the fall, and at least that part of my heart would be mended.

Haley sent two grooms over to hose off our horses while we got the next two saddled. Regina watched from her stall, probably wondering why she wasn't being included in the cross-country fun after we'd put her in a trailer and dragged her over here. "You would have hated being home alone, sweetie," I told her.

She pinned her ears at me.

"Pete, your mare needs you," I told him, and he went over to give her some attention. Regina loved one human. This horse switch would never have worked if the shoe was on the other foot and I needed an Advanced ride.

Haley stood nearby, holding Forest's reins while she waited on us. She watched Pete disappear into Regina's stall and then looked at me. "Is that mare coming back?"

"I don't know. I hope so."

"You're taking your horse back, aren't you?"

I nodded.

"Good," she said. "He's a nice horse for Pete, but I can see how he matches up with you."

Haley had just spent the past hour making me feel pretty good about my riding, and so I finally felt comfortable enough to ask the thing that had been on my mind since we'd set off this morning. "Have you heard anything about my horse Danger Mouse being for sale?"

Her eyes widened. "No. Is that why you didn't bring him today?"

So they hadn't told anyone yet. At least, they hadn't shopped him to Haley yet. But I could appreciate that Mickey's absence from my barn was still being kept quiet. When word got out, I'd know for sure that I'd lost him for good.

"We're working on it," I said.

"Well, good luck," Haley said. "But to me, the best thing you can do is own your own horse. Get a syndicate to help you if you must, but don't believe the hype about having a stable of wealthy owners. They are more unpredictable than the horses."

I was learning that. "Thanks," I said, and took Jim Dear out to the mounting block, reflecting that although he wasn't my top choice, at least sweet little Jim was mine, free and clear.

Rise and shine," I called to Pete the next morning. "Literally, because we overslept."

"Did we oversleep, or did I get out of bed and shut off our alarms so we wouldn't have to get up this morning?"

I smiled at him and tugged the duvet down to the trailer floor. Unperturbed, he snatched up his fleece robe and pulled it over himself. "This has to be the last cold morning. It's March already."

"I think it's going to be over eighty degrees by the end of the weekend."

"So, on cross-country day?"

"Probably."

It was Friday, time for last-minute spa preps before the event on Saturday and Sunday, but we had to wait for the sun to warm up the dry air before we could get going with any bathing plans. At least the blankets had kept the horses from getting too filthy last night.

"Any of you going to the event this weekend will be wearing rugs tonight and tomorrow night, even if it's a million degrees out," I announced to the crowd at large as we dumped feed. "We don't have Lacey or Becky to help us anymore, so this is a shoestring show. No grooms, no extra bathing."

"She's right," Pete added. "I'm not giving anyone a bath half an hour before we're expected in the dressage ring." And he gave Barsuk, who liked to decorate his dappled coat with green-and-brown manure patches, a hard look.

We spent the morning on quick tune-up rides, schooling each horse in the dressage movements that tripped them up the most—with Dynamo, it was transitions between collection and extension; with Jim Dear, it was straight lines. He seemed to have been born crooked, I thought with exasperation, trotting him up one more imaginary center line with my legs aching from trying to anticipate his next wobble left or right and moving to straighten him out before his hooves followed his spine.

"This would be easier with an actual dressage arena," Pete pointed out, watching me push him into a square halt in the near-enough center of the ring. "A round jumping ring is not helping you teach him about straight lines and squared-off turns."

"It's one of those things you never really think about until you're faced with the problem," I agreed. The outdoor jumping ring at High Springs had gently curving corners, like many others. They were safer for cantering horses and riding lessons, but dressage horses were asked to go deep into corners and then bend their spines tightly to turn through them, like cars turning on a city street.

Without the guidance of a rail, it was hard to teach such an unnatural concept to novice horses like Jim Dear.

"The *next* place will have a dressage ring," Pete muttered.

There was just enough time after riding to give them soapy baths and do some quick trims of ears, fetlocks, and bridle paths before we headed to our afternoon jobs.

"Any updates from Lindsay?" Pete asked as we grabbed sandwiches in the trailer.

I thought back to the most recent text conversation we had. I was still begging her for reassurances; she was still saying she was on top of it.

"She seems to have a secret plan to push through a purchase without Eileen knowing it's me."

"A secret, evil plan?"

"If that's what it takes. I'll talk to her this afternoon, she has a lesson."

"Who would have thought a sixteen-year-old would save the day?"

"If she really does, I'm going to hire her as a working student. I can't let a girl like that get away."

"Oh, Jules." Pete regarded me with mock sorrow. "Surely she deserves better than working for *you*."

Lindsay's secret plan, it turned out, was to cut me out of the deal. At least, my name.

"We're not raising *you* the money anymore," she explained over her shoulder. She was grooming William before her lesson. I leaned on the wall and watched her work with him, noting the way she responded to his slightest twitch or tail swish, immediately amending whatever she was doing to please him. "We are raising money to buy the horse. I took your name off all the copy. And the accounts."

"The copy?"

"The copy—the *words*. You're out of the emails, the website, everything. Control-F, 'Jules Thornton,' delete." She knocked off the dirty curry comb against the wooden wall, leaving behind concentric ovals of matted hair. William clearly thought Florida winter was over. "Control-F means the *Find* command on a *computer*," she explained, emphasizing her words as if speaking to a toddler.

"I know that," I protested.

"Anyway, we're strictly in the Danger Mouse business these days."

"You think Eileen's going to buy that?"

Lindsay grinned and picked up a hot-pink body brush. It glowed against her slinky black riding top, matching the fringe of her bangs. The teal hadn't lasted long. "We're going to raise so much money, she'll forget you ever existed. She and Carrie both will be falling over themselves to accept our offer. And if they ask who we're going to put on him, we'll just say we haven't finalized our plans yet. Just wait and see. The money's still going to come in."

I let my head rest against the wooden wall behind me and closed my eyes.

"What makes you think that? Seems to me if people don't know I'm involved, they have less reason to buy the horse."

"People will like it even better now that it's a conspiracy." She knocked dirt, dust, and loose hair into the atmosphere with obvious relish. It was nice to see Lindsay enjoying horses again. "So if everyone can keep their mouths shut . . . we'll buy your horse without your help."

If everyone kept their mouths shut! I could've cried. I could've laughed. I definitely could've done both at once. Lindsay had deftly taken over the campaign, turning it from "buy Jules her horse" to "buy a nice eventer for ourselves, why don't we?" A great idea . . . if only horse people were well-known for *hating* gossip and *never* spilling secrets to the first acquaintance they ran into at the feed store—or to those human gossip pollinators, farriers and vets, driving hundreds of miles a day and carrying away bits of stories with them, spilling a little more of every tale that brushed them at each new barn.

"Jules! Jules! Jules!" The voice was urgent.

My eyes flew open. I whipped around, expecting some sort of horse emergency, blood and guts everywhere, or broken tack at the very least, but just saw Jordan, sans horse, running up the aisle, her cheeks flushed with embarrassment or excitement, her book bag banging at her hip. She'd just gotten dropped off, by the looks of it. What could she possibly have to say to me that required yelling down half the barn when she hadn't even passed her horse's stall yet?

"Good Lord, you scared me," I told her. "What on earth do you want?"

Jordan stopped in front of me and hesitated, shifting her weight from one dusty paddock boot to the other. Her eyes twitched from me to Lindsay and back again. Finally, I obliged her silent request, shoving off the wall and heading down the aisle, Jordan at my heels.

"What?" I hissed as soon as we were a few stalls down from the crossties.

"I just wanted to tell you we donated," Jordan whispered, her cheeks even more pink now. "I know the website says it's to purchase a share of Mickey, but it's so you can keep riding him, right?"

"How did you even find out about that?"

"It was all over Facebook," she said. "Haven't you seen it? Anyway, it *is* for you, right?" Jordan's face turned anxious. "We did the right thing, didn't we?"

"It's for me." I looked back down the aisle, where William's big warmblood head was nodding from the crossties. Lindsay ducked under the closest rope, smiled at me, and disappeared again. I shook my head. I didn't know why she was doing this—maybe just because she liked to win—but I owed her. And I'd owe everyone if it all went down in my favor . . . I'd owe them so much I didn't know how I'd begin to deal with the pressure. But payback was a problem for another day. "Thanks, Jordan."

When I came home from teaching, Pete was finishing putting rugs on everyone for the night. The weather was less chilly, and would be back to the regularly scheduled Florida programming tomorrow, with temperatures up in the eighties, but horse show prep decreed these horses had to stay clean tonight, and stay clean they would.

"How did it go?" he asked as I slipped out of the truck. He

only meant my evening of riding lessons, but somehow it felt like more. I busied myself with luxuriating in Marcus's greeting for a moment, kneeling down and presenting my cheek for sniffing and one lick (the maximum I allowed, and only because he liked it so damn much), so I wouldn't have to answer right away.

"It went," I said finally, standing up and disentangling myself from Marcus. "Lindsay took my name off the website and the emails, but some people know I'm still involved. Jordan came up and told me her family was buying in specifically to help me out. So I guess . . . I don't know, Pete. I guess they're going to try and buy him and then put me on him. But I'm afraid it won't work if my name's off the deal. It was supposed to be this emotional thing, trying to keep a partnership together, look how great we've done and look how much better we can do in the future . . . and instead it's just buying into a horse. One more horse in a world stuffed with horses."

I leaned over the closest stall wall and looked at the horse within. Regina lifted her head and glared at me, to let me know *she* was not just one more horse.

"My apologies," I told her, putting a hand to her neck. She pinned her ears and shook her head at me, but I lingered by her stall anyway. Something about her had changed. "Her bandage is off," I said slowly, realizing her forelegs were bare below the knee for the first time in months. They looked hard and tight and clean, except for the arch of black scarred skin and scattered white hairs where she'd been cut by the wire. Her hoof was in one piece, with just a ripple to betray where the crack in the coronet had been.

"That part is finally over," Pete said, his voice weary instead of triumphant. "So now we see. Either she holds up to light work, or she doesn't and we have a broodmare. I'll start her on walks in the next couple of weeks, probably once Penny Lane is ready to head up north and I have more time."

"I'm happy for you, Regina," I told the liver chestnut mare, and she pinned her ears again, looking more like an adder than a horse. I backed away from her stall before she got more serious and removed part of my face.

"She's very happy too," Pete assured me. "As you can see."

It would be so good to have Regina in training again, I thought wistfully. Pete needed his big horse back . . . even if getting her back into eventing condition would take at least until autumn. If she could stay sound.

"So, soon we'll all be back on our own horses, if everything goes well," Pete said, echoing my thoughts.

"I guess so."

"You don't sound very sure."

"Who can be sure of anything anymore?"

"That's true." Pete looked at the horses for a moment, the smooth lines of their backs beneath their green-and-blue plaid blankets. Their heads, of course, were buried in hay, out of sight. "Well, everything's done out here. Do I smell chicken or is that just wishful thinking?"

"Actually yes, you do!" I retrieved a big plastic bag from the truck, once again achieving Marcus's undivided attention along the way. "Publix fried chicken, potato salad, cowboy beans, rolls, and sweet tea. Compliments of Lindsay's mom, who is very excited about Lindsay's new lack of free time, and also that I'm handling this big class project for her by being the subject."

"Oh, hell yes," Pete moaned, pretending to stumble to his knees. "We're going to eat this for days."

We watched TV on Pete's laptop and set about destroying the chicken. I went at a crunchy, greasy thigh while Pete demolished an entire breast, then started plowing through the potato salad while

I concentrated on carbs for a little while, dabbing two Hawaiian sweet rolls directly into the margarine tub.

"It's going to be a good event this weekend," Pete said eventually, putting a big spoonful of cold cowboy beans on his plate.

I nodded. "I'm almost too tired to think about it with everything that's been going on, but at the same time it feels like we'll be getting back to our real lives."

"Maybe we shouldn't have taken so much time off."

"Well, it's done now. Game back on, until we move again."

"About that . . ." Pete poured more sweet tea into our glasses. There was enough sugar in each ounce to keep me up all night, but it was too good to bother worrying about right now. "Have you heard back from anyone? Like Grace?"

"About a job?" I hated the idea of working for anyone else, but if we were going to have a barn . . . "Not yet," I said. "I don't know what Grace is going to do."

"Shame," Pete said. "I thought her moving up here might be our best shot at moving into a proper farm again."

"Maybe." I ate another roll. I was becoming all bread. I would be Jules, the Carbohydrate, and I would die happy. "But I think that if Grace buys a place up here it will be a downsize, anyway. She won't need us. She has Anna to be her manager, besides."

"So, no room for us?"

I shook my head. "I think Grace was a dead end. I shouldn't even have brought it up, to be honest."

Pete started to reply, but his phone buzzed, cutting off his words. "Hang on, this is Rick," he said, picking it up. "Hey! Rick! Just eating dinner, no problem—" He slipped from behind the table as he spoke, and went out the door into the night.

Marcus looked up at me, and then at Pete's plate.

"Why not," I said, and pulled a decent-sized chunk of meat from the chicken Pete had abandoned, handing it over to Marcus. "At least you don't take phone calls during dinner."

I picked up my own phone and started scrolling aimlessly through Instagram, looking at other people's horses, other people's dogs, other people's barns. One thousand equestrian accounts on my Instagram and all our lives appeared so similar, they could have been interchanged without anyone noticing. I didn't know if this was reassuring or depressing.

The minutes passed slowly, and I got tired of looking at other people's versions of my life. I'd paused the show we'd been watching, but when Pete didn't come back in what I considered a polite amount of time, I turned it back on. He could finish it on his own time, I thought. I switched from sweet tea to beer.

A half hour had gone by before Pete came back inside, his face drawn and his eyes worried. I hit Pause again. "What happened?"

"Just a lot of talk." He sat down and went back to his cold chicken as if nothing had happened.

"About Rogue?"

"We did discuss Rogue, yes."

"And? Did you at least think about what I told you yesterday?"

"I told him I'm keeping my nose clean." Pete sighed. "I'm giving the kid a lesson on her horse next week. We're going to figure this out once and for all. Either she agrees she can learn to ride him and we fix the problem, or she decides it's too much and she sells him to us."

"You're doing the right thing," I said, feeling the insufficiency of my words. He was risking losing the horse he wanted so badly because I told him it would upset me. I hadn't realized what a big deal that would be until this moment, but now I could see Pete was making a professional and emotional call based entirely on me. I wondered if I'd do the same thing for him. "It will work out in the end." ·

"I hope so," Pete sighed, stretching out his legs. "It doesn't usually, though. Anyway, he didn't care that much about Rogue. That was all me."

I looked at him. You didn't spend half an hour outside on the phone, with a chilly wind blowing, while dinner grew cold on the table, talking about dropping the ball on purchasing a horse the caller didn't really want. He avoided my gaze, studiously rummaging through what was left of the chicken, trying to decide which piece he wanted. "So what's *actually* going on?"

"Christ, Jules," Pete sighed, shaking his head. "What do you think? Exactly what you said was going to happen. He heard about a nice horse on the market and wants in before the word really gets out there."

I had picked up a roll, but now I put it down. I stared at Pete.

Pete's gaze met mine. "He wants to buy Mickey."

24

I WAS OUTSIDE again before he had a chance to say anything else, Marcus hard at my heels. It was a testament to my dog's loyalty that he'd so quickly abandoned the prospect of more chicken in order to follow me, and I leaned down to give his ears a quick rub without slowing my strides. "Thanks, buddy," I told him. "I need a friend like you tonight."

The shed row was dark, but I could hear the sounds of teeth grinding hay and tails swishing pointlessly against nylon rugs, making sight unnecessary. I ran my hands along the stall guards until I came to the third one and slipped underneath the cotton webbing. In a moment I had my forehead pressed against Dynamo's warm neck, his copper mane scratchy against my skin. I wrapped my arms around him for dear life.

"I gave you to Pete and it's been the longest winter of my life," I told him, my voice hushed against his bulk. Those smooth muscles I'd worked so hard to bring to life, that swan's neck curve I'd conditioned and sculpted out of a solid lump of hard gristle. "Now he thinks he's going to have Mickey, too? It's too much, Dyno. It's too much. They have to stop asking this of me."

"No one is asking anything of you." Pete's voice cut through the darkness, hard and angry. "You didn't wait one second. You didn't stop to ask me what I told him. You assumed the worst and ran away."

"You're not going to turn him down, Pete. You *just* said you're going to stop chasing Rogue. I thought you were doing it for me. But I can read between the lines." I didn't bother lifting my head from Dynamo's neck, and he shifted anxiously. I knew I'd look ridiculous hanging on to him if he decided to take a few steps toward Pete. I loosened my grip on his neck, hoping he'd steady and go back to his hay. "You'd be an idiot not to take Mickey. But it's not fair and it's not right and I'm not okay with it and—"

"I couldn't possibly take him," Pete said harshly. "I can't believe you'd think that of me. And I told that to Rick. I told him Mickey was your horse and there was no way it could be otherwise. I said he should buy Mickey for *you*."

"And what did he say to that?" He hadn't said he'd do it, or Pete would've led with that good news.

Pete was silent.

"That good, huh?"

"It's not important, but he said we'd shared horses before, so he didn't see how this was different."

This was different because one was a gift from my heart, I thought, and one was taken from me.

Dynamo grew tired of my hanging off his neck and started to take a lap around the stall, forcing me to let go and listen to his blanket rustle in the darkness. When I looked up, I could see Pete's silhouette as he looked in at me, the orange glow of the light over the trailer casting him into blackness. The shape of him was all there, but I couldn't see his face. With the shadows blanketing his features, Pete was just another man who'd gotten an opportunity denied me by the boys with the money.

"Sometimes I resent you more than I love you," I said suddenly.

"I know," Pete replied, his voice resigned.

"And you're okay with that?"

"I just keep thinking that someday it will be better. For both of us. And you won't have to resent me anymore. I keep waiting."

I nodded, forgetting it was too dark to matter. Dynamo came back to my side and went back to nosing through his hay. I put out a hand to touch him, then stopped. I ducked out of the stall again. "If you had Mickey, he'd be in our barn."

"Don't."

"I'd know he was safe."

"It's not what you want."

"It might be . . ."

"Trust me, Jules." Pete slid an arm around my shoulder, drew me close to him. "For both our sakes, you don't want this."

I'd gone outside without my phone, and when I went back in, there were a few messages from Lindsay on the screen. I opened the app and read through them silently. Then I started to laugh. *Hard.* Enough that Pete, escorting Marcus back inside, gave me his oh-God-she's-cracking-up face.

"I'm not crazy," I assured him, choking on my own giggles. "I don't think. Read these."

He took my phone cautiously and scrolled through the messages. The eyebrow went up. "Everyone at the barn wants to go to the event with you?"

"They're not even my students. Well, aside from Lindsay and Jordan and one or two others. They're Rosie's. And that hunter trainer who comes out on Saturdays." I didn't mention the group lesson I'd taught a week ago. I took the phone back and looked at the messages again, reading the ending aloud.

We really want to see what eventing is all about, Lindsay had typed, with such attention to writing out full words and using actual punctuation, she must be serious. *Everyone is ready to do something new. There will be about a dozen of us if everyone actually shows up. What do you think?*

"What do you think, she says, like I even have time to say no. This is about tomorrow!"

"Well, what *do* you think?" Pete asked. He looked at me with barely concealed glee. "Are you ready to be Camp Counselor Jules?"

"I'm barely nice enough to go out in public, let alone shepherd around a group of kids while also competing. And you'll need help! I can't do it."

"You *can't* tell them no," Pete said in a mockingly shocked tone. "You'll break their little hearts. And they'll be trapped in a life of hunter rounds until they wake up one morning, sixty-five years old and never having gone beyond a cautious hand gallop in a nice, safe arena with the gate latched closed."

"Well, I can't tell them yes. I can't possibly event my two and help you with your horses as well with a load of kids following me around. Not to mention this is an event, not a hunter show. The barn area, the warm-ups, it's all way wilder and more open than what they're used to. Someone will get in the way and get hurt."

"But they're all experienced with horses. Someone can hold a horse, someone can help you with water buckets, you'll have a spare hand every time you turn around. And when it's time to concentrate, you can tell them to go the arena, watch, and learn."

I stared at him. "You're serious. You think I should say yes."

"I think you don't have a choice," Pete said. "What, you're going to disappoint a bunch of little kids who look up to you? This is your chance to be a hero, Jules. You can't resist that kind of attention. It's the Little Juleses in real life."

I looked at my phone. It had gone back to the lock screen: a picture of Mickey gazing straight at the camera, his black-tipped ears pricked at me, his nostrils flared so that I could see the pink deep within. I missed him with a wave of longing that was absolutely nauseating. But for a few minutes just now, I hadn't been thinking about him at all.

"Plus, free grooming," Pete said.

That was pretty convincing. Lindsay and Jordan were old enough to help with the horses unsupervised. The other kids could be utilized for group activities like filling water buckets or wiping off tack.

And hey, maybe this kind of distraction was just what I needed—something so scary and un-Jules-like, I wouldn't have time to worry about what might have been, or what definitely wasn't to be, or what other awful things might await. "Fine," I said, and started typing a reply while Pete hooted with laughter and dug around the fridge for a beer.

Before I put my phone aside, I swiped through my camera roll and changed the lock screen photo, choosing a profile shot I'd taken a few days ago of Jim Dear. Just for my peace of mind, I told myself, admiring his kind brown eyes peeking from beneath a wispy black forelock. Not because I was giving up on Mickey.

25

SATURDAY MORNING, I found myself in a familiar setting, doing something totally unfamiliar: standing by the dressage warm-up with a gaggle of kids spilling around me. There were eight of them, all looking excited, taking in the controlled chaos surrounding them. Even Lindsay had a bright expression on her normally guarded face.

And no wonder, because there was plenty of beauty to take in. All around us, extremely fit event horses were being painstakingly shaped into elegant frames by stone-faced riders. Florida spring had come at last, with a hot dry sun gleaming in a cloudless sky overhead, and every horse gleamed with elbow grease, polishing spray, and the vigor of good health. We'd been watching Pete school Dynamo for his Intermediate dressage test, but he'd gone to the far end of the field to warm up away from the other horses, so now we were watching whoever trotted past.

The barn kids' parents had come, too, and now they didn't know what to do with themselves. They stood mostly apart, in a cluster of confused adults, looking uncertainly around them at the dozens of circling horses and black-hatted riders. The dressage warm-up—indeed, the entire event—took place in a fairly massive pasture, studded here and there with cow patties that hadn't been picked up and pulverized by the bush hog. A low ring of trees darkened the distant perimeters, but otherwise we were standing on a broad, shadeless prairie.

The dressage arenas, warm-ups, jumping arena, and the various pop-up tents and trailers required for the judges and ground jury, the greasy horse show food and show secretaries, the vendors and paramedics, had all mushroomed in the lonesome pasture's center like a medieval fair, with canvas tents flapping and straining ropes humming in a stiff March breeze. The air smelled of French fries and diesel exhaust from a nearby generator, enthusiastically pumping power to the eventing encampment.

I let them all take it in for a few minutes while I tried to decide what on earth to say about it. *This is an event,* I could say. *They come in all sizes, and on all sorts of properties, but they generally look more or less like this in the end.*

Horses, tents, and more horses.

"It must look different from a big hunter/jumper show like HITS," I said eventually, and the group nudged a little closer to listen to me. "You're used to all those barns and permanent buildings and arenas, right?" There were nods. "Since events require so much land for the cross-country course, unless it's a massive equestrian center, they usually end up on chunks of land in the middle of nowhere, like this. But it's a good atmosphere, lots of friends getting together, and all here to see what our horses can do . . ." I was babbling. I closed my mouth and let them look around again. The event itself could do the talking, I thought. They'd figure it out.

Haley Marsh trotted by on a good-looking chestnut. She waved. "I see you brought a cheering section today!" she called.

I waved back, and the kids followed suit. Now we were Haley's cheering section, too.

Across the dressage warm-up, an unremarkable stretch of grass cordoned off from the rest of the planet by PVC posts and looping white rope, Pete picked up his reins and asked Dynamo for a trot. The chestnut horse arched his neck, picked up his hind end, and bounded forward. I felt a little prickle of pride up the back of my neck. *I'd* done that.

"We don't really show on the big Ocala circuits like the other barns," Jordan volunteered from behind me. "It's too expensive. I don't think we need those fancy barns and arenas, and anyway," she added in a slightly defiant tone, "I don't think I want to just ride in hunter rings anymore."

I turned around, impressed. Jordan's cheeks were pink, but her pointy little chin was set. Behind her, the others were nodding in agreement. "So have you all decided in the first five minutes that you're going to be eventers now?"

Jordan shrugged, not willing to stick her neck out. But Lindsay spoke up. "Did we not make that clear before? We are done with boring old hunter courses! We want to gallop around and jump logs now."

"I just thought you were still thinking about it, I meant."

"Well, we thought about it. And that's why we're here." Lindsay gestured over her shoulder, toward the parents. "They need to see how safe this is before they say yes."

"Safe?" I echoed. "I can't promise that. We have an ambulance sitting next to the cross-country course all weekend."

Lindsay's mother had walked over while I was talking. "As long as it isn't chasing them around the course, like in horse racing," she said. "This one has been talking about riding racehorses, too." She gave her daughter a disapproving look.

I glanced back at Lindsay, who gave me a diabolical grin in response. "I never should have introduced you to Alex."

"I know eventing is dangerous," her mother said. "But riding horses is dangerous. I think we've all accepted that." She looked at her fellow parents. They all looked pretty resigned to their fates.

Rosie's going to kill me, I thought. "Okay," I said out loud. "Since I only have two horses to ride, this is a good day to hang around and ask questions. But if I'm busy and I don't answer you, don't worry about it, okay? We can talk about it another time."

There was a synchronized performance of head-nodding.

"We can help," Jordan offered. "If you need anything."

"Of course you can," I said with a grin. "Eight working students, a two-day event with dressage and show jumping on the same day? It's my lucky day!"

Everyone looked pumped.

By the end of the weekend, I thought, *they'll be hooked.*

Dressage took up the morning, and by the time I was wrapping up my ride on Jim Dear, Pete was already prepping Dynamo for show jumping. He was in tenth place after dressage. Not a great spot, but he was staying optimistic. A lot could happen in the jumping phases. I sent Lindsay to the warm-up arena with him, after packing a bucket with ice water, horse cookies, a damp sponge, and a granola bar.

"What's the sponge for?" she asked.

"Wipe his mouth before he goes into the arena. We want him to look fresh and neat, and Dynamo's a slobberer."

"And the granola bar?"

"If Pete gets hangry, feed it to him."

Lindsay saluted and marched off after Dynamo and Pete.

I turned to the rest of my tiny army. "It's time to get Barsuk ready for show jumping, so who wants to give Jim Dear a shower and a graze session?"

Heather and Jordan volunteered. While they led him to one of the shared hoses for a shower, I gave the rest of the crew their assignments. In a few minutes we'd assembled my jumping tack, grooming kit, and Barsuk himself, who looked startled but pleased with the crowd gathering around him. I handed Melanie my phone. "Take video and we'll post it, okay?"

Pete was back before we went over to the warm-up ourselves, Lindsay looking so triumphant she might as well have been the one in the saddle. "He's up to fifth place now," she announced.

Pete grinned and hopped down from the saddle as the kids, and some parents who had wandered over, cheered. He joined me alongside Barsuk while Lindsay took Dynamo's reins with a proprietary air and started unfastening bridle straps. "What do you think of the pit crew?" he murmured in my ear.

"Actually kind of fun," I whispered back. "And it turns out Tomeka is a world champion at getting manure stains off fetlocks, so, obviously she's hired."

Tomeka wasn't the only one with a knack for grooming. Jordan brought back an immaculate Jim Dear and stalled him with fresh hay while Heather refilled his water buckets. Lindsay had Dynamo stripped of tack and on his way to the hose before anyone thought to help her. And Tomeka armed herself with a can of cornstarch she found in my tack trunk before we took Barsuk to the warm-up arena, promising that she'd whiten his socks before we jumped our round. Melanie still had my phone, and was apparently getting footage of every move for future publicity.

I had a team!

We had a team. Lindsay marched Dynamo off to graze, and

Jordan hung back to help Pete with Mayfair, while I took the bulk of the crew to the warm-up. Parents trailed behind, bemused but willing.

I was still thinking about the novelty of all those kids helping us as I trotted Barsuk around the warm-up, taking care to stay close to the rail and allow the horses moving at a canter to have the inside of the ring. Trying to show multiple horses without help had been just one more problem at the back of my mind, and now these barn rats had appeared like magic to be our little helpers—and they were really good at it! I hoped Pete and I put in nothing but good performances for the rest of the weekend. I wanted to really sell them on eventing—because now that I had them, I knew I needed to keep them.

As Barsuk moved smoothly into a canter, I glanced at the kids in their spot along the rail. Someone was talking to them. Another trainer. I tightened my fingers on the reins without meaning to, and Barsuk tugged back, shaking his head. He was a sensitive horse, alert to my mood. *Focus on the ride,* I told myself. *No one's poaching your students.*

But what if that trainer did steal them away? I looked across the arena. The trainer was well-dressed. She bent her head to listen to their questions and nodded as she responded. Probably telling them how great they'd do in her barn. Barsuk thundered around the short side of the arena and I brought him back to a trot as I neared the cluster of children.

They looked up, and so did the trainer. I exhaled, a burst of relief along with a short laugh at how silly I was. Haley Marsh smiled at me, and raised a hand to say hello. "I was just telling them how lucky they are to be here with you and Pete," she called. "Incredible examples of how horsemen should treat their horses and each other!"

I felt myself blushing. "Thank you. That's very kind."

"Just the truth," Haley said. "You look fabulous up there, Jules. Go show these guys how it's done!"

I think we showed them how it was done.

It wasn't the best weekend for finishing scores. But everything we did was correct, and only the eventing gods could say why Jim Dear stopped at the palisade on cross-country, a jump he'd seen and jumped before without issue, and they were probably up to no good when Barsuk spooked at a jump judge sitting innocently beneath a sun umbrella by the water complex and jumped so crooked that my boot took out the pole on the right, leaving a jagged gash across the leather. Between the two of them the horses racked up more penalty points than I'd had in years, but at least they completed the event sound and happy, and the kids learned an interesting lesson about how riders don't always finish on their dressage score.

Pete had a better time of it, finishing in third place on Dynamo and winning his division on the perfect, saintly Mayfair, who never put a hoof wrong the entire weekend.

But the real winners seemed to be the kids. They figured out their roles and dug into them, making cross-country day a breeze. Jordan proved to be a thoughtful groom, taking reins of horses as they came back from competition without being asked, offering sips of water to both mounts and riders, wiping off boots and bits with a washcloth she'd discovered in a tack trunk, fetching bridles and tightening girths at just the right moment. I was ready to hire her on the spot. Lindsay took over the logistics of organizing everyone else and kept the crew hard at work skipping out stalls, fetching cold drinks, adding last-minute polish to leather, and clipping numbers onto headstalls and breastplates. When I came out of the cross-country dripping with sweat—the promised heat had arrived—Tomeka was waiting with a cold Diet Coke, a roll of mints, and a wet towel. "For your neck," she explained, taking Jim's reins in one hand and offering up the towel with the other. "You cool off, I'll walk the horse."

I dropped the reins, settled the towel in the gap between my helmet's harness and my safety vest's top-most panel, and took a long, thankful gulp of fizzy soda. Jim's breath was coming fast—the heat had taken it out of him, too—and when I opened my eyes again, I saw that as we were walking, Tomeka had unbuckled both his flash noseband and his cavesson, and was offering him a mint. "Thank you," I breathed.

Tomeka smiled up at me. "No problem," she said cheerfully. "Just doing what I'd like someone to do for me after a hard ride."

In all my time as a working student, and all the time I'd spent teaching my own students, I'd never once thought of an event groom's vocation in such simple terms. "That makes a lot of sense."

"It usually does," she said simply. "About most things."

We drove home under blue skies on Sunday afternoon, Pete's blue and yellow ribbons fluttering on the dashboard. The kids who had made it out for day two—Tomeka, Jordan, Lindsay, Ricky, and Maisey—had all left before us, dragged protesting into minivans and sedans by their exhausted parents. But despite their sweaty disbelief that they'd spent two days in the middle of nowhere, watching their kids help two trainers show horses in a competition they'd never seen before, every single parent had said thanks, and looked as if they'd meant it.

They thanked *me* for all the help I'd gotten this weekend. This, I thought, was why trainers amassed vast quantities of students. It wasn't because they enjoyed teaching so much that they needed to fill as much of their time as possible with riding lessons. It was because eventing didn't just take a village . . . it took a damn army.

"This was fun," I remarked, sliding off my paddock boots and wiggling my toes in relief. "A really nice way to kick off the rest of our season. Some lessons learned, sure, but fun."

"And you have enough new students now to fill up an entire week." Pete grinned at me. "Dreams do come true, my sweet."

I stuck out my tongue at him. "They won't all come ride with me. What about the two that didn't come back today? Yesterday must have been plenty."

"They both had previous commitments or they would have been back for day two. I asked."

"You're so nosy," I scolded, but I looked out the window to hide my smile.

They all wanted to come back, did they? Well, wasn't that something?

I flipped my thumb up my phone screen and checked the blogs for writeups on the event, curious to see if anything interesting had happened that I'd missed while I was riding or helping Pete or keeping an eye on the kids. I skimmed an *Eventing Chicks* post listing the winners, noticing a cute picture of Dynamo trying to eat his ribbon as a steward tried to fix it to his headstall and screenshotting it for future use, and then spotted a sidebar link to a previous article with a headline that made my breath catch.

Your Next Superstar: Unicorn Favorite Danger Mouse on the Market!

It felt really *real* now. It was one thing to make some posts asking people to help keep him in my barn. It was another to tell the world that my horse was really gone. On the market. This wasn't about Jules saving Mickey anymore. This was about who was going to get him next.

I clicked so fast I hit a Rockwell Brothers ad above the link instead, and then had to swipe the screen frantically to get back, let the page reload, and scroll down to the link again. When I finally got to the story, my heart was pounding so hard my vision was swimming. Would it say where he was? Would there be any info on potential buyers? All weekend, I'd wondered if anyone there had been approached about Mickey—maybe someone was watching me ride my other horses, feeling bad for me, even as they planned to buy my former ride. But apparently not, if Carrie and Eileen were breaking their media blackout to let the world know he was available.

Little white pony outgrown? Rejoice and get out your check-book, because the ultimate unicorn is looking for a new rider. We don't know why Jules Thornton is out of Danger Mouse's saddle after the duo's impressive winter season ended abruptly after Glen Hill Farm's winter three-day event. But we do know he's for sale—privately. What does that mean? It means you're not going to see an ad on our classified page with his price, that's for sure. But if you have the right connections and maybe pass a credit check, you can visit Danger Mouse at Shannon Mulligan's Thousand Oaks Farm in Ocala. And if you go, please send us pics! We're all missing our favorite mouse.

I sighed. Was it good news? Yes, and no. Yes, I knew where he was now—Thousand Oaks was an impossibly fancy private eventing barn not far from Briar Hill. Plus, no mention of Eileen and Carrie's decision to keep me off their horse. But he sounded expensive. That mention of a credit check was a joke, but it didn't do anything for my mood. What if the asking price was higher than even what Miss Secret Plan Lindsay could handle?

"Everything okay?" Pete asked.

"Mickey got a mention on this blog. He's at Thousand Oaks."

"Shannon's place?"

"You know her?"

Pete had always moved in more rarefied circles than I had, thanks to his famous grandfather. I watched big-name trainers from the warm-up ring and tried not to get excited if I happened to be standing next to one studying the course map before show jumping. Pete grew up going to their houses for lunch and riding their daughters' outgrown ponies for sales videos.

"She used to come over to Briar Hill when I was a teenager, before I went overseas to train. She'd bring her young horses and ride with my grandfather. He was good with babies."

"That's kind of cool."

"Briar Hill was like that while he was alive." Pete sighed and a line creased along his jaw. "Everyone came there to ride with him."

His voice wasn't quite as steady as before, and I was sorry I'd brought it up. I didn't have a thing to say in response. *I'm sorry* was a bit weird for a death that had occurred years and years ago, and *Hasn't it been a while?* was definitely wrong. Losing his grandmother, and then the farm, must have made his grandfather's passing feel like it had happened all over again. I considered several responses and then settled for placing my hand on his thigh. The tense muscle in his jaw relaxed, and we sat in silence for a few miles. The towering pines flashed by in uniform rows, flashes of golden sun bursting between them and striping the road ahead of us with a ladder-like pattern of dark and light.

"So," Pete finally said, moving on with admirable composure, "does that blog post say what they're asking for him?"

"Nope. Says he's for sale privately. I can only imagine what that could be hiding. Six figures? They couldn't possibly get that for him, could they? He's still so inexperienced." It had occurred to me that this whole mess might be traced back to someone suggesting they'd pay an ungodly sum and giving Carrie and Eileen ideas about what they might be sitting on. Did I think Mickey had a shot at international competition? Of course. But he was untried at the upper levels. "They're being unrealistic if that's the case."

"Saying it's private doesn't necessarily mean they're asking for a lottery winner. They just don't want a ton of people who have no real intention of buying him."

"I guess." I leaned my head back on the seat and studied the endless interstate in front of us. "I just wish I knew if the Danger Mouse Project really has a chance of raising enough money for him. Since Lindsay took total control of it I don't know what's going on. But if they buy him . . ."

"If they buy him, everything's solved," Pete finished for me.

"Unless there's something in the sales contract about not putting me on him."

He looked at me suddenly, then shifted his gaze back at the road. "They wouldn't."

I shrugged. "We're talking about horse people, Pete."

He nodded and suddenly seemed to need to concentrate very hard on the road. We finished the trip in silence.

There was simply nothing else to say, after all. The worst of behaviors could be explained, and expected, when you just remembered you were dealing with horse people.

26

ANOTHER WEEK PASSED with little change in our lives. The days grew warmer and longer. The brown pasture began to sprout little tendrils of green, hopeful blades pushing through the dry brown thatch of last year's grass. The horses got a few days off after the event, and came in from a full day's turnout with sweaty flanks and flared nostrils from the heat of the strengthening sun. I taught my usual riding lessons and fielded more questions from the kids' parents about eventing—would they need new tack, how long would it take for them to be competitive, that sort of thing.

Pete went to Penny Lane one evening to teach Rogue and his owner, and came back with no more answers than before he went. "She did fine on the flat," he said when I pushed him for an update. "And she didn't get unseated when he bucked after jumps."

"You told her he likes going cross-country, though, right?"

"Yes, and she said she wasn't interested in riding outside of the arena." He shrugged. "I guess we'll see."

"And what about Mickey? Is Rick going to make a bid?"

"Rick's on vacation in Costa Rica until next week. We'll talk when he gets back."

He should stay there forever, I thought.

By Thursday we were back to riding everyone, hacking them out with a long, easy trot up the hill to High Springs Equestrian Center, and walking home as the pine shadows stretched across the driveway. Pete had a rare evening off from Penny Lane, which felt like a preview of our life to come, as the winter show circuit ended and the hunter/jumper trainers started to pack up their Florida operations and head north. They had a migratory life, following the show circuit north, working their way to upstate New York by summer's end.

We managed to agree that it was nice to have some time off, without bringing up the growing concern that yet another income stream was trickling to its natural end. We were both just trying to relax, as if we weren't spending all our time out of the barn on our phones, sending out emails and looking for a property that would hire us as trainers and managers, saving us from the mess we had gotten ourselves into with this far-flung little hideaway in the woods.

"I liked it here," I remarked as we rode up the lane. "I'll miss it when we do go."

"I know you did." Pete nudged Mayfair closer to Jim and put a hand on my thigh. "It was a good idea. It got us through a rough time."

We'd been living in a horse trailer and I'd lost my horse, so maybe it hadn't been the best idea. Or maybe we never could have seen this coming, and I couldn't blame myself, as much as I'd like to. "Thanks," I said gratefully, right before Mayfair snapped at Jim Dear's inquiring nose and he leaped to the side to escape her.

Up at the equestrian center, there were boarders all over the place, and I was regretting leaving our hack so late. Rosie generally did not like us riding in the arenas when they were receiving heavy use from the people who actually boarded at the barn. But she was teaching a lesson in the jumping ring and didn't have time for more than a glare at us before she got back to shouting instructions.

But it was quite a glare.

"This was a bad idea," I said, reining back Jim Dear. "We're going to get in the way."

Pete swung Mayfair in a circle around us. "We'll just stop in the barn and say hello to all your fans, and then we'll head home. It'll look like we never planned on using her arena."

I nodded in agreement, then turned as someone called my name. Lindsay was standing in the barn aisle. "Come here," she yelled. "Something to tell you."

I lifted my brows at Pete.

He trailed after us and pulled Mayfair up a few feet away, in case whatever Lindsay had to say was private. I leaned down, hoping she had something good to say about the Danger Mouse Project, but she shook her head at me. "Come into the barn. Just bring Jim along. My mom wants to talk to you guys. *Both* of you."

The barn seemed pitch-dark after the golden sunset outside. With Rosie out in the ring, no one was in charge and the assortment of barn kids hadn't thought about flipping on the overhead lights. It took a moment for my eyes to adjust to the dim aisle, and avoid colliding with the kids running back and forth between crossties and tack rooms and stalls, their horses in various states of grooming and riding prep. I spotted Ricky and Maisey, the brother-and-sister duo who rode a pair of Connemara pony crosses, bickering over a girth in the door of the boarders' tack room, and shook my head, relieved I didn't run a barn like this. It was great the kids were interested in eventing and we'd had fun over the weekend, but I still didn't see myself with a lesson barn. I didn't want them around *all* the time.

"There's my mom," Lindsay announced when we reached the far end of the barn, where a covered patio had been built into what originally would have been a set of crossties. A group of women were sitting around a metal patio table, chatting and looking at their phones. I recognized most of them from the event; these were my students' mothers. A soda machine hummed against the barn wall, but it was easy to draw a conclusion from the red plastic cups and brown bag on the table that these ladies had moved beyond Diet Coke. Lindsay's mother put down her cup and waved her phone at me. I smiled in response, then glanced back at Lindsay, utterly confused.

Lindsay grinned. "I gotta get back to William," she said, a hint of laughter in her voice, and disappeared into the barn.

Lindsay's mother stood and nodded to the others, who raised cups or phones or manicured fingers in salute, and then walked over to me.

"Jules," Lindsay's mom said. "How are you?"

"I'm fine," I said, pushing Jim Dear's head back before he ran a drooling mouth over her outstretched hand. I put my gloved hand into hers, and felt her strong grip. I tried to remember her name. In my head, she was only "Lindsay's mom." Come on, Jules, think! What was it? *Robin.* That was it. "Nice to see you, Robin. You look very professional in that suit."

She brushed imaginary hay from her very red power suit. "Very professional, but much less comfortable than I'd like. I should bring a change of clothes for evenings like this. We like to get together after work every now and then. The Horse Show Moms." She waved her hand at the women behind her, and I noticed most of them were also wearing office getups. The kind of clothes I'd never owned and hopefully never would.

"I get to wear Spandex all day," I said with a grin, gesturing to my breeches. "I know I'm lucky."

"Living the dream," Heather's mother called from behind Robin. "Why did my mom tell me I had to go to law school?"

"I wanted to be a vet," Melanie's mother said, pulling at her blazer lapel. "And I haven't been on a horse in fifteen years."

"Tell me about it! It's all about Heather and Heather's horse. Wait until she goes away to college . . . we'll see who gets that horse then."

There was a round of laughter that did not sound totally innocent to me. I realized I was in the company of at least a few ex-riders and immediately felt a strange combination of sorrow and superiority.

Robin smiled tolerantly at the banter, as if she had a point to make and not much time to make it. I decided to help her out.

"So, what can I do for you?" I asked in my professional trainer tone, and she immediately looked relieved.

"Well, to be brief," she said, "we want to lease a property and put you in charge of it."

I stared at Lindsay's mom—*Robin,* I had to call her Robin. I was an adult; we were both adults. Hanging out with teenagers and horses too much could confuse a person sometimes. "I'm not sure . . . *What?*"

She grinned, a surprisingly human gesture from a woman I was instinctively intimidated by. "A farm. Nothing too outrageous, but a barn, some paddocks, some arenas. We're going to go in together and lease a property, and we'd like you to be the manager, teach our kids, and put together a solid riding team. Since they're all eventing-crazy now, they can't get what they want here, and we"—Robin looked around at the other women and smiled—"don't want to be split up in the divorce if everyone has to find new barns. No one will have enough open stalls, so we can't all move together any other way."

I put a hand on Jim Dear's neck to steady myself. I was dizzy and I definitely wasn't hearing correctly. If I was, Lindsay's mom—

Robin—had just told me she wanted to give me a job. And that couldn't be right. Wishful thinking and hallucinations, what a combination. I looked around for a place to sit down and found a handy hay bale someone had left out. I sank gratefully onto it, feeling the tiny knives of cut hay press through my thin breeches. Robin was watching me closely; all the mothers were staring at me. I looked down at my dusty boots and concentrated on my breathing. Jim Dear, happy with this turn of events, pulled at the hay bale, chewing awkwardly with his flash noseband still fastened below the bit.

"Are you all right?" Robin asked. "We thought you were looking for a more permanent situation than that pasture down the road."

So she had really said it. "This feels very sudden," I said, for lack of anything more intelligent to contribute. A barn, students, boarders—just offered to me? How had this happened?

Robin unfolded her arms and peered at me. "Do you need a bottle of water? Something stronger?"

Jordan, passing by with her saddle over her arm, glanced at me and grinned. "I'll get her a Diet Coke."

The little devil knew just what was going on.

Still, I could really do with a Diet Coke.

Or something stronger. I glanced over at the brown bag on the table, its telltale bottleneck peeping from the top.

"Thanks," Robin called over her shoulder to Jordan before turning back to me. "See? That's just what got this started. The kids all love you. We went out to dinner after the event Saturday night and talked it over. Here's the deal. The kids want to event. And we don't want to get stuck paying the bills on horses they're bored with. So we've done the numbers and eventing is a better value than hunters, at least at the top levels. We can get through a weekend for a couple hundred bucks and call it a month. If they're showing A-circuit, they want to stay for five weeks and pay a grand a week. That's just not in the cards for any of us." She paused as Jordan reappeared, passed me a Diet Coke with a wink, and went back to tacking up her own horse. "But we do know of several farms in the area we could take out an annual lease on. And this isn't Ocala—land prices aren't sky-high here. It's not a crazy idea with enough people investing. *You* just have to pick the one you like and sign on as manager, and we'll be in business. It'll be a co-op situation."

"An eventing co-op," I said wonderingly, and took a gulp of Diet Coke. The bubbles fizzed in my throat. The chemical tang was like a tonic to my confused brain. "All of you will share ownership, or the lease. And the farm expenses," I added, making sure I wasn't somehow getting landed with those.

"And your salary," Robin said. "Doesn't that sound like a good plan?"

It sounded amazing. It sounded too good to be true.

It sounded like if they'd just offered this a few weeks ago, I'd still have Mickey—or at least a better shot at buying him.

My face must have clouded, because Robin shifted impatiently. "You don't like the idea?"

I shook my head. "No—I love the idea. It's perfect. I don't know how to thank you." I stood up on wobbly legs, to face Robin eye-to-eye. Her eyebrows were elegant slashes, turning every glance into a challenge. I thought that Robin's immense strength of will combined with Lindsay's casual genius was going to produce something powerful someday. Then I realized that if Lindsay was handling the Mickey syndication, and Robin was chairing this eventing co-op, I would owe this mother-daughter team my very career. It felt a little like having the Medici family offer to sponsor me. They were just as capable of ruining me as they were of making me.

"One condition," I said daringly. "Pete comes with me, and we have space for our horses. We need at least ten stalls."

Robin arched one weaponized eyebrow at me. "Ten?" Her voice made it clear I was pushing my luck.

"We still have some sponsors and owners, plus our own horses," I explained. I didn't want her to think we were beggars, with no one else interested in our services. "Pete has an owner actively shopping for a new upper-level horse. He has an upper-level horse coming back from stall rest later this month, and two good young horses. I have a young horse and an upper-level horse, plus there's, um . . ." I trailed off, not knowing what she knew, or any of the parents knew, about the change in direction the Danger Mouse Project had taken once Eileen had insisted I couldn't buy him.

But Robin knew exactly what I hadn't said. "We're working on the syndicate. The co-op will take that over once it's underway as well," she assured me, simultaneously informing me that a syndicate was in the works. That must be Lindsay's secret plan. "So you'll have three horses. We hadn't counted on Pete, but I see how it adds up. Lindsay wasn't exactly clear on his situation. But that's okay, because more trainers just means we can do more business. Right." She tapped a talon on the table. "Sound good, guys?"

There were nods, a few whoops, and a couple of raised cups in response.

"Perfect," Robin announced, taking it as a yes. "I'll bring this back to the board and we'll call you in a few days. We should have some properties to show you."

"Already? There's a board and everything? Before you even asked me?"

"Jules," Robin said in a fond tone, her eyes dancing. "You weren't going to say no."

They're going to own you," Grace said briskly.

"They're going to own you," Alex said doubtfully.

"They're going to own us," Pete said dubiously. "But," he added, "if they own us, at least we have someone to pay our bills."

"My thoughts exactly," I said. "So we're going to do it?"

"Was there ever any doubt?"

"Of course not."

Pete leaned over and kissed my forehead. "When do I meet our new masters?"

"It's the entire group from the event last weekend. You met them. And put their children to work."

"Well, at least they're already fans."

Robin called two days later to let us know my provisions were accepted and we were permitted ten stalls. "That takes one property out of contention," she said. "But we have three others for you to look at. This weekend?"

It was mid-March and we had events every other weekend until May. All I wanted to do on my free weekends was sleep. "That sounds perfect."

"I'll text you the address and time of the first one and we'll make a day of it."

Too small, too wooded, and just right: like Goldilocks, I surveyed the three farms placed before me and took the one I liked best.

Fifteen acres, with a long old-fashioned center-aisle barn on a hilltop, and a little cinder-block rancher right next to it. The barn was empty and cobwebbed, but I liked the solid feel of the white-painted cinder-block stalls and the airiness of the bars that replaced the upper halves of the stall fronts and adjoining walls.

The center four stalls had been enclosed—on one side, two had been adjoined to create a big tack room with lockers along each wall, and on the other there was full bath with shower, and an office. In the office, a cracked green chair from the Nixon administration showed its stuffing. The Formica desk seemed to be of equal vintage. I wondered how many mice lived in its drawers.

With all this the barn still boasted an astonishing thirty stalls: room for everyone in the co-op, plus our horses, plus more boarders in the future.

We all split up and prowled around in little groups of two or three, looking out the square windows at the surrounding fields, sloping down to the endless pine forests surrounding the farm; the white-sand arena, just right for a jumping course, which needed new fencing and weeding; the concrete-sided manure pit, which was perfectly designed for a removal service to come and scoop out regularly. We could put in a dressage arena on a flat sweep of ground near the barn, and add some cross-country fences in the fields. There was even a small paddock behind the barn just right for one horse, where Regina could go out and talk over the fence without getting into trouble with other horses.

Someone had put a lot of thought into this place, a good forty or fifty years ago, and now we'd add on to it, making it the perfect eventing factory.

And it would last, unlike my first foray into farm management. I leaned on the cinder-block wall and felt the cool strength within. This was the kind of barn that stood up to hurricanes, tornadoes, and tough recessions.

"The house is three-bedroom, two-bath, and has beautiful

views of the pastures," the real estate agent announced once we had finished murmuring to one another about the barn and fields. "You can rent it out separately if you like."

I glanced at Robin, wondering if we were still going to be living in the horse trailer. She gave me a smile in response and turned back to the realtor. "That will be the trainer's residence. Let's go in and see it."

I was afraid the house would be as dusty and cobwebbed as the barn, but luckily it was just dusty. I felt like we were walking through an empty time capsule of Old Florida—not the woodsy, pioneer-built Old Florida of Grace's little house down near Orlando, but the concrete-and-stainless-steel of midcentury rockets-and-orange-groves Old Florida. The terrazzo floors echoed back our footsteps as we walked through its long, narrow rooms and through low doorways; white walls stared down blankly and long windows with dented aluminum casings looked out on the barn and pastures. In an antique bathroom, I flicked the light switch and found myself staring at my reflection in a gold-flecked mirror, with light bulbs above it glaring like in a Hollywood dressing room.

Pete came in and laughed. "You're a star!"

"This would need to change a little."

"We can just unscrew some of the lightbulbs, bring down that wattage."

I turned and smiled at him. "This is a good house, Pete. Solid. It's literally the opposite of a horse trailer."

He leaned forward, his lips close to my ear. "Worth selling your soul for?"

I nodded, my chin bumping his shoulder. "What's left of it, anyway."

27

WE MOVED IN two weeks later, the horse show kids' trailers lining up to drop off their charges. We helped handle skittish horses as the kids led them down the ramps and into their stalls. The bedding was laid deep and the water buckets were full, the feed room was organized and the tack lockers were sparkling clean and wide open, waiting for each boarder to slide saddles into place and hang bridles from the hooks.

We'd had plenty of time to prep the barn, thanks to bad blood with Rosie. I knew we couldn't avoid the drama, but I'd still felt bad when she'd called me into the office, about twenty minutes after the first two parents pulled her aside and gave their notice.

"Get out by April first," she fumed. "And don't come up here again. No lessons, no riding, nothing."

"I'm sorry," I said.

She spun her chair around and looked out the window until I walked out of the office.

I knew she'd be cursing my name up and down at every feed store, tack shop, and horse show for the next few years. Ah, small-town horse businesses. You got used to the gossip after a while. To people like Rosie, everything was personal, even if it really, really wasn't.

The upside of my newfound free time was that I had plenty of time to get the new barn whipped into shape. Pete had a few shifts at Penny Lane to work, but otherwise we went all out on beautifying and horse-proofing the property.

We rented a power washer and took turns blasting the spiderwebs and old birds' nests from atop the rafters and cinder-block walls. We wandered the fences with hammers and nails, tacking up loose boards. Robin presented us with a debit card attached to the co-op's brand-new bank account, and we bought buckets, feed mangers, brooms, manure forks, wheelbarrows, crossties, and dozens and dozens of double-ended snaps.

It was the most fun I'd ever had, putting that barn together. Even its few drawbacks were easily managed. The low-slung roof could have been a liability in hot weather, but the big windows and open upper halves of the stalls let the daily breeze wash through the barn and push the heat of the day on through. The cinder-block walls could be dangerous for any horse who kicked, but Pete had visited a citrus packing house near Ocala that was wrapping up for the season, and picked up rolls and rolls of used conveyor belt. We'd bolted those to the walls of several stalls, guiding the horses who were known kickers to those boxes as they arrived. The rubber padding wasn't as shock-absorbing as purpose-made stall mats, but it still put a nice buffer between hooves and wall.

And the house! I fell hard for the house. We took one of the trailers down to Ocala to get our things out of storage, and soon we were all set up. White cinder block and low-slung like the barn a few dozen feet away, the house had an Old Florida sensibility I couldn't get enough of. The louvered windows on the back door reminded me of the condos in my grandparents' neighborhood along the Gulf Coast, built before you needed to be a billionaire to have a beachfront view. (The sale of that condo had funded, in part, the inheritance that had gotten me to Ocala in the first place.)

Of course, we weren't actually in Ocala. We were still up in Alachua County, closer to Gainesville and the University of Florida, with all its students and keggers and football games, than we were to the Horse Capital of the World, where we'd thought we'd spend our lives among our own kind. But we were close enough.

And we had clients who wanted us here.

The first night in April was cool, breezy, and moonlit, and we had our own house and our own farm, and for a few rare moments, everything felt like it was coming up Jules.

The windows of our little house were still uncovered. There'd been no blinds left behind by previous residents, and we didn't have any curtains of our own. I liked the bare windows. There wasn't anyone nearby to see in, and I'd lived in deep country long enough not to fear that there were strangers lurking in the darkness, peering inside. I leaned my forehead against the cold glass of the living room window and gazed past my reflection to admire the barn. A few aisle lights stayed on all night, and under their dim blue glow I could watch the horses as they moved restlessly around their new stalls, pushed their heads out of their open windows, pricked their ears at the scuttling night noises of rodents and ghosts. Barn Kitty stalked past, tail held high, as she made her evening rounds. The oak tree in the front yard creaked in the northwest wind, scraping its branches along the metal barn roof. The sound was like nails on a chalkboard, but I loved it; it reminded me of so many other barns, so many other oak trees, so many other chilly spring nights in the brief calm before summer.

So many other horses, shuffling through their shavings and

dragging their hay piles around their stalls, waiting for summer nights spent outside, grazing in lush pastures.

Well, summer would arrive soon enough, and we would have good grass here; the soil was strong and rich. I could tell by that granddaddy oak just a few feet away, spreading its branches over the barn and house. I could tell by the thick thatch of dry brown grass, already struck through with little spikes of green, carpeting the slowly wakening pastures. Good grass and good breezes. They'd be so happy, all my lovely horses. They would love it here so much.

"I love it here," I said, my words bouncing backward from the glass at my lips, and behind me I heard Pete chuckle in acknowledgment.

He was rummaging through boxes we'd brought up from our storage unit, putting books on the low shelves he'd set under the windows on the other side of the room. I loved these old-fashioned windows, their Old Florida feel. They were set a little too high on the walls for modern tastes, but stretched the length of the room, with old metal frames that pinged when you flicked them. With the living room spanning the central width of the little house, they would keep the space constantly flooded with light, even on cloudy days.

I felt a happy sense of anticipation of all the hot afternoons when I would retreat to this oasis, settle into our own deep-cushioned couch, and slip one of those training manuals off the bookcase for inspiration and rejuvenation. With the barn just a few steps away, snagging a few minutes to refresh myself when the weather turned oppressive would be simple . . . and so much better than an air-conditioned tack room.

Plus, I realized, there'd be an army of children here all summer to help with barn chores.

"Why don't you come over here and sit with me?"

I turned around. Pete had finished emptying his boxes and was settling onto the couch, tipping a bottle of something purple-red over two wineglasses—also salvaged from our storage unit. I recognized the wide bowls and slim stems from the china cabinet in the dining room back at Briar Hill. Stemware: the sort of thing grandparents left you, even if they never really thought about leaving them to you.

"You really took everything out of the house, didn't you?" I observed with amusement, settling down beside him. "Did you leave anything for the estate people?"

"If they want them, they can come and get them." He turned his dark blue eyes on mine, and I saw the tired lines sagging around them. I might have fallen in love with our new farm, but Pete was not going to forget Briar Hill anytime soon.

And if I really let myself dig around in my own thoughts too much, I'd have my own sorrows to distract me.

It had been three weeks since they'd taken Mickey. The chances were solid that several buyers had been out to try him. There was even a distinct possibility he'd been put under contract. The vet could be scheduled to come out and do a prepurchase exam this week.

Tomorrow. Yesterday. I didn't know where Lindsay's project was in raising the money to buy him, and I was afraid to ask. If I said anything, I might jinx the whole scheme.

There was one bright side, I reflected. With Lindsay running things so expertly, I'd never needed that meeting with Amanda to talk about syndication.

Pete handed me my glass with grave ceremony. The dark red depths of the wine looked gloomy beneath the blue-white light our cheap IKEA torch lamps were pouring onto the low ceiling.

I supposed wine, even grocery store wine, did not like being surrounded by the cheapest furnishings possible.

But the wine was still pretty, the color of blackberry juice when it pools at the bottom of a bowl after the berries have been devoured, still warm from the sun. I could almost taste those summer flavors on my tongue, plucked from the side roads and riding trails around my childhood barn. I'd gathered berries from the prickly bushes until my fingers were stained purple. It felt like a hundred years ago, when I was a kid riding bareback on a half-wild pony, snatching a few moments to myself before the clock called me back to barn duty. I'd always been working. I'd always *be* working. I'd cast my lot when I was just a child, and so had Pete. But even with endless labor and horses always needing more and more attention, every now and then you could lean down from the saddle and pluck a few berries.

We clinked glasses solemnly, and the rims hummed for a moment, competing for our attention with the constant rasping of the oak tree branches outside.

"To new beginnings," Pete said after a moment, when the glasses had ceased their singing. He looked dissatisfied. "That sounds kind of dumb. It's been done to death."

"To getting it right this time," I suggested.

He nodded. "To getting it right . . . this time."

We both took sips, both puckered our mouths a bit, both plunged bravely on toward a celebratory tipsiness we thought we deserved—or maybe were obligated—to feel. Cheap wine wasn't as good as blackberries, nor did new beginnings really cover all the emotions I was feeling. In that whirlwind of twelve days—yes, it had only been twelve days from looking at the property to moving in—I hadn't had a moment to think about Mickey or Eileen or Grace or Gallant Rogue, things which had been of such dire importance before. I'd barely even talked to Alex since I'd told her about the offer, although she'd been excited to have a nice new place to bring Tiger for lessons. And I'd forgotten I was mad at Pete for reconnecting with Amanda. The world had retreated. I already regretted how quickly it would barge back into our lives.

"What's going on?" Pete asked, settling deeply into the couch and holding his glass up to the light. "You look more preoccupied than a person getting sloshed on cheap wine should look."

"All the things we've been ignoring."

"The truck insurance coming due?"

"Shit, really?"

Pete smiled mirthlessly. "Oh, that wasn't it?"

"I'm worrying about Mickey, and you know it."

"Yeah," he said. "I do."

I missed him so much. I felt his loss every time I walked up the barn aisle and looked into each stall, peering through the bars to check on the horses that were left after two years of turmoil had stripped the others away, one by one. I loved them even more because they'd been with us through all that drama.

It was still shocking to me that I was down to two horses. Dynamo and Jim Dear were all that was left, and a year ago I'd had a full barn. Now I'd do anything for these two, who had survived everything my bad luck had thrown at me. I wasn't sure I could even bear to sell Jim Dear now. It had been a wrench to sell the others last year, even though they'd paid my bills for quite a while. When you have horses with you through hurricanes and high water, you get to loving them, even if loving horses was once the worst mistake you thought you'd ever make.

"I won't let Rick buy him," Pete said softly.

"Thanks," I said. But if the syndicate didn't come through,

I still wasn't sure I wouldn't prefer Mickey in our barn, safe and happy, even if he was Pete's mount instead of mine.

"I know what you're thinking."

"And?"

"You'd feel better because he'd be in the barn. But it would be a blow to your career. You'd be marked as my assistant. People loved how selfless it was of you to hand over Dynamo. But now when you take him Advanced next winter, they'll give me the credit. You know that, right? And if I take over another horse for you, they'll give me the credit for everything he does at Prelim. You'll be the nice girlfriend who gets Pete's horses ready for him."

I took a long sip of wine. Then another. I wanted to feel it tingling in my fingers, I wanted to feel it wavering in my mind, muting all the feelings Pete's words were dredging up.

I drained my glass and poured another. I looked at the books on their shelves, their spines stamped with the names of the greats who had come before me. I'd always wanted to be one of them. Pete was right; I'd given him Dynamo and lost the chance to be the one who took him all the way, to the uppermost level of eventing. I was on shaky ground, one step away from being demoted from partner to assistant. I couldn't risk that.

But I wanted my horse that I loved, too.

I'd changed, I realized. I'd changed so much from the girl who had first come to Ocala, ready to fight tooth and nail to get to the top. I'd softened in ways I could never have imagined, as if life had ground away the sharp edges that had defined me for so long. And maybe I needed those sharp edges still, or I wasn't going to make it. Maybe now was when the real struggle began—when I had to pretend I was the toughest girl in the room.

Pete was looking at the books too, his eyes roving across the titles. I rubbed a calloused hand along his shoulder, a finger along the smooth skin of his neck. He smiled, but he didn't look at me. Pete had changed, too. I just wasn't sure if he'd grown softer, or harder.

Pete went out for a late night-check after the wine was gone, and I picked up my phone with quiet intent. I clicked the browser and swiped quickly through some bookmarked blogs, looking for any updates. If Mickey had been sold and it went public, one of these gossipy sites would have the news. When I didn't find anything, I did a couple of quick web searches, just to be sure a forum hadn't posted the news first.

"Danger Mouse sold" only brought up references to a British cartoon from before I was born. By the time Pete came back in, Marcus wagging behind him, I'd put the phone back down, my curiosity sated and my mood strangely deflated.

I'd been hunting for news, and I was just disappointed because there wasn't any, I told myself. But I wondered if that was the real reason. Maybe, I was just hoping this would all end so I could move on.

"You rescheduled the next lesson with Rogue's owner for this week, right?" I asked, hopping up to give Pete a quick kiss.

"Yeah, and this will be my one and only chance to get a yes out of her, because after that they're going to make plans for the summer. If she decides to keep him, they have to get their travel plans finalized. After Florida, it's off to Virginia, and then Saugerties for the summer."

"Shame we can't go to upstate New York for the summer." I sighed. "Must be nice being a rich teenager."

"Maybe someday we will," he said. "This seems like a step in the right direction."

"We're now riding instructors," I pointed out, speaking a little more sharply than I should have, thanks to the wine. "A year ago we were strictly trainers. Is this the right direction, or just making the best of a bad situation?"

Pete shook his head at me, and his expression told me I was missing the forest for the trees. As usual. "Jules, remember how you wanted to ride fewer horses, better?"

"Yes," I answered cautiously.

"Well, don't you think this is the way to do it? Make your money teaching, spend your free time getting intense with a couple of handpicked horses you love?"

I sat down on the couch, a hot blush flooding my cheeks. "I never thought about it that way."

"You don't have to get dramatic about it. You just missed the memo that everything was going to be all right."

"I think you're the one who is still struggling with that reality."

Pete eyed the empty wine bottle with regret. "You're better at losing your home than I am, I admit."

"It sucked," I said. "But then I had something better."

He didn't look up with an instantly meaningful look in his eyes, didn't take the bait at all, but that was fine, because this wasn't a rom-com. I said it anyway.

"I had you."

And then it was a rom-com after all. The sultry romantic part at the end, with lots of kissing, and a slow fade to black.

28

LINDSAY SWAGGERED INTO the barn on a sunny Tuesday, a few days after the move, while I was knocking mud off Jim Dear. After a day's turnout he looked more like a house mouse than a horse, all gray-brown mud from a pretty but perhaps unfortunately placed stream at the bottom of the gelding pasture. It might make for a nice water jump once we'd gotten around to building some cross-country fences, but at the moment the stream was only good for a certain type of horse who enjoyed coating himself from head to hoof in a thick barrier of dried mud. There wasn't a dandy brush in the world that was strong enough to handle this clay, I was thinking. I needed a pickax and a steady hand.

"I do declare, that animal looks like he was lost in a cypress swamp during a hurricane," Lindsay said in a cartoon drawl. She sounded like Blanche from *The Golden Girls*.

"If I ever get this mud off him, I'll show you the scar he got from an actual hurricane," I panted. "You riding today?"

"Of course. Mommy Dearest thinks I'm going to the American Eventing Championships in about four months, so I guess I'd better figure out my Starter dressage test before April's over." Lindsay dropped the drawl. "It's *possible* she'll be disappointed."

"I wish I knew how to explain to them that it's more than changing saddles," I admitted. "Everyone's parents seem to think pretty much the same thing—you guys are already advanced, so they don't see why you have to start with something called Starter."

"Screw Starter." Lindsay snorted. "Ricky wants to do Baby Grasshopper or whatever it's called, where the cross-country course is literally just poles on the ground."

"So you guys have been doing research."

"Every day when we go to the library for study hall, Mom," Lindsay mocked. "Of course we have. We've been professional juniors for years. Some of us, anyway," she amended. "Ricky and Julia have never done the A-circuit. Neither has Jordan. But Tomeka and Maisey and Heather used to compete with me out of Linda Drysdale's barn. Weekends at HITS, the whole hairy mess."

"All of you together? I didn't realize so many of you had that much experience."

"We were pony kids together. We shared garter straps and hot dogs out there in the trenches."

"Intimate."

"Linda always has about fifty kids riding out of her barn. We formed cliques. Our clique was the 'get us the hell out of here' group."

"So, she's a big-name hunter trainer?" I'd never heard of her.

Lindsay raised her eyebrows. "Man, it's a different world in eventing."

I took the sarcasm for a yes. I went back to slapping the dandy brush across Jim Dear's back. He shuddered, closing his eyes in appreciation.

Maybe he got so muddy just to enjoy the act of getting clean again.

Lindsay leaned against the nearest stall wall, apparently in no hurry to start riding, despite the fact that we had less than two hours until sunset and there were no lights over the arena. I drew the brush over Jim Dear's shoulder and uncovered the long, jagged scar there.

She gasped, starting forward, and traced a finger across the indentation. It zigzagged over his shoulder and finished in a short but savage little gully through the meat of his neck. "What did that?" she breathed. "I didn't notice it when you were riding him at High Springs. The arch of his neck must hide it."

I shrugged. "A two-by-four? Part of the barn roof? Everything was collapsing all at once. I was with my working student under a fleece cooler in the tack room, just hoping we wouldn't die."

"Where's the working student now?"

"She gave up on Florida and went back up north." I wished she hadn't, but at the same time, I couldn't fault her instincts. Where would I have put Lacey when Pete and I were living in a horse trailer?

Lindsay was quiet for a few moments. I let her trace the scar again with one black-polished fingertip while I retrieved my hoof pick and started digging the clay out of Jim Dear's hooves. I was just adding to the mess; the barn aisle was an absolute disaster zone around him, with piles of mud and hair ornamenting the concrete.

When Lindsay spoke again, it was barely above a whisper. "You've really been through some shit, Jules Thornton."

I burst out laughing. "Oh God, Lindsay. You have no idea."

There was a crunch of wheels on gravel out front, and then a car door slammed. I heard a shout of greeting, and laughter. The boarders were arriving.

I'm running a boarding stable. I felt a sudden flood of panic. A lesson barn full of other people, bringing their own drama and infighting and wants and demands every single day. I thought of the quiet of the annex barn back at Briar Hill, before everything had fallen apart. When it was just Lacey and me, listening to the radio and working our way through riding and barn chores, with Barn Kitty slipping in and out of the tack room with mice and lizards between her jaws, and Marcus snoozing in the sun. I wanted that back. I wasn't cut out for this public version of equestrian life.

The joy of setting up the new farm had obscured the reality: a barn without Mickey, a barn full of kids that were going to be my problem, a barn provided to me by clients I'd never wanted. I wasn't ungrateful, I was just terribly afraid things were not going to work out. The most worrisome part was how much power the co-op would have over our lives. One wrong move, and we could find ourselves out on our asses, homeless with a string of horses to care for. Again. I knew this was just how the horse business worked, but that knowledge didn't make the possibility any less frightening.

I can't do this.

Lindsay looked down the aisle and for a moment I thought I saw the same thoughts written across her face. Then it was gone; she was lighting up and heading down the aisle to greet her friends, the people she'd helped bring together and place under my wing. Either Lindsay was more well-adjusted than I'd ever been, or she was better at faking it. I felt a bit jealous of her, whatever the answer was. Because right now I felt nothing but serious anxiety.

Jim Dear stomped next to me and I got back to business, strapping on his brushing boots and pulling my cross-country saddle out of the tack room. We were going out for trot sets, so at least I could have some quiet time in the empty pasture while the kids were up here clowning around with their horses. Pete was off with Rogue and his owner, giving the lesson that would seal their fate, and I hadn't scheduled any lessons for Tuesdays yet. There was still a fighting chance that this sunny spring evening would belong to me alone.

I hadn't counted on the tenacity of teenagers.

"Wait, where are you going?" Tomeka squealed when she saw Jim in the crossties, finally clean and tacked to the nines in boots and martingale and hunting breastplate.

"Are you going galloping? We want to watch!"

"We want to *come*," Maisey insisted, slipping up beside Tomeka. She was tiny, like a junior jockey, and always appearing where you least expected her. Neither of them had ridden with me before, yet both of them were insistent eventing was where their hearts and futures lay.

"I'm just doing trot sets," I said. "There's nothing exciting about trot sets."

"We can be tacked up in five minutes," Jordan assured me. "Wait right there!" And suddenly all of them were off, flying around with grooming kits and saddles and hard hats and chaps, while Jim and I stood in the center of their little hurricane and waited it out with surprised faces we couldn't quite straighten.

"Shit," I told him, and he flicked an ear at me with a gesture that could have been agreement, or annoyance.

So there I was, jogging Jim Dear along the lower edge of the big field I'd designated the gelding pasture, where the evening shadows pressed against the hillside from the neighboring pine plantation, with a gaggle of show riders trailing after me in an unkempt cavalry charge. None of them rode out of arenas very often, and all of them were experiencing varying degrees of anxiety, for their horses and for themselves. William had spent the first ten minutes walking on his hind legs, which Lindsay managed with a grim expression and a set chin, rather like my own. Even Jordan's aging Sammy managed to put up a fuss, trotting sideways all the way down the slope, including the steep parts where I encouraged everyone to walk downward in a straight line, not at an angle.

"Because if you're going down a hillside at an angle," I explained, "and your horse trips and falls, he'll fall sideways and land on top of you."

"And then flip over a few times and destroy what's left of you," Lindsay added with her usual helpfulness, and I couldn't say she was wrong.

"But if you're going straight down and he falls?" Tomeka asked, reining back her little bay gelding and looking at the hill before us with trepidation.

"You're sitting far enough back that you can balance him, or shove off to one side if you can tell he's going to flip," I told her. "If you're not sure you can balance him, choose pushing off to one side over taking your chances in the saddle. Eventually you should be able to feel the difference, but a good emergency dismount is never a bad idea."

Tomeka's eyes widened and I knew she was thinking of the groomed surface and safe fences of the jumping ring back at High Springs. It wasn't my job to scare them, I admonished myself. Without their parents paying the bills, this farm wasn't mine. And this time, we really had nowhere to go if everything went to hell.

Now they trotted behind me fairly quietly, happy to be on flat ground for a few minutes before we started up the hill. I'd warned everyone to pay close attention to their horses as we trotted back up. If anyone felt like they were losing their hind ends and getting tired, they were to find a buddy to walk with and drop back from the group. The last thing I needed was strained muscles before we even got started with lessons.

"Some of them will feel the need to canter," I added. "And that's okay, just get off their backs and hang on." There were some wide eyes in the group, but no one actually dismounted, so I figured they were up to the challenge.

I turned around to check on my ducklings for the twentieth time. "Are we all doing okay?"

There was a collective nod from the students. Sammy was trotting sideways again, but Jordan was just posting away with a resigned expression on her face.

Her clear determination gave me hope for her future in eventing. When you learned to accept the shenanigans your fit event horse gave you, you lived a longer, happier life. Most of the time, the airs above the ground just stemmed from an exuberant outlook on life. When they didn't come from a happy place, it was generally pretty easy to figure out—although the fix wasn't always obvious, as Mickey had once proved.

I pushed him out of my head. I wasn't going to think about Mickey. Not right now. Not with all these kids out here, depending on me to teach them how to love my sport.

"Okay," I shouted. "When we go up the hill, I want everyone in two-point. Sink your weight into your heels, but keep your shoulders back and think about keeping your body upright. Don't tip too far forward. Some of you are going to find yourselves cantering. Just be quiet and try to bring your horse back to a trot without any drama. If you don't, you don't. It's not a huge deal. Cantering is just a reaction to not being fit enough to trot uphill. Got it?"

"No drama," Tomeka replied. "Got it."

"Let that be your mantra," I said. "Here we go!"

We reached the corner of the pasture and I turned Jim along the fence line, feeling his hindquarters reach underneath him as he tackled the sudden incline. His neck arched and I lifted out of the saddle, my weight in my stirrups and my hands alongside his withers, just pressing against his tangle of dark mane, out of his way but ready to help if he needed me.

Behind me I heard a few squeals and laughs, and a rumble of hooves as someone burst into a plunging canter. The hoofbeats came up rapidly on my left and I turned to see Tomeka, her hands loose on the reins while once-plain Merci tackled the hill like a mighty Himalayan summit. "He looks like a warhorse," I told her approvingly. "You're sitting him nicely."

"I've never felt him move like this," she gasped. "It's incredible."

I laughed. "You're not riding hunters anymore. This is just the beginning."

Tomeka sat down slightly and Merci settled back into a trot, puffing hard with every stride. She posted to keep his rhythm steady. I watched her while Jim Dear did his own thing, trotting uphill with his usual work ethic.

Tomeka just might be a little diamond in the rough. Her instincts were impeccable and her seat was elegant.

Even Merci, who had been pretty dull to watch in the arena, looked like a different horse with his ears pricked and his body engaged. But then again, I could say that about all of their horses. Everyone was interested, happy, and ready to move forward.

We hit the top of the hill and the whole group seemed to be huffing and puffing, with the exception of Jim, for whom it was just another Tuesday. I brought him down to a walk and the others clustered around me, panting as hard as their horses. Hill work built up everyone's endurance. There was a lot of excited chatter about the way horses reacted to the hill, with some cantering and some nearly stopping and a little bit of bolting in between, but I held up a hand and they gradually quieted.

"We're going to walk for three minutes and then we're going to trot again. This time we're going to trot down the hill. Stay back, keep your leg in front of you and your seat out of the saddle as much as possible, and if your horse starts to stumble, pull up and walk. Just like going up, find a buddy so you're not asking them to separate from the herd. How is everyone's breathing?"

There was a conspicuous silence as they struggled to find an answer. Fair enough, I thought. We'd have to talk about taking TPR after this, too. How had today turned into one big riding lesson? I took a breath and began.

"Okay, guys. Let's talk TPR. It stands for temperature, pulse, and respiration. Here's how we're going to start observing your horse's breathing . . ."

29

I HAD EVERYONE helping feed dinner when Pete came into the barn, Marcus trotting at his heels with an adoring look that said Pete had brought home something tasty and Marcus had gotten a bite. I wondered if it was celebratory fast food or disappointment fast food.

He slipped into the feed room as the last of the students loped out with a feed bucket and closed the door behind him. I dropped the scoop back into the trash can of pellets and busied myself wedging the lid on tight, then fastening it with a bungee cord. I didn't ask how the lesson with Rogue's owner had gone; he would tell me without any prompting.

"She rode him very well," Pete said, his voice even. "I was impressed, and I told her so."

"He didn't buck?" I didn't turn around. I reached onto the shelf where the supplements were and began screwing on the lids more tightly. Vitamin E. Selenium. Electrolytes. Bee pollen. Farrier's Formula. More vitamins per horse per day than I took in a year.

"He bucked, but she rode him through it without any problems this time. She didn't understand that he does it because he's excited. She just . . . didn't understand him." There was a catch in his voice, as if he was disappointed that he'd helped the girl figure out her horse.

I thought about what I'd told the students earlier, about riding through their horses' excitement. How well they'd all seemed to grasp the concept of their horses enjoying themselves, and running sideways, bolting forward and jigging because they loved being out in the field, not because they were trying to be naughty or because they were unhappy. This kid could be another refugee rider in our barn, if Pete played his cards right. If Pete wanted her around, if she decided she was going to keep the horse he wanted so much, he could probably convince her to abandon the jumper classes that made Rogue crazy and come join us on the dark side.

I replaced the last tub of vitamins on the shelf and hesitated before turning around, out of things to busy my hands with. The feed room was barely lived in yet, still clean and uncluttered, and there were no cobwebs to fuss over or out-of-place medicine scoops to find homes for. I had to face Pete, and it was shameful of me to put it off. I just felt bad that *my* evening had been so surprisingly rewarding, when his had obviously ended in disappointment.

Beyond the feed room door, I heard a shriek of laughter and recognized Jordan's giggle, and I felt a surprising lift of happiness at all the good that was about to happen in this barn. We were building up the next generation of eventers. This was important.

I turned around, ready to convince Pete that even if all was lost with his horse, we had bigger things to devote ourselves to right here in our own barn.

Pete was grinning.

"What?" I asked, shocked.

"She wants to sell him to me," Pete said, his voice now incredulous, as if he still couldn't believe it. "She said he wants out of the ring, and that I understand him. She says she wants him to be famous."

I sat down on the metal trash can, its cold ridges biting through my breeches. "That's insane," I said thoughtlessly.

But Pete knew what I meant.

There was a knock on the door. "Are you two necking?" a bored voice called.

Pete arched an eyebrow at me. "Which one of your heathens is that?"

"That's Lindsay," I assured him. "You can always tell because she's *rude*." I shouted the last part so Lindsay was sure to hear.

"No, you are," came the witty retort.

"And super clever." I got up and opened the door; Pete was too busy laughing. "We're having a staff meeting about what the hell we're going to do with all of you."

"You should give us all paid apprenticeships so we can learn at your feet and bask in your greatness."

"Paid? That's not how the horse business works, sweetie. You want to be in my barn all afternoon, following me around like a lost duckling, you better be prepared to work it off later."

"Of course I will," Lindsay said, and then some of the others wandered up, empty feed buckets in their hands, encouraging me to tell them what to do next, and there I was.

Being Laurie.

Pete was on the phone to Delannoy before we'd finished watering everyone for the night, letting him know they could proceed with the offer on Rogue. Then he went down the aisle to the empty stall next to Barsuk, a prime corner spot with two windows that he'd laid claim to the day we moved in, imagining his new horse standing there, pulling at hay, coming to see him with pricked ears, rumbling a welcome deep in his chest. I'd seen little of Rogue but enough to know he was that kind of horse, expressive and full of character. He was probably going to make us crazy, always opening gates and figuring out how to destroy things sold as "indestructible." But a lot of good event horses had that quality. It was a rare horse who managed to be both intelligent and well-behaved.

Lindsay sidled up to me as kids started to disappear into their parents' cars for the night, shouts of "See you tomorrow!" and the sound of car doors slamming in the dark parking lot. "I think you should know the offer is in on Mickey," she said.

"What? Who's handling all that?"

"My mother. She worked out the syndicate details, it got really lawyer-y and I had to bow out. But it's based on all the work I did for you. She just pared it down. We have ten majority owners, and then about twenty minor investors who are basically just getting bragging rights. And they'll show up at events and cheer you on, which'll be pretty fun, I guess."

"So, thirty people are putting money into this." I thought about the hundreds who had wanted to help. "Is that everyone who wanted in?"

"No," Lindsay said. "The syndicate is the barn parents, plus some grandparents who wanted to help out. It's basically all in-house. Mom said it would be too unwieldy with a thousand people from all over the world. But," she added, "I did make a fan club for everyone who chimed in that they wanted to invest. It's five bucks a month and you're going to make them a video message every month. We have about two hundred subscribers so far. Don't worry, I'll remind you and handle the uploads."

I stared at her. "Lindsay, this is insane. I don't know any other way to describe it. How did you make all this happen? The co-op, all these horses, *Mickey*?"

Lindsay looked around, satisfied with the empire she had created. Her pink bangs were growing out, I noticed, along with the color. The dark roots were being allowed to take over and the shocking pink was tucked behind her ears, almost out of sight. "I just wanted to see what I could do," she said eventually.

I thought about her fearsome mother and her always-busy father, whom I'd only seen once. I thought about how angry and resentful she'd been back in January, when I'd met her. Lindsay had done all of this to show that she existed, that she mattered. I felt a very unfamiliar urge to pull her in for a hug, but instead I just put a hand on her shoulder and squeezed.

"Look at what you did, Lindsay," I said in wonder. "Look at what you've created."

Everything felt so right, I didn't expect the call later that night. Already showered and wrapped in a plaid robe against the cool night, the windows open and the gentle sound of sighing horses floating through the screens, I answered the phone with a feeling of confusion while Pete glanced at me, eyebrow arched questioningly.

It was Grace. I glanced at the carriage clock Pete had unearthed from a box and placed atop the simple flat shelf of the modernist mantel. Nearly nine o'clock. Entirely too late for a phone call in our world. "Grace? What's going on?"

"I'll tell you what's going on," she said crisply. "I tried to buy Mickey and he's already sold."

30

BREATHE.

Breathing is good. Breathing is important. Just keep doing it. In and out.

Don't mind that your heart's not beating, don't mind that your head is spinning.

Just keep breathing.

Don't mind that you don't want to, not one bit.

"Jules?" *Grace is still breathing, Grace is still perfectly alive and in control of the situation. Must be nice to be Grace.* "Do you know anything about this?"

"I don't," I croaked. "I had no idea he was sold."

"It's not your people?"

"I don't know. I *hope* so. Lindsay said they were putting in an offer. I guess it could be? It seems soon though. I don't know. Wouldn't she have said? Wouldn't someone have called me?" I was babbling.

"Well, whoever got him, it's done." Grace sighed. "I'm sorry if it isn't your offer, Jules. I know you two were close. It's still possible, though, that whoever bought him will put you back on him."

Sure. Anything was possible. Putting me back in the saddle after Eileen and Carrie very publicly removed him from my barn? That was possible. Like my being selected for the United States Equestrian Team tomorrow was possible.

"Why were you trying to buy him?"

"Oh," Grace said, sounding embarrassed. "I sold the farm."

For the second time in five minutes, I stopped breathing.

Why, when everything seemed like it was coming together for me, did the world start falling apart?

"You *can't* have sold the farm," I gasped, and it was more like a sob, because it felt like something had ended while I wasn't looking. I was supposed to have been part of this, part of Grace's big move, but instead she had gone and sold Seabreeze while I was busy with the thousand moving parts of my own crazy life.

"I didn't think I could sell it either," Grace said with a chuckle. "But in the end, it was pretty simple. They gave me a huge offer and I would've been crazy not to take it. Sentimentality doesn't pay the bills. We both know that."

"So you and Anna are . . . moving up here?"

"I was going to," Grace said, with the air of someone admitting a weakness. "But my students were adamant that I stay in the area. So we are looking to buy a place north of Orlando. Apopka, or maybe up in Lake County. Still close enough for a commute for my clients. But this way we'll have more space. Grass pastures, even. So it's going to be better for everyone, in the long run. We have six months to figure it all out. And if I haven't gotten a place by then, I'll tell the buyers they can wait another six months. They're not going to go to court to move a barn full of horses just to build another condo tower—it's the kind of thing the local news goes crazy for. They'll wait until I'm good and ready."

"So you're not going out of business or anything?"

She chuckled. "I was going to buy you a horse, right? What does that tell you? I thought I'd dabble in a beautiful investment that would never pay me back a penny. If that isn't staying in the horse business up to my neck, I don't know what is."

I slithered my way back onto the couch, not really conscious of how I ended up on the floor to begin with. "Okay," I said. "Okay."

"What's that mean?"

"It means I'm really, really happy for you."

"Thank you," Grace said, and I would swear I could hear the warmth of her smile through the phone. "And you have a new farm too. For a little while I thought we might end up together, but . . . I think this is for the best."

"I do too," I replied sincerely. "Me too."

"And you're okay?"

I chewed my lip for a moment before answering. "I'm okay. I'll wait and see what happens."

Pete looked at me as I ended the call. "Text Lindsay."

I was already typing.

What do you know about Mickey? Did anything happen with the offer?

There was an unbearably long pause, during which I alternated between staring at the phone and burying my face in Marcus's fur.

Finally her reply came through.

Mom says it's best not to talk about it at all. But the offer is out there and supposedly they're considering it along with several others.

How long are we supposed to wait?

Another pause.

I don't know. Until it's complete. Insurance exam and every-thing, mom says.

She says there is legal stuff and it could get complicated.

I groaned.

Pete looked alarmed.

"There's more than one offer," I said.

"What are you going to do?"

"I have to sit and wait. Just like I said to Grace."

After a sleepless night, I went outside and started taking pictures, and it became my therapy and my revenge and my hope, all at once.

I walked around the farm in the rosy glow of sunrise, songbirds bursting into a noisy chorus as they shook out their wings and chased gnats through the clear air. Barn Kitty stalked lizards; Marcus snuffled at jump poles. Regina watched me through her window, and a few other horses nickered for breakfast. But it was too early. This was my time. I took pictures of the tidy pastures, searching for the lines of fencing that weren't leaning, still crooked from years of abandonment.

Eventually we'd tighten up those posts and repair some of the broken boards, but for the moment they were good enough. Everything was good enough for the horses, and some of it was good enough for my pictures.

I took pictures of the barn aisle with the neat line of horses leaning over their stall doors, ears pricked, eyes expectant and fastened upon me, waiting for their morning grain with barely restrained anticipation. I took pictures of the arena, its white sand groomed in tidy deep furrows after a few turns with the antique harrow we'd found in an equipment shed and happily put back into use. I took pictures of the oak tree, towering between the house and the barn, to give perspective: this is how close we are, and this is how deep our roots will grow, beneath this ancient tree. This is how sturdy and strong and unbroken we are, after everything you've done.

I sent them all to Eileen. One picture per text, one text per minute, for twenty minutes. It was probably a little psychopathic, but I couldn't care. I could scarcely think. My thoughts scattered around me, shards of glass from a wantonly shattered vase. Something beautiful that had been broken, without hope of repair. And for what?

My only linear thoughts were about chores. First horses are fed hay, and then breakfast. Then horses go outside, except for the first ride of the day. First tack up, then ride. Jim Dear was walking on a loose rein, my feet were swaying free alongside the dangling stirrups, and until a bird fluttered up in front of us and startled him, sparking a tiny spook, I wasn't aware of the actions that made it all happen. I was on autopilot, until Jim *made* me react.

"Settle down, Poppy," I said soothingly, sitting back in the saddle to bring his surprised jog back down to a walk. "Just a big bird, nothing to fuss about."

He responded by shoving his head down toward the dirt, tugging the reins through my hands, and heaving a tremendous sigh.

"That tiny bird must have been more traumatizing to a big strong horse than I realized," I told him. "You gonna make it?"

My phone buzzed in my pocket and I pulled it out, set it on a nearby fence post, and kept riding. I didn't look to see who was calling. Probably Eileen. Now that I'd sent the pictures, now that I'd had my little breakdown, I didn't care what she had to say. I'd block her number if she kept calling. I was over it. We were done. But she had to know what she'd given up. She had to know what she'd lost with her impatience. This farm was the sunshine waiting after all that rain. We'd pushed through the storm and found the end of our rainbow. It was too bad she didn't have the strength of character to endure it with us.

If Eileen, or Carrie for that matter, wanted to talk to me, they could get into their luxury SUVs and drive out and face me, right here on my farm. I was done inviting them into my life, slobbering for their horse and their money. I had clients now who loved me and wanted me to succeed, and if they weren't what I'd ever expected, that didn't make them any less life-saving.

Times had changed, that was all.

Jim Dear snorted and I rubbed his neck with one hand. At least he was mine.

31

"EVERYONE CIRCLE AROUND me!" I shouted, and five obedient riders on five varying-degrees-of-obedient horses closed in. They danced around my horse and me like a carousel, bays and grays and chestnuts snorting and sidling and giving the huge open fields around them wary sidelong glances, as if they couldn't quite believe they'd been plucked from the safety of their fenced-in show ring and dropped here, in the middle of absolute-fucking-nowhere. To be honest, their riders didn't look much better.

We were on Haley Marsh's gorgeous cross-country course. The massive expanse of grass pastures and oak forests, all dotted with fences from Beginner Novice to Intermediate, was quite a change for my little flock of ducklings. Besides our weekly endurance sections in the broad grassy slopes of the gelding pasture, they hadn't ridden outside of the farm arena.

I had before me a little quintet of accidental agoraphobes, not sure the yawning emptiness stretching all the way from the barn to the tree-lined horizon wasn't somehow going to crush them, like a submarine diving too deep into endless seas.

To me, though, all this space was heaven. And I knew that

soon, this lot would agree. They'd chosen this life, after all. They'd convinced their parents this was the way forward, the way to stay in horses forever. I knew from experience that once you talked your parents into spending a fortune on something, heaven help you if you went back on that interest. There were probably professional equestrians out there with medals bouncing around their necks after successful jumper or dressage rounds who lived their entire illustrious lives suppressing the fact that they had really wanted to switch to team penning back in seventh grade.

I wouldn't let my students regret this decision.

"We're out on forty acres with no fences except the kind you jump," I told them. "What happens if your horse runs away?"

Faces turned to me, grave, before they went back to managing the tribal dances their horses were shuffling through.

"The answer is nothing happens, if you keep your seat and don't panic. Every single one of you has galloped with me in the gelding pasture. Every single one of you has controlled your horses even when they're hot as hell in the warm-up ring. Right?"

I waited for nods and eventually I got them.

"You all remember how the emergency brakes work, right?" This was the term I used when I taught them to slide their grip up one rein and yank upward, useful for chaotic runaway situations. I vaguely thought I remembered Laurie calling it a pulley halt or something like that. "Emergency brake" did a much better job of driving home its importance *and* its specificity—because except in life-or-death situations, a horse's mouth must still be considered sacred ground.

There were more nods. A couple of riders, Jordan and Lindsay among them, quietly experimented, doubling the reins in one hand and sliding the other hand along the free side without actually tightening their hold.

"Okay, so if you stay balanced and your horse doesn't stop when you try to hit the brakes, what happens next?"

There was silence. A few questioning glances.

"You're right," I announced. "Nothing happens. Your horse runs for a while. Eventually, you get him to stop. And he'll stop. I promise. None of you are on half-broke Mustangs galloping toward the promise of their beloved herd just over the horizon. You're on a bunch of well-trained warmbloods, and their beloved herd is right here. No one's leaving on their own. That's not how horses work. If you turn back toward us, chances are you'll come to a neat little halt right next to us without even asking for it."

Lindsay grinned. She was always the first one in the group to push past her fears. She looked around at the nearest cross-country fence, a pleasant enough pile of logs, and pointed at it. "Should we start here?"

That's my girl, I thought. "Absolutely," I said. "You ready to go first?"

"I got it," Lindsay said confidently, and we broke ranks to make room for her to circle and find the right approach for the log fence.

I rode back over to a lone oak tree about thirty feet away, where Pete sat in its shade, his feet kicked free of Mayfair's stirrups. The late-April day felt summer-warm, although I knew it wasn't even close to the misery we'd experience in another month or two, and the tree's cool shadow seemed to reach out and embrace me as I crossed the line from light to dark. "You abandoned me out there with the tadpoles in the blazing heat."

"A wise trainer always teaches from beneath a tree."

"Probably true. I'm pretty new at this."

"They look great."

"I thought if I stood there and shouted at them while they feel out this kind of jumping, they'd just get tense and nervous. They're good riders, they don't need to be micromanaged."

"And a fence of that size can't hurt them," Pete agreed. "I think you're going to be good at this."

And that might have been the biggest surprise of all: I was good at this, and I liked this.

A bigger surprise even than the email I received a week after Grace's call, when the Danger Mouse Project issued a press release announcing that they had successfully purchased Danger Mouse in partnership with Alachua Eventing Co-op, and would be immediately placing him back into training with Jules Thornton.

A bigger surprise than the apologetic voicemails from Eileen, and later the apologetic emails from Eileen, and still later the moment I'd actually accepted the call, spoken with her, and accepted her apology once and for all—and asked her not to contact me again.

A bigger surprise than Rockwell's secretary sending the papers to renew our sponsorship for another year, guaranteeing us more clothing, tack, and equipment in exchange for relentless social media posts, and of course, more wins.

But I was used to surprises. After these past couple years in the horse business, all I knew for sure was nothing was guaranteed. Nothing was predictable. And all our hard work, all our tears, and all our mental breakdowns might be for nothing. We spent all our time and money and sanity producing horses who jumped piles of logs fearlessly, horses who trotted through sandboxes with exacting precision.

What exactly was it all for? I didn't know; maybe so we felt like we had some control over this life. I just knew it was what I did, it was my passion and my pride and my culture and my community, and I'd keep training horses until I couldn't lift myself out of my bed in the morning. And then I'd probably just holler out the window at whoever was doing it for me.

It took luck, for sure. But it also took a pretty broad view of what luck really was. Because here I was, surrounded by students, doing exactly what I'd never wanted to do, and I was pretty damn happy.

If that wasn't luck, I didn't know what was.

As Lindsay cantered William over the little fence, jumping it with show-ring panache, my phone chimed from the little pocket on my saddle pad. I pulled it out and smiled.

"Alex," I answered. "Where have you been?"

"California," Alex said nonchalantly. "Do you even look at Facebook?"

"Not if I can help it. I have staff for that now," I added, watching Lindsay trot back to the group. "Listen, I can't talk right now. I'm teaching a cross-country lesson."

"Without me?" Alex screeched. "I'm offended."

"Hang on," I said, and raised my voice to riding-instructor level. "Jordan, give him leg before the fence or he's going to just step over it. Demand some effort, woman! Alex," I went on in a normal voice, "you can't just go off racing horses in the middle of spring. We have to get your horse in eventing shape."

"Some of us have jobs," Alex said.

"I have a job. I'm a riding instructor." I grinned at the words. So crazy. And yet I was having so much fun.

"I want to come ride with you," Alex said. "I'm missing out!"

"Well then, get Tiger up here," I told her. "There's plenty of room."

Room for Tiger, room for Mickey, and room for a half dozen more horses—all of them representing chances for me, for Pete, for everyone we knew to move up and move on. Eventing was a tough sport, and the only way to thrive in this game was a little good luck. Well, it looked like we finally had some.

ABOUT THE AUTHOR

Natalie Keller Reinert is the award-winning author of more than twenty books, including the Eventing and Briar Hill Farm series. Drawing on her professional experience in three-day eventing, working with Thoroughbred racehorses, mounted patrol horses, therapeutic riding, and many other equine pursuits, Natalie brings her love of equestrian life into each of her titles. She also cohosts the award-winning equestrian humor podcast *Adulting with Horses.* Natalie lives in north Florida with her family, horses, and cat.

www.nataliekreinert.com